For the Sacramento Valley Rose

You were with me from the start. Thank you all for your support, encouragement, and friendship.

Praise for ***Kiss Me, Kill Me***

"[A] riveting new series . . . Lucy continues to be a fascinating and enticing character, and her ongoing development adds depth to an already rich brew of murder and mystery. Brennan rocks!"

—*RT Book Reviews*

Praise for ***Love Me to Death***

"A world-class nail-biter . . . Brennan is in the groove with this one."

—*New York Times* bestselling author LEE CHILD

"This pulse-ratcheting romantic suspense from Brennan delivers intense action, multifaceted characters, and a truly creepy bad guy . . . [A] fast-paced, engrossing read."

—*Publishers Weekly*

"Twists and turns in this dark drama make it creepy and compelling in the extreme!"

—*RT Book Reviews* (starred)

Praise for ***Original Sin***

"Brennan shows a deft command of all things both normal and otherworldly in crafting one of the best tales of its kind since Dean Koontz and Stephen King were still writing about monsters. There is no shortage of those here and the result is a new genre classic."

—*Providence Journal*

Praise for ***Fatal Secrets***

"A master of suspense, Brennan does another outstanding job uniting horrifying action, procedural drama and the birth of a romance—a prime example of why she's tops in the genre."

—Top Pick, *RT Book Reviews*

"A fast-paced, action-packed romantic suspense."

—Romance Junkies

Praise for ***Sudden Death***

"Brennan knows how to deliver."

—*New York Times* bestselling author
LISA GARDNER

"This very satisfying read presents loads of action that keeps the pages flying—and makes one wonder how much is pure fiction and how much of it could really happen."

—BookLoons

Praise for ***Tempting Evil***

"*Tempting Evil* is an old-fashioned potboiler in all the right ways, chock-full of tried and true hallmarks of the genre."

—*The Providence Journal*

By Allison Brennan

If I Should Die
Kiss Me, Kill Me
Love Me to Death

Original Sin
Carnal Sin

Sudden Death
Fatal Secrets
Cutting Edge

Killing Fear
Tempting Evil
Playing Dead

Speak No Evil
See No Evil
Fear No Evil

The Prey
The Hunt
The Kill

IF I SHOULD DIE

A Novel of Suspense

Allison
BRENNAN

BALLANTINE BOOKS • NEW YORK

If I Should Die is a work of fiction. Names, characters, places, and incidents are the products of the author's imagination or are used fictitiously. Any resemblance to actual events, locales, or persons, living or dead, is entirely coincidental.

A Ballantine Books Mass Market Original

Published in the United States by Ballantine Books, an imprint of The Random House Publishing Group, a division of Random House, Inc., New York.

BALLANTINE and colophon are trademarks of Random House, Inc.

Grateful acknowledgment is made to Rench Audio for permission to reprint an excerpt from "Big Branch" music by Rench, lyrics by Tomasia, performed by Gangstagrass featuring Tomasia. Available at www.renchaudio.com. Reprinted by permission.

Love is Murder was originally published as an ebook in 2011.

ISBN 978-0-345-52041-8
eISBN 978-0-345-52042-5

Cover photograph (woman): Tom Grill/Getty Images

Printed in the United States of America

www.ballantinebooks.com

9 8 7 6 5 4 3 2 1

Ballantine Books mass market edition: December 2011

ACKNOWLEDGMENTS

Though writing is a solitary profession, many people help with the details. I want to especially thank those who helped make the details so much richer in this story.

First, Rench of the band Gangstagrass and Tomasia who granted permission to use their lyrics to lead this story. I bought the album after hearing the intro to the television show *Justified*; the songs inspired me and set the tone for this book.

Thanks to Joel Margot with Argus Thermal Imaging Products who answered my many questions regarding air surveillance. The extraordinary Margie Lawson and her husband, Tom, who lent me their expertise about aircraft. The Sacramento FBI regional office is always willing to help, especially Special Agent Steve Dupre, media liaison and all-around great guy who responded to the most arcane questions I could come up with, including researching the history of badge numbers. And also FBI SWAT Team Leader Brian Jones, who let me role-play in a variety of training scenarios, including a recent medic-training session, which helped tremendously for the field-medic details in this book. If I got anything wrong, it's my own fault.

For seventeen books, the Ballantine team has really shined. Without my amazing editors Charlotte Herscher and Dana Isaacson, I wouldn't have this book to share with my readers. Gina Wachtel's enthusiasm and smile are contagious, and I truly appreciate her efforts. Thanks especially to Linda Marrow and Scott Shannon for being supportive from the very beginning. And of course the unsung heroes—the production, sales, marketing, publicity, and art departments.

I am blessed with amazing friends and family. My smart and diplomatic agent, Dan Conaway, who took me on mid-career with both faith and a vision. My blogmates at Murderati and Murder She Writes who keep me sane and focused. My mom and best friend who's my biggest fan and strongest supporter. My kids, all five of them, who make me love them more each day, even when they drive me crazy. And of course my husband, Dan, who tolerates my hectic schedule, late nights, and wild questions. I couldn't do any of this without your support and understanding.

And last but certainly not least, I want to thank my readers who have embraced Lucy Kincaid and love her as much as I do. Writing a series character is both new for me and exciting, and I hope you enjoy this and future Lucy and Sean thrillers. To keep up with the latest news about my books, please visit my website at allisonbrennan.com where you can read excerpts, watch book trailers, sign up for my quarterly newsletter, and follow me on your favorite social media website.

Who's the outlaw, quick on the draw
Cast the first stone if you don't have a flaw
Who fills the jails, who lives above the law
White collar, black market, who's rich, who's poor

—"Big Branch," Gangstagrass feat. Tomasia

PROLOGUE

Three months ago

Guilt led him down the dark, cold passage many times that winter.

The weeks of unrelenting snowfall kept most people indoors, huddled in houses with poor insulation and roofs threatening to cave under the pressure of snow and ice. TV newscasters called this an epic winter, though upstate New York had seen it all before.

Jamming his ski poles into the deep snow, he slid to a halt at the main entrance of the abandoned Kelley Mine. The sun inched over the smooth, round mountains, chiseled against the blue sky. He stared at the entrance, frozen in fear and deep pain, as the clear February morning crept up to minus twenty degrees as dawn broke.

The rock and wood barrier appeared impassable, but a hollow spot to the left—visible from only one angle—gave easy access to the mine. He removed his skis and slipped through the opening into the dark tunnel, storing his equipment in an alcove off to the right.

Numbing cold had already seeped into his bones through the many layers of clothing, but he was used to it. Trekking down the main tunnel, he hunched over to avoid hitting his head, a flashlight illuminating the area right in front of him.

The only sounds were his footfalls on the frozen ground and the blood pumping through his veins, its relentless roar an echo in his head. As the tunnel slowly led him deeper into the mountain, his anxiety fueled his imagination. She wasn't there. She was a ghost. She would seek revenge.

He bit back a strangled sob. In life, she had been kind and smart and forgiving. Would she be different in death?

His foot slipped on the edge of a deep hole, rocks falling down the vertical exploration shaft.

"Stupid," he whispered, as he pushed his back against the rough wall, trying to calm his racing heart. Dammit, he had known about the hole in this passage! How could he have wandered so far into the most dangerous area of the mine and missed the turn? There were a dozen exploration shafts and he knew exactly where they were because he had the only set of maps that had been updated by the last engineer, with all the added tunnels and shafts marked.

In the years since the mine closed, a half dozen people had lost their lives here. Everyone had heard the stories. Like three decades ago when Paul Swain and his pals were getting stoned in the mine, and Mike Stine fell to his death down one of these shafts. They never recovered his body. Some people didn't believe it was an accident, but no one dared question the Swain family. Lawson Swain had kept Spruce Lake alive until his death, when Paul took over. And even though he was in prison on drug charges, most people suspected Paul was still very much in control of criminal enterprises in Spruce Lake.

But the truth was far more terrifying.

Ten yards back he found the right tunnel. Thirty feet down, it spilled out into an open space, not much bigger than a long, narrow garage, which had long ago stored mine equipment. Two tunnels shot off the room. He didn't know where they went. He'd never been this far into the mine, except . . .

He turned his flashlight toward the woman who haunted him.

She was unchanged, lying so peacefully he could almost pretend she was sleeping. His eyes burned.

He knelt at her side, reached out to touch her, then stopped himself.

"I'm so sorry." His voice broke and he began to shake. Gutless. This should never have happened. She should never have died.

He bowed his head and prayed for forgiveness. For strength.

He prayed for survival.

He remembered not her death but her smile, her sassy mouth, her quick wit. He'd loved her.

Love? You're a fool. You killed her.

He hadn't killed her, but he'd let it happen.

And you think there's a difference? Woe is the man who ignores the truth.

He remained kneeling until the cold was so bitterly unbearable that he feared he wouldn't make it back out. Would that be so bad? To die here? Every time he came, he thought the same thing. Take a few pills, lie down next to her, sleep. The subzero temperature would take care of the rest.

But others depended on him. He had responsibilities and obligations. If he disappeared, the town he had once loved, the town that had once saved him, would be doomed.

His soul was already doomed. There would be no forgiveness, no redemption. Truly, the only thing that kept him alive was the fire of vengeance burning inside.

He pulled a limp white flower from his pocket. He didn't know what it was called, he wasn't much into gardening, but she had loved them. It was wilted from being frozen, then being stored in the warmth of his pocket. Before leaving, he placed it on her chest, barely able to resist touching her.

ONE

Present day

Sean Rogan watched Lucy stretch with the grace of a cat, her thick, wavy black hair falling across his bare chest. She sighed as she relaxed on top of him, her dark eyes closed, a half-smile on her face.

There was little Sean enjoyed more than early-morning sex with Lucy.

For the first time in months, they were alone—no friends, no family, no stress—sharing a secluded cabin in the middle of the Adirondacks. Just the two of them. Lucy didn't seem to realize how much she'd needed this vacation—already, after one night, she was looking more rested than he'd seen her in months. Sean hoped their change of plans to help his brother Duke's friend wouldn't put a damper on their week together.

"This is perfect." Lucy kissed his chest. "I wish it could last."

A faint, nagging fear that such unadulterated happiness would come at a cost marred Sean's good mood. He knew Lucy was talking about their time alone, but he couldn't help but think she had been reflecting on their relationship.

"Luce?"

"Hmm?"

What should he say? That their vacation could last forever? Should he call her out on her skepticism? If he asked her to explain her comment, she'd overthink her response, and worse, she'd put her shields back up. He'd worked hard at getting her to put down her armor; it was these rare moments when she was entirely comfortable that he savored.

"Up for a hike this morning?" he asked instead.

Lucy didn't sound as though she noticed his hesitation. "After breakfast. I'm starving."

Sean laughed.

She leaned up and looked at him, her eyebrows raised. "What's funny?"

"In the four months I've known you, not once have you told me you're hungry, let alone starving."

He grinned, then reached up and tickled her ribs. Her spontaneous laugh was genuine, such a rare sound that every time he heard it he remembered how much Lucy needed him to remind her of the good in life, and forget the evil from her past.

"This is war!" she declared. Before Sean could tighten his abs in resistance, she tickled the sensitive sides of his stomach. He tried grabbing her hands as he laughed, but she enjoyed winning far too much to make it easy for him.

"Stop. Please."

"Say Uncle."

"Uncle."

She stopped, and he flipped her onto her back. "Now that you woke me up—"

"You mean you weren't awake when we were having sex?"

"That was just a prelude, Princess."

She tensed, and for a moment Sean thought he'd done or said something wrong. He was about to ask her what it was when she said, "Do you smell something?"

Her hair, their sweat . . . and something else he recognized only as she spoke. "Smoke."

They jumped up and pulled on the clothes closest to them.

He grabbed his backpack and they ran out the door, the scent of burning wood palpable as soon as they stepped outside.

They sprinted down the shadowy trail to the main lodge. Dawn had just broken over the mountain ridge, casting a fresh but pale light all around. A growing plume of dark gray smoke rose from the trees, and as soon as the lodge came into sight Sean saw smoke pouring from an open kitchen window. Several flickers of orange flames glowed through the thick smoke, but the fire hadn't reached the external walls.

Sean instantly took in the scene: twenty-two-year-old Adam Hendrickson at the water tank struggling with the hose attachment; his older half-brother Tim bolting across the center clearing, his face a mask of disbelief and rage; the Spruce Lake Inn manager, Annie Lynd, at his heels, her long, dark red braid trailing down her back.

There was something else—a sound in the background, growing fainter. A motor? Had the saboteur who had caused the Hendricksons' extensive property damage over the last several months now moved up to arson?

Sean scanned the area. Partly obscured by the barn a lone figure dressed in black rode slowly away on an ATV, glancing over his shoulder at the house. When he saw that Sean had spotted him, the rider sped up and disappeared into the trees, hightailing it away from the lodge.

Sean caught up with Tim and gestured toward the fleeing arsonist. Sean said, "I need an ATV."

"In the barn—"

"I'll get him! Take care of the fire." Sean sprinted toward the barn.

Lucy caught up to him as he turned the ignition in the ATV. "Be careful," she said.

"Always." He took his gun from his backpack and threaded his holster through the loops in his jeans. "I'll switch my cell to radio, better to communicate short distances. I'll keep in touch."

Sean sped out of the barn. The arsonist had left a light trail of exhaust, the ground too moist to kick up much dirt. But Sean found the tire tracks in the soft earth and stuck with them, picking up speed, driving the ATV with as much confidence as he drove his Mustang. He lowered the face shield on the helmet and leaned forward. The bastard had picked the wrong way to escape—Sean was boldly proficient on any sort of wheels, from motorcycles to SUVs.

The Yamaha Raptor he was riding had terrific responsiveness. He reached fifty miles per hour on the straightaway leading into the woods, though he suspected he could push it faster. Any other day, he would enjoy being on this powerful mechanical beast, but today, he had a job to do.

He was at a slight disadvantage in that he didn't know the area. Whoever was sabotaging the Hendrickson property was most likely a local, born and raised in the Adirondacks. The saboteur also had a big lead—Sean couldn't hear the other quad over his own engine. Without a line of sight, Sean pursued on instincts alone, following the fresh dirt trail the arsonist's ATV left in its wake.

The trees where Sean had seen the rider disappear came quickly into view, and Sean slowed to maneuver down a trail barely wide enough for the quad. Branches cut into his bare arms and he pulled his elbows in. The cold morning air seeped into his bones, his adrenaline keeping him from shivering.

The trail wound dangerously through the trees, a foot-worn path unsuitable for ATVs. Only the newly turned soil told Sean he was heading in the right direction.

The path came to a sudden end and Sean almost drove straight into the lake. He breaked rapidly and turned ninety degrees, fishtailing. Though the drop was short, the sheer ledge led directly to the water below. Sweating, Sean leaned forward and to the left, using his weight to balance and maintain control.

For a split second, he thought he'd stall out; the quad sputtered and jerked. He eased up on the throttle, rolled back an inch, then gunned it. The engine roared back to life, and Sean let out a relieved sigh.

He pushed on along the edge of the lake. The initial cold Sean felt wearing only a T-shirt and jeans had given way to overheating, sweat dampening his shirt. He barely registered the sharp sting of pine needles on his neck when he came too close to a low-hanging evergreen.

The trees thinned out and Sean found himself in a clearing about half the size of a football field. It appeared to be a seasonal camping spot, with two wood pits on either side.

The asshole he was pursuing had spun donuts in the area in an attempt to confuse him. "You'll have to do better than that, prick," Sean muttered. He ignored the disturbed campground and looked for where the other ATV had exited the clearing. Sean grinned when he found it after less than a minute.

The rocky trail turned steep quickly, and a sharp turn took him in the opposite direction of the lake. The terrain was becoming more difficult the higher he climbed up the mountain, with large branches that crunched under the quad's wide tires. Sean was forced to slow down to circumvent a rock that, had he hit it, would have flipped the vehicle; at thirty miles an hour he'd probably have broken his neck.

But that meant the arsonist had to slow as well. The chase might end when one of them ran out of gas—Sean hoped it was the other guy.

A sharp bend in the path nearly sent Sean down the mountainside fifty feet. His back wheels spun off the edge. He was losing ground and almost jumped from the ATV to save his life when the front wheels caught traction and he lurched forward.

The quad stalled, and he took a moment to breathe. He wouldn't do anyone any good if he ended up dead.

In the sudden silence, Sean heard the other rider,

much closer than he thought. He saw that the path peaked only twenty yards away; the arsonist sounded like he was right on the other side.

Sean restarted the ATV and cautiously drove up the steep, narrow path until the grade evened out. He then saw the man in black, picking up speed on the downhill slope. He doubled his speed, but the guy was increasing the distance between them. He noticed Sean and added speed. Because he wore a helmet, Sean couldn't see his face; he was skinny and not too tall, and his neck was pale. A short, skinny white guy would fit any number of people in the town. Sean needed to catch him.

The arsonist veered east, away from the ledge, and picked up speed as he sailed through the trees. Sean followed suit. Rocks and fallen trees from the recent winter littered the landscape. The guy was still increasing the distance between them, and when he topped a hill he disappeared from view.

Sean reached the peak and saw the other rider far in the distance, halfway across the clearing, on an old logging road or mining road. Spruce Lake had been a successful mining town for over a hundred years, up until the midseventies. If this was a mining road, they were closer to the main highway than Sean had thought.

Sean used all the power in the Raptor to fly down the packed dirt and rock road. The arsonist glanced back, but his face was hidden by the helmet's face shield. Sean was definitely getting closer. He'd have to maneuver the guy into a canyon or trap him somehow, or hope that Tim had called the sheriff and a helicopter was on its way. Wishful thinking—even if they had a chopper in Canton, it couldn't get here this fast.

He'd have to wing it. The arsonist was zigzagging

to either side of the wide space, looking for an escape; Sean now had the advantage: with both his skill and the Raptor's power in open space, he closed the distance between them to fifteen feet.

The other rider headed toward an obscured path. But he was slowing down and messing with the dash. The guy jerked forward and his wheels caught in a rut. He released the throttle and jerked again, nearly hitting a tree. Panicked, he overcompensated and turned one-eighty, facing Sean.

Sean rode straight toward him, hoping to force him back to the trees where he could block his escape route. Sean was bigger, stronger, and—he hoped—faster.

The other quad's engine was sputtering and a faint whiff of oil told Sean it had a leak. He wouldn't be getting far. Sean went full throttle until he was only feet away, spun into a controlled stop, and leapt from his quad toward the man in black.

Sean tossed his helmet and sprinted toward the guy. The quad stalled out, and Sean tackled him as he tried to run. He head-butted Sean with his helmet before jumping up, his helmet falling to the ground. Sean stood and drew his weapon in one motion, standing cautiously only feet from the arsonist.

He was practically a kid. Sean was surprised that he was so young—he might have been eighteen, but Sean suspected younger. Clean-cut, sandy blond hair, and pale blue eyes that looked both angry and scared shitless. He reminded Sean of himself when he was a teenager, shortly after his parents died. He'd been wild, angry, and felt abandoned—determined that if he was bad enough, his brother and legal guardian Duke would wash his hands of him. His brother never had, and Sean had finally overcome his anger and deep sadness.

"My name's Sean Rogan. I can help you, but you need to own up to your actions."

"Fuck you."

Sean would have said the same thing when he was a teenager. Probably had.

"You're not leaving here; I'm not letting you. We can dance around all morning, or you can make this easy."

Sean looked from the kid's eyes to his hands, assessing if he had a weapon or was going to bolt. Sean hadn't wanted to draw his gun on an unarmed kid, but he didn't know whether or not the kid was carrying.

"I'm not going to hurt you."

"That's why you have a fucking gun on me?"

"We're going back to the Hendricksons'."

The kid was trying hard not to shake, but Sean saw the telltale signs of fear. He didn't want to face the Hendricksons anymore than the police.

"You don't want them to know you're the one who's been destroying their property?" Sean said. "I get that. Believe me, I did some dumb-ass things when I was your age."

The kid snorted.

"Even worse than arson."

That got the kid interested. Sean didn't elaborate, but said, "We'll work this out, okay? If you're honest with me, I promise, I'll help make this right."

The kid's face changed, from caution to dark sadness. "You can't," he said quietly, looking down.

"You don't know me, you have no reason to trust me, but I mean what I say."

Sean mistook the downcast eyes as shame or consideration, he realized, when the kid bolted like a rabbit along the edge of the logging road.

He fired his gun into a nearby tree, hoping the sound would make the kid stop. It didn't.

Sean went after him. Faster, he quickly caught up and was about to tackle him when the kid turned sharply right, off the road. Sean followed, picking up speed, about to tackle the kid, when he veered again to the left. Sean took two more steps forward as he turned, and the ground gave way with a startling *crunch.*

His foot broke through brittle wood. A sharp cracking sound cut through the forest. Sean was falling, the sensation startling him completely, though his reflexes had him reaching for something to stop his descent. Wood and dirt slipped through his fingers. He continued to fall, shouting for help even as the daylight disappeared and he plunged into darkness.

I'm going to die.

As he thought of his death, he thought of Lucy, and then he hit the bottom of the narrow pit, his left arm twisting painfully beneath him. He cried out, his body writhing, and an excruciatingly sharp pain hit him in the thigh. His head ached and he couldn't see. The only thing he heard was ringing between his ears.

But then faintly, from seemingly down a long tunnel, a young man's voice said, "I'm sorry. I had no choice."

And then silence and darkness blocked out everything.

TWO

When I was ten, I wanted to kill my brother.

I pushed him off the roof because I caught him searching my room for money. I was half his size and five years younger. I may have been born with a vagina, but I've always had more balls than he ever did.

He only broke his arm. I went down to the front yard and broke his fingers for good measure. He's lucky I didn't cut off his hand like they do to thieves in some countries.

When I turned fifteen, my daddy's best friend tried to force me to suck his dick. I shot him in the balls.

I don't suck dicks.

Daddy took care of that problem. I didn't kill the prick, but he's dead.

Amen.

Before he got himself killed, Daddy always warned me that my temper would get me in trouble. I listened. Common sense taught me I had to control the Amazon inside. Can't push my brother off the roof because he's family, and blood is all we can count on. Can't shoot someone in the balls because it's messy, and messes are hard to clean up.

I hate messes. Yet time and time again, I'm forced to clean up other people's shit. I never forget who created the problem in the first place. The threat of punishment keeps people in line. Revenge is a dish best served cold? I say revenge tastes good any way you can get it.

My oldest brother calls me a monster, but I prefer Amazon. A mythological race of warrior women stronger, better, smarter than everyone else. And my temper has served me well, when necessary. No one screws with me, that's for sure.

Returning to Spruce Lake after all these years was the last thing I wanted to do. It felt like being kicked back to the street turning tricks as a twenty-dollar whore after pulling in two hundred bucks an hour as a call girl. The saying that when you want something done right, do it yourself pounded in my head, taunting me. If I'd just had the damn Hendrickson property burned to the ground last year, I'd never have to step foot in St. Lawrence County again.

Yet here I was. Waiting at the curb of the tiny airport for my driver, who was late.

It wasn't that there was anything particularly wrong with my hometown, other than I hated every square mile of the pit, but I'd grown into a city girl with city girl instincts. If Spruce Lake wasn't essential, I would have simply ignored the situation and let the good old boys handle the problem, not caring whether they got themselves arrested or killed. But not only was that wretched piece of mountain important for my business, it was critical at this point in time.

My reluctance to return was somewhat due to some old grievances related to my last visit. But when had

I ever let a threat stop me? I would face any problems head-on, like I did everything else in life.

If I hadn't left Spruce Lake, I would never have met my husband, now deceased and burning in Hell, thanks to me. I used everything Herve taught me, used everything he had—his knowledge, his money, his life.

If I hadn't left, I would never have learned more than my brother about the business. I wouldn't be feared and worshipped, and I would never have the power to run such a vast operation from afar.

But part of leadership was punishing the weak, and my people were acting like a bunch of fucking hillbillies. I didn't even want to take ownership of the motley crew. Not a clearheaded, forward-thinking brain among any of them.

Maybe I didn't hate my hometown, I'd just outgrown it. I would have been happy to have a house here to relax and keep my eyes on things, but business in the city was too intense. And about to get busier.

If only I could put an end to that resort. If I could control the damage from the arson fire. If only the Hendricksons had postponed their plans until next summer, I wouldn't have to resort to any extreme measures.

Another thing my daddy always told me: avoid murder unless there's no other choice. I haven't always followed that advice, but I always had a reason to kill, damn straight.

My ride finally drove up, thirteen minutes late. I probably wouldn't have shot him if he were later. It would have been just one more mess to clean up.

But he didn't have to know that. Fear would keep him in line.

THREE

Lucy accepted the water from Annie Lynd and greedily guzzled the sixteen ounces. Her throat was raw from the smoke, and soot covered her skin and hair. She watched as the Fire and Rescue team did their job of extinguishing the fire and checking for hot spots.

"The fire's out," Tim said as he approached, taking a water bottle from Annie. "The kitchen's a total loss." He kicked a metal chair and it skidded across the wood porch.

Annie spoke timidly. "We can use the kitchen in Joe's house until—"

Tim cut her off. "How can we open at all? What if we had guests here when that fire started? What if someone got hurt?" He turned to Lucy, fury and helplessness in his eyes. "Have you heard from Sean?"

She shook her head. It had been nearly an hour, and she'd been trying to reach him for the last ten minutes.

"Unless we find the asshole behind the vandalism and fire and put him in prison, this is just going to continue," Tim said. "I'm not putting my guests at risk. I'll just— I don't know." Collapsing on the porch swing, he glanced at Annie. "Sorry I snapped," he said before burying his head in his hands.

Lucy pulled out her cell phone. Sean had set up GPS tracking so they would be able to find each other any time—after a couple of harrowing situations, Lucy didn't object. He'd set it up so no one else could track her phone, only the principals at Rogan-Caruso-Kincaid, his security company.

His phone was sending out a strong, steady signal nearly three miles away. She frowned and tried him a second time through the walkie-talkie feature. No answer. Maybe there was too much interference, though she didn't think she'd be receiving his GPS signal if there were.

She said to Tim, "We need to find Sean. He's been stationary for at least the last twenty minutes. Do you have two more quads?"

Tim shook his head. "The arsonist took one, Sean the other." He looked at her, concerned. "What's wrong?"

"He's not answering my page."

"Where is he?"

She showed him the map on her phone.

"That's Travers Peak, near the Kelley Mine," he said. "We can drive there—it's accessible through an old logging road off the highway. I'll get my truck."

"I'm going to grab a first aid kit," Lucy told him. "I'll meet you back here."

Annie called after her, "I'll put together food and water in case you need it."

Lucy ran back to the cabin, her lungs still burning from helping put out the fire. The police hadn't arrived yet, but Spruce Lake was so small it didn't warrant a police force or even a substation. Tim had reported the crime to the sheriff's office in Canton. They were sending an investigator and she wanted to be here to talk to him. But first she had to find Sean.

Lucy didn't tell Tim he should have brought the police into this situation sooner, because he now understood his mistake. Maybe they could have prevented this expensive attack. The good news was no one was hurt, the fire hadn't spread to the rest of the lodge, and there was another kitchen that could be used. But if she and Sean couldn't find the culprit, it was clear by Tim's reaction that he wasn't opening the resort as scheduled on Memorial Day weekend, a real shame because Tim and Adam cared so much about creating a viable economy for the dying town. She hoped Sean had some idea who was behind this after his pursuit.

After packing a duffel bag with emergency supplies she ran back to the lodge, where Tim was waiting in his truck.

"I still can't reach Sean," Lucy said, as she climbed in.

"Are you getting his GPS signal?"

"It hasn't moved."

Lucy couldn't dismiss her worry. It wasn't like Sean to not check in—not when doing something like this. If he was moving, she wouldn't be as concerned, but he'd been driving an ATV over unfamiliar terrain pursuing an unknown arsonist who might have a gun. Sean was smart, but he wasn't invincible.

"Ever since the sabotage began, I've been trying to figure out who would do this," Tim said as he drove down the private road. "Maybe I was wrong—maybe it isn't someone who doesn't want tourists. Up until now, he only went after small stuff, easily fixable. Disabling my truck. Stealing supplies during construction—I started ordering twice what I needed. It's not about the money. I have more money than I know what to do with. It's that this resort will be good for the town. I've done all the comparables; I know it'll work."

"Arson is a big step up from theft and vandalism."

"That's why I'm wondering if it's personal. Maybe someone hates me. I just can't figure out why. I wasn't raised in Spruce Lake. I don't know anyone."

"Adam does."

"He left five years ago, when he went to college. I can't imagine someone would hold a grudge that long."

Five years was nothing for someone dead set on revenge. "We need to talk to him," Lucy said.

Tim turned off the road onto a two-lane highway. Two miles north was the main road into the town of Spruce Lake, but Tim turned south. "The logging road is four miles down the highway."

When Tim turned onto the logging road, he slowed down as the truck bounced over rocks, branches, and potholes. Lucy spotted an ATV partly hidden in the trees, about twenty feet down from the logging entrance. "Stop! Is that your ATV?" she gestured.

Lucy barely waited until Tim braked. She jumped out and ran into the woods. It was definitely the yellow Raptor that Sean had been driving, parked between two trees. The keys were in the ignition.

Lucy glanced at the GPS on her phone. Sean's cell phone was transmitting half a mile directly southwest of their location. He could have lost his phone while pursuing the arsonist, but that didn't explain where he was now.

Tim caught up with Lucy and checked the gas gauge. "It still has fuel." He held his hand over the engine, then touched it. "Warm, not hot."

Lucy looked around the woods for a sign of the second ATV. Not only was it not within sight, but there was only one set of tracks. It was unlikely that Sean would have pursued someone on foot then just left the ATV here—or would he?

Tim ran down to the highway, then across it. She didn't see anything that gave her a clue as to what happened to Sean. She walked a wider circle, still picking up no signs that there was more than one rider. She followed depressions in the mulch that led back to the logging road, forty feet from Tim's truck, then ended at the packed gravel and dirt road. She knelt. It was nearly impossible to make out tire impressions, but gouges from taking off too fast clearly came from a vehicle wider than an ATV. Several drops of fresh oil stained the gravel near where the tracks stopped.

Tim returned and said, "Nothing. No sign of foot or vehicle traffic or the other ATV."

She rose and gestured to the oil spot and four gouges. "Someone was parked here and left quickly. We need to find Sean's phone." She didn't want to say it out loud, but he could be lying injured anywhere between here and his phone. Finding the phone was a starting point to tracking him down. Then she would contemplate the idea that he'd been forced to leave with the arsonist.

Except that there was only one set of tracks leading from the ATV to the car.

Tim handed her the keys to his truck. "Continue

down this road until you reach the signal. I'll take the quad and retrace its route, and hopefully we'll meet up at some point."

Lucy nodded. She ran back to the truck and got in the driver's seat. Deep pits and debris littered the path in front of the vehicle. Lucy was forced to drive slowly, and it took her nearly ten minutes before she saw the other ATV.

She stopped the truck and jumped out. She could hear Tim's ATV in the distance, but with the echo couldn't gauge how close he was.

On the ground was a blue helmet—the one Sean had been wearing. She smelled some sort of fuel, but it wasn't gasoline. She looked under the vehicle and saw a large dark spot on the ground.

There were signs of a scuffle, the dirt freshly turned, branches broken, bushes trampled. She followed the destruction and saw Sean's backpack next to a tree.

She searched it. All his emergency supplies were there, including his phone.

The ATV, the backpack, the helmet—everything but Sean. And no sign of the arsonist.

Lucy bit her lower lip. Sean was resourceful, smart, even cunning at times—there had to be a logical explanation as to why his things were here, while he wasn't.

"Sean, where are you?"

Tim drove up, stopping close to where Sean's helmet lay on the ground. Lucy said, "Did you find anything?"

"Nothing."

"There was a fight over there," she pointed to where she'd found Sean's backpack, which she now had over her shoulder. "I found his pack and phone."

"We need to be careful," Tim said. "There are several ventilation shafts for the mines in the area, and it's easy to miss the warning signs. The mines are all closed now, but they're still dangerous."

"We'll start where I found the backpack and go from there." Her pulse raced. "How deep are these mine shafts?"

"Fifteen, twenty feet, some deeper. They're narrow, six to eight feet wide, used for ventilation and to haul supplies in and out. They've been boarded up for years."

They followed the tracks which made a sharp turn to the right. They skirted a tree stump, and Tim said "Watch your step." He gestured toward a bright orange tie around one tree. "See that ribbon? There's a shaft around here." He looked, then pointed. "There."

Lucy saw a gaping black hole in the ground. Except for a few broken boards along the edge, the wood was gone.

"Sean—"

Footsteps led to the hole's edge. Only one set ran away. The side had caved in, lower than the ground by a foot, as if someone might have pulled a chunk of earth with him when he fell.

Tim pulled her back. "Hold it."

"He's in there. I know it."

"Go slow. Test the ground with each step."

Lucy did exactly as Tim instructed, though it was killing her. She got down on all fours at the edge of the pit. "Sean? Sean! It's Lucy! Are you there?"

She heard only the echo of her own panicked voice.

FOUR

The pain started in his chest and radiated out to his limbs.

Sean wondered if he'd been shot.

It was very cold. Moldy and damp. He remembered. He was in the basement of that bastard who'd kidnapped Lucy. Cold, snow all around . . .

As he took a deep breath the pain suddenly sharpened and he fully regained consciousness. He wasn't in a basement; that real-life nightmare had occurred months ago. He pushed the memory aside and recalled that he had been chasing a kid—and the kid led him into this pit, whatever it was.

A mine.

Forty years ago, Spruce Lake was a booming mining town. But the mines had long been abandoned. No one would find him.

He shifted just a fraction, and his right arm sent sharp pains through every nerve in his body. Broken? No—it wasn't his arm, but his shoulder. And something was wrong with his leg, but he couldn't see anything in the darkness.

He heard something—faintly, far away. His name.

The volume increased, the panic in the voice forcing him to open his eyes and try to call back.

Lucy.

He couldn't speak; his lungs had little air from his hitting the hard packed earth. He slowly drew in breath, practically tasting the damp, moldy dirt. The pounding in his head was painful and thick. Worse than his worst hangover.

"Sean, please!" Lucy cried from above. Her voice was clearer, and she wasn't as far away as he'd thought.

A rock was jabbing him in the thigh, and he began to move, but a sudden, sharp pain made him cry out. He tried to mask his pain with a cough.

"Sean?"

He coughed again. That hurt, too, and he worried about a cracked or broken rib. He'd cracked a rib before, and that was certainly no picnic.

"Lucy," he called with difficulty.

"Thank God. Are you okay?"

"Peachy."

He was lying facedown, his mouth coated with dirt, his jammed shoulder rendering his entire right arm useless. He used his left arm to help push himself onto his back, and he cried out again. A dislocated shoulder could be easily fixed, but until he could force it back into place the pain was nearly intolerable.

"What happened? Sean?"

He couldn't respond until the initial wave passed, fearing he'd pass out again. He'd dislocated his shoulder twice before, he knew how to pop it back in—if he could stand. He moved his leg. It wasn't broken. That was a big fat plus. But something was wrong with it.

"Dammit, answer me, Sean Rogan!"

"I'm still here, Princess." He tried to sound normal, but his voice was scratchy and weak. He could make out faint light from above, but his vision was cloudy. The entrance to the shaft was partly blocked by trees and shrubs, but there was enough light for him to see shadows. He judged that the shaft was about eight feet square and twenty-five feet deep, but his vision blurred again as he tried to focus on his immediate surroundings. He closed his eyes, though in the back of his throbbing head he knew he shouldn't because he probably had a concussion. How long had he been out?

"Tim is here with me. We're going to get you out."

Though it hurt like hell, he pulled his body up so he could sit against the wall. The pain helped wake him up, and he didn't know whether to swear or be grateful.

He realized as he righted himself that a sharp, squat piece of rotten wood protruded from his jeans. Blood seeped from the wound and he didn't know how deep the oversized splinter was embedded.

He leaned against the side of the mine shaft, his dislocated shoulder bumping against the rock, and he grunted.

"Sean? Where are you injured?"

"My shoulder. Dislocated." He felt like puking, which wasn't a good sign. His head was still spinning.

"I'm coming down there," Lucy said.

"No!" The effort to shout exhausted him. He couldn't have Lucy down here. What if he was dying? He didn't want her to watch him die.

Stop being so melodramatic, Rogan. You're not dying.

It sure as hell felt like it.

"Unless you tell me that if I toss you a rope you can climb out on your own, I'll be there in two minutes."

"Lucy—"

A deep, male voice said, "Sean, I have equipment in my truck to get both of you back up. Give me a couple minutes and I'll lower Lucy down."

It was useless to argue. How else was he going to get out of this pit? He just didn't want Lucy to see him like this.

But of course Lucy could handle it. She could handle anything life handed her. Even him in this condition. He just . . . hell, he didn't know what he was thinking. The pain was making him stupid.

He closed his eyes again. He thought he heard Lucy talking, but it was far away.

"Sean? Hang tight. Okay?" Kneeling at the edge. Lucy braced herself when she heard no answer. She squeezed back tears. She was usually so much better at closing off her emotions, but Sean was in a bad way and she was pretty certain he'd passed out again.

From behind her, Tim said, "Lucy, let's get my gear."

She didn't want to leave Sean, but the faster they gathered the equipment, the faster she could get down there and check out his injuries. A dislocated shoulder she could fix. But there was more. No one could fall that far unscathed. His arm or leg could be broken. His back. He could have a concussion. He wasn't responsive, and that worried her more than the shoulder.

Tim's truck wasn't far, and he had plenty of rope and mountain gear. "I only have one harness," he said. "I'll lower you down, and you strap Sean in and I'll pull him up."

"How can you do it alone?"

"Alone?" He patted his truck. "I have a winch."

She tried to smile, but it felt unnatural and forced.

Tim squeezed her arm. "We'll get him out. He's going to be fine."

She had to believe it.

Lucy watched Tim's vehicle cautiously approach the mine shaft. There weren't many trees blocking access, but the bushes and fallen branches left over from winter storms made it cumbersome even for the large four-wheel drive. Finally, the truck was in place.

Tim called down. "Sean? You doing okay?"

"Yep." His voice was faint.

Lucy checked Tim's equipment. The harness was simple and lightweight, primarily used for rappelling, not rescue. But it had a metal ring to attach the rope, essential to Sean's release since he wouldn't be able to pull himself out.

She strapped on the harness, attached the rope, and checked all the buckles.

"You've done this before." Tim handed her a small flashlight.

"Only in training. My specialty is water rescue, not getting-my-boyfriend-out-of-a-mine-shaft rescue." Her attempt at humor was weak, but Tim smiled.

She quickly rappelled down the side of the mine shaft. She landed hard, but kept her balance.

"Impressive," Sean said, his voice strained.

"I live to impress you," Lucy said as she removed the harness. She wasn't one for playful banter, especially when she was so tense, but it relaxed Sean. Little light made it down this far and she turned on the flashlight.

He'd pulled himself into a slumped position against the rock and dirt wall. She smelled blood, and looked at Sean. Wood protruded from his leg, and his jeans were soaked in blood. She averted her eyes, just for a second, to gather her strength.

"You smell like smoke," Sean said.

"I got a little dirty putting the fire out."

"You okay?"

"Much better than you," she said. "I think—" She hesitated, a familiar smell flitting under her nose. She breathed in, smelling mostly soot and her own sweat. She exhaled and breathed in deeply.

Then she identified it.

A decomposing body.

Lucy had worked for a year in the morgue; she knew what a dead body smelled like. This was subtle, but still putrid, likely from the dampness in the tunnels as well as bacteria and molds that feed on body tissue and organs in such an environment. It smelled like cold storage, when organic matter breaks down extremely slowly.

It's probably an animal. A large animal.

It was much colder down here than on the surface. How cold did it stay in the summer months? She had no idea. But it was spring now, and if someone had fallen into this pit last year, the body could have frozen and just now started to thaw.

She pulled a more powerful flashlight from her backpack and shined it around the area. There was little except broken wood, some old, rusty tools, and a pitch-black corridor leading off the mine shaft—no telling how long the tunnel was or where it led. But no dead body in sight.

"You're not thinking of exploring the caves?" Sean said, half-joking.

"Of course not."

She knelt next to him and stared at his leg.

"It's just a splinter," Sean joked without humor. Then he said, "It hurts, but not half as much as my arm."

She inspected his dislocated shoulder. She wasn't a doctor, and would have at first thought it was broken. But she trusted Sean's assessment. "We'll have to secure it—"

"Just pop it back in."

Lucy stared at Sean under the flashlight, which made his face appear extremely pale. A sheen of sweat coated him even though it was frigid. "What?" She knew exactly what he meant, but hoped he wasn't asking her to do it.

"Duke usually helps. You have to—"

"I know *what* to do, but I don't want to."

She sounded childish. Adjusting a dislocated shoulder was agonizing, and she didn't want to hurt Sean.

"I can't do it alone, Luce. I need you."

She let out a long breath. "Okay." She had no a choice.

"Do it fast."

"Hold this." She handed him the flashlight. "Relax."

Sean tensed. "Maybe—"

"*Relax,*" she repeated. "If you're tense I could damage something. You have enough injuries as it is."

"Okay." She felt him try to calm his muscles, but he began shivering. It *was* cold down here, and his injuries and blood loss could put him into shock.

"Count to three, okay?" she said.

"All right." She didn't touch him yet, but positioned her hands so she could push and twist the shoulder back into place in one smooth move. "One," Sean began and forced his body to relax.

She grasped Sean's shoulder with one hand and pushed against his chest to hold his body against the cave wall. She pushed and barely heard the bone pop back into place over his sudden scream.

She bit back her own cry. He was right—it had to be done—but she didn't have to like it.

Sean's eyes squeezed shut and the muscles on his neck stood out. He'd dropped the flashlight and it rolled a few feet away, casting a ghostly light over their surroundings.

"I'm sorry, I'm so sorry," she said.

Sean was shaking. She took a blanket from her backpack and put it over his chest. She didn't want to accidentally bump the wood in his leg. He grabbed her hand and squeezed.

"It's okay," he whispered through clenched teeth.

"I hate to hurt you." She held a water bottle to his lips and he sipped.

She sat with him for a long minute. Dislocated shoulders were painful, but putting them back in place was twice as bad. Fortunately, other than general soreness, the pain dissipated quickly.

He swallowed, drank more water, then breathed deeply. "Better."

"Your head—"

"Yes, I probably have a mild concussion. I was knocked out for a minute or three. But other than a growing bump on the side of my head and a whopper of a headache, it's fine. Not even bleeding."

"Much." She wetted a clean piece of gauze and

wiped dried blood and dirt from his scalp and face. Sean was so much like her brothers—take a beating and still get up fighting, even when they needed to lay low for a while. "I'm keeping an eye on you tonight, since I'm pretty certain you won't let me take you to a hospital."

"I'd have to be unconscious before you could get me anywhere near a hospital."

"I need to take care of your leg," she said. "Drink some more water."

"Bossy nurse, aren't you?"

She smiled. "I'm sure you're not a model patient."

"I'll be a great patient. Especially if I'm bedridden with you."

She snorted. "One-track mind."

"We're still on vacation, Princess." He paused and gave her a half-smile. "We *were* on vacation, until someone nearly burned down the lodge. You know what this means, right?"

"Don't—"

"Exactly. This doesn't count as our vacation. I should never have let Duke convince me this would be a quick and easy assignment."

"Well, except for your clumsiness, I'm glad we can help Tim. He's heartbroken about what's been happening." She assessed Sean's leg with the flashlight. The bleeding seemed to have stopped, but she couldn't be certain it wouldn't start up again. "I'm going to cut your jeans."

When her hand brushed against the wood, Sean ground his teeth against the surge of pain.

"Sorry."

He'd need a tetanus shot, antibiotics as well. She

carefully cut away the material. "How did you end up at the bottom of this mine shaft?"

"Just lucky."

"We found the ATV you were riding by the highway."

"The kid busted his quad. I chased him, he did a quick turn and I slipped right in here."

Lucy stopped what she was doing and looked at Sean's face.

"An intentional trap?"

"I think it was a spontaneous idea on his part."

"You said he was a kid?"

"No older than seventeen or eighteen. He's not doing this alone. He was scared of someone. I'm going to find him. I almost had him convinced to trust me—then he bolted. I suspect he planned to circle around back to my quad in the hopes I'd left the keys in and he could get to it before me."

"You *did* leave your keys in it."

He shook his head. "I was stupid. Rookie mistake."

Lucy gently pulled away the scraps of material. She pulled an emergency combat tourniquet from her first aid kit—the C-A-T used by the military and EMTs were not usually found in an over-the-counter kit, but she'd enhanced her supplies. She wrapped it around Sean's thigh above the stake and cinched it into place.

"I'm going to pull this straight out, pour water on it, then—"

"Just do it."

Lucy laid out the rest of her supplies and propped the flashlight on her backpack. This time, she didn't count. She assessed the angle, then pulled the stake straight out of Sean's thigh. Nearly an inch of the sharp wood had gone in. She poured water liberally over the wound.

His eyes were closed, his jaw clenched, his face covered in a fresh layer of sweat. The grime and dirt from the mine coated his skin, his dark hair falling forward over one eye. She needed to get him someplace warm, clean, and dry.

She patted the injured area with a thick wad of gauze, then checked the bleeding. The tourniquet was doing its job. She hadn't thought any major arteries had been hit, considering the location of the stake, but she wouldn't remove the tourniquet until they got him out of the hole.

She held the gauze there for a long minute. Tim called down. "Lucy? Sean?"

She looked up. The sunlight was brighter. It was eleven in the morning, though it felt as if much longer than four hours had passed since she and Sean first smelled smoke.

"I'm bandaging his leg, then I'll get him ready to bring up."

She lifted the gauze. The skin was red and starting to turn purple. She sprayed antiseptic on it and Sean's body jerked. She bit back another *sorry,* took a fresh bandage from the kit, and taped it on the wound.

"You're good for now," she said.

"A minute," he said.

She packed up the first aid kit, then sat next to Sean and took his hand. "You're going to be okay," she said, more for herself than for him.

He put his arm around her and held her head to his chest.

She squeezed back tears. Why was she about to

cry? Sean was *fine*. It might take him a few days to go running, but he hadn't broken anything, he hadn't *died*.

A tiny sob escaped.

"Luce?"

"It's nothing."

"I'm okay. You know that."

"I know."

He kissed the top of her head, and that made the tears fall. She didn't understand why she was so upset. She'd get Sean out of this pit, take him to the cabin, watch him all night to make sure the concussion didn't cause him more problems, and by tomorrow . . .

What if he'd died?

There were so many things she wanted to tell him, things she didn't know how to say. The thought of Sean dying terrified her. She'd lost people in her life, people she cared about. Her cousin. Her ex-boyfriend. Her brother Patrick had been in a coma for nearly two years and though she prayed daily, she never thought he'd wake up. That he'd survived and was now back to his old self was a miracle.

With all her hard-fought strength, her ability to close off her emotions, she found her walls crumbling as she pictured Sean sprawled on the floor of the mine shaft, dead.

To Sean's credit, he didn't try to get her to talk about it. Maybe he understood her better than she did—he seemed to get her even when she was confused.

"Are you ready?" she asked.

He looked down into her face. Her breath caught at the emotion twisting his face. "I love you, Lucy."

Say "I love you." Tell him.

She wanted to, but not here. Not now. Her feelings were all jumbled, fear and relief and an aching rawness.

She kissed him instead. "How's your shoulder?"

"Sore, but functioning. I'm more than ready to get out of here."

Lucy helped Sean put on the harness while he remained sitting, since he couldn't put much weight on his bandaged leg. Then she helped him stand. He leaned heavily on her, showing Lucy that he was in more pain than he wanted to admit. "You're going to have a lot of bruises," she said.

"I'll expect you to kiss every one of them. You might have to bathe me, too."

"The sacrifices I'm going to have to make." She wondered if she could get a doctor to come out to the lodge.

The scent of decay hit her again. This time, Sean hesitated, too, and looked down the tunnel.

"I smelled it when I first came down," Lucy said.

"No," he said, knowing what she was thinking.

"I won't go far. I promise. Just check it out. If I don't see anything within a few feet, I'll turn around." She clipped on the hook to the harness belt. "I'm not reckless, Sean. It's most likely an animal. But just in case—" She didn't say it.

"And if you don't check it out now, you'll be back here tomorrow."

"How do you know me so well?"

Sean kissed her lightly. "I know you better than you know yourself."

A sudden unease crept up the back of her neck at the truth of Sean's statement. She called up to Tim. "He's ready!"

Tim said, "Okay, Sean—I'm starting the winch."

After an initial jolt off the ground, Sean was lifted slowly to the surface. He used his good leg to keep himself from hitting the wall, his hands holding the rope.

Once he was out of the shaft, Lucy breathed easier. She called up to Tim, "Make sure Sean gets water and blankets. I'll be ready in a few minutes."

Lucy picked up a stick to mark her way—she wasn't taking any chances of getting lost. She aimed her flashlight toward the tunnel that led from the ventilation shaft.

She knew very little about mines, but was aware that they could be unstable and extremely dangerous. Because there was no active mining, she suspected her greatest danger would be from unmarked openings or debris left over from the mining days.

Using the stick to scar the wall, which was mostly rock with some wood supports at the base, Lucy left a trail to follow back to the pit.

As soon as she stepped into the tunnel, the unique, putrid scent of decaying flesh increased. She proceeded slowly as the tunnel veered slightly to the right, shining her light on the ground to make sure it was solid before continuing forward. Glancing back once, she could barely see the light at the beginning of the tunnel and noted that she was on a gradual downslope as well as the curve. The roof seemed to be shrinking.

Claustrophobia gripped her for a minute. Breathing deeply, she calmed herself.

But the silence continued to claw at her, more terrifying than the dark. A complete void of sound. No water, no creaking, not even the sound of scurrying rodents. Shouldn't there be mice or *something* here? She didn't know, but it was logical—not that she wanted to encounter a diseased, flea-ridden rat. Only her movement made noise.

The smell of the decaying body grew stronger.

Each footfall carefully placed, Lucy continued. One. Two. Five more feet. The light behind her disappeared. The roof brushed the top of her head, and she hunched over. A small rise of panic grabbed her spine, slithering up to her brain, paranoid warning signals silently shouting

run run run

but no one was here. She had nothing to be afraid of but her own fear. She would not let it win. She counted her steps to focus on something tangible in her battle against her nerves.

Suddenly, she stepped into a wide area that seemed even colder than the pit Sean had fallen into. She stopped to get her bearings, pulling her down jacket closer around her, though that did little to warm her. Shivering, she shined the light on the far walls and estimated that the long, narrow space was about twenty feet long and ten feet wide. Four-by-four wooden support beams were placed in the center, but they didn't look strong enough to hold up anything.

Here, the miners had kept tools and other supplies. A makeshift stone table had lost one leg and leaned awkwardly in one corner. A metal chair, old and rusted, rested on its side against a wood-reinforced dirt and rock wall. Two tunnels branched off the room—one narrow like the tunnel she'd come from; the other a bit wider with a metal track laid on the ground, disappearing into the dark beyond the scope of her light. An old mining cart with metal wheels sat at the end of the line.

She couldn't go farther into the mine without putting herself at great risk, as well as worry Sean while he was injured topside. She'd inspect the room, and that was all. Besides, it was below freezing down here—in the eerie light, her breath looked like smoke.

She skirted the wall and shined her flashlight all around, turning in a slow circle.

Lucy bit her cheek to keep from screaming.

Next to the tunnel from which she'd emerged was a horizontal cutout in the wall—about six feet wide and four feet high and lined with wood planks—possibly used for storage, possibly as a makeshift bed for a miner.

It was a stone coffin now.

The corpse's long blond hair fanned around her, dull and limp from dirt and damp. Her hands were crossed at the wrists over her chest. Her legs were straight. She was dressed in dark slacks and a once-white blouse that was streaked with dirt and grime. Her eyes were closed, her mouth slack, and her skin had a blue, waxy, molted appearance.

Swallowing uneasily, Lucy approached the body. She looked down, not knowing what she expected to see—maybe physical signs of violence, or something else that might indicate whether this was an accident or murder.

The body didn't look as though it had been dead for more than a few days, but the skin didn't look quite right, either. It was hard to tell with the long-sleeved blouse and pants. The odor of decomposition was most definitely stronger here, telling Lucy that under the material there were bacteria at work.

On the surface the woman *appeared* to be dead three or four days, but this chamber felt like the cold storage room at the morgue. Cold enough to freeze a body and slow the rate of decay. The woman could have been dead for a few days, or months. Without an autopsy, there was no way of knowing.

Lucy's eyes were drawn back to the victim's hands, as they were positioned oddly on her body, cupped over her breasts.

Lucy's peripheral vision caught movement and she jumped.

The victim's mouth moved and Lucy stifled a scream, certain she was seeing something that wasn't there. Lucy shined the light fully on the woman's face. The cheeks were moving. Her mouth was partly open. The glare of the flashlight revealed thousands of tiny maggots filling the orifice.

Lucy blinked, frozen for a moment, and involuntarily pictured Sean. Insects and rodents devouring his body until it was a skeleton. If they hadn't found him, he would have died here, too.

Lucy ran back the way she came, wishing she had never seen the body.

FIVE

"Thank you so much for coming," Lucy told the semiretired doctor who'd agreed to make a house call when Sean refused to go to the closest hospital in Potsdam.

"No trouble, no trouble," Dr. Sherwood Griffin answered, looking across the room at the patient in bed. "Just wake him every couple of hours, check his eyes and reflexes, give him the pain meds every six hours. He'll be sore but I've seen far worse."

"I'm not taking any pills," a pale and exhausted Sean mumbled from the bed.

Lucy sat down next to him. "Can I convince you to sleep?"

"Yes."

"By morning, I guarantee you'll be wanting something to knock out the pain." Griffin grinned, revealing crooked white teeth.

Sean didn't return the physician's smile. He took Lucy's hand and pulled it to his chest, forcing her to lean over him. Through clenched teeth, he said, "Get him out of here."

She kissed him lightly. She had an impulse to lie

down next to Sean and make sure he was really okay, even though she knew he was going to be fine. She'd been periodically shaking since returning from the mine shaft. She didn't understand her unusual reaction, considering she'd been around plenty of dead bodies at the morgue and none of them had affected her the way the dead blonde had.

"I'll be back in a few minutes," she told Sean.

He nodded, still glaring at the doctor. When Sean had found out that Sherwood Griffin doubled as a veterinarian, he'd almost agreed to go to the hospital.

Lucy walked Dr. Griffin down the path toward the main lodge. The sun had just set, the sky glowing orange, pink, and purple. She wanted a moment of peace and silence to absorb the stunning beauty of the scene, thankful that Sean was alive.

But the doctor had something else in mind besides quiet contemplation. "I heard Tim say you found a body in the mine."

"Yes."

"Probably a hiker. We've lost more than a few in my sixty-nine years. Think because we have rolling hills and some good trails they can just do what they like, but there's plenty of danger if you don't know what you're doing." He looked her over, top to bottom. "You're a city girl. What were you doing near the mine?"

Tim hadn't told the doctor about the vandalism, and Lucy wasn't going to. "I've done my fair share of camping."

He laughed. "Your hands are too pretty to spend much time outside."

Though his comment could be a compliment, his

tone was one of derision. She'd already considered the lost hiker theory, but the positioning of the body didn't suggest accident. Possibly natural, but more likely not. Someone had specifically arranged the body.

However, she asked, "Have you heard of any hikers gone missing recently?"

"Nope, but that don't mean much. If anyone's missing, they'll be posted at the Fire and Rescue."

"Where's the station?"

"We're too small for our own substation, but about twenty minutes southeast, up the mountain near Indian Hills, there's a good-sized station. Handles a much larger area than just our little dot on the map. When I was little, we had over four thousand people in Spruce Lake and our own pump engine. Now, less than four hundred." He shook his head.

Tim emerged from his house. He extended his hand to the doctor. "Thanks for coming out, Doctor. Please send me the bill."

"Glad to do it, Tim." He looked over at the lodge and frowned. The smoke and fire in the kitchen had blackened the walls outside the windows. "I heard you had a kitchen fire. Word is it was arson."

"Word sure gets around fast."

"The Getty boy is on Fire and Rescue, and he's sweet on Trina. You tell Trina something, the entire town knows by sundown."

"The sheriff is sending an investigator tomorrow," Tim said.

"And what about the body in the mine?" Lucy asked.

"They will need to bring in equipment, the coroner,

and a detective. Everyone should be here by eight in the morning."

Lucy thought of the woman spending another night exposed like that. Someone somewhere loved her—a husband, a parent, a sister, a child. Her family deserved to know what had happened as much as she needed a proper burial.

"Where's Adam?" Griffin asked, changing the subject. "Haven't seen him around much lately."

"He's blowing off some steam," Tim said. "This resort is his brainchild, and he's really upset."

"Well, Tim, some things just aren't meant to be."

Odd comment, Lucy thought.

"I'll check on your guest in a couple days," the doctor continued. "Holler if you need anything, Ms. Lucy. I'm overdue for my nightcap at the Lock & Barrel. Maybe you should spend more time in town, Tim. Get people used to seeing your face. Bring Adam. Might make them a bit friendlier to your wild ideas for Joe's land."

"A resort is hardly a wild idea," Tim said. He rubbed his face. "I just don't know who would do this."

"I'm sure it'll all work out," Griffin said as he got into his car.

Lucy frowned as she watched him drive off. The doctor had contradicted himself. Some things "aren't meant to be" followed by "it'll all work out"? Maybe she'd misunderstood, or he was thinking about something else, but his words lingered in her mind even as his car disappeared from sight.

Tim turned to Lucy. "So Sean's okay?"

"Sore, a few stitches in his leg, and he hit his head pretty good. But he'll be fine. He's resilient."

"That's a relief." He turned back toward his house. "Would you like some coffee? Something stronger? I'm not much for liquor, but we have some beer."

"No, thank you. I'm going to go back and sit with Sean."

"I'll walk with you."

They started back up the trail that led to the cabin, discreet ground lighting guiding them along the path. "What did the doctor mean about people getting used to seeing your face?" Lucy asked.

"My parents divorced when I was five." He stopped walking for a moment, looking out at the lake through the trees. The sun had set, but the twilight made the lake sparkle darkly. "My mom brought me to visit my dad once a year until she remarried, but she'd always hated this place. The isolation. The quiet. The last time I was here, before my dad's funeral, I was sixteen. Adam was three. I barely knew my dad, and I don't know my brother. Didn't," he corrected, "until last year."

He said nothing for a long minute. "Adam lived here until he was ten. His mother divorced Dad, too—my father wasn't the easiest person to live with. Stubborn and set in his ways, but he loved this land and in a certain way he had the patience of a saint. My best memories here were going fishing. Adam ended up spending every summer here. I've wondered that if my mom wasn't so bitter, I might have had the same summers Adam had."

They started walking again. "Adam loves this place," Tim said, "and I've grown to love it. I know he's quiet, but all this stuff that's been happening is tearing him apart."

Lucy thought a conversation with Adam Hendrickson was overdue—perhaps without his half-brother Tim around.

She said, "I think it's a given that your saboteur is someone you or Adam knows, someone you'd recognize. Sean said the arsonist was a teenager. There can't be too many in a town so small."

"Everyone in Spruce Lake goes to school in Colton. But maybe it's not someone from town. There are a lot of small communities in the area, outside of what's considered Spruce Lake. At least three villages of more than two hundred people."

"Whoever it is knows the area well," Lucy said. "And they have a huge stake in making sure you don't open this resort." She stopped outside the cabin. "Can you put together a list of everyone you can think of who might have a reason—however lame it may sound to you—to stop the resort? Personal or financial."

"Duke already asked for the same thing, and I told him there's no one."

"Either someone hates you—or Adam—so much they want to hurt you personally, or they have a financial interest in ensuring you don't open this resort."

"Adam would have said something."

Another reason to talk to Adam alone. Maybe he hadn't been as forthcoming with his brother as he should have been. Or he just needed to be asked the right questions.

"What about your father? Any enemies? Close friends?"

"None that I know of. My dad was stubborn, but everyone liked him."

Except Tim couldn't truly know that, Lucy realized, if he rarely visited.

She stopped outside her cabin. "Is the coroner coming here in the morning or going straight to the mine?"

"They didn't say. I suspect they'll check the body first, then talk to us."

"I'll meet them at the mine then. I'm hoping they'll know who the victim is."

"Victim?"

"The death may have been natural, there's no way of knowing without an autopsy, but the position of the body was deliberate. I guess I'm wired to assume she was murdered."

They said good-bye at the cabin's doorstep. Lucy stepped inside and glanced at the bed. Sean lay right where she'd left him, on his back, eyes closed. He still looked pale, but he didn't appear to be in distress.

"Sean, it's Lucy. Wake up."

Sean moaned when he heard his name. "Ten more minutes."

"Good," Lucy said. "You're okay."

Sean felt Lucy sit on the bed next to him. He opened his eyes and tried to glare at her for disturbing his sleep but it hurt his head too much. His leg throbbed as if it had been stitched by Dr. Frankenstein, making his sore shoulder feel downright good in comparison.

"Who beat me up?"

Lucy sighed. "Are you trying to be funny or trying to scare me?"

"I guess I'm not funny when I'm in pain." He winced as he pulled himself up on the bed so he could lean against the headboard. Lucy put a pillow behind his head. He smiled. "Maybe I should get hurt more often, if you're going to play Florence Nightingale."

Lucy rolled her eyes at him, but he saw a hint of a grin. "I don't want to keep you up too long."

"I'm awake."

"You need to sleep."

Sean took her hand. "The faster we come up with a strategy, the faster I can go back to sleep."

"You're a rotten patient."

"So you've told me." Sean shifted to get comfortable. His leg itched, but when he touched it the pain shot up to his back.

"The doctor left some Vicodin," Lucy said.

"Hell no. That stuff is nasty. Do you have any aspirin?"

"That's like using a water pistol to put out a fire."

"I'm not taking pain pills."

"Fine, Tylenol it is, and your antibiotics."

"Yes, Doctor Kincaid."

She shook her head and read the bottles that the doctor had left. Sean never tired of watching Lucy, even now when he was hurt and exhausted. Her black hair hung over one shoulder in long, silky curls, damp from the shower she'd taken when they'd returned. Her profile was aristocratic without being sharp. Her skin revealed her half-Cuban heritage, neither light nor dark, but a perfect blend. Lucy had no idea how beautiful she was or how much he loved her. He'd told her many times, of course. He couldn't hold it back once he'd realized how strongly he felt. That she hadn't yet admitted that she, too, loved him wounded his ego a bit, but he knew her feelings for him scared her. He'd seen it especially today, in the pit, when she'd realized his injuries might be serious.

She handed him three Tylenol and an antibiotic. He took the pills and a swig from the water bottle she offered.

"Learn anything interesting about what's going on around here?" he asked.

"We need to talk to Adam," Lucy said. "He spent every summer here, but Tim hasn't been here since he was sixteen, not until his father's funeral last year."

"We should go into town tomorrow as well."

She glanced at his leg.

"I'll be fine."

"I doubt you'll be able to walk."

"I didn't say walk to town."

"Can't you just take it easy for a day?"

Sean took her hand and squeezed. "The kid on the ATV is in some sort of trouble. I can help him."

"That *kid* nearly killed you."

"He's scared." At the look on Lucy's face, Sean quickly added, "I'm not saying he had no choice, I'm just saying I can get to him."

"You think if we just drive through town you'll be able to spot him?"

"Not really, though I might. But I want to have a drink at the local watering hole, talk to people, watch them, see what we can learn."

Lucy frowned. "That tone—what do you have planned?"

"Nothing specific—yet."

"Now that the Sheriff's Department knows about the vandalism, they'll be on it."

"I haven't seen a cop since we got here. They didn't exactly rush over here after the arson fire, but I'm not going to step all over their investigation."

"All right, we'll go *if* you're feeling up to it. I don't want you making yourself sick."

He ran his fingers down her cheek. "I'm fine, Lucy. Just sore. We'll leave first thing in the morning."

"Maybe not first thing—the coroner and a search-and-rescue team will be here tomorrow morning. To retrieve the body from the mine. Can you wait to go to town until I get back from there?"

"I'm coming with you."

"Not back down in the mine!"

"Tonight, I feel like shit. But tomorrow, it's back to work." He paused, seeing the worry in her eyes. "What about you? Sure, my body took a licking, but that dead woman really shook you up."

"I think she was murdered," Lucy said. "Her body was posed. She was fully clothed, but something was wrong. If I hadn't suddenly lost my nerve and run away, I might have noticed what struck me as off." Lucy stared at a blank wall, but Sean knew she was picturing the morbid scene.

"You're cold."

She shook her head.

"Then why are you shaking?" He pulled her down to lie at his side. The tension in her body was from more than the gruesome memory.

He rubbed her back until she finally relaxed. When she closed her eyes and rested her head on his shoulder, he breathed easier. "What happened down there?" he asked quietly.

Lucy didn't immediately answer, but Sean knew she wasn't asleep. Her heart was beating too fast, and her hand absently rubbed his chest.

"If we hadn't found you, you would have died." Her voice cracked at the end of her sentence. "For a split second, I saw you instead of the woman. Lying in that alcove."

"But you did find me. And I'm not completely helpless." She didn't respond to his reassurance, and he kissed the top of her head. "Princess, I understand."

Lucy had been scared of losing him and she didn't like being scared. She didn't know how to interpret or respond to the complex emotions about their relationship. It was as if admitting she loved him would jinx it, or put one or both of them in physical jeopardy.

Sean understood all this about her, even though she had never voiced her fears. They lived dangerous lives, and that wouldn't change. Sean would no more tell Lucy to dump the thought of becoming an FBI agent and take a nice, safe teaching job than she would demand he quit Rogan-Caruso-Kincaid and sell computers.

And even if they did take an easier road? Sean suspected trouble and danger would follow them—or they'd seek it out. Lucy could not turn away from someone in need, nor could Sean ignore someone being bullied.

Lucy's deep compassion for others was one of the many reasons Sean had fallen in love with her.

Her breathing evened out as her body relaxed. "I love you, Luce," he whispered and closed his eyes.

SIX

All the years I spent learning how to control my reactions, and in less than ten minutes Reverend Carl Browne had me enraged.

"What the fuck *were you thinking!" I shouted, my voice echoing in the large open space.*

We sat in a church pew in the chapel, just him and me, though now I rose in fury, standing in the aisle. If I didn't get this anger out of my system, I'd kill him, and that would be disastrous.

I simply couldn't believe the pathetic reasons Carl gave for his decision to torch the Hendrickson place. It all boiled down to panic.

"You were scared," I continued. "You freaked out. If you were anyone else, you'd already be dead."

He bristled. "Remember who you're talking to, little girl."

"Just because you were my father's closest friend doesn't give you a free pass to be an idiot," I said.

He reddened, his hair looking even whiter. Twelve years ago Carl might have been called distinguished; now he just looked old.

This day had exhausted me. I'd spent twelve hours

checking and double-checking on every cog in my operation. Amazingly, everything was running perfectly smooth, except for the issue with the Hendricksons. But I had figured out how to handle that, and while it would be some time before I exacted my revenge on the family, I could wait.

Business took precedence over revenge.

"I have a plan," I told Carl, "and for it to work, you need to call off your dogs. No more petty vandalism and definitely no more fires."

"If the resort isn't shut down by Sunday, we lose everything," Carl said.

I stared. Damn, I wanted to kill him. Just for stating the obvious, as if I were some kind of imbecile.

"Thank you," I said, looking down at him in the pew. "What would I do without you reminding me of my own business plan?"

He didn't flinch, nor did he look scared as he stared up at me defiantly.

I slapped him hard. Not expecting it, he almost fell out of the pew. A red mark darkened his skin. A spot of blood welled on his lower lip.

"This is my town, Carl. Mine. *Just because I left doesn't mean I handed it over to you. Remember, Preacher, I know what you've done, so don't think one second about going against me."*

If my first plan didn't work, I had another. But I wasn't about to strategize with Carl. He'd pissed me off. Instead I said, "The resort will be shut down before Sunday because the Hendricksons want to close it, or are forced to, but it will be done without the ridiculous shit you're pulling."

"You've been gone too long."

"That sounds like a threat, Carl."

He hesitated. Good. Maybe he had finally realized I was dead serious. Maybe he saw in my eyes that I wanted to gut him.

My cell phone vibrated. It was my stupid brother.

"What?"

"We have a problem," he said with deep seriousness.

"Oh for shitsake, don't be so melodramatic! Spill it."

"A woman's body was found in the mine."

I closed my eyes. I felt like I was on a roller coaster. "Don't tell me it was the bitch."

"I don't see who else it could be."

Was the universe conspiring against me? First Carl panics, and now my idiot brother calls me without even first verifying all the facts.

"Find out if it's her, then bring me the person responsible for fucking up a simple body dump!"

I threw the cell phone across the church. It hit the large wooden cross behind the altar and fell to the floor, shattering in three pieces. "God-fucking-dammit!"

Carl rose. "Watch your mouth in God's house!"

I really wanted to kill this fool. First for being stupid, now for daring to correct me. Instead I laughed. "That's rich, Carl. You've broken more of the Ten Commandments than I have." Smirking, I walked to the back of the church. Without turning around, I said, "Find out everything about the body in the mine. Who found her, if they know who she is, anything else the cops might know. Before sunrise. My patience has left the building."

SEVEN

Jimmy Benson sat on a bar stool at the Lock & Barrel, his draft halfway to his mouth.

I'm a dead man.

He drained the rest of his beer and put down the mug. It hit the counter with a thud. He froze, eyes on the mirror behind the bar, searching for evidence that someone, anyone, was watching him.

The Lock & Barrel was the only business in Spruce Lake open past six p.m., the only place to get dinner and a drink and talk. Even on a Wednesday night in a town of 386, the place was nearly half filled with two dozen patrons.

It was soon to be a town of 385, Jimmy thought. Because he was getting out of Spruce Lake tonight one way or the other—on foot or six feet under.

Was everyone looking at him, or was it his overactive imagination?

Reggie, the Lock & Barrel's longtime bartender, gestured toward his empty mug. After his shift, Jimmy usually had three beers, but he'd had only one since he arrived twenty minutes ago. He hadn't even finished his shift; he'd left sick. After he'd gotten the call about the arson, he knew his nephew was in way over his head. He actually felt sick. But anyone who was watching would only notice he was nervous.

He nodded at the barkeep. "Thanks." He put a small handful of nuts in his mouth, being as casual as possible as he eavesdropped on Doc Griffin's conversation with the waitress and two regulars. Not that he had to concentrate; Woody Griffin wasn't keeping his voice down.

Someone had found her body. Jimmy had heard it on the scanner this afternoon. He wished Woody knew more, because Jimmy had to know how this happened. But then Woody switched topics and talked about the fire and vandalism at the Hendricksons' place. About how no one wanted outsiders here. The others nodded in agreement.

Jimmy knew the truth. They *all* knew the truth, but wouldn't say it aloud. Easier to act like rednecks than criminals.

Jimmy picked up his fresh beer and sipped, leaned back, and saw Gary Clarke in the mirror. Standing across the room, staring directly at him.

Jimmy looked away, but he still felt Gary's eyes on the back of his head.

The body had been found around noon, and Hendrickson would have immediately called the police. That meant the information had been out there nearly nine hours. Plenty of time for the wrong people to find out that Jimmy hadn't followed orders. That had to be why Gary Clarke was here.

The creaky front door signaled a new patron. Jimmy glanced discreetly at the mirror to see who entered. His pulse raced.

Shit.

Slipping off the bar stool, he casually walked toward the bathroom. But as soon as the swinging hall doors closed behind him he turned left, into the kitchen.

"What's up, Jimmy?" Omar Jackson—the cook and only black man in Spruce Lake—smiled brightly.

"Not much." Unable to fake a smile, he kept walking. He didn't know if Omar knew what was what, or if he was as ignorant as he pretended. Maybe he feigned ignorance to stay alive.

Or maybe he was neck deep in the same shit Jimmy trudged through.

Avoiding conversation with the cook, Jimmy exited out the back door, then walked briskly around the corner to his truck.

As soon as he slid into the driver's seat, the bar's front door opened wide. Three men emerged and headed his way.

Jimmy floored it. No use pretending. They knew he hadn't made the body disappear. There was no way they'd let him live. They didn't know why he'd survived this long. It was as if he was made of Teflon; he'd been told that now and again.

He had known the risks when he put Victoria's body in the mine. He was no saint, but he wasn't a killer nor could he treat her body like garbage. So what if he'd disobeyed orders. He hadn't believed she'd ever be found.

Going home would put his nephew at risk. The only way Jimmy could protect his nephew was to disappear.

He sped up, his old truck squealing in protest. He glanced in the rearview mirror.

Gary Clarke's brand-new black F-250 was gaining on him.

Jimmy floored it. At first, his truck didn't respond, then it lurched forward as he picked up speed with the decline in the road toward Colton.

He *might* make it to Colton, but then what? Go to the police? He would have laughed if he wasn't so terrified. He wasn't safe in prison or out.

He fumbled with his cell phone and dialed the only person who might be able to help. The only person he might be able to trust.

"Jimmy? You can't call me. Not now."

"Help me! Someone found her body! Now Gary and—"

"I can't help you."

"You have to! Dammit, you promised to protect me!"

But the line had gone dead.

He dropped his phone, sobs racking his body. His sister had asked him for one thing: to protect her son. The last five years he'd thought he was doing the right thing, keeping their enemies close, doing odd jobs, keeping the kid in school. The kid was going places.

But not if Jimmy couldn't protect him. The one person who promised to be there wasn't.

The Colton Reservoir was coming up. Behind him, Gary Clarke was still gaining. If they caught him, it would be a lot more painful than what he planned to do. Maybe he'd survive. Maybe he'd escape.

Speeding up just as he crossed the short bridge, he turned the wheel sharply to the right, using the lip of the walkway to jump the railing. The bottom of his truck scraped the metal, and for a moment he thought his wheels would catch, Gary and his pals would drag him out of the truck and do horrible things . . .

Then he was up and over, flying in the dark, falling down, hitting the water hard. His head banged against the steering wheel on impact, and the last thing he thought as he drifted into unconsciousness, the water rapidly rising around his legs, was:

I'm sorry, Abigail. I tried my best.

EIGHT

Even though she didn't believe he'd take her up on her suggestion, Lucy still tried to talk Sean out of going with her to the mine Thursday morning so he could rest. He drove her to the site in the rental SUV he'd picked up at the airport, parking behind three official vehicles.

"I suppose you won't wait in the car," she said.

He raised an eyebrow skeptically. "Give it up, Luce."

She grumbled, but opened the passenger door. Why was she surprised? None of her four brothers would have been waylaid by a two-story fall or a dozen stitches.

She walked—Sean limped—to where a sheriff's deputy and rescue worker stood at the edge of the mine shaft watching their approach. Apprehension rose in her chest as they neared the open pit.

"Hello," Sean called out, raising his hand in a friendly wave.

"Lost?" the deputy asked.

"Not at all," Sean said. "I was the lucky guy to fall down there yesterday."

The cop didn't smile. "You're lucky you didn't break your neck."

Lucy's stomach flipped. Was her inability to rid her mind of Sean's fall a sign of post-traumatic stress? She couldn't control her body's reactions, and that was unlike her.

"That's what I said, I'm a lucky guy." All humor was gone from his tone. "Sean Rogan. Lucy Kincaid. Lucy found the body."

He didn't say anything about their backgrounds. If people knew he was a P.I. and she was an FBI recruit, it would be harder to quietly gather information.

"Deputy Weddle. This is Al Getty, Fire and Rescue. You're staying at the Hendrickson place?"

Sean nodded. "Is the coroner down there?"

"Just lowered their equipment."

"I'd like to join them," Lucy said. "I found the body and can show them where she is."

At first Weddle looked as though he would argue. Then he said into his radio, "Ham, you there? Over."

"What do you need? Over."

"The little lady who found the body wants to join you. Over."

There was a long pause. Weddle didn't take his eyes off her. Was he laughing internally, or suspicious?

"Shaffer says send her down. Over."

Weddle said to Lucy, "You heard him."

"Are you sure you want to do this, Luce?" Sean quietly asked.

"She's been on my mind—I want to make sure I saw what I did."

"Excuse me?" Weddle said. "You want to make sure you saw *what*?"

"The way she was posed."

"Posed," he said flatly. When she'd first approached, Weddle's casual posture had led her not to consider him much of a cop, but now his eyes assessed her with a suspicious glint.

"She was flat on her back, arms crossed over her chest. It didn't seem . . . ," she searched for the words, ". . . a natural way to die." She zipped up her jacket, remembering how cold it had been in the mine yesterday.

"Boss?" Getty said.

"Strap her to the chair."

Getty buckled Lucy into a rescue seat with a full five-point harness secured around her thighs and over her shoulders.

"Ready?" he asked.

She nodded, holding Sean's blue eyes as she was lowered down.

I love you, he mouthed.

"She's going to be okay down there?" Weddle asked Sean.

"Yes," Lucy heard as Sean and the cop disappeared from her view.

Down below, Ken Hammond, the Fire and Rescue supervisor, introduced himself and the deputy coroner, Frank Shaffer, as he unhooked her.

The smell of decomposition Lucy had identified yesterday seemed to have dissipated, but she figured it was because of the severe overnight temperature drop. She made a mental note to check the high and low temps over the last few weeks, though she didn't know why she'd need to do it—the coroner would handle the death investigation. Shaffer motioned for her to lead the way.

"I marked the walls with a stick," she said, shining her light on the tunnel walls. Her faint scratches were still there.

Hammond said, "Smart move. These mines have some odd tunnels. I've been down here before with the Army Corp of Engineers to assess damages after cave-ins. Even the maps they have aren't completely accurate. I don't know if anyone knows these caverns anymore."

"What was mined?" she asked as she walked carefully down the tunnel to the room.

"Iron primarily, but they found a vein of titanium in the thirties, which helped keep the mine in business during World War II and the Korean and Vietnam wars. It slowed down after the Second World War, but it wasn't until the midseventies that they completely shut down.

"My dad and granddad worked down here," Hammond continued. "I think everyone in town is attached to this mine one way or another."

Lucy stepped out of the tunnel into the larger cavern, bracing herself.

"I've never been on this side of the mine," Hammond said. "This was a secondary vein, built in the midfifties. They needed the ventilation shafts because the air quality—"

"Where's the girl?" Shaffer interrupted.

"She's in a large cutout in the wall." Lucy turned and shined her light. "Right here."

She stared.

The slab was empty.

Her face froze in a blank expression as she shined her light slowly around the area. The broken chair. The old tools. The two tunnels. This was where she had been yesterday. There was no mistake.

She looked back at where the decaying body should be. It was still missing.

"Maybe you went down one of these other tunnels," Hammond said.

Lucy shook her head. "She was right here." Her voice cracked on the last word and she steeled herself. She was a professional; there was an explanation. She just had to figure it out.

She saw Hammond and Shaffer exchange glances they might have thought were discreet, but they believed she was either an idiot or an attention-seeker.

"We're going to check out the tunnels," Hammond said. "Wait here."

Lucy stared at the empty hole.

She hadn't imagined the dead body. She hadn't made up the maggots in the woman's mouth, or how she lay. She didn't have nightmares last night over a figment of her imagination, dammit!

Less than twenty-four hours ago there was a dead woman *right there.*

Someone had moved the body.

Who? Why?

She shined her light on the floor. A dead body, even a diminutive woman like the blonde, would be heavy and awkward. One person couldn't easily carry her, not without disturbing the dirt, unless he had help.

The ground yielded little information, especially with her lone flashlight. She needed an evidence kit and bright lights to make out any faint marks on the hard surface. Did she see footprints? Were they hers? Too large. Shaffer's or Hammond's? She couldn't tell just by looking.

Whoever moved the body had help. Or . . .

She spun around and turned her flashlight to the tunnel with the tracks. The mining cart that had been there yesterday was gone.

NINE

Hands clasped firmly in her lap, and resisting an overwhelming urge to pace, Lucy sat stiffly on the worn couch in Tim Hendrickson's living room while Deputy Sheriff Tyler Weddle asked her questions. Sean sat next to her, watchful and protective, but he was keeping his mouth closed—which was rare, but probably a good thing since she was about to throttle the cop.

"Ms. Kincaid," Weddle said, "I understand you were highly stressed when you were in the mine. Your boyfriend was injured, you were—"

Lucy interrupted. "I know what I saw."

"There was no body down there."

"There was no body there *today*, but it was there yesterday. You need to get a trained crime scene team down there to look for trace evidence."

"I think you watch too much television." Weddle exchanged a smug glance with Ken Hammond, who stood next to Tim by the front door.

Lucy bristled. "I have—"

Sean cut her off. "You're out of line, Deputy."

Lucy frowned. She didn't like being talked to as if

she were a fool. She had seen a body. She could close her eyes and picture the woman: dark blond hair; extremely pale skin with a blue tinge; white blouse and dark slacks, and something else . . . something that flitted in and out of her mind as soon as she attempted to focus. But it was the deceased's arms crossed unnaturally over her chest that had Lucy the most intrigued—and concerned.

The deputy questioned, "And someone went down there and did what? Moved the body? To where? Why would someone do such a thing?"

Sean said, "It's no secret that I fell down the mine shaft. Word travels fast in a small town. Maybe whoever was hiding the body felt the need to move it."

"That's a bit of an assumption," Weddle said.

"Hardly." Sean leaned forward. "There was a body exactly where Lucy said it was."

Lucy knew Sean was irritated that the cops were treating her as if she were crazy, and she wasn't tickled about it either, but she put aside her frustration and tried to see it from their point of view. She was a stranger, she'd been through a traumatic incident, and she seemed to be seeing things that simply weren't there.

"I apologize." Weddle didn't sound at all sincere. He stood. "I'll contact the sheriff and give him your statement. He may send a team down there, or maybe not. The mine is extremely dangerous. There are exploration shafts that go down a hundred feet, caved-in ceilings; it hasn't been maintained in forty years. But he'll probably want to at least check out where you thought you saw the body."

"Where I *did* see a body," Lucy said.

"That's what I said."

"They need to search thoroughly," Lucy pushed. "They only did a cursory inspection—"

Hammond said, "There were some signs that someone had been down there recently, but nothing significant. I'm not going to put anyone at risk—we need a current map of the mine and additional team members."

"The lighting was poor, but if you—"

"Ms. Kincaid," Weddle interrupted. He took a step toward her, intentionally crowding her as a method of intimidation. "We're going to check out your claim, but we must follow safety protocols."

"I understand," she lied. Every muscle itched to defend herself. "I can look at missing persons pictures, see if I recognize her," she offered.

"I'll have the station shoot you over what we have. But there's no one local who's missing, and no lost tourists. Probably a waste of time."

"It's my time to waste," Lucy snapped. She rose from the couch, and brushed past the cop.

"I'll let you know if anything turns up," Weddle said. "About the body or the arsonist."

Lucy didn't have any confidence in Weddle's ability. Surely, the sheriff would show more professionalism when he read the report.

Tim walked Weddle and Hammond outside to their truck.

As soon as they were safely out of earshot, Lucy said, "Sean—"

"I know what you're going to say, Luce. But until we know what's going on with the vandalism, we need to keep a low profile. Announcing you work for the FBI or trained as a forensic pathologist doesn't equal 'low profile.' "

"It's murder, Sean! The police need to make that young woman's death a priority."

"I agree, but let's see what they do in the next twenty-four hours before we blow our cover. Give them time to do their job. You said the body *could* have been down there for months—another day isn't going to make much of a difference."

Even though she understood his reasoning, Lucy didn't agree with Sean. They were in Spruce Lake because of the vandalism. Now that there was an arsonist endangering lives, the gravity of the situation had increased. If word got out about their credentials, it could spook the saboteur into hiding—or possibly even escalate the sabotage. But that didn't mean the police couldn't uncover their identities with a little looking—an Internet search would easily yield Sean Rogan at RCK East, a private security company, and Lucy's involvement with a couple of FBI cases might have her name popping up in the media. Lucy didn't think that just because Spruce Lake seemed to be living in the past, the authorities didn't have basic tech skills and an Internet connection.

"Luce?"

"You're right," she said.

"I have a feeling your mind is working overtime."

Before Lucy could respond to Sean's comment, Tim stepped back inside the house. "I think they're taking you seriously, Lucy."

"I hope so."

"You didn't tell them why we were here?" Sean asked.

Tim shook his head. "As far as anyone in Spruce Lake knows, you're friends of mine. End of story. I didn't lie, didn't expand. But the cops have your names and addresses."

Sean nodded. "That's the police—unless the conspiracy is huge, our information shouldn't get out of the Sheriff's Department."

"In a town this size, anything's possible," Tim said.

"Let's keep our cover for the next couple days and see what happens. If it gets out quickly, then we'll need to rethink our strategy." He stood and stretched, then tried to hide his limp.

"It's a little early for dinner," he continued, "and I have some work to do. If you'll excuse us, Tim."

"Of course."

Lucy and Sean left, but instead of going to their cabin, Sean led the way to the lodge. The scent of wet, burned wood still clung in the air. "I saw Adam go inside when we drove up with Weddle," Sean explained.

They found Adam Hendrickson upstairs in one of the rooms, salvaging what he could after the fire in the kitchen.

"Adam," Sean said, "we need to talk."

"Sure." He sniffed the mattress deeply. "I can't tell if I'm smelling smoke in the mattress, or if that's just because I can't get the stench out of my nose."

"Give it a couple days. We can move everything to one of the other cabins, air things out, see what can be saved."

"This is going to delay the opening. Why would someone do this?"

It was a rhetorical question.

Sean pulled over a straight-back chair and sat, his leg throbbing. "Tim said you were close to your dad, closer than he was."

Adam shrugged. "I spent every summer here, even after my parents divorced. Dad didn't talk much, but he was one of those guys who didn't need to. You felt like he just knew everything under the sun. I was raised in Syracuse, but Spruce Lake is my home." He paused. "He'd talked about turning this place into a family camp, but he never got around to it. I think he enjoyed having the lake to himself."

"Did your dad have any enemies? Anyone who—"

Adam shook his head and leaned against the wall. "Everyone liked Joe Hendrickson."

"Maybe it dates back further. When he was younger. Or his family."

"Like the Hatfields and McCoys? The only thing along those lines might be that my grandma—she died when I was little—was a Kelley. Her family owned the mine until they sold to the government, then had a lease to keep mining. The Kelleys used to own all the land around here, but sold most of it off."

"Who owns the mine? The federal government?" Lucy asked.

"As far as I know. Or New York State. We're northwest of what most people consider the Adirondacks, but we're technically in the same mountain range as the state park."

"It sounds like the Kelleys made a good deal," Sean said. "Get paid for the land by the government, but still be able to mine and pull out resources."

"I really don't know," Adam said.

"Maybe someone held a grudge, doesn't want you

to be successful? Did anyone lose big when your family sold off the other parcels?"

"No—the thing is, my grandmother sold the land to people who'd been paying rent for years to the Kelleys—sold it cheap, too, from what my dad said, telling people all the rent they'd paid over the years could be used toward the purchase."

"When was this?"

"Before I was born. I was three when she died, and in her will she forgave all the outstanding loans. My dad was the same way, you can ask his best friend, Henry Callahan. The big ranch you passed on your way here? That's Henry's place."

"Would you introduce us to Henry?" Sean asked.

"Sure, why?"

"At this point, I don't know. Someone is trying to shut you down and I want to find out if it's personal—against your family."

Adam looked stunned. "Personal? I don't believe that."

"Can we talk to Henry Callahan tonight?"

Adam nodded, but now seemed preoccupied. "Sure. I can arrange that."

"Someplace out in public," Sean added. "See if we garner any interest from strangers." It was time they shook things up and see who reacted.

Lucy was quiet as they walked back to the cabin.

"Tell me why you're ticked off," Sean said when he opened the door.

"I'm not."

"Is it because I want to go public? Meet with Callahan and push some buttons?"

"No."

He didn't push. He crossed over to the desk in the corner and booted up his computer. Lucy stood at the wall of windows overlooking the lake, arms crossed over her chest. He watched her out of the corner of his eye. Her chin tilted slightly upward, the posture she assumed when she was trying to form an argument.

He sent an email message to his partner Patrick, Lucy's brother, giving him a rundown on what happened as well as a request for some needed research. As he typed, he watched Lucy's mouth turn down. She was ready. He suppressed the itch to smile. He knew Lucy well.

She said, "A dead body trumps arson."

"You think we should have shown our cards."

"Weddle treated me like an idiot. I don't think they're going to take this seriously, no matter what Tim said. Why on earth would Deputy Weddle think I'd *lie* about seeing a dead woman in the mine?"

"I don't think that's—"

"And someone moved her. That means someone who knew we found the body went there last night to get her out. Why?"

"To cover up a murder?"

"Exactly. Yesterday I wasn't sure if her death was natural or inflicted, but I wasn't thinking straight. There is no logical way for her to *naturally* die in that position. Maybe she was killed in or near the mine, and it was the only place the killer could think of leaving her. Maybe it was an accident—and someone panicked and didn't want to go to the authorities."

"Tim said no one in town is missing."

"No one from *Spruce Lake* is missing. What about

the surrounding areas? Potsdam or Canton? A camper from last summer? Spruce Lake is small, but the highway winds through the state park and could bring people from all over passing through."

"What do you want to do?" Sean asked, though he knew the answer.

"Go back down in the mine, first thing in the morning."

"I knew you were going to say that."

"I'll understand if you're not ready—"

"I'm not letting you go alone."

"How's your leg?"

"Fine." It hurt like hell. "What do you expect to find?"

"I don't know. Maybe nothing. Or maybe a clue to her identity. How she died. How she was moved. Who she was. A confession etched on the wall of the tunnel, I don't know. I just feel like I need to go down there and do *something*."

And that was the crux of the problem, Sean realized. Lucy felt helpless and her need to find justice for the dead woman—to give her family peace—overrode the details of the plan. If she didn't search for answers, she wouldn't be able to put it to rest. The woman would be on her mind, a tragic puzzle with no solution. Even if Lucy went down in the mine and found nothing, at least she would feel that she had done everything she could.

"All right," he said. "We go down first thing tomorrow morning."

"Thank you. And—would you mind if I asked Patrick to pull all missing persons in the area? Not just

St. Lawrence County, but all of upstate New York? Maybe the adjoining states?"

"Already done." He grinned at the surprise on her face and leaned back in the chair, hands behind his head.

"Why didn't you tell me?" Lucy stared at him with such a quizzical expression that Sean laughed.

"You never have to hold back with me, Luce. Your mind is a computer. You go through all the arguments you can think of to get your point across, and then bring them up one by one until you get your way."

She looked both confused and sheepish, not sure if what he'd just said was a compliment. "I don't understand what you mean."

"Brainstorm with me. Give me all your ideas, the good and the bad, and we'll go through them together. You don't have to justify your reasons for anything, not to me."

"That's not what I was doing."

"Yes you were. Maybe you don't see it."

She shook her head and turned away.

What had he said wrong? He wanted Lucy to know that he *knew* her, how she thought, how she felt, so she never felt that she had to put on an act for him. She didn't have to sell him on her ideas. With her family and her colleagues, she was always hesitant to stand by her theories, though she was rarely wrong. Sean wanted her to have the confidence she deserved without tacit approval from Patrick or the rest of her family, or even him.

He stood and limped over to her, his leg stiff from sitting too long.

"You can say anything to me, Lucy."

"I know," she said quietly.

"Good." He kissed her, a long, soft kiss that generally was a prelude to taking her to bed. He wished they had more time alone—she was still preoccupied, and it felt important to find out what she was thinking. "Luce, I mean it."

"Sometimes I think you enjoy this game of yours a little too much. Trying to read me, so proud when you get into my head. And you're good at it. Really." But she wasn't smiling, and Sean felt a chill run down his spine. "I like that you understand me, and I love that you're so supportive. But sometimes I feel manipulated, like a puppet, when I explain something you already figured out."

"I don't mean to—"

"I know you don't." She squeezed his hand. "If I thought you were doing it to make me feel foolish, I wouldn't be here. You know me, Sean, better than anyone. Which is kind of scary considering we haven't known each other for long. So think about that—knowing me, how I would feel if someone *was* manipulating me."

Sean realized he had made a critical mistake with Lucy. "Sweetheart, I would never do anything to hurt you. You know that, right?"

She smiled and nodded, but Sean saw that she'd put her shields back up, the invisible barrier that he hated. She should never feel defensive around him.

He wanted to push. Instead, he said, "I think it's time to go into town and see what crawls out of the woodwork."

TEN

An audible hush descended on the half-filled Lock & Barrel when Lucy and Sean made their entrance with Adam Hendrickson. All eyes turned to the group as they crossed the room to an empty booth. They sat, Adam on one side, Sean and Lucy on the other.

The crowd resumed talking. Quietly, making no pretense that they weren't looking at the threesome.

"You sure know how to kill a party," Sean said, bemused. "I swear, this place is right out of Deadwood."

"Until these past few months, I'd have said Spruce Lake wasn't as violent or colorful," Adam said. "Now, I don't know."

Lucy looked around. Small, round lopsided tables littered the dark, scuffed wood floor and a row of booths lined the far wall. Behind the worn bar was a beveled mirror to watch the crowd. The mirror itself was an antique. Much of the bar and its décor was old but durable, adding a certain raw charm. A sign on a small stage in the back declared that Bo Crouse and the Miners were playing from eight-thirty until closing on Friday and Saturday, and the specials were written in Day-Glo chalk near the kitchen: Unlimited barbeque ribs for $6.99 and draft beers for a dollar.

Black-and-white photographs of the Kelley Mining Company lined the walls. Kelley had been the only major employer in Spruce Lake for decades. Mining equipment hung from the ceiling and an old mining cart was showcased in the corner, reminding Lucy of the cart she'd seen yesterday in the mine.

A bald, middle-aged man worked behind the bar, and the lone waitress—a skinny blonde in her midthirties who wore too-bright makeup and too-tight jeans—approached the table with a warm smile that didn't quite reach her tired eyes.

"Adam Hendrickson! You haven't been by in forever. And you brought friends." She appraised Sean as if he were a *Playgirl* centerfold and she the lucky photographer.

Adam introduced Sean and Lucy. "They're friends visiting before the resort opens." He looked over at them. "Trina was always nice to me when I visited in the summers."

"Your arrival was always exciting! City boy visiting us hicks for two whole months. A cutie, too. Anything to liven up this town." She then did a double take on Sean. "You're the one Doc Woody was talking about!" Trina looked at Sean's lap. "Twelve stitches, huh? Did it hurt?"

Sean gave Trina a self-deprecating nod and dimpled half-smile. Lucy had seen him turn on the charm like a faucet, and it never failed—whether the women were young or old, attached or single.

"Not much," he said modestly.

While they talked about the "excitement," as Trina

called it, a sprinkling of pinpricks crawled up Lucy's spine. They were being closely watched. She discreetly assessed the room. Many patrons were glancing over at them every now and again, but no one seemed unduly focused.

It would seem odd to most people that Lucy had a vivid physical reaction to being watched. In the past, she'd blamed her discomfort—and occasional panic—as remnants of her attack seven years ago. And, in the past, her reaction was psychosomatic; she'd felt as though she was being observed even when she wasn't.

It had taken her years, but she'd learned to distinguish the difference between the psychological tension when she was in a large crowd and the real tension caused by undue attention. Sean had taught her to trust her instincts. Just because she couldn't tell who was watching their table didn't mean there wasn't someone watching. And here? They were the strangers. She tried to dismiss her feelings, but she couldn't stop the sensation crawling down her spine.

Adam said, "Trina, I know I'm getting the ribs, but could you bring a couple menus for my guests?"

"Sure! Can I get y'all some drinks first? We're running a special on Miller in the bottle. Jon got a deal from the distributor." She winked and walked off without waiting for them to agree to her recommendation.

Adam smiled. "Don't tell her anything you don't want the world to know."

"She might come in handy," Sean said.

"She hasn't changed. No one has, really," Adam said.

"Do you know most of the people in here tonight?" Sean asked.

Adam looked around, none too discreetly. "I recognize most everybody, though not all by name." He smiled broadly and waved at an older, clean-cut man who walked in to the chime of two bells over the door. "It's Mr. Callahan."

Henry Callahan smiled broadly at Adam, who stood to shake his hand. "Adam! Good to see you, son," Henry said.

"Thank you for meeting us," Adam said, sliding over so Henry could sit.

Lucy wished they'd met in private, though she'd understood Sean's reasons for making the meeting public. She didn't know how forthcoming anyone would be in such a public venue. The bartender was watching their table, his face expressionless.

Adam introduced the group. "I haven't been in here in months," Henry said with a long sigh. "I'm getting old."

"But you own the Lock & Barrel," Adam said.

"Not anymore, I gave it to my nephew a couple years ago. Jon had already been running the place for years, and with Emma doing poorly, I don't like being out of the house as much."

"I'm sorry to hear Mrs. Callahan isn't well."

"Growing old wears you out." But he smiled. "I'm glad you called, Adam. We've only talked a few times since Joe's funeral."

"Tim and I have been busy."

"Joe would be happy that you and Tim are here, working together."

"Not everyone is," Sean said.

Henry shook his head. "I heard about the fire. Al Getty said it destroyed the kitchen?"

"Yes. We salvaged all that we could, and Tim is working out a plan to see if we can make the repairs in time for the grand opening."

"When is that?"

"Memorial Day weekend."

"Adam said you and his dad were close friends," Sean said, steering the conversation toward their goal.

Henry smiled. "We grew up together. My dad was the foreman at the mine, worked for Joe's in-laws, the Kelleys. Faced changes, the mine closure, the town dying. Births, deaths. Change hasn't been kind to Spruce Lake."

"Tim and I think the resort will be a good change," Adam said. "But someone has been vandalizing our equipment for months. And with the arson—we don't know if we're going to be able to pull it off."

"People get set in their ways, and change scares them."

"The town is dying," Adam repeated. "The resort will create jobs and industry. It's a good thing!"

"I agree, son, I do, but after everything that happened with the Swain family, people don't exactly like the idea of strangers around. That left a sour taste."

Lucy said, "Who are the Swains?"

"Satan's spawn," Henry said, the words sounding odd coming out of the mouth of such a soft-spoken man. "Six years ago, Paul Swain finally went to prison. Followed in his father's footsteps, that's for sure."

"What were they convicted for?"

"Lawson Swain, Paul's dad, was a couple years older than Joe and me. A big bully. Went to prison for killing his girlfriend. And everyone knows he killed his wife—the mother of his kids—though no one could prove it."

"Where is he now?" Sean asked.

"Lawson is dead. Rumor has it he led a prison riot, and was stabbed to death by a fellow inmate with a knife made from a tube of toothpaste. But Paul was already ten times shrewder than his dad. Paul was the one and only drug dealer in Spruce Lake. Hooked a whole generation of kids, but not just here. He was selling everywhere. What did they call it? Distributing? Had a house where they made that chemical drug."

"Methamphetamine?" Lucy prompted.

"That's it, I think. Well, there was a big sting, and Paul and a dozen others were arrested. The press—state *and* national—were here, reporters from television to newspapers to radio. We all had short tempers then. The way the media depicted our little town was nothing short of slander. As if we were all drug dealers. They didn't understand that anyone who stood up to the Swains were dead. We just did what we had to do to survive. And that's why most of us don't cotton to strangers."

"You mean you knew what was going on?" Adam asked.

"We didn't *know,* not as fact, but Joe and I suspected Paul was doing something illegal. It was easier to ignore it. Safer." He shook his head. "Your dad only had you two months out of the year. He only showed you the good side of Spruce Lake."

Adam seemed distraught, and Lucy said, "What happened after Paul Swain went to prison? Did things improve?"

"That's a matter of perspective."

"Perspective?"

"The devil you know . . ." Henry's voice faded away.

"Henry," Adam began, but then Henry smiled meekly and waved his hand.

"Ignore me. I'm just feeling old today."

Lucy glanced at Sean. He was thinking the same thing she was—something secret was going on and Henry Callahan knew what it was. But he was scared or too intimidated to talk.

Sean said, "What do you think about the vandalism at the Hendricksons'? Is it simply someone who doesn't want change or someone who doesn't want growth?"

"I honestly don't know. Tim . . . he may be Joe's son, but he's not like Adam. He hasn't been here in years. People don't know him or trust him." Henry looked at Adam. "You're part of Spruce Lake. Tim isn't. No one's going to trust him."

Lucy suspected it was more than that. She said, "The vandalism may be about distrust of Tim, but it's also about stopping the resort. Who benefits if the resort doesn't open?"

"I think the question you should be asking is, who is *hurt* if the resort opens?"

Henry excused himself and shuffled to the bathroom, stopping twice to talk to patrons.

"What does he mean?" Adam asked.

"The devil you know," Sean muttered.

"Excuse me?"

"I need more information about the Swains, and what happened to their drug operation. I think there may be a new player in town, far more dangerous than local boy Swain."

"But what does that have to do with the resort?" Adam asked.

Lucy explained. "If there's a criminal enterprise in town, anything that upsets the apple cart is a threat."

Lucy again felt the chill of being watched. She glanced at the bar, and this time saw a man staring right at her. He had stringy brown hair to his shoulders, a red plaid shirt, and a partial beard. Seeing her look his way, he winked. She turned away.

Sean picked up on her discomfort and followed her gaze to the bar. "Who's that guy?" he asked Adam.

"Gary Clarke," he said. "Don't know anything about him, just that his family has been in town forever."

"And the guy he's sitting with?"

"Andy Knolls. He owns the Gas-n-Go. One pump, small grocery store—we passed it driving in. He's a nice enough guy, used to give out lollipops whenever kids came into the gas station."

"We need to put together a Spruce Lake family tree, so to speak," Lucy said. "Maybe if we can see the connections between the people in town, something will stand out."

Sean said, "I'll ask my partner in D.C. to run backgrounds on the Swains, Clarkes, and Knolls. What about other property owners? Who borders your land, other than the Callahans?"

"Everything on the eastern side of the highway is

state land—part of the Adirondack State Park system. South of us—some is county and the rest is privately owned, I think."

Henry returned and sat back down. "Adam," he said, "I hope you take this advice in the spirit in which it is offered—your father was my closest friend. There's a reason why he never tried to open a resort. Maybe you and Tim need to rethink your plans. Just for a year or two."

"I thought Dad just wasn't organized. He didn't like the paperwork and permits. I remember when he built the house, he complained for years about county regulations."

Henry sighed and shook his head. "That was part of it, for sure, but he understood that Spruce Lake isn't Lake Placid. We like our quiet way of life. But, Tim is like your father. Stubborn. I'm sure he doesn't want to postpone. I wish there was something I could do to help."

His eyes were on a man approaching their table. He was about Henry's age, but taller and with more hair—all of it silver. His pale blue eyes were magnified behind thick glasses, and he shook Henry's hand warmly. "Henry Callahan, how are you? And Emma?"

"I'm well, thank you. Emma has her good days and bad days."

Henry introduced the group to Reverend Carl Browne.

"Adam," Browne said, "it's been good seeing you in church. Maybe you can bring your brother once or twice."

Adam smiled sheepishly. "I try."

"I was sorry to hear about the fire. I hope there wasn't too much damage."

"Nothing that can't be fixed."

"Did I see Jon come in a few minutes ago?" Browne asked.

"I didn't see him," Henry said, looking around. His eyes came to rest on a man coming out of the kitchen. Presumably Jon, he was speaking with a wiry man with skin darker than a moonless night. The black man wore a well-washed white smock and chef's hat. After a brief conversation, he went back to the kitchen and Jon Callahan waved to their group.

Henry's nephew, current owner of the Lock & Barrel, was in his midforties. He stood straight, though was no taller than Lucy's five feet seven inches. Physically trim with conservatively cut dark, graying hair, he wore pressed jeans, a turtleneck, and a sweater. His watch looked expensive, but Lucy supposed it could have been a knockoff. She didn't pay much attention to fashion.

Lucy didn't know whether Henry was simply tired or wasn't thrilled to see his nephew. But as Jon stepped up to the table, shaking hands like a politician, Henry smiled. "Hello, Jon."

"Uncle Henry, you should have told me you were coming by! I would have had dinner with you."

"I took your aunt on a drive today," Henry said. "It was such a lovely spring day, but she's a bit worn out and went to bed early. I thought I'd take advantage of the longer days to stop by for a drink, pick up some supplies."

"I can bring you anything you need; all you have to do is ask."

"You do more than enough, Jon. Have you met Adam's friends?"

After introductions, Henry said, "I should go and check on my wife. She still gets around all right, but I don't want her becoming disoriented in the dark."

He said his good-byes and left. Lucy exchanged a glance with Sean. He silently agreed that the conversation was unusually brief, as if Henry didn't want to stay around talking to either his nephew or Browne.

"Would you like to sit?" Adam asked them.

"Just for a minute," Jon said. "It's Thursday night and I came in to run payroll. Not a big staff, but it takes time."

"I'm going to hit the road, too," said Browne. "Nice to meet you folks. If you're around this weekend, please stop by the church. Don't matter what faith, just a short little sermon and a nice little choir. Ten a.m."

"Thank you," Lucy said. "That sounds lovely."

The minister left and Jon pulled up a chair from a neighboring table. "I'm sorry about the trouble you've been having on your property," he told Adam.

Adam nodded. "Do you have any idea who might be doing this?"

"You probably know everyone in town," Sean added quickly. "Anyone unusually upset about the resort plans?"

"Everyone has an opinion. Mostly, we don't want change, even if it might be a good thing. But I don't know who's behind the vandalism, Adam. I wish I did, sorry."

Jon paused, then added, "Maybe if you just held off

a year or so, let people in town get to know Tim, get reacquainted with you, you can start fresh."

Lucy was instantly suspicious. That was almost the *exact* same thing Henry Callahan had said.

But maybe since Henry and Jon were related, they talked often, and since right now the resort was number one on everyone's minds, if they had come to the conclusion that postponing the resort was a good idea, they both could have espoused the viewpoint as if it were their own. It was a plausible theory, though Lucy wasn't certain their response wasn't somehow orchestrated.

Sean said, "Jon has a point."

Lucy and Adam both looked at him. His face was blank, or rather, Lucy thought, *intentionally* blank. He had a plan.

"I'm not waiting," Adam said, stubborn. "The police will find out who did this." He turned to Jon. "The Spruce Lake Resort will help revitalize the town. Bring it back to the way it was when my dad was a kid."

"Have you thought that maybe people here like the quiet life?" Sean asked.

"Jobless and depressed?" Adam countered. "I don't think so."

"We're doing fine," Jon said. "Look, Adam, I'm not wholly opposed to the idea of bringing in tourists. Right now just isn't a good time. You and Tim settle in, take your time, and then I'll be there helping you. But right now, people are skeptical and, to be honest, scared of change."

"That fear doesn't justify burning down our property!" Adam said.

"Of course it doesn't," Jon said calmly. "I have an idea. Do you want to hear it?"

Adam frowned and said nothing. Sean said, "Sure. I'll pass it on to Tim."

"It's really simple." Jon smiled and looked from Sean to Lucy and back. "Tell Tim if he slows down, I'll meet with him in a couple weeks, he can lay all his plans out for me, and I'll help him sell the idea to the people of Spruce Lake. I think what they're really scared about is how fast this is all happening. Joe only died last spring."

"Fourteen months ago," Adam said.

"And in a town like this, it feels like weeks, not months." Jon rose and shook everyone's hand. "I'm happy to come out to talk to you all."

Sean said, "I'll talk to Tim."

"Good. By the way, how do you know him?" Jon asked.

"From the city," Sean said.

"Right. New York."

"Boston," Sean corrected.

Lucy watched Jon Callahan leave. "He was trying to trip us up, see if we really know the Hendricksons," Lucy said. "He knew Tim lived in Boston."

"The question is why?" Sean asked.

"Jon Callahan?" Adam shook his head. "Henry was my dad's closest friend. They've been neighbors their entire life."

"Henry isn't his nephew," Sean stated plainly. "Henry said something that has me thinking this is a bigger situation than a couple good old boys not wanting tourists in their town. *Who would be hurt if the resort opens?* It's a different way of looking at the same problem, but it was how Henry said it. Someone will lose big if you open. And Henry Callahan knows—or suspects—who that is. The fact that his nephew was pushing you to postpone the opening is a big, fat red flag."

"At this point," Lucy said, "I wouldn't be surprised if the whole town was in on it."

ELEVEN

Lucy was dreaming one of those dreams where initially you have the illusion of control. In the dream, it was dusk, the sun sinking into the foothills. Each day began in birth and ended in death. Why was she so melancholy? This was a dream! She could make it a happy one.

She smiled as Sean walked up the leaf-strewn, gravel road toward her, the sun no longer setting but high overhead. She was so warm. He kissed her. She sighed and closed her eyes, her body leaning against his. Sean was always hot, her personal electric blanket.

"Lucy."

She opened her eyes and it was sunset again, this time the sun gone along with Sean, the sky rapidly darkening. Dead leaves skittered across the dirt and an icy wind stung her bare arms. She looked down at the raised bumps and wondered why she would have gone out in this thin blouse without a sweater.

But this was a dream, she reminded herself; she could give herself a sweater. Something warm, thick, and soft. She had to find Sean.

She squeezed her eyes shut and huddled in the

sweater, the wind nearly blowing her over. She had to find Sean before it was too late. What did that mean? Too late for what?

Fear clawed at her, just beyond reach. Foreboding gripped her chest, her heart racing, and she knew deep down where she rarely looked that all good things must end.

"Lucy!" a distant voice called.

She opened her eyes and for a moment she thought she was awake and wondered why she was outside. It was dark, the air cold and still, a full moon casting odd, blue-gray shadows over the mountainside. The trees. The ground. The dark, bottomless hole . . .

"Lucy, help!" It was Sean!

"Where are you?" He was deep in the pit. But the pit wasn't a hole, it was a tunnel. She ran in, chasing his voice, as the tunnel spiraled down, steeper and steeper. She was Alice chasing the white rabbit, only there was no light, no hope, and time had already run out. The blackness surrounding her had taste and texture, like the crypt at the morgue, thick and tangible, suffocating her. She ran, her hands skimming wet rock walls, the coppery taste of blood filling her mouth. She began to tumble down, faster and faster, a scream trapped in her throat until . . .

She was kneeling next to Sean as he lay at the bottom of the mine shaft. "You're okay," she said.

Light surrounded Sean as he smiled at her. "Hey, Princess, I know you love me."

"How?"

But he just smiled and reached up, his brilliant blue eyes sparkling, bluer than blue, bluer than was natural. This was the dream she wanted. Sweet and warm and full of love. She wanted to lose herself with Sean, forget everything but this moment in time. His hand rubbed her neck, her hair looping in his fingers, and he brought her lips to his. Sean's patience, his greedy but steady kisses, his powerful fingers, replaced her fear with desire. And maybe it wasn't the words of love, but the actions that mattered. Sean had shown her something she never thought she'd have. Never thought she was capable of receiving . . . or giving.

The sound of water, like a winter stream, began softly, steady drips, as they kissed. As Lucy relaxed, the running water intensified, pounding around her like a waterfall. Lucy broke the kiss. The light was gone and the fear returned tenfold. Sean screamed from far away, and when she searched with her hands where he had been, all she saw was blood.

Water flooded the mine and she swam toward Sean's cries of pain, her body thrown against rocks, cuts stinging. She couldn't breathe. Water poured into her mouth and she was drowning . . .

. . . until she was spit out into the pit of the mine, where she'd found the dead woman. So cold. So silent.

"Sean," she whispered. "Where are you?"

On the ledge, the dead woman was back. Lucy crawled over to the body and kneeled in front of it. A flower bloomed in the corpse's hands.

A scream came from deep in the mine, echoing through the rock chamber. Lucy shook her head, eyes squeezed shut, trying to get rid of the sound.

"Lucy," Sean whispered.

She smiled, and turned to him.

Sean lay where the dead woman had been. His eyes

stared at her, but they saw nothing, drained of color. He grabbed her left hand and put it on his chest. It was wet, slick and messy and bright red.

"No no no no!"

In her other hand was a gun.

Sean had been trying to gently wake Lucy as soon as he realized she was caught in a nightmare. Night *terror* was more appropriate, as sweat covered her body and she thrashed in her sleep.

"Lucy, wake up, please." He tried to control his own panic because he didn't want her to hear him so worried. Her hands were ice cold and she was shaking, a faint whimper coming from her chest that had Sean on edge. He'd never witnessed one of her nightmares lasting this long or deep.

He pulled her from the bed, hoping the motion would jerk her awake.

"Lucy, it's Sean. Look at me!" He shook her limp body. She stiffened and threw her head back, her dark eyes open, glazed and filled with pain.

A sob caught in his chest, and he held Lucy tightly against him. Her heart raced as fast as his, as if they'd both just run a marathon. She wrapped her arms around his neck, her face pressed against his chest, her body still shaking violently.

"I've got you," he said. "I've got you."

Sean had never been so scared as when he couldn't wake up Lucy, knowing she was suffering. Knowing he couldn't stop her pain. He wanted to hit something. The people who hurt Lucy all those years ago were dead. If they weren't, he'd kill them himself. The urge toward violence was unlike him. But he couldn't think, not where Lucy's pain was concerned, and he ached keeping his feelings bottled up. She'd told him that her nightmares had all but disappeared in the seven years since her attack, until a few months ago when her rapist had been found dead only miles from her house.

"I—I—I—" Lucy's teeth were chattering and she couldn't form her sentence. Sean sat on the bed with her, grabbed the down comforter from the floor, and wrapped it around her.

"Shh," he whispered. He'd let her talk if she wanted, though hearing her speak of her attack would shred him inside. He braced himself.

"You were dead." Tears streamed down her face.

"What?" It wasn't the same recurrent nightmare she'd been having? He was relieved, but uncertain. He cleared his throat. "I'm right here, sweetness."

She pressed her clammy forehead against his chest, his T-shirt fisted in her hands. "I need you." Raw emotion clouded her voice.

Sean rocked her. He hated that he felt better knowing her bad dream wasn't about the attack. He pushed aside his anger and focused on Lucy's heart. Because that's exactly what this was about—her, him, *them*. Though she'd handled his fall down the mine shaft professionally, he'd known she was worried about more than his injuries. That she'd had something to do helped her deal with the fear of losing him, but in sleep her defenses were down. All the barriers she'd put up to protect herself, gone.

"I need you, too, Princess."

She shook her head. "Not the same."

"Yes, it is the same." He kissed the top of her head.

"I love you." Lucy held back a cry, and he pulled her closer. "Don't be scared of my feelings."

"Not yours. Mine."

"I know." She wouldn't admit she loved him. She didn't want to need him. He knew she did, but it would take time and patience for her to accept it. He'd never been patient about anything in life, until he met Lucy. She had spent years learning to be alone, to protect her heart and her mind and her body. He'd been methodically working his way beneath her barriers because he needed her to lower her shields—at least when she was with him.

"How? How do you always know?"

He shrugged and kissed her. "I just do. I know you were scared yesterday when I was at the bottom of the mine shaft. I know that you didn't want to give voice to your first thought that I was dead. Finding the woman's body made you think, what if you hadn't found me? What if I died down there?"

"Don't—" She swallowed a cry.

Lucy still didn't want to think about that, and Sean's rhetorical question had her picturing the bullet in his chest, just like the nightmare she was still trembling from.

Sean said, "Luce, you're the strongest woman I know."

She didn't feel strong, not now. "It's not the dead that get to me." Lucy struggled to find words that wouldn't make her sound childish. "I killed you, Sean. In my dream, I was holding the gun."

Lucy had killed two men, but it was the first—one of her attackers, seven years ago—that had her constantly questioning her morals and ethics.

She'd shot Adam Scott in cold blood, six bullets to the chest. And she didn't regret it, not for one second of her life. What terrified her was the lack of guilt—no remorse, no doubt that if she had it to do over again, she would still have shot him. Revenge? Justice? Or was this lack of remorse akin to sociopathy? What if she was walking the line between the good guys and the bad? How could she tell the difference?

What was she capable of? How far would she go for justice?

She'd let the FBI report conclude it was justifiable homicide based on extreme emotional distress. Scott had shown her rape live on the Internet while thousands of sick perverts watched, believing she had been a consensual partner playing the part of a victim. She would never forget the lie she hadn't corrected:

Ms. Kincaid believed that Scott had killed her brother, Dr. Dillon Kincaid, in the moments before she arrived at Dr. Kincaid's house and saw Scott at the scene.

Scott had not pointed a gun at her. She had known Dillon was safe; she'd seen him. She'd taken her father's gun with the sole purpose of killing Adam Scott.

Lucy had been forced to talk to shrinks about her rape and the shooting. And she had played the stalwart victim. Only, she didn't know how much of it was truth and how much deception. Maybe all of it was an act. She'd finally told her parents that she wasn't talking to one more psychiatrist or rape counselor or priest. The tightrope she'd walked during the months before she moved cross-country to attend

Georgetown University had been unbearable because she didn't feel at all like herself. It was as if her entire life was happening to someone else, and she was observing it as a bystander. The more she looked at herself from the outside, the more distance she had from her own emotions. And she liked becoming focused, cool, and unemotional. It wasn't happening to *her;* she was merely an observer. She had never broken down, not then, and didn't want to now. Moving to D.C. had given her the space she needed to distance herself from her own thoughts and sensitivities. Until now.

All these complex and foreign emotions about Sean were dangerous. After seven years of keeping her feelings under tight lock and key, she was out of control. What if the fates made her pay for her actions? Justified killing or not, understandable or not, Adam Scott's murder had been premeditated and calculated. And wouldn't it be just the perfect sick cosmic joke to take away the one person who had so easily picked the lock that had guarded her thoughts, feelings and—ultimately—her sanity?

"Lucy?"

Sean touched her damp face carefully, as if she were precious to him.

Tell him you love him. Tell him.

She kissed him.

"I need you." She hated that she couldn't say the words. She wanted to, but fear shut her down. Sean wanted her to; it hurt him that she hadn't, though he'd never tell her that. She saw it before he hid his disappointment.

But if she said the words out loud, she feared what was so special between them would suddenly end.

"I'm here, Princess." He held her face, planting soft, gentle kisses on her lips, the kind of kisses that made her melt, and in her current state melting would turn into a meltdown, and she couldn't have that.

You overthink everything.

She turned off her inner critic, which seemed to be taking Sean's side in everything. Lucy needed to be in control. She couldn't give it up, and love meant no control. It meant sacrifice and heartache and being lost in another person. If she could just keep the barrier up a little while longer, to figure out what this all meant, where it was going, how she was going to survive.

Lucy straddled Sean, reaching for the hem of his shirt and pushing it up, her cold hands warming against his chest as she opened her mouth and kissed him fully, no soft sweetness, no doubts that she wanted to make love. No more talking about her feelings or his feelings or thinking about anything. She could lose herself in the moment because that's what this passion was—a moment in time.

She needed to be lost. She needed to stop thinking.

Sean wanted to savor Lucy, to show her that he needed her as much as—maybe even more than—she needed him. He was arrogant and fun-loving and he played it loose with the law if he had to, but at heart he'd been waiting for a woman like Lucy to give him purpose and meaning in his wayward life. She completed him, and he needed her to understand what that meant to him.

But she didn't give him time to think, and he never wanted to go slow when Lucy turned on the switch and craved him. He needed that from her, her faith and passion, because now was the one time she gave herself over to him, trusting him with her body and her deep, unspoken need for unconditional love.

In the back of his mind warning bells rang that something was going on with Lucy, that it was important, and maybe now was the time to push her hard and force her to tell him what that beautiful head was thinking. But when he opened his mouth to speak, she locked onto him, her kiss hot and unstoppable. Not that he wanted to stop. Her hands massaged his chest, her fingers digging into his muscles just short of the point of pain. She didn't stop moving, her hands, her mouth, her long legs pressing against the outside of his thighs as she sat on him fully arousing him.

His hands moved under her long T-shirt, skirted over her hips, up the soft curves of her athletic body. He loved how she was both soft and hard, her muscles tight and strong but her skin smooth and delicate. His thumbs reached for her nipples, pushing in gently but firmly until he heard that pleasurable gasp he loved, emanating from deep in Lucy's chest.

Sean watched Lucy pull off her shirt, revealing her body. The scars that cut across her breasts still made him angry, but he never showed it. She'd close up, cut him off, worry . . . Right now, all he wanted was to show Lucy she was perfect.

He brought her breasts to his face and kissed them, savoring the weight of them first in his hands, then in his mouth. She leaned into him and he almost didn't realize she was pulling down his boxers with her toes until they were tangled around his ankles. Her full body pressed against his, and he wrapped his arms tight around her, but she shrugged them off as she sat back up.

She touched his penis and he groaned. "Luce—"

His voice was scratchy. He wanted to tell her to wait, slow down, let him relish her, but it was too late. She rotated her hips until he started to penetrate, then all at once she pushed down.

Sean grabbed her ass and held her tight against him as he attempted to regain control. But that was a fruitless endeavor because Lucy didn't sit still. Slowly, she moved her hips in circles, giving and taking pleasure. She reached for his hands and clasped them, pushing their joined fists into the bed for leverage. She adjusted her knees on either side of his body and picked up the pace of her lovemaking. Her back arched, and he watched her, amazed at how beautiful and sexy and innocent and wanton she looked, all at once. Her head tilted back, her long, elegant neck begging to be kissed, but he couldn't lean up without breaking the intense moment. Her eyes were closed, her skin flushed and slick, her mouth parted. She licked her lips, not intending to arouse him further, but because she didn't know what a turn-on it was, it made him all that much more greedy for her body.

Lucy had made her mind a blank. No thoughts, just the physical sensations that drenched her body, drowning her inner voice, burying her fears. Sean was inside her, his hands clutching hers, his muscles clenching and relaxing, then contracting even tighter as he came closer to the edge she was about to go over. Fast, little foreplay, but she didn't need it or want it. She was learning more about her body and Sean's body and ways to set them both off. The explosion was becoming seductive, a drug she craved more now than ever before.

"Kiss me," Sean said, his voice gruff.

She leaned down, shifting her pelvis, and he groaned beneath her. He let go of one of her hands and grabbed her head, bringing her mouth to his, devouring her lips, his tongue mimicking his penis. He wasn't moving in and out, he was moving in and deeper, and her body shuddered all on its own, shaking as his orgasm ignited hers. Sean swallowed her cry as he held her body tight against him, his muscles rigid.

"God, Lucy," he muttered as she felt his final release.

Sweaty, she collapsed on top of him, all liquid and hot and satisfied. She sighed, her mind still empty as her body came down from overdrive. Sean's rapidly beating heart soothed her. She could stay like this forever.

Sean felt Lucy drifting off to sleep. He shifted her to his side, and she murmured into his chest, "That was nice."

"Only nice?" he whispered, trying to pull a blanket around Lucy even though she wasn't budging. He maneuvered the comforter back onto the bed and put it over them. Too hot for him, but Lucy would get cold.

"Very nice?" Her eyes were closed but she had a half-smile on her lips. He kissed her. "Perfect?"

"Honey, that was too fast to be perfect."

"That's okay."

"Why?"

"No time to think."

Long after Lucy fell asleep, Sean thought about her comment and wondered what she meant—or if she even realized what she'd said.

TWELVE

Lucy didn't know what she'd been expecting to find in the mine when she and Sean ventured into the cavern on Friday morning, but nothing jumped out at her as odd. In the storage room, she stared at the spot where the dead woman had been lying two days ago and saw nothing but rock and dirt.

"What do you want me to do?" Sean asked.

She hadn't wanted Sean to come down with her. He still wasn't one hundred percent after his fall, and though he tried to hide the pain she knew his leg hurt. However, now she was relieved she wasn't alone in the dark, frigid space. It seemed ridiculous to be scared of something that wasn't even here. It was like being in a haunted house. Purely fiction, the imagination creating all sorts of implausible outcomes because of fear.

She gestured to the alcove. "She was right there."

Their breath was visible. Though nearing fifty degrees topside, it was still below thirty here underground.

Why would someone keep the body in the mine?

To store it.

Down here it was as cold or colder than the crypt at the morgue. A body would decompose slowly or, if frozen, not at all.

Sean took her hand. "Do what you need to do," he said.

She closed her eyes. She wanted to see the woman as she had been, the unique and musty scents of the cave triggering Lucy's memory.

Her hair had been limp and darker than true blond, but that could have been because of the moisture. The skin had been only slightly molted, very pale, showing no obvious physical decomposition. But in these cold environs, the body could have been there a week or for months.

"She was laid out straight, flat on her back," Lucy said, glancing at Sean. "Her arms were crossed over her chest. She wore dark slacks—not jeans—and a very dirty white blouse. No jacket or sweater."

"Odd for this climate."

Lucy nodded. "Her skin tone was almost identical to the corpses in the cold storage room at the morgue, but given her clothes, it stands to reason she was killed in a warm place, or at least not outdoors. I can't see why the killer would have removed her coat, but not her other clothes, unless there was something on it that would identify him."

"What about her shoes?"

Lucy sighed. "I didn't look."

"You saw them—you just don't remember. Close your eyes again."

She did, but didn't know how this would help. She hadn't made a conscious observation about the dead woman's shoes, and she didn't want her imagination conjuring something.

But as she mentally assessed the body as she'd seen it, she realized she *had* seen something. "Dark. Flat. No shoelaces. Loafers maybe, some sort of slip-on."

"Good," Sean said.

She smiled, pleased that she'd remembered the detail.

"Last night you said something bothered you about her hands. What?" Sean asked.

Her arms had been crossed . . . but something else was there, something had caught Lucy's attention.

It hit her.

A flower.

Lucy opened her eyes. "I didn't really register it before, but there was a flower on her chest, between her hands. Not in her hands, but laid on her chest, the stem tucked under her wrist. It wasn't big, and it was shriveled and brown, but I was too distracted to notice more."

"Distracted how?"

A chill went down her spine. "The maggots. In her mouth."

Sean ran his hand up and down her back. "You didn't tell me."

"I didn't want to think about it."

"What kind of flower?"

"It looked more like a weed, all dried out like that. But it's clear—someone intentionally placed it on her chest."

"As if visiting her grave."

She shivered. That meant nothing—the killer might never have come back after leaving her here. He could have killed her and left the flower as a sign of remorse or part of some sick ritual. She wouldn't know until she knew more about the victim herself.

She inspected the area closely with her flashlight. There didn't seem to be any trace of bodily fluids or signs of blood or struggle. That didn't mean they weren't there, only that they weren't visible to the naked eye.

However, where the woman's head had been, Lucy spotted several strands of dark blond hair.

"Sean!"

He saw them, too. "Do you have plastic bags?"

"I can't tamper with evidence."

"I didn't see any crime scene tape up. Or warning sign. And where are the cops?"

True. After talking to Deputy Weddle yesterday, it was clear that the Sheriff's Department wasn't taking Lucy's statement seriously. Maybe they believed her, maybe they didn't, but Sean was right: they weren't here searching for evidence, nor did they blockade the area off.

She handed Sean her flashlight. "Shine the light there—I'm taking a few pictures."

Though she had no cell phone reception, the built-in camera took photographs just fine. She snapped several of the area, then zoomed in on the hair. She wished she had a high-end digital camera for better quality, but her phone would have to do.

"Her head rested here," she said.

Emboldened, Lucy gave the alcove a thorough examination, taking more pictures, before moving on to the area surrounding the slab. There were faint footprints in the hard-packed dirt, but there was no telling which ones might have belonged to the men yesterday or to whoever removed the body. A serious police investigation would get impressions and compare the footprints to those of the two rescue workers, as well as hers and Sean's. If one set didn't match anyone, it might lead to the person who had moved the body.

"A dead body isn't easy to carry," Sean commented.

"But not impossible. He was strong, or had a partner. There are no drag marks—dragging her body would be noticeable, even on this hard floor. If we assume she was here for a while and frozen—"

"It's still twenty-eight degrees here, and it's already nine," Sean said, looking at his phone.

"Can you get historical data when we get back up?"

"Absolutely. What do you want? I'll run it as soon as we get in the truck."

"Temperature, high and low, for the last year," she said, brow knitting. "I don't know how to extrapolate it into underground temps, though."

"I can write an algorithm for it, but it won't be perfect. Underground, both heat and cold are retained, depending on the surface temps. You'd want a geologist to interpret the data, based on the location of this room, the type of rock, pulling in any data from when the mine was operational."

"I'll write down what I need if you can figure out how to get the information."

"That I can do."

"The maggots are important—if it was warmer, flies would breed and lay eggs at a faster rate. The maggots would turn into flies in days. But the cold inhibits them.

They could have been dormant for weeks—months. It's too cold down here for insect activity."

"What are you thinking?"

She didn't want to speculate, because she honestly had nothing to go on but conjecture. But Sean liked to brainstorm.

"This might sound stupid . . ." she began.

"Try me."

"Under normal temperatures, the life cycle from egg to adult fly is twenty-four days. It's very predictable. What affects their life cycle most are cold temperatures."

"And it's too cold here for a twenty-four-day life cycle?"

She nodded. "If she was killed here, then any flies would have remained dormant until the temperature rose."

"I haven't seen a fly down here."

"Neither have I. It's still too cold, but they *could* have been here at some point if there was a change in temperature. I'm not an entomologist, and this is all coming from a long-ago forensic biology class, but the larvae I saw in her mouth were about three days old. They wouldn't have gotten to the pupa stage for another five to six days."

"So you think she could have died three days ago?"

"Five days—three days before I found the body. If she was killed then, it wasn't here."

"Because there are no flies."

"Exactly. The key point is that flies lay eggs within minutes of death," Lucy continued, "so if she was killed in town, for example, the eggs would have been laid there."

"So you think she died five days ago?"

"Possible, not likely—not based on her skin tone."

"Can eggs be laid and then not hatch?"

"Yes."

"So she could have been killed months ago, and only because it's spring and the weather is warming the eggs hatched."

"Exactly."

"But not last summer, because they would have hatched long ago."

She smiled. "You should be a scientist."

He shrugged. "Well, I did go to M.I.T. I might not have been paying too much attention, but some basic knowledge seeped into my thick head."

There was something about his tone that sounded odd to Lucy, almost regretful. She wondered what had happened back then that had him unusually melancholic. Before she could ask, Sean continued.

"A frozen body wouldn't have been easy to move."

"Quite right," she agreed.

He shined his light slowly around the eerie space while Lucy looked more closely at the ground.

Yesterday, when she'd been down here with Hammond and Getty, the men had walked down each of the two tunnels for several yards. She considered it now, only because Sean was here with her. But Tim had warned them that there were cave-ins, holes, any number of dangers. And she had no idea where the tunnels led, or how to get to the main entrance from here. They could follow the tracks, but the dangers in the mine stopped her from suggesting it. Still the tracks were a clue. There was no evidence that the killer had moved the body up the mine shaft that Sean had fallen down. And the cart was missing. She wasn't foolhardy—she wasn't going to risk her life wandering down a deadly labyrinth without solid evidence.

"We should have asked Tim to take us to the entrance of the mine. The killer took the cart to move the body, he couldn't have gone up the shaft."

"When we're done here"—he glanced around—"maybe we should go down the tunnels—"

"No," she interrupted. "There are too many unknowns. We'll go down a few feet, but that's it."

"What specifically are you looking for?"

"Anything that looks out of place. We should start where I saw the mining cart."

They walked over to the narrow tunnel, just wide enough for a cart and little more. Its ceiling was low, just an inch taller than Lucy's five feet seven inches.

Sean squatted, resting his weight on his good leg. "The tracks are freshly scraped, see?"

She saw the rust missing in gouges, possibly from the metal wheels of the cart. "How long ago, do you think?"

"Two days."

"How about if you didn't know I saw the cart here just two days ago."

"I'd say these marks were made not more than a few weeks ago, at most. Seriously, the rust would have started to grow back. Not fully, but enough to lose that sheen."

She took pictures of the markings and the track itself.

"Hammond followed the track down twenty feet," she said, "and didn't find anything. This probably leads to—" Something moved in the corner of her vision.

Lucy turned her head, dipping her flashlight to the packed dirt floor between the metal tracks. She sucked in her breath, stifling a startled cry, her stomach clenching painfully beneath her ribs.

On the ground, several maggots flopped slowly, stymied by the cold and lack of nutrients now that they had fallen outside of the corpse. Finally, solid evidence the killer had moved the body down this tunnel after Lucy's discovery had been made public.

Her heart raced and she scanned the area with her light. About two dozen of the translucent white insects littered the path, some of them dead, some of them having moved much farther down the tunnel.

Sean whistled under his breath. "That's pretty damn conclusive. I can't believe they missed this yesterday."

"They were looking for a body," she said. "They weren't thinking crime scene evidence."

"They should have been."

Lucy hesitated—she didn't want to tamper with evidence. Quickly, before she could change her mind, she picked up three of the maggots with tweezers, then sealed them in a small plastic jar. She wrote the day and time and where she'd found them on the label.

The simple, methodical act of evidence collection calmed her more than her admonitions that she was a professional and shouldn't get freaked out by bugs.

She turned around and swept the room again with her flashlight, from the angle the killer would have seen. The only reason the body had been moved was because it had been discovered. The dead body could have stayed down here forever, decomposing over the summer, until all that remained was a skeleton.

"Dozens of people knew I found the body," Lucy said.

"Thanks to the quack doctor who you let sew me up."

"That, and the Fire and Rescue and the Sheriff's Department and anyone *they* told."

They gave the ground one last going-over, and that was when she found it. Shriveled and brown, almost lost in the dirt, was the flower that had been on the woman's chest, right next to where the cart had been. Lucy almost picked it up, but instead took a picture.

Sean watched her. "The flower?"

"Yes." She packed everything up. "I'll call Weddle and lay out our theories when we get back to the lodge and suggest he send someone down here ASAP. They can learn a lot from those little maggots. They may be able to get her DNA. Until we know the identity of the victim, where, why, and how she died will remain a mystery."

They returned to the ventilation shaft. Lucy stared at where Sean had been lying, unconscious, at the bottom of the pit. It had been a long drop—he could have broken his back. It could have turned out so much worse.

Sean watched where Lucy rested her eyes, then looked back at her. Her expression was filled with loss. He'd thought that after Lucy's nightmare last night, then her urgent lovemaking, she'd purged the fear that had grown after his fall and the tragedy that might have been. He realized by the stricken, desolate look in her dark eyes that she was still struggling. She'd merely avoided addressing her feelings, and he'd let her. Was he so scared of losing her that he let her skate by on something so fundamental? Was he strengthening her emotional barriers because he was too afraid to see her in pain?

She'd told him about her nightmare, her fear for his life, but he realized that he'd dismissed it as leftover from the shock of seeing him after the fall. There was far more to it than that. For the first time, he didn't know what she needed. All he could do was reassure her.

"Lucy, I'm fine." He put his hands on her shoulders and tilted his head so she couldn't avoid looking at him.

When she shook her head and plastered a fake smile on her face, he wondered what she was now trying to hide. The mine shaft was no place to discuss this, but Sean knew if he didn't push her now, it would be twice as difficult to get her to talk later, when she had time to suppress her feelings.

"Let's get out—" she began.

"Talk to me, Princess," he interrupted.

"Not now." Her voice wavered. She leaned up and kissed him. "Later." But she didn't look him in the eye.

She pushed on the extension ladder to make sure it was secure, then motioned for him to go first. He began to argue, but she said, "You can't put all your weight on your leg, I'll hold the ladder so it doesn't move as much."

"You are a bossy nurse," he said to lighten the tension. He kissed her firmly. "I'm holding you to your promise."

Sean climbed up the ladder. Lucy was right, his thigh was throbbing, and it helped that she kept the ladder from bouncing with his weight.

He didn't know why he hesitated; maybe it was the repetitive training his brother had put him through, but for some reason he stopped an inch away from the top.

Slowly, he peered over the edge.

His truck was where he left it, right on the edge of the overgrown logging road about twenty yards away. Birds chirped in the trees; a light breeze rustled the leaves. The sky was blue; the air was crisp.

But something felt wrong. Electric.

Sean slipped off his backpack and tossed it over the edge, five feet away.

A rifle echoed, hitting the ground next to him, a plume of dirt jumping into the air.

Fuck.

"Sean?"

Lucy's voice was concerned, but not panicked.

"Stay there," he commanded. He already had his gun in hand, but a handgun against a sniper rifle was like a match against a flame-thrower.

Which direction had the shot come from?

He pictured the area surrounding the mine shaft. Trees and foliage surrounded them on three sides; the only exposed side was the logging road. On the other side of the road were more trees, but the ground sloped down.

Based on the trajectory of the exploding dirt, the sniper was higher than the ground. Up a tree?

He didn't have binoculars on him, and the tree line was thick on the opposite side of the road, roughly a hundred yards away. A good sniper could take him down as soon as he climbed out.

He assessed his surroundings as best he could without a clear line of sight. To his left, the trees were thinner, but to the right there was a low rise. If he could get out on that side, he could use the natural rock formation and foliage to hide.

Then what?

He wasn't going to leave Lucy here, but he needed to get to the truck. He could drive it closer to shield Lucy when she got out. But a good sniper would go for the gas tank. What he needed to do was get out, determine where the sniper was located, then provide cover for Lucy. They wouldn't go directly to the truck; they'd head into the woods. There was no guarantee the sniper didn't have a partner. In the pit, they were sitting ducks, but no way was he going deeper into the dangerous mine.

He pocketed his gun and took out his cell phone. He had a weak signal.

He sent Tim a message.

Sniper at the mine. We're going to run for the highway. Need pick-up ASAP.

Ideally, he'd like to sit tight and wait for the cavalry, but he didn't know how long that would take, or if the sniper had friends. They could come after them here and he and Lucy would be trapped in the tunnels, with no idea of where the danger spots were.

He climbed back down the ladder.

"I have a plan," Sean said moving the ladder to the

right side of the ventilation shaft. "Leave everything except your gun."

Lucy frowned.

"Luce—" He couldn't believe she was poised to argue with him. She was smarter than that.

Lucy shrugged off her backpack, retrieved her Glock, and then the small bag with the jar of maggots. "If that's the killer out there, I'm not leaving the evidence here for him to destroy." She shoved the paper bag down her shirt, which was tucked into her jeans. She zipped up her dark jacket.

"I'm going to climb out, roll into the bushes to the right, and whistle. You get up this ladder as fast as you can when you hear it, but don't show yourself. I'm hoping he'll shoot at me so I'll know exactly where he is. On the second whistle, count to three and get out, as low as possible, and roll over to my position; I'll provide cover."

She nodded, her jaw tight, and Sean kissed her quickly before he scaled up the ladder.

Lucy watched as Sean paused at the top, gun ready, every muscle poised, listening—feeling—for movement. Sean didn't have to tell her how screwed they were—the sniper had plenty of time after spotting Sean to come closer. He could be standing at the edge of the mine, ready to shoot both of them as soon as they emerged.

She had her gun pointed at the edge, even though she had a very limited view of the surface. She looked for movement, shadows, anything that put Sean in jeopardy.

Sean gave her a hand signal that he was moving. He moved fast for his size, and five seconds later she heard the report of a rifle. It hit the spot where Sean had emerged.

Heart pounding, she almost didn't hear his whistle. She quickly climbed the ladder and waited at the top. She tilted her head to spy where Sean was, but couldn't see more than the bushes immediately in front of her.

Sean whistled again, and he was much closer than she'd thought. She counted to three, then saw Sean pop up on his knees, shielded by a boulder, firing his .45 at an angle over her head, toward the opposite side of the logging road.

She climbed out and scrambled over to him, lying low, her gun out.

Sean emptied his cartridge, popped it out into his hand, and slammed back in a reload.

"I can't see him, but he's shooting down at an angle— I think he's in a tree. We can run for it because it'll take him time to get down." He gestured behind them. "I'm going to cover you while you run to that clump of trees. Then you cover me. Once we're there, he won't have a line of sight."

Lucy nodded.

Sean used his fingers to count to three, and Lucy bolted, staying low, making herself as small a target as possible. Sean shot steadily toward the treeline until he was out of ammo; he reloaded and Lucy got into position. She could barely see the truck from where she was, but Sean had been aiming a bit south of it.

She caught his eye and nodded. She fired her Glock, calm and focused, knowing if she screwed up, Sean's life was at risk. It angered her that someone was shooting at them; in fact she was more angry than scared.

There was one lone rifle shot, then nothing.

Lucy reloaded when Sean was on his knees at her side.

"Okay?" she said.

"Let's go. That last one came from ground level."

How he knew that, Lucy didn't know, but she wasn't going to question.

They ran through the trees in a zigzag pattern. Sean was falling behind, limping. Lucy slowed and he shouted, "Move it!"

If Sean thought she was leaving him behind, he didn't know her. She kept the lead, setting a steady pace that pushed Sean but gave him a little slack. He had to have noticed, but he didn't comment again. She cut through the path that the ATVs had forged the other day. There was no further gunfire, no sound of a vehicle or anyone in pursuit, but Lucy wasn't about to stop and wait for a possible ambush.

The gully along the side of the highway was deep and muddy but Lucy jumped into it, rolling onto her stomach and looking back the way they'd come, gun ready, her eyes scanning the distance to see if anyone was in pursuit. Sean did the same less than thirty seconds later.

They both breathed heavily, but Lucy did her best to control her breathing to minimize noise. She hadn't heard anyone coming after them, nor had she heard gunfire, but that didn't mean someone wasn't following, waiting to hit them after they thought they were safe.

Sean pulled out his phone. "Tim's almost here."

Lucy looked behind her. "Tell him we're about fifty feet from where we found the ATV yesterday."

Sean typed in the message while Lucy kept watch. "I don't think our shooter followed us," Sean said. "Once we got into the woods, there were no more shots."

"But why shoot at us in the first place?" Lucy didn't expect an answer. It made no sense that he'd let them go.

She heard a truck on the highway and cautiously peered behind her. It was Tim's old red truck, followed by a newer Jeep that belonged to Adam. They drove slowly and as they neared where she and Sean lay in the gully, Sean stood up and waved. Tim pulled over.

"What the hell happened?" he asked through the open window.

Lucy jumped into the backseat and Sean into the front. "Someone shot at us as we climbed out of the mine."

"I brought Adam for backup. Are we going back to your truck?"

Lucy deferred to Sean. He considered. "I think the guy is gone. He didn't come after us, but he could be waiting until we return. We go back, get as close as we can to the driver's side, and I'll use your truck as a shield." He glanced back at Lucy. "You stay with Tim—provide cover."

Tim made a U-turn on the two-lane highway. Adam followed. Tim used his radio to tell Adam the plan, then added, "You go first down the logging road. Get behind Sean's truck and take out the rifle. If someone is there, he'll know we're serious."

"Got it," Adam said, and sped past them.

The turnoff wasn't far, and Adam made the turn in his black Jeep, driving as fast as he could on the rutted, unpaved road. Tim followed.

By the time Adam was in view again, he had the door of his Jeep open, an AR-15 over the top of the window frame, scanning the area across the logging road.

Sean jumped out and got into his own truck. He looked around quickly, assessing potential dangers, but nothing seemed out of place . . .

. . . except a blank envelope on the dashboard.

He still had on the gloves from the mine. He opened the unsealed envelope and removed a single piece of white paper on which was typed:

IF I WANTED YOU DEAD, YOU'D BE DEAD.
GO HOME.

THIRTEEN

Sean slammed the door. He handed Lucy the unsigned note as he scanned the horizon.

"We should get out of here," Tim began. "He could be—"

"He's gone. He gave us a warning." *Bastard.*

Sean continued to assess the landscape. If the sniper was telling the truth, he intentionally tried *not* to hit them. But the shots came close enough to make him believe, at the time, that the shooter wanted them dead. Or maybe when he missed, he wanted Sean to think it had been planned. Either way, he was enraged.

"He was up in a damn tree," Sean said, having a hard time reigning in his temper. "I don't think he stayed around long enough to clean up his brass."

He started down the logging road toward where the shots had been fired.

Tim followed. "You can't go out there. He could still be around."

"Dammit, Tim, he could have killed us!"

What Sean wanted to say was that the shooter could have killed *Lucy.* When he found out who it was, he'd pummel him. But his anger wasn't going to help them here and now. He reined it in. "He's gone. I'm sure of it," Sean said with as much calm as he could summon from inside. "If there's any evidence out there about who this bastard is, I'll find it." Lucy nodded at him. Sean was relieved that she understood. "Keep your eyes open, Luce."

"Of course."

"I'll go with you," Tim said. "Adam, stay with Lucy."

Sean had identified the area where the shots originated. Heading that way, he noted three possible trees in the distance the sniper could have climbed, all the while scanning the area to make doubly sure he wasn't wrong about the bastard's departure.

If I wanted you dead . . .

First the tricky maneuver that led to his fall into the mine, then someone taking shots at him, now further threats. Sean had to find out if the vandalism was related to the shooter, because if it was that meant the dead girl was also connected.

The first tree Sean approached had a large, freshly broken branch near the ground. Sean looked up and noted several cracked branches.

"He shot at us five times," he said. "I want the brass. There's a good chance he didn't wear gloves when he loaded."

"I'm shutting down the resort," Tim said.

Sean stared at him. "You'd give in to these scare tactics?"

"He could have killed you."

"This is my battle now."

Tim clenched his fists, showing a rare anger. "Like hell it is."

"Dammit, Tim, he went after *me*. I'm not backing down, not until I find him."

"I have to postpone the opening. I have a lunatic shooting at my guests."

"We're hardly guests."

"It doesn't matter. It's only three weeks until my first *real* guests arrive, and I couldn't live with myself if something happened to one of them. If we stop these people before then, great, but I'm still not opening until it's settled."

Delaying the opening was exactly what both Henry and Jon Callahan had suggested the night before. Was the shooting to underscore this so-called suggestion? The vandalism had escalated from property damage to arson to attempted murder.

If I wanted you dead, you'd be dead.

"Let's find the brass first," Sean said. "Then, I want you to meet with the Callahans. Jon Callahan told us last night that he wanted to talk to you about postponing the opening. Suspicious, don't you think?"

"You can't think that the Callahans are behind this—why?"

"I'll find out. They want to play hardball—I invented the game."

A chill ran through Sean's body. How easy it was to fall back into his old life, an existence prone to lawbreaking and violence. His brother Duke had, as a condition of opening RCK East, made Sean promise he'd stay on the right side of the thin line.

"We can straddle the line, Sean, but we can't cross it."

His brother had cleaned up Sean's background, but it wasn't lost on Sean that Duke was more than willing to tap into Sean's expertise and old network when necessary. It was only when Sean wanted to do it that Duke balked, fearing his brother would slip back into his old bad habits. Bad habits? That was an understatement.

Looking back toward the trucks, he extrapolated where the shooter had to have been situated, then walked behind the tree he suspected was ground zero. Scanning the ground, he circled outward. The bullet casings could have been ejected quite a distance, depending on the type of gun, the wind, and the angle of the shooter.

He found a casing about ten feet from the base of the tree, on the right side.

Pulling tweezers from one of Lucy's evidence bags he'd grabbed when they'd returned to the truck, he used them to pick up the brass.

A .270-caliber Winchester round. Very common among hunting rifles, particularly for deer and other large game. Here in the Adirondacks probably every household had a rifle, and half of them fired .270 bullets.

But it wasn't hunting season.

He dropped the casing into the bag.

Tim said, "I called Duke last night."

Sean barely controlled his flash of anger. "You called my brother, why?"

"To fill him in on what is going on. I've known Duke nearly twenty years; I wanted his advice."

Of all people—dammit, his brother? For years Sean had been working to get out from under Duke's thumb, to run the East Coast branch of the California-based RCK without unnecessary interference and unwanted advice.

"And what did he say?" Sean asked, though what he wanted to ask was *How did I screw up?* Because no matter how much Duke said he trusted him, he had never truly stopped second-guessing his little brother's decisions.

"He said he'd have done everything exactly as you've done. Also, that he'd tap into other contacts for the background checks your partner is running. He told me to have you call him if you needed anything."

Sean swallowed uneasily. He hadn't expected that.

"But," Tim continued, "I'm not so sure about any of this anymore. How did anyone even know you and Lucy were at the mine?"

"That's why we're upping the ante," Sean said, though he didn't have a firm plan in place. He spotted another casing, three feet from the first. He put it in the bag.

"What's your plan?" Tim asked.

"We'll talk at the lodge. I have a few details to work out."

Meaning he didn't know what the hell he was doing, but he wasn't going to sit around and wait for the shooter to come after him.

It was time to go back to the Lock & Barrel, look everyone in the eye, and declare war.

FOURTEEN

Lucy paced the short length of Tim Hendrickson's living room in the small house next to the Spruce Lake lodge. She'd been livid that it'd taken two hours for Deputy Weddle to arrive after the shooting, but nearly exploded when he focused on their excursion into the mine rather than the attack.

"Someone *shot* at us," she repeated. How long was he going to ignore the more serious crime of attempted murder?

"We'll get to that," he said, "but first I want to know why you went to the mine when it's a possible crime scene."

"When you were here yesterday, you gave no indication that the missing body was a priority, and there was no police barrier blocking access to the mine."

"It's in the middle of the woods," Weddle said. "I didn't think I needed to tell people to keep out. The sign near the mine shaft says the same thing."

She bit back the urge to explain the difference to him. "We didn't disturb anything," she said with forced calm. This cop brought out the worst in her.

Tim leaned forward from his chair at the table

across the room. "Deputy, my guests could have been killed. This has all gotten out of control."

"There's nothing that tells me there's a connection between the guy with the rifle and the vandalism you've been having," Weddle said. "For all you know it could have been a hunter and he didn't even know you were there."

"That doesn't explain the note," Tim said.

Lucy glanced at Sean. He sat on the couch watching the deputy with a deceptively casual expression. He'd been so angry after finding the sniper's note in their truck, and uncharacteristically silent after Weddle arrived. She forced herself to stop pacing, but she couldn't sit.

"I'll take it to the sheriff and see what he thinks," Weddle said, "but at this point, we have more important issues to discuss, such as interfering with my investigation."

"What investigation?" she snapped, unable to keep the sarcasm from her tone.

They'd decided not to mention she'd picked up three of the maggots they'd found. She felt uncomfortable keeping the information from a cop, but he hadn't taken her seriously, and she didn't trust him. His attitude today told her they'd made the right choice. She'd already packaged up the bugs to ship to a lab once she figured out exactly where to send them for the fastest, most accurate analysis.

"There were strands of hair on the rock," Lucy continued, "and the maggots I'd seen in the woman's mouth were in the tunnel opening, right where the cart had been. It's pretty clear someone used the cart to move the body."

Weddle looked ill as she spoke, and Lucy was silently pleased. Childish, perhaps, but this cop wasn't making anything easy. She'd been around law enforcement officers her entire life and expected them to do the job; most did. Weddle was one of the few who seemed both clueless and incompetent.

"I ran you both. You live in Washington, D.C., not Boston," Weddle said.

Lucy frowned. "Boston? We never said we lived in Boston."

"You *said* you were friends of Tim Hendrickson from Boston."

"You know what they say about 'assume,'" Sean spoke up for the first time.

Weddle didn't get the insult. He continued. "And you, Rogan, should have told me you're a licensed private investigator. You're just on vacation?"

"Yes," Sean said curtly. "When we found out about the vandalism, we told Tim we'd help him get to the bottom of the situation."

"And found a dead body." His voice dripped with sarcasm.

Lucy exclaimed, "The body was there! I told you there is evidence, but it needs to be collected immediately to avoid any more degradation. The larvae need to be collected as soon as possible and sent to a lab. They'll be able to dissect them and detect human DNA, to prove that they grew inside a dead body, and possibly yield enough DNA evidence to identify the victim."

"Ms. Kincaid, I appreciate your diligence, but you need to leave this investigation to us. You tampered with evidence by returning to the mine. We may be a small county, but we're not hicks and we know what we're doing. You should have told me you worked at a morgue."

She had left her position three months before, but evidently her official records hadn't caught up with her status. She didn't correct him, but said instead, "Then you should believe me. And the fact that someone shot at us—they may have been trying to scare us away so they could destroy that evidence!"

"Which you've given them ample time to do since you breached the crime scene."

"*Now* you're calling it a crime scene?" She began to pace again. She hated confrontation, but couldn't seem to stop her anger from spilling out. "You're missing the point! Someone shot at us! I don't know if it's related to the dead body or the vandalism, but I don't like being shot at."

"That wouldn't have happened if you didn't go back to the mine," Weddle snapped.

Lucy clenched her fists, and Sean rose from the couch and put his hand on her arm, halting her movement. Usually she was the one who tried to calm Sean down.

"Deputy," Sean said, "you're out of line."

"No. You and Ms. Kincaid need to stand down. Both the arson and the dead body are police business." He, too, rose and stared at them, his face flushed with anger. Unjustified, as far as Lucy was concerned. "If I see either of you interfering again, I will arrest you."

"With all due respect," Sean said, though there was no respect in his tone, "Tim hired me to stop the vandalism and protect his property. I'm not backing off."

"You haven't done a very good job."

Now it was Sean who looked ready to deck the cop. Lucy took a deep breath and said, "Are you going to collect the evidence, or do you think I should call the FBI?"

Weddle's face reddened. "It's our jurisdiction. We'll decide if we bring in the Feds." He eyed Sean. "I have no problem with you playing mall cop on the Hendrickson property, but you'd better watch yourself if you leave these grounds, because my department doesn't want your help or interference."

Weddle swaggered out, brushing against Sean, as if daring him to fight. Tim looked stunned at the exchange but followed the cop out, and Sean slammed the front door behind them, causing the windows in the small house to rattle.

"He's the epitome of every reason I hate cops!"

Lucy winced. Sean didn't mean it literally, but she knew he had issues with law enforcement, many of them justified from his personal experience. And Lucy was no Pollyanna when it came to law enforcement—there were good and bad cops, without a doubt. Her older brother Connor had been forced to quit the police force when he turned against a corrupt cop. Her sister-in-law Kate had been unjustly accused by the FBI of getting her partner killed. But most police officers did the job right and they did it well.

Sean ran both hands through his hair. "I don't trust that cop. We have no idea who the players are. For all we know, he could be involved with trying to shut the lodge down. He could have killed that woman or shot at us."

"Quite a conspiracy theory you've got going there," Lucy said.

"You can't trust him."

"I don't."

"Not all cops wear white hats, Lucy," he continued as if she hadn't spoken.

"You think I don't know that?" Why was Sean so confrontational with her? Because of his deep-seated animosity toward law enforcement? "I know *exactly* how you feel," she continued. "You've made it perfectly clear. The world isn't black and white; no one is a saint. The bad cops on the street make me sick, but most cops aren't like that. They might not bend the rules enough to suit you and you might not like the restrictions they have to work under, but take away the rules and what do you have? Vigilante justice. And we know where *that* leads."

"Lucy, I'm—"

She cut him off. "And how are you going to feel about *me* when I'm wearing a badge?"

She was so angry—at Weddle, at the sniper, but mostly at Sean, because deep down he'd scratched at a doubt she still couldn't articulate: would she be able to follow the strict rules required of the FBI? When could they be bent? If Spruce Lake's Sheriff's Department didn't do anything about the missing dead woman, could Lucy let it go? Or would she break the law to see true justice done?

"How I feel about you won't ever change, whether you have a badge or not." Sean rubbed her arms. "I shouldn't have to tell you that."

She swallowed uneasily. "Maybe you don't realize how hostile you are toward authority." But her anger, and deep-seated worry about Sean's attitude, began to fade.

"This is a ridiculous conversation. We agree that Weddle is an asshole cop and is either incompetent or guilty of something. So why are we arguing?"

She hesitated, torn between forcing Sean to address his issues and letting it slide to keep the peace. Sean took that moment to extend the olive branch.

He stepped closer and held her face in his hands. "I wish I'd never agreed to help Tim. We need time together, alone." He studied her eyes, wanting her support and affirmation.

It felt as if Sean had been in her life for years, but it had been only three months since they'd grown intimate, and they rarely had any time alone together. He knew everything about her past—but what did she really know about Sean's history? He'd had issues with authority ever since he'd been expelled from Stanford after hacking into his professor's computer to expose him as a pedophile, but that wasn't the whole story. There was much about Sean's past she didn't know.

Nevertheless, Lucy absolutely trusted Sean's deep-seated drive to help those in trouble. "You couldn't turn your back on somebody who needed you," Lucy said, "and we must do what we can for Tim and Adam."

"We're good, right? You and me? That's my main concern."

He looked worried. Sean had told her that he needed her more than she needed him, and she didn't believe it. But for the first time, she saw fear of loss in his eyes.

"Lucy, I'm sorry I overstepped."

She shook her head. "I overreacted. We agree that Weddle is a problem. Do you really think he could be involved in what's going on with Tim?"

"I need to call in some help." He smiled, though the humor didn't reach his eyes. "You probably thought you'd never hear me say that."

"You're right." She smiled back, grimly.

"I suspect the sniper will try again, when he realizes we're not leaving, I need Patrick up here to watch our backs."

"What about the bullet casings?"

"I'll send those to RCK West. Duke has an interest in this case; he'll be happy to run them."

"What about the missing persons reports?"

"Patrick is already working on it; we're not going to let that go. I promise."

Lucy nodded. "I'm going to the cabin to take a shower. I still feel dirty from the mine."

"I'm going to Canton to overnight the casings to Duke."

"Why Canton? Isn't that nearly an hour away?"

"I'll stop by the Sheriff's Department and follow up on the vandalism report Tim made, check on the arson investigation. Maybe file a report against Weddle. Do you think there's a crime for being an asshole?"

She tried to conceal her grin. "Sean—" she said in warning.

"I won't get into trouble, but the only way to find out if Weddle actually reported the vandalism is if I check it out in person. I'll follow up on the evidence in the mine as well, make sure the sheriff knows it's down there, find out if Weddle was blowing smoke up my ass about a detective coming in to investigate. You may find this hard to believe, but I can be diplomatic when necessary."

"True. But there's a reason Patrick usually handles law enforcement when you're working a case."

"I'll be fine." He hugged her, but his mind was elsewhere.

Tim walked in and said, "I don't know why Deputy Weddle acted that way. I tried to talk to him, but he's adamant that we're to stay away from the mine."

"It's on your property," Sean said, taking Lucy's hand.

"My property surrounds it, but the mine itself is still on a ninety-nine-year lease to the Kelley Mining Company. Though the mine used to be in my grandmother's family, the estate sold it long ago."

"We should find out who owns the mine, what they have planned, what it's worth. It could be they have plans for the area that your resort would hinder."

Tim looked skeptical. "Certainly nothing's been going on with the mine since I came back from Boston."

Lucy shook her head. "Except murder."

FIFTEEN

I kept quiet after my pet cop told me what had happened at the Kelley Mine. I didn't know what made me angrier: that Tim Hendrickson's friend was a private investigator or that someone had tried to kill the two interlopers.

I'd taken over my brother's office, such as it was. Made a few aesthetic adjustments to suit my taste, rearranged the furniture so no one could sneak up behind me through the door or window. Ian had arrived that morning and watched from the corner. He didn't like Tyler Weddle any more than I did.

"Who fired the shots?" I asked my cop.

Tyler's Adam's apple bobbed unsteadily. "I-I don't know. You made it clear—"

"Yes, I made it perfectly clear that you all were to stand down. I'm giving the Hendricksons time to do the right thing, and I'm confident they will. The fire was a dumb move, but what do I expect from idiots?"

I didn't bother waiting for an answer. "It's Friday. We have two days"—I looked at the clock—"just under fifty-eight hours to make sure the resort project is dead. Now a private investigator is snooping around. You think shooting at him is going to scare him off?"

"I didn't—"

"And what is this so-called evidence left in the mine?"

"The girlfriend works at a morgue, apparently. She noticed things no one else would have noticed."

"What things did she fucking notice?"

Tyler shifted his feet. He knew better than to sit without an invitation, and I hadn't issued him one. "Some hair and, um, some bugs she said were on the body."

"And were they from the bitch's body?"

He actually turned green. "Yeah."

"You didn't clean up your mess very well, did you?"

"It was Jimmy—"

I put up my hand. I wasn't going to discuss Jimmy with anyone. He was the thorn in my side. I couldn't kill him and I couldn't let him live. Not when everything I'd been working toward for six long years was finally happening in two days. I swear, that bitch was haunting me from her grave. I should have cut her up and fed her to the pigs like they did in the good old days. I might just do that to Jimmy. And Tyler. Hell, I should fucking buy stock in a hog farm!

"You were supposed to make sure the job was done, and you let him go down there alone. That makes it your fault and your responsibility." I stared him down. He was sweating. That made me as happy as I could be considering the mess in front of me. "What, are you scared of the mine? Of the dark? Ian, look at the big, bad cop who's scared of the dark."

Ian grunted, his eyes on Weddle.

"It's all taken care of, really." Tyler glanced at Ian, then faced me.

I didn't like what I was hearing.

"What do you mean?"

"I heard on the scanner this morning that Jimmy's truck was found in the reservoir."

I froze. My heart just about stopped. "What?"

"They have to drag the bottom because his body wasn't in the car, but—"

"Go back. What did you do?"

He backtracked. "It wasn't me, I just heard about it. Carl said he had to clean up some loose ends, and I assumed—"

Carl Browne.

After we inked the deal Sunday, Carl Browne was a dead man.

I looked Tyler in the eye and pictured him dead, too.

The images calmed me.

"Get rid of any evidence still in that mine today and I won't punish you," I lied smoothly.

"I will. I promise. Thank you."

"Did the girl and her P.I. take anything with them?"

"No."

"You know that for sure? Like you 'knew' Jimmy had dumped the bitch in the Hell Hole?" The Hell Hole was the deepest exploration shaft, drilled in the 1940s during the height of World War II. An accident resulted in three men falling to their deaths—more than 150 feet. My daddy used the Hell Hole whenever he needed to disappear someone. I suspected skeletons were stacking up down there like cordwood.

"They would have told me," Tyler said. "I threatened to arrest them for obstructing justice."

I simply didn't believe that Tyler had any skill in reading people. If he had, he would know he was already dead.

"Good. Take care of the evidence and report to me when it's done."

"Yes, ma'am."

"Go."

"Ian," I said after the fool left. "I'm not happy."

"I can see why. What do you want me to do?"

"I need you to discreetly search Jimmy Benson's house. No one can know you were there. Anything you find that even remotely connects back to me or my family, bring to me."

"Of course."

I had no need to tell Ian the entire truth. If he found what Jimmy had on me, he would instantly think traitor, and that would suit my purposes, but I didn't think he'd find anything. I'd already had Jimmy's place searched after my brother turned on me, and found nothing. But I had to believe the threat—and if Jimmy was dead, the information could be leaked.

My instincts were on fire. Something was wrong. I needed to know everything going on in town, starting with the strangers.

"I want everything on the P.I. Sean Rogan and his bed buddy Lucy Kincaid," I told Ian. "Start with how they know Tim Hendrickson, and then move into their backgrounds. What kind of cases he works. What the bitch does at the morgue. Where they live, siblings, parents, everything."

"Not a problem."

Nothing was a problem for Ian. He was perfect for me. Young, beautiful, strong, smart—and he did everything right the first time I told him. I've gone through so many personal assistants I've lost count. The longest running was Zachary, who was with me almost two years before I found him screwing a cheap whore. It pained me to kill him. What a waste.

Ian had been with me for seven months, and was amazing in all parts of his job. After my one failed marriage, I'd never again give control to a husband. Killing husbands was a messy business because there were official marriage records and crap like that. A hired, under-the-table assistant was far preferable.

"We're going to have some fun tonight."

His blue eyes sparkled. "The cop?"

I grinned. Ian got the same thrills I did.

"May I kiss you?"

My skin tingled. "You may."

He came around the desk and kissed me. I reached down and touched him between his legs. He was already growing hard.

I pulled away. "Save it. We've got a lot of work to do today." And no way was I wasting time screwing.

Ian walked over to the couch and opened his laptop. "Sean Rogan. Lucy Kincaid. Let's see what I can find."

"While you do that, I have people to punish."

I couldn't tell from his look if he was concerned about my safety or merely disappointed he couldn't participate.

"I'll be fine," I assured him, "and I promise to let you help with the fun punishments later."

"You're so good to me."

SIXTEEN

Lucy showered until the hot water turned cold. Her head ached from both lack of sleep and the friction with Sean.

She was drying her hair when her phone rang. It was her brother Patrick, Sean's partner at RCK.

"Luce, I emailed you a link to the missing persons reports I pulled."

"I'll look through them right now." She put her phone on speaker and quickly gathered her damp hair into a ponytail.

"I used your criteria—Caucasian women between the ages of twenty-five and thirty-five who went missing in the Northeast during the last nine months. I narrowed it down to forty-seven women, blond or light brown hair, between five foot four and five foot eight. Since the files are large, I posted them to my server and you can view or download them from there. I can broaden the search if necessary."

At Sean's computer, she logged into her email. "I hope she's here."

"I just got off the phone with Sean; he told me what happened. I got a seat on the last flight to Albany tonight, then a commuter plane first thing in the morning. This was supposed to be a vacation for you two."

"This is the second vacation I've had where a dead body has turned up. Maybe I should stay home."

She was half-joking, but Patrick was serious. "I started the background checks Sean asked for. The Swain family popped immediately. The father died in prison—he got twenty-five-to-life for killing his girlfriend. The oldest brother, Paul Swain, is in prison for manslaughter and drug trafficking. They tried to make a case against his brother Butch, but nothing stuck. Butch was suspected of bribery, extortion, and manufacturing methamphetamines."

"Do you know if there's an active investigation?"

"I called around to the usual places, didn't hear of anything ongoing, but that doesn't mean squat half the time. The word is when Paul Swain was sent away, his operation dried up. Nine people went to prison. He was the brains, Butch was the brawn."

"Where's Butch Swain now?"

"His legal address is in Colton, about twenty miles from Spruce Lake. There's a younger sister, Roberta, who went to college in Florida, and I can't find anything on her since then."

"Really?" Lucy teased. "You're stumped?"

"Hardly. I'm digging. I think she probably got married, which is why I have nothing on her maiden name. I can't find a marriage record in Florida or New York, so I'll broaden the search. Anyway, I wanted to make sure you got my email with the missing persons records. Let me know if your mine lady's not there, and I'll broaden that search, too."

"Thanks, Patrick."

"Watch out for Butch Swain. Even though word is he isn't a sharp tack, he could have acquired a new partner. I told Sean the same thing."

"Does anyone think the little brother has a new meth lab up and running?"

"I called Noah, and he's putting a feeler out with the DEA about drug activity in St. Lawrence County. There was nothing on the FBI radar, at least with the Swain name or Spruce Lake attached. They're focusing on labs in Massena now, which they believe picked up the slack when the Swains went out of business."

"Take one down, two more pop up."

"Got that right. Luce, I don't know what's going on in Spruce Lake, but keep a low profile until Sean gets back. I wish he hadn't left you alone."

She sighed. Long ago she realized that she'd be forever coddled by her family. "Patrick, I'm not alone. Tim and Adam Hendrickson are both here. And do you remember I'm practically an FBI agent? When I have my badge, will you still tell me to be careful?"

"Yes."

She laughed. "Fair enough."

"And you'd better have your gun on you now."

She glanced across the room to where her Glock was partly hidden on a bookshelf. Sean had given her security measures to follow since they became involved, many of which she'd already learned from her oldest brother, Jack, a former army sergeant. There was another gun hidden in the bathroom and a third under the cushion on the couch.

"I have it covered," Lucy told Patrick. "Nothing we've found indicates the vandalism on the resort is drug related. Did you run the other names Sean gave you?"

"There's nothing much on Jon Callahan. He's originally from Montreal, but after his father died when he was twelve, his mother sent him to live with his Uncle Henry in Spruce Lake. He went to college in Connecticut, became a naturalized citizen—easy because his dad was an American—and settled in Spruce Lake. He owns a lot of property—most of the town, in fact, that isn't owned by the Hendrickson estate."

"How did he make his money?"

"He's a lawyer specializing in international law—no criminal law, all civil. He's with a major firm based in Montreal with a U.S. office in New York City, very respectable, seems to work primarily in intellectual property rights, contract law, estate planning. I'm going to look at the type of work he specializes in."

"But how can he practice law living in the middle of nowhere?"

"With technology these days, he wouldn't necessarily have to go into an office. He gave you the creeps?"

"No. He seemed to be the most normal person I've met here; maybe that's why he stood out. Very smooth, like a good salesman."

"Absolutely, we need to *especially* watch out for the normal people."

"Very funny. What about Reverend Browne or Callahan's uncle?"

"Henry Callahan worked for the Kelley Mine as a young man. Married Emily Richardson when they were both nineteen, right out of high school. They have no children. When the mine closed, he enlisted in the army, served five years stateside as a mechanic.

Opened his own shop in Colton. It went under a few years later and he retired early."

"He has a huge spread of land next to the Hendricksons'. Where did he get the money?"

"The Richardson family, inheritance. Mostly land, little cash."

"Henry and his nephew Jon seem complete opposites," Lucy said. "Middle-class blue-collar worker and wealthy international lawyer. How did Jon pay his way through college?"

"I didn't go that deep; all this is basic intelligence. You want me to give them both a full rectal exam?"

"You're full of humor today, Patrick."

He laughed. "Oh, and the local reverend. He's lived in Spruce Lake his entire life, owns two acres in town where he has both a house and the church. His father was the preacher before him. Looks like the only time he's left the county for any length of time was four years' divinity college in Ohio."

"Thanks for everything," Lucy said.

"On another note, when I said low profile, I meant in more than just staying safe. You know how Sean can get, and the last thing I want is for him to in any way jeopardize your future with the FBI. He should never have let you go down to that mine again. What were you thinking?"

The conversation went from cordial to confrontational real fast. It took Lucy a moment to respond. "Sean doesn't *let* me do anything. The local deputy disregarded everything I said. No one was handling the investigation, and that's something I know a lot about."

"You're not a cop—yet. Watch your step, Lucy.

Sean isn't going to think about your future when he's on a case. It's one of the reasons he's so good, but it could damage your career."

Lucy's stomach dropped. Patrick had voiced the largest obstacle in her relationship with Sean. She didn't want to think her brother was trying to put a wedge between them, but he'd made it clear three months ago that he didn't think Sean was good for Lucy. They had somewhat of a truce, but Lucy felt Patrick constantly assessing her, as if waiting for moments like these to sow dissent.

"It was my idea to go back to the mine," she said evenly. "I take responsibility for any repercussions."

When Patrick didn't respond right away, she added, "No one else seems to care about the fact that a young woman was murdered."

"Lucy—" he began, then stopped himself. "I understand. Just be cautious."

"I'll see you tomorrow." She hung up, wishing Patrick hadn't scratched that issue. It made her wonder if everyone she cared about was waiting for her relationship with Sean to self-destruct.

Lucy had no illusions that she was normal. One horrific mistake seven years ago had changed her life forever. She had survived her attack, but had become a different person. She was so focused on her career goals, her careful planning, that life passed her by. What normal person turns down a shot to be on an Olympic team? But though she swam on her college team, she couldn't make the commitment necessary to train for the Olympics. Seven years ago it had been one of her dreams, but no longer. What normal person goes to college year round—and one night class—in order to get the units necessary for a double major? What normal person moves from one law enforcement internship to another, building a résumé solely to get into the FBI?

Being busy—swimming, studying, working—had saved her. She hadn't had time to think, had no time to feel sorry for herself. And she was proud of what she'd accomplished.

But she also had no close friends from college, because she hadn't had time to socialize. Her one serious boyfriend before Sean had been a cop she'd met through one of her internships. She didn't know how to have fun, didn't know what to do when she wasn't working or training or exercising.

Until Sean.

Simply, he made her happy. He'd taken her ice skating, flying, and now on vacation—such as it was. A couple of weeks ago before he went out of town on a case, he'd taken her to a G-rated kids' movie. And he'd laughed as much as the kids surrounding them, giving her an all-too-rare carefree feeling.

Sean seemed to understand her, to *know* her so well that sometimes it scared her.

Maybe that was why their earlier fight was so disturbing. It was the first time that he couldn't read her mind—when he didn't push her to explain herself, or reveal what she was thinking as if she'd said the words out loud. Though it was unnerving at times, she'd come to depend on the unspoken connection.

And thanks to Patrick, the conflict with Sean continued to eat at her as she meticulously went through each missing woman in the file.

SEVENTEEN

After sending the bullet casings to his brother Duke at the RCK main office in California, Sean headed to the St. Lawrence County Sheriff's Department. It was housed in a large building with numerous other county departments, including the property records.

In the sheriff's office—a small, clean, functional space—Sean was pleased that they acted professionally, but frustrated he couldn't get any real information. He used all his charm on the fifty-year-old secretary, but she just smiled sweetly and told him someone would contact him, or he could wait until one of the detective sergeants was available. Essentially, "kiss my ass" but in the nicest way possible.

Sean left his contact information, because waiting would drive him up a wall. If he was lucky, someone would call his cell before he left Canton. He much preferred face-to-face meetings because half of what he learned in conversation came from body language, which revealed what someone *didn't* say.

He found the property records office, filled out the paperwork, and sat at one of the early 1980s monitors. They all fed into a larger mainframe but didn't store any data. Searching for property records by parcel number was easy, but the actual records were on either microfiche or paper, depending on how old. New transactions were in a different database, but Sean wanted to learn more about the ownership history of the mine.

Bureau of Land Management leases would be federal, but Sean could get those online when he got back to Spruce Lake. Right now, he was more interested in the mine and surrounding property. He pulled all the files and didn't see anything unusual.

He went to the new computer terminal that housed all property transactions for the last decade. He searched all parcels in the Spruce Lake area—and was surprised when Jon Callahan's name popped up on almost every record. When Patrick told him Callahan owned the majority of the property, he hadn't realized it was divided into so many individual parcels. To contrast, he looked up the Hendricksons' property. They owned one large parcel of over five hundred acres; Callahan owned dozens of parcels anywhere from one acre—the lots in town—to upward of one hundred acres.

The transfer dates on Callahan's properties were recent, starting about seven years ago. Most of them, however, were during the last two years.

Sean sweet-talked the clerk into letting him download the information to a flash drive, rather then waiting for her to burn a CD or print out the documents. He left wondering if Jon Callahan wanted Tim's property, and if so, why? Property could be a good investment, but Spruce Lake was in a depressed area.

After finishing his research, he was almost back to the turnoff to Spruce Lake when he saw the sign to Colton, ten miles to the north. He glanced at the time. Nearly three in the afternoon—maybe he could get to the high school in time and catch sight of the teenage arsonist.

It was worth a shot.

St. Lawrence County had its share of crime, but compared to the rest of New York State, it was a safe place to live. In fact, Detective Sergeant Kyle Dillard had lived pretty much everywhere in New York and Pennsylvania, and he was set on raising his kids and retiring in Canton. While the bitter winter got to him from time to time, the St. Lawrence Valley was one of the most beautiful and serene places to live—without hordes of people to mess with his peace.

While Kyle handled a variety of calls from murder to petty theft, the bulk of his duties were investigating traffic fatalities. The roads were not kind, especially to inattentive drivers and those unfortunate enough to cross their path.

He'd just come from a particularly nasty crash—a truck went over the guardrail up on Route 56 outside Colton two nights ago, landing in the reservoir. They didn't have the equipment to bring the vehicle up until this morning, and when they did, there was no dead driver behind the wheel. The truck was being taken to the police yard for inspection while a team was finishing up the preliminary accident report, based on the physical evidence. Kyle was certain drunk driving was the cause. Based on the skid marks leading to the crash site, the truck had been going far too fast for the road. While there was no body, the driver could easily have been thrown from the truck and be at the bottom of the lake. They'd searched up and down both sides of the lake downstream and found nothing. They'd send down divers this weekend.

The truck was registered to James Benson. He had a deputy working on finding next of kin for Benson, a firefighter stationed up in Indian Hills. He was a single man of thirty-two with no offspring.

All Kyle wanted to do now was go home to Laurie and the kids and forget the senseless accident. Play some games, maybe barbeque some ribs, and listen to his three boys laugh.

"Hello, Margo," he said to the secretary/clerk/office manager. He didn't remember Margo's official title, but the Sheriff's Department would fall apart without her at the helm.

"Mrs. Fletcher called about the duplex on the corner of Elm and Sycamore. Three visitors between midnight and four a.m."

"Maybe Mrs. Fletcher should take an extra sleeping pill," Kyle muttered. The woman slept so lightly that she could hear a fly snore.

"The courthouse called to let you know that Jeremy Fisher cut a deal on the assault charges and you won't be needed in court on Monday."

"My day just got better."

Margo looked at him blandly and said, "And a private investigator stopped by regarding a case he said Deputy Weddle is working."

Kyle took the business card and message from Margo. *Sean Rogan, Rogan-Caruso-Kincaid Investi-*

gative Services, Eastern Office. Sounded impressive, but P.I.s liked to bullshit. When he'd been a cop in Philly, he'd dealt with enough low-life P.I.s that he didn't hold out hope that Rogan was any different.

He expected a message from Margo, but Rogan had written the note himself.

Detective—

I'm inquiring about the status of the investigation into the missing body of the female victim found in the Kelley Mine on Travers Peak outside Spruce Lake, as well as the statement myself and Ms. Lucy Kincaid gave to Deputy Weddle regarding evidence visually identified in the mine this morning, specifically hair strands and insects first observed on the dead woman before she disappeared.

I've been retained by Tim Hendrickson, who owns the property adjacent to the mine and has been the subject of escalating acts of sabotage aimed at preventing him and his brother from opening a family resort, which was approved by the county. I am interested in the status of this investigation as it may be related to my own. Please contact me at your earliest convenience.

—Sean Rogan

"I'm lost," Kyle said.

"According to Deputy Weddle's report, he closed the case yesterday after Fire and Rescue determined it was a crank call."

"Crank call?"

"No body was found in the mine."

Kyle was royally confused. "Track down Tyler. I want to talk to him before I call this P.I. back."

"Yes, Detective." She picked up her phone.

Kyle went to his small office and pulled up the report on the computer. A call came in from Hendrickson on Wednesday about an arson fire and the corpse in the mine. Two different locations. The arson investigation was active and assigned to the county fire marshal's office. Standard. The other call was a prank?

Something didn't jibe. He read Weddle's notes.

. . . No body was found in the mine at the location Ms. Kincaid identified. They searched the immediate area, but no sign of any body, or evidence of violence, was seen. The area where Ms. Kincaid claimed to have seen the body is heavily shadowed, and an overactive imagination could easily have "seen" a dead person. When questioned, Ms. Kincaid admitted she didn't approach the "body" but ran back to the mine shaft. This officer doesn't believe the false report had been malicious, but simply a scared young woman who saw "something" in the dark.

Weddle had closed the case. So what evidence was Rogan talking about?

"Margo?" Kyle called out into the main room. "Did Weddle log in any evidence today?"

"No, Detective."

"Have you reached him?"

"He's off duty. I left a message."

Kyle glanced at the clock. 3:10. Typical of Weddle and a few others who didn't raise a finger after they clocked out. When their budget was slashed and overtime had to be preapproved, half the deputies protested by clocking in and out right on time. Most went back to the old way, but a few, like Weddle, didn't.

Kyle didn't have a college degree, but he'd been a cop for over twenty years. A good cop. He smelled something rotten, and feared it was his own deputy. Kyle almost called the P.I., then decided to wait. He needed something more than his gut instinct before he brought the situation to the sheriff, who was currently in Albany fighting for more funding. Ever since the state screwed the counties in the last budget, they'd been unable to hire more deputies, upgrade their computer system, or perform more than minimal maintenance on the county jail. Tyler Weddle had better have a logical—and provable—explanation for the conflicting information or Kyle would string him up.

The only thing Kyle hated more than an unrepentant criminal was a bad cop.

Margo buzzed him. He didn't want to answer—thirty minutes until he was off-duty—but of course he did.

"We found Mr. Benson's next of kin," she said. "He's the legal guardian of his seventeen-year-old nephew."

Kyle rubbed his face. Damn. A minor.

"Do you want me to have a deputy inform the family?"

"Where does he live?"

"Spruce Lake."

"Send me the address; I'll do it." Kyle's instincts were buzzing. Spruce Lake, of all places—he never heard anything out of that dead mining town for the last six years since Paul Swain's drug operation was busted, and in two days there was a report of arson, a dead body, a missing dead body, and now a firefighter was apparently dead in a car accident, but his body couldn't be found.

He definitely wanted to pay a visit to Spruce Lake.

As Ricky pulled out of the high school parking lot that afternoon, he thought he saw Sean Rogan, the guy he'd tricked into falling down the mine shaft.

He had to be wrong.

When he looked again, he didn't see anything but a blur of the white truck as it made a U-turn and went in the opposite direction. Ricky tried to breathe easier, told himself his mind was playing tricks on him, but that didn't help. It was guilt, he knew, that had him on edge. He was relieved Rogan hadn't died, but he hadn't been able to eat or sleep much in the last two days. He knew he'd survived the fall—everyone in town had heard about the friend of Tim Hendrickson's who'd fallen down the mine in pursuit of an arsonist—but that didn't appease Ricky.

He kept his eyes on the rearview mirror until he was confident that Rogan, if it had been Rogan, wasn't following him. He decided to take a roundabout way home, partly because he really didn't want to face his uncle right now. Uncle Jimmy had been furious when he first found out Ricky had been working for Reverend Browne. That was months ago.

"I've done everything to keep you safe and out of harm's way," Jimmy had said. "Make sure you go to college and get out of this backwater. And you're

walking right into the shit. Who are you, Rick? Are you your mother's son or your father's son?"

Ricky hadn't spoken to Jimmy for a week after that. His uncle *knew* how he felt about his father. Ricky wanted to do the right thing, but he no longer knew what was right. And Jimmy was a hypocrite. He was in deeper illegal shit than Ricky.

He promised to lay low, but Ricky had been terrified after Rogan had fallen down the mine shaft, and he had to tell Jimmy the truth. Maybe Jimmy wasn't still upset with him. He couldn't be madder at Ricky than Ricky was at himself.

He felt awful about setting the fire. He hadn't wanted to do it in the first place. He hadn't wanted to do anything to Joe Hendrickson's place. He'd liked the old man, missed him more than he'd miss his dad if *he* croaked.

The reason he agreed to help Reverend Browne was because he hated Adam Hendrickson. Adam hadn't even remembered him.

Ricky didn't know Tim, the older brother, but Adam spent nearly every summer here. They'd gone fishing half a dozen times. The last time, Adam was seventeen and Ricky was twelve, two months before his mom died. Joe had taken them on an overnight fishing trip. They'd camped under the stars and Ricky desperately wished that Joe was his dad and Adam was his brother and his mom wasn't dying.

Stupid, stupid childish fantasy.

Adam didn't even *remember* Ricky, and why should he? Ricky had been a runt until recently, and when Adam went to college he stopped visiting Spruce Lake. That was fine with Ricky. He had Joe all to himself. He started helping him with chores every Saturday. Joe paid him, but Ricky did it for the company, not the money.

Then he died. A heart attack, Doc Griffin said. Ricky had found Joe on the kitchen floor when he'd come by the first Saturday in March, over a year ago. After that, he started doing odd jobs for Reverend Browne.

"I'll help make this right. I mean what I say."

Ricky felt queasy as he remembered Rogan's words. Why would a stranger offer to help him? Rogan was a friend of Tim Hendrickson, which meant he was one of them. And even if he tried to help, what could he do? Ricky just needed to lay low, stay out of Rogan's sight, and eventually the dude would go home. The resort wouldn't open, and everyone would finally relax. Get back to business as usual. It was the whole resort thing that made everyone crazy. And while Ricky understood the resort wouldn't be good for the town's illegal business, he didn't understand why everyone was so freaked out.

He turned down a long, bumpy street that bordered the so-called town of Spruce Lake. The potholes were so bad he had to work on his alignment damn near every month. The sad houses mirrored their occupants—tired, sagging, appearing older than their years. Everyone had big lots filled with cars and junk. The skinny Doberman across the street from his house barked at Ricky, teeth bared. The chain-link fence didn't keep the attack dog in the yard, but the rope he was tethered to did. Ricky suspected that one day, the dog would bust the rope and rip out someone's throat.

He pulled into the carport, relieved Uncle Jimmy wasn't home yet. He worked a three days on, three days off schedule at the fire station. Ricky went in through the side door, dumped his backpack on the kitchen table, and opened the refrigerator. Nearly empty, but at least the milk was fresh. He took the container, drank half from the bottle, and put it back.

As he closed the refrigerator door, his peripheral vision caught movement to his right. He glanced around, looking for something to defend himself with, when he recognized the intruder.

"Hello," Sean Rogan said. "Now, why don't you tell me why you tried to kill me? Spare no details. I've got all the time in the world."

EIGHTEEN

Sean stared the kid in the eye. First reactions tended to be the most honest.

The kid was scared, but ready to defend himself. A survivor. Cocky and cautious, a familiar combination. So much like the young Sean Rogan that he could have been looking at himself in a mirror fifteen years ago.

Still, because he, too, was a survivor, Sean watched the kid's body language for signs that he had a hidden weapon. Sean didn't think so—but there could be a gun under a table or cabinet.

"I could kill you for breaking into my house," he said.

"So James Benson is your dad? He seems kind of young to father a teenager, but anything's possible."

The kid couldn't hide his surprise. "You followed me?"

"I thought you'd spotted me at the school, but I didn't need to follow you," Sean replied. "I tagged the license plate number, ran it, found the registered owner was James Benson at this address."

Benson lived in town, one of the few side streets off

the main road that intersected the highway two miles west. About half the nearly four hundred residents lived in the one-mile-square "town" on large parcels with small, ramshackle homes where the "newer" houses, like Benson's, were still more than fifty years old. The rest of the town lived in the "country" on acreage, but most of the houses were just as rundown.

"I didn't want to follow you," Sean continued. "Didn't want you to do something stupid like drive off the road trying to get away. This way, I could do a little research. Like figure out that James Benson is an employee of Fire and Rescue. And he's one of the few residents here who still owns his house. Very interesting to me, since Jon Callahan owns seventy percent of the properties in Spruce Lake. Been buying them up for the last couple years."

At the mention of Callahan, the kid tensed.

"I offered to help you," Sean said, "and you tried to kill me."

The kid spoke. "I didn't want to kill you."

"You're lucky my girlfriend is smart and tracked me down. Otherwise, I could have died down there. So right now, you have two options. I haul your ass to Canton and have you arrested for arson and attempted murder or you tell me what the fuck is going on, starting with your name."

Sean watched the teenager weigh whether he was serious or not. Sean let him stew.

Finally, he said, "I don't want your help."

"Fair enough. Come with me."

"I ain't going anywhere." He backed away, eyeing a butcher block of knives.

Sean was getting pissed. "Look, kid, I can draw my gun faster than you can grab one of those knives, and that's not taking into account that I doubt you know how to throw a knife with any accuracy. I want to help you. But you have to want help. You can think there's no way out, that you're drowning in whatever shit you're stuck in, but I promise you—there's *always* a way out. Might not be pretty, but when you're drowning and someone offers you a life preserver, you'd be smart to grab it."

Sean held out his hand. "You know my name. I don't know yours."

"You found Jimmy, I bet you can figure it out."

Jimmy. That meant either an older brother or an uncle.

"Let me tell you what I think is going on. I think Jimmy has you doing something you don't want to do. That he's mixed up with some people and got you mixed up with them, too. First you start small—basic sabotage. Slows construction at the Hendrickson place, costs them a bit of money, but doesn't stop them."

"You don't know what the fuck you're talking about."

"Jimmy has you by the throat, and he's going to get you killed or in prison if you don't take my help." He held out his card. "I'm being straightforward with you, kid."

"Jimmy's not—" He cut himself off and grabbed the card. Stared at it as if it were a lifeline, his face trying not to show how worried he was. How scared. How protective of Jimmy.

"Jimmy's not what? Maybe I should just hang out

here until he gets done with his shift, talk to him, find out if he knows what you've been doing while he's been working seventy-two-hour shifts." Sean pulled out a kitchen chair and sat down. He leaned back, pretending to relax.

"You can't stay here. You gotta leave." His voice cracked as he looked at the closest exit.

"I don't want to play games with you. But you nearly killed me, and worse? You scared my girlfriend. I want to help, but right now I don't like you much. Give me a reason."

The kid looked up as if asking God for help, but not expecting any.

"Start with your name. First name, that's all."

Through clenched teeth, he said, "Ricky."

"Good. I don't know what's going on in this town, but I'm pretty sure you—and Jimmy—aren't orchestrating it. I will find out the truth."

A car door slammed and Ricky jumped. Panicked, he craned his head toward the kitchen window, so he could see down the driveway. "You're a liar," he said to Sean.

Sean looked out. A sheriff's truck was parked behind Ricky's car, but the man who was walking up the weed-infested path wasn't Deputy Weddle. This guy was ten years older and out of uniform, though he had a badge clipped to his utility belt next to his gun.

"I didn't call the cops, Ricky."

"Right."

"I'm not lying."

"Prove it."

There was a knock on the door. Sean glanced

around, motioned toward the bathroom at the end of the hall. "I'm not here."

Ricky looked skeptical, but Sean walked to the bathroom and quietly closed the door. A moment later, he heard the front door open.

The house was small and the walls were thin, so Sean was able to hear nearly everything the cop said.

"Are you James Benson's nephew?" he asked.

"Yes," Ricky said. "Why?"

"I'm Detective Sergeant Kyle Dillard. What's your name, son?"

"Ricky. Where's Jimmy?"

"Do you have any other relatives in town?"

"No. What happened? Did he get hurt? Why didn't his chief call me?"

"He wasn't hurt on the job," Dillard said. "May I come in a moment?"

There was a long pause, then Sean heard the door click close. "I'm really sorry, son, but your uncle's truck went off the bridge outside Colton Wednesday night. He's presumed dead."

"Wednesday?"

"I gather you haven't missed him for the last couple days?"

"He was on duty."

"I spoke to his unit. They said he left sick Wednesday afternoon. You didn't see him?"

"No. Are you sure? You said presumed dead. He could be okay?" Ricky was trying to sound brave, but his voice cracked at the end. Sean wished he could go out there and stand by him. Ricky needed someone in his corner, now more than ever.

"It took some time to assess the scene and bring the

truck up. I'm looking into the cause of the accident. I don't think anyone could have survived."

Ricky wasn't talking, or he spoke too quietly for Sean to hear. It was a minute later when the detective said, "Are you sure I can't call someone for you? A teacher or friend maybe?"

"I don't want to talk to anyone!" Ricky's grief turned to anger.

"You're over sixteen, I can't force you into custody, but I can get you a temporary place to stay in Canton if you don't want to be alone tonight."

"I said *no*! I just need to know what happened to Jimmy."

Silence again. Sean strained to hear. "I understand," Dillard said quietly. "You didn't know he'd left duty?"

"No."

"When was the last time you spoke with him?"

"Tuesday night. When—" Ricky hesitated. Something in his tone made Sean suspect he was lying. "When can, I mean who—what happens now?"

"You don't have to make any decisions. I would advise you to talk to someone—a minister maybe, or your uncle's boss. Someone will help you make the decisions that need to be made, but you have time. Do you know if your uncle had a will?"

Ricky didn't say anything but he must have shook his head, because Dillard said, "I can call Chief Homdus for you. I know him personally; I'm certain he'll help. Go through your uncle's papers."

"I'll call him," Ricky's voice was rough and Sean suspected he was trying hard not to cry. He closed his eyes for a moment. He knew how Ricky felt. He hadn't wanted his brothers, or sister, or anyone else, to see him cry after his parents were killed. He hadn't wanted to be around anyone, especially people offering their condolences. He'd sat through their funeral like a stone, and as soon as they were buried, he bolted. Duke didn't find him for nearly a week. Sean hadn't wanted to be found, but when he was fourteen, Duke was better at tracking him down than Sean was at hiding. Today, Sean would know how to disappear.

What happened to Ricky's parents? Why was he living with his uncle? Had he just lost the last of his family?

"Are you okay to be alone? I asked the chief not to say anything until I spoke with you. I'm pretty certain if you don't call him, he'll be coming by later."

A few minutes later, the front door shut. Sean exited the bathroom and when he didn't see Ricky, he looked out the window. The teenager stood in the driveway talking to the detective. Sean didn't like this—what was Ricky saying that he didn't want Sean to hear? He almost walked out to confront him and turn him over to the detective as an arsonist. But Sean couldn't quite bring himself to do that. He'd had Duke on his side when he was an angry, grieving teenager; Ricky had no one. Sean couldn't send him to juvie. It could force the kid over the line permanently. And by the body language, the detective gave no indication that Ricky was telling him anything related to Sean or the fire. Still, something felt unsettled, and Sean continued watching.

Detective Dillard drove away a few minutes later, and Ricky stared after him. When he turned toward the house, Sean saw his face, red and wet with tears, the anger that he couldn't control. Sean knew how that felt. He'd cried once in front of Duke and hated that his brother had seen him so raw. He turned his head, giving Ricky a moment of privacy.

He glanced around the small, tidy house. The furniture was clean but worn, the sofa so faded and threadbare that Sean could tell that the pattern was small flowers only by the edges. It wasn't a pattern a man would choose; in fact, though there weren't any frills, the furnishings themselves had a feminine touch. He walked over to a well-stocked bookshelf in the corner. On the top was a photograph of a young pretty blond woman. As he picked it up, he heard the engine of Ricky's Camaro.

"Shit!" He ran out the front door, but Ricky had already backed out. Sean was parked down the street to stay out of sight, and he wouldn't be able to catch up. Especially since his leg still ached, and his short sprint out of the house sent searing pain up his nerves.

Sean limped back inside, scratching the outside of the stitches through his jeans. He put the picture back on the shelf, angry with himself. He'd known Ricky didn't want to talk to him; the kid had taken the first opportunity to bolt.

Sean had a hundred questions for the kid, starting with the coincidence that the day Ricky set fire to the lodge and Lucy found a dead woman, Jimmy Benson called in sick and died in an alleged car accident.

Sean's instincts drummed home that Ricky was in danger, but he didn't know where to look for him. He glanced around the house. At least he had a place to start.

Sean started in Ricky's room and quickly learned that he was a fairly tidy kid. His closet was packed to the ceiling with winter gear, books, shoes—some obviously too small for a teenager—and junk. His desk was cluttered, telling Sean he spent time there. He opened a letter from the College Board and was mildly surprised that Ricky had high SAT scores—nearly as high as Sean's. He flipped through some old papers, all A's, a couple of B's. Good student, and there were letters from two colleges outside New York State that had sent him information about early enrollment.

There was no laptop or desktop computer in his room. Did he have one in his backpack or car? Sean searched the desk. Every drawer was cluttered—magazines, pens, junk. Except the only thing in the bottom drawer was a baby-blue box.

Sean hesitated only a moment before he opened the box. Inside were letters in flowery handwriting, and for a split second he thought they were love letters.

And in one sense, they were. From a mother to her son.

Sean felt uncomfortable reading the personal letters, all dated more than five years ago. But he quickly got the sense of why Ricky's mom had written them.

She had known she was dying.

When Ricky was eight, she was diagnosed with breast cancer. She wrote a letter every couple of months to her son. First, she had surgery. Later, the cancer returned and she started chemotherapy, but stopped after only one treatment. The tone of the last few letters changed dramatically.

The last one was dated December 2, five years ago.

Dearest Ricky,

I visited your father today. I know you will be angry. I'm sorry it has to be this way, more than anything I want to see you grow up, go to college, find a girl to love, raise a family. You are my bright light as I wait for my Lord to take me.

My time is coming. When you get this I will be gone. I love you more than anything on earth, and I will do everything to protect you. That is why I had to see your father.

I never lied to you about your dad. People say horrid things about him. Many of them are true. But he never hurt me, not once, and he loves us. With me, he was gentle and kind and sweet. Most people never saw that side of him. Forgiveness is not easy, harder I suspect for a twelve-year-old man. But I forgave your dad. I hope, someday, you can do the same.

My brother will be your legal guardian. I've already filled out the paperwork and your father signed it. Jimmy is a good man, loyal and trustworthy. He will do everything to protect you. Anything to keep you away from the Swains.

Your father told the monster that he would destroy her if anyone hurt you. He always said he had a card to play if he had to, and for you and you alone, he's willing to use it. You need to understand what this means. If your father is forced to reveal the evidence he has hidden all these years, the monster will be locked up for life, but your father will be killed in prison as a traitor. He will do this because he loves you. He will do anything to protect you.

If I had any money, Jimmy could take you far

away from here, give you a different name. But you'll be safe here. There are people watching out for you.

I am not scared of dying, sweet son. I have put my soul on the mercy of my Lord. I know you will cry for me. My only regret in dying is not being with you. But do not mourn me. In Heaven, there is no pain. There is no suffering, no betrayal, no monsters. There is only pure love. As you read this, know that I am at peace.

Do not be sad long, my son. My love will be with you forever.

—Your mother, now and always

Sean read the letter twice, committing it to memory. Most kids who lost a parent didn't have a letter.

For Sean, it had been so sudden he didn't believe it. It felt as if his mother—both his parents—had been ripped from him. No good-byes, no apologies, no peace.

Sean pushed aside his anger about his parents' plane crash and took a picture of the letter with his cell phone.

Sean skimmed the rest of the letters, but nothing revealed the identity of the monster she mentioned in her last letter.

Folded at the bottom of the box was her marriage certificate and Ricky's birth certificate. Her name was Abigail Benson.

Her husband had been Paul Swain.

Ricky's father was Paul Swain, a convicted killer.

Sean put the box back exactly as he'd found it and sent both Patrick and Duke a note about what he'd uncovered. Since Patrick was heading to Albany tonight, Duke could get answers faster, Sean hoped. The letter was written a year after Swain went to prison, and Sean suspected that what was happening in Spruce Lake today related directly to Paul Swain's drug-running days.

There are people watching out for you.

Sean knew who had the answer to his questions. First, he needed to find Ricky Swain; then he'd pay a visit to Paul Swain.

NINETEEN

Lucy sat alone in the cabin and stared at the picture of Victoria Sheffield on Sean's laptop.

She looked like the woman Lucy had seen dead in the mine. Blond hair, long and wavy, five feet six inches tall and one hundred thirty-five pounds. She'd been missing for just over four months, since January second, and if alive, would turn twenty-eight at the end of the month.

Lucy had seen the woman for only a few minutes. Was she now imprinting someone with a similar appearance? Could she trust her memory?

Victoria Sheffield's file was sparse. She had been last seen in Albany, New York, but it didn't list where specifically, nor did it state what she was last seen wearing or driving.

None of the other women had caught Lucy's eye. The shape of the face different, the hair too dark, the nose wrong. But Victoria . . . Lucy was ninety percent certain it was her.

It would fit. She went missing in early January, could easily have been preserved in the mine without any decomposition, yet she wasn't dressed for the weather. No visible sign of what might have caused her death, but she could have been suffocated, poisoned, any number of things that would leave no obvious external marks.

The Albany FBI office had issued the alert, which was odd—standard missing persons were usually issued by local law enforcement. She dialed the 800 number. As soon as she reported that she may have information regarding Victoria Sheffield, her call was transferred.

A minute later, a deep voice came on the line. "Ms. Kincaid?"

"Yes."

"I'm the assistant special agent in charge, Brian Candela. You saw Victoria Sheffield?" His voice was gruff and to the point.

The number-two guy in the Albany FBI field office was taking her call, before an agent even verified her story? That alone told her this was an extremely important case for the FBI. Her curiosity was definitely piqued.

"Yes, sir. I believe so."

"Believing you saw her and seeing her are not the same thing. Either you saw Agent Sheffield or you didn't."

Lucy sat up straighter. "*Agent* Sheffield?"

"I'm not at liberty to discuss the circumstances surrounding Agent Sheffield's disappearance. Where did you think you saw her?"

"I'm on vacation in the Adirondacks, in a small community called Spruce Lake on the edge of the state park. On Wednesday, I was in the Kelley Mine outside of town and saw a dead body that matches Victoria Sheffield's description. I reported it, but when authorities arrived the next morning, the body had gone missing."

"Which agency did you report to?"

"Sheriff's Department. I don't think the responding officer took my report seriously. But I assure you, it's not a prank. I'm an agent-in-training scheduled to report to Quantico later this summer."

Candela asked, "Is there someone I can call to verify your identity?"

"Special Agent Noah Armstrong." She gave Candela her training supervisor's office line and cell phone number.

"Please hold."

Lucy stared at Sheffield's picture on the computer. She had been only a couple years older than Lucy. She couldn't have been an agent for long.

What happened to you, Victoria?

Several minutes later, Candela came back on the phone. His tone changed just a fraction, a bit more cordial, but still brusque. "Agent Kincaid?"

Lucy's heart skipped a beat. Technically she was an agent-in-training, not a special agent, but a small thrill went through her. "Yes, sir?"

"I just spoke with Noah Armstrong and he vouched for you, confirmed you are on vacation in Spruce Lake. Please tell me exactly what happened from when you found Agent Sheffield's body until now."

After Lucy related her discovery of a body down in the Kelley Mine, there was dead silence. Lucy went on, getting a bit nervous, but reciting the facts of the case kept her calm and focused. She explained in detail, finishing with the disappearance of Sheffield's body.

"You mean to say the body was moved?"

"That's the only explanation."

"Did you photograph the scene?"

"Today I did, but when I found the body I honestly didn't think of it. I was in the mine to rescue Sean, since he'd been injured."

"Why did you go back down?"

"To look for evidence. As I mentioned, I didn't feel the police had taken me seriously because the body was gone when they arrived."

"What evidence?"

The conversation now sounded like an interrogation. Lucy told him what she and Sean found in the mine that morning and the reaction of the sheriff's deputy. She concluded, "I used to work for the D.C. Medical Examiner, and I've been trained in evidence collection. I followed all protocols." Except for the fact that she wasn't supposed to be down there in the first place. "I understand that I had no authority to do so, but the deputy sheriff who responded essentially believed that I was making it up. I didn't know when, or if, they would go back to the mine to search for her body. The mine is unstable and dangerous, according to Fire and Rescue. But I know what I saw, and I know someone went down after I reported her and removed the body."

"Are you suggesting that someone in the local police department had a part in this?"

"I wouldn't rule it out. This is a small town—by dinnertime, I suspect everyone knew there was a body in the mine."

"And why didn't you contact me immediately?" He sounded both angry, and upset.

"I didn't know who she was. After her body went missing, my brother Patrick—Sean's partner—pulled all the missing persons files for the Northeast that matched the description I gave him. She's the only one who is close."

"Close? You mean you may be wrong?" He sounded hopeful.

"I'm nearly certain it's Agent Sheffield. But I was only with the body for a few minutes." She didn't want to give him false hope, but she couldn't swear it *was* her.

"You said she could have been there for months or days—explain."

"I'm not an entomologist, so I'm really just making a guess, and I don't like to do that."

"You need to understand that no one has seen Agent Sheffield since December twenty-third."

"The missing person's report says January second."

"She filed a report, via email, on January second, but no one has spoken to her in person since December."

"She was undercover?"

"It's a classified investigation, and as an agent-in-training I don't think you have the clearance."

She winced at his tone, but understood. A message popped up on Lucy's screen. It was from Noah.

Call me when you're done with Candela.

She said. "Based on the appearance of the body, I think she was frozen. Not in a freezer, but naturally, in the underground mine. No freezer burn or ice that indicates a mechanical unit was involved in any way, and because her body was flat—arranged that way, would be my guess, based on the positioning of her arms—I'm guessing she was down there prior to full rigor. Mean ing, less than twelve hours after her death."

"Was there any sign of a struggle or injuries?"

"No outward cause of death. No bruising around the neck to indicate strangulation—though, to be honest, I don't know how or if freezing would impact her appearance."

While she was talking, Sean walked in. He was about to speak, but saw she was on the phone.

"Send me the photos," Candela ordered.

"Of course." She had already downloaded the photos to Sean's laptop. She zipped them into one file.

Candela gave her his email, then said, "I need the name and contact information of all people involved in the search for Agent Sheffield."

Lucy typed everything she had in the email as she told him the same information. "Thank you. I'll be in touch," he said, then hung up.

Lucy turned to Sean. "Well, that was Albany FBI. ASAC Candela." She shook her head, still trying to absorb all the information Candela did share with her. "I identified the body. Victoria Sheffield. She was an FBI agent."

Sean sat across from her. "FBI? What was she doing here?"

"He wouldn't say. I think he was surprised. She disappeared between December twenty-third and January second."

"A Fed is missing and it's not plastered on the national news?"

She turned the laptop around and showed Sean the missing persons report. "It doesn't even say she's a federal agent in the report. There's nothing about her, other than her photo and description."

"If they didn't want anyone knowing she was a Fed, maybe they have an active investigation."

"He didn't give me any details."

Sean stood and looked out the window. It was getting late, the sun was setting to the southwest, and Lucy wondered what had him so preoccupied. Usually he preferred to talk out possible scenarios.

"What is it?" she asked.

"I found the arsonist. His name is Ricky Swain."

She leaned forward, palms hitting the desk. "*Swain?*"

"The son of Paul Swain."

"What happened?"

"After I went to Canton—which was mostly a wasted trip—I made a detour to Colton and waited until school got out. I spotted him and ran the plates."

Lucy raised an eyebrow as Sean related what had happened at James Benson's house.

"What did you find in Benson's house?" she asked, ignoring the obvious fact that it had been an illegal search.

"Letters from Ricky's dead mother. One in particular stands out." He plugged his cell phone into his laptop, scrolled through, then turned the screen to face her. "Read this."

Lucy scanned the image of the letter, not only absorbing the information it contained, but wondering if this beautiful but sad letter was partly the cause of an uneasy vibe she was getting from Sean.

"What do you think Abigail meant by the card her husband had to play? And why would their son be in danger?" Lucy frowned, looking at the letter again. "If we take what she's writing at face value, she was genuinely concerned about her son's safety."

"It's vague, but Ricky must know who the 'monster' is."

Lucy reread the letter slowly. Three sentences stood out.

He will do everything to protect you. Anything to keep you away from the Swains.

Your father told the monster that he would destroy her if anyone hurt you.

"Sean, why would Abigail write that her brother Jimmy would do anything to keep Ricky away from the Swains? Ricky *is* a Swain." Lucy added, "And the monster she writes about is a woman."

"Patrick found only two female Swains in the immediate family," Sean said. "The woman who married Butch and the younger sister."

Lucy looked at the notes from Patrick. "Kathy Davis Swain married Butch fourteen years ago, so she was in the family during Abigail's illness. And Roberta Swain moved to Florida sixteen years ago, but Patrick couldn't trace her after that. She'd be thirty-four now."

Sean leaned over and sent Patrick and Duke a message. "I'll get them working on it, because you're right—Abigail was very concerned."

"And yet look what's happened anyway. Her son is involved in something extremely dangerous."

"I need to find Ricky again. The kid's scared shitless. And now his uncle is missing and presumed dead. This is no coincidence—it's all connected."

"He could be setting you up. Can you trust him?"

"Hardly, but I'm not going to dismiss him as a lost cause. The kid has been through hell. What if Benson wasn't the paragon of virtue his sister thought he was? What if he got in deep with whoever took over the Swain drug operation? *Or* something worse?"

"Patrick said there's nothing on law enforcement radar."

"Yet you found a dead federal agent in the mine. There's something we're missing!"

Sean had a point. They had only a few pieces of the puzzle and none quite fit.

"Ricky wasn't scared of his uncle," Sean said. "In fact, if anything, he seemed protective. And his reaction to Benson's death was real enough. He's hurting."

"What are we going to do about it?" Lucy asked. "Obviously, the kid is in trouble, but he nearly killed you."

"He knows how to reach me, and I think he will try to make contact. If not today, I'll track him down tomorrow. After I go to the prison to talk to Paul Swain. He has the answers I need."

Lucy didn't like that idea, though she had to admit it sounded logical. This situation had exploded far beyond simple vandalism. "Do you think he'll cooperate?"

Before Sean could respond, her phone rang. "It's Noah," she said.

"Word gets around fast," Sean mumbled.

"The FBI needed to verify my credentials," Lucy said as she answered the call. Sean and Noah weren't friends, though Lucy appreciated that both made an effort to be cordial.

"Hi, Noah," Lucy said.

"You didn't call." Direct and to the point, as always.

"Sean came in and I was filling him in on the details."

"This situation sounds serious."

"I'm going to put my phone on speaker, if you don't mind."

Noah paused. Sean wasn't looking at her, but his jaw was tense. "Fine," Noah said crisply.

She put her cell phone down on the desk and turned up the speaker volume. "It's just Sean and me," she said.

"Rogan," Noah said in greeting.

"Agent Armstrong," Sean said formally.

Lucy ignored the tension and asked, "Do you know what Agent Sheffield was investigating when she disappeared?"

"Enough to know you're in dangerous territory. Candela asked me to come to Albany. He'd like you to join us and debrief the task force."

"What task force?"

"I don't know who's involved, but it's related to Sheffield's case. She was working undercover for the white-collar crimes squad."

"White collar? Bribery and political corruption?" Hardly her area of expertise.

"They also handle intellectual property rights, corporate espionage, major fraud. From what Candela said," Noah continued, "I gather that not only was Victoria Sheffield exceptionally good at her job, she loved it. About three years ago, illegal DVDs started popping up in Canada. Piracy is nothing new, but these were special—top quality. An international task force was created, and last summer they'd identified an operative they felt could be used."

"Who?" Sean asked. This was definitely his area of strength, particularly corporate espionage.

"Candela didn't say. When they were about to take

down the ring, Sheffield discovered that the piracy was just a small part of the operation—and that she still hadn't identified the leader. They agreed to a delay, then her communications became sporadic. She met with her boss and her Canadian counterpart before Christmas, told them she was close, and would contact them on January second—after a big meeting that was supposed to take place between the principals. She was scheduled to visit her parents for Christmas but never showed."

"Why didn't the FBI pull her in earlier?" asked Lucy.

"Her parents said that she canceled her trip, that she was working a big case and couldn't get away. They didn't know anything was wrong until the FBI contacted them in January."

"But her last communication was January second?"

"She sent her boss an email that said the meeting was canceled and she'd let him know when it was rescheduled, that she needed to lay low because her contact was suspicious."

"What the hell were these people thinking?" Sean said, shaking his head. He didn't look at Lucy, and while she sensed he was irritated, she hadn't expected him to react so strongly.

"Because she was on vacation, no one considered—"

Sean cut Noah off. "It just seems to me that you either have a rogue agent or an incompetent office."

Lucy bristled. "We don't have enough information—"

"They want you to brief them in Albany, but they're not sharing what they know. You're going in blind."

Noah spoke up. "We'll have a full briefing. I agree, there are some apparent abnormalities in this investigation, but we're assessing it with limited information. Candela isn't going to reveal sensitive information over an unsecured line."

Lucy changed the subject back to Sheffield's disappearance. "Does the FBI think the January second message was fake?"

"They didn't say, but that's my read on the situation. Her contact is missing, presumed dead, or in hiding."

"White-collar criminals don't tend to be violent," Lucy said.

"That's in the past. Financial crimes now top $400 billion annually. That's a lot of money to kill for."

"Then how did she end up in the middle of nowhere at the bottom of a mine?" Lucy said.

"That's the million-dollar question."

"Or the 400-billion-dollar question," Sean interjected.

Lucy glanced at Sean. He was staring out the window, but every muscle was rigid. "When are we going to Albany?" she asked Noah.

"Tomorrow morning. Patrick will be on a commuter flight that gets in at seven-fifty a.m. It turns around and goes back to Albany at eight-twenty a.m. I'd like you on it. I'll pick you up at the airport."

"Of course," she said. "Whatever I can do to help."

"In the meantime, both of you be careful. If they'll kill a Fed, they'll kill anyone. Patrick told me someone already took shots at you."

Sean said from across the room, "It was basically a message to get out of town."

"You tend to have that effect on people," Noah said, a modicum of humor in his voice.

Sean didn't smile, however. "I gathered up the shell casings and shipped them to RCK in California. I'll let you know if Duke uncovers anything."

The tension returned, Lucy could practically feel Noah's frustration through the phone. She quickly added, "I collected a few insects in the cave. I'll bring them with me to Albany."

"Thank you," Noah said. "Watch your back, both of you. I'll see you in Albany, Lucy." He hung up.

Lucy watched Sean as he continued to look out the window toward the lake and colorful sky as the sun sank on the horizon. "We'll find out everything Albany knows about the case," Lucy said. She wished she understood what was bothering Sean. He was usually up front about everything, especially with her.

"Maybe it's better to get you out of town for a day or two," Sean said.

"Excuse me?"

"It's heating up here, and—"

"And you don't think I can handle the pressure? Yes, it's dangerous, but we've both been in dangerous situations."

"That's not what I meant."

Lucy wondered what Sean really thought. He was always more than willing to explain what he meant, but he didn't elaborate now. "You can understand why the Albany office would want to ask me questions, but—"

"It's *fine*." He turned to face her, but she couldn't read him. "A sniper shot at us today and I couldn't do a damn thing about it. I'd rather you were away from here, at least until I can figure out what the hell is going on."

She was stunned. He was talking about her as if she were a hindrance to his job, as if he couldn't work the case if he had to worry about her. She didn't know how to respond, whether to be angry or upset or ask him to explain himself. Or maybe this was why law enforcement agencies frowned on lovers working together. Breaking deep-seated male protectiveness over women, especially women with whom they were romantically involved, was difficult. Yet two of her brothers had married FBI agents and didn't have this problem. Was it her? Did she act needy or incompetent?

She was missing something. Sean had always been supportive of her career choice—aside from his general animosity toward law enforcement. He'd always stood up for her. Yet he stared at her now, as if egging on an argument. She just didn't have the energy to go at it again.

"All right," she finally said. "We need to pick Patrick up at Oldenburg at seven-fifty and my flight leaves at eight-twenty."

"I'm going to the Lock & Barrel," Sean said. "I'm going to drop some bombs tonight and see what happens." He kissed her, but it was a light peck, out of habit, without any real emotion. "Keep your eyes and ears open; don't leave the cabin without a gun. Adam and Annie are here; I'm bringing Tim with me."

She didn't ask to join him.

TWENTY

I'm used to people lying to save their ass, but I couldn't be one hundred percent positive whether Carl was *telling the truth. He swore up and down that not only had he* not *told anyone to take a shot at the P.I and his bitch, but he hadn't heard that anyone had gone off on their own.*

He did, however, have a hand in Jimmy Benson's truck going off the road.

He said, "I told them to bring me Jimmy alive. They said his truck just lost control and went into the water."

I didn't buy it. Trucks don't just lose control.

Carl was a problem on many levels—he thought he was in charge and he had manipulated the loyalty of the team I'd put together. He'd stayed in Spruce Lake and people here trusted him.

Which was why I couldn't pepper him with shot-gun pellets and watch him slowly bleed to death, however much I wanted to.

People were scared of me, and I could work with that, but until this deal was finalized on Sunday—and

Carl had to be alive for the final handshake—killing him was not an option.

That put me in a bad mood.

Coupled with, of course, the problem of the shooter.

I didn't ask for Ian's advice often, but on issues like this he sometimes had good insight. We were already halfway to Potsdam to meet my pet cop and make sure he finished his last job.

"Carl swears he knows nothing about the sniper."

"Do you believe him?" Ian asked.

"Unless he's become a far better liar over the years."

It wasn't solely because I thought he was telling the truth; a sniper wasn't Carl's style. Did someone want to fuck up my operation? Killing a civilian would bring in cops I didn't control during the next critical forty-eight hours.

"The clients," Ian said discreetly, "could have sent an advance team."

"Without me knowing?" I changed the subject. "What did you find at Benson's place?" I asked.

"Nothing that would indicate Jimmy was playing both sides," Ian said. "But I did spot the P.I. Sean Rogan in the neighborhood."

My instincts vibrated. "How close? Benson is right off the main road."

"At the intersection, headed toward Hendrickson's place."

That could mean something or nothing. I needed to assess Rogan myself. "Did you dig anything up on him?"

"Not much. He is who he says he is—a private investigator out of Washington, D.C. From what I could put together, he specializes in computer security. Grad-

uated from M.I.T. That's near Boston, could be where he met Hendrickson."

Something didn't feel right. Hendrickson was at least five, maybe ten, years older than Rogan. "Dig deeper."

"I already have the word out. I'll have reports coming in tonight."

"And Lucy Kincaid?"

"We may have a problem there. When Weddle said she worked for the morgue, I was able to track her down easily. Thing is, she doesn't work there anymore. She left three months ago. They told me she could be reached at FBI Headquarters."

I slammed my fist on the dashboard. "Fuck!"

"I think it's a coincidence—she has no ties to Albany."

"I don't care; it's too risky."

I weighed my options. She couldn't be an agent—not after only three months—but she definitely knew *Feds. If she went missing or turned up dead, others would start snooping.*

For all I knew, she'd already called in her buddies.

And if the Feds identified the dead bitch, everything would come tumbling down. All I needed was two more days.

Ian pulled into the Potsdam town limits. "Let's do this quick," I told him. "I need to get back to Spruce Lake. It's time everyone knows I'm back."

TWENTY-ONE

"I'm not quite sure what you hope to accomplish tonight," Tim told Sean as they sat in the truck outside the Lock & Barrel.

Sean was barely listening. He wanted to go back and set things right with Lucy, but he didn't know how to explain it to her.

It wasn't her fault that Sean had a flash of jealousy whenever Noah Armstrong's name was mentioned. Lucy had never said or implied or even *hinted* that she was more than a friend and colleague to Noah. She had done nothing to make Sean believe she wasn't committed to him alone—except she'd never said *I love you.*

Foolish, really, for him to come back to that. For years he'd cringed when he heard his ex-girlfriends declare their love, because he didn't believe it and he didn't feel it. And since he'd never stuck with any of them for long, he couldn't imagine that they were being honest with him, or themselves.

But Sean had known he loved Lucy almost from the beginning. And his feelings had only deepened since.

Maybe it was the methodical way Noah had insinuated himself in Lucy's life. Like quietly cutting through red tape when Lucy's FBI application was held up. And there was no way Sean believed for a minute that Noah didn't have everything to do with Lucy being assigned to him while she waited for a slot to open at the FBI training academy.

However, when it came right down to it, Patrick was the problem. Patrick thought Noah was better for Lucy than Sean, and had made that clear in more ways than once. He'd said as much, and it had festered in Sean's head like a tumor. Growing darker and blacker until just the mention of Noah—the by-the-book G-man—made Sean see red. He had to shut down, otherwise he'd explode and say something that could jeopardize his relationship with Lucy. He had to get his reaction under control before he tried to explain it to her.

If he even could.

He put all of it aside to focus on the task at hand.

"Sorry," he said to Tim, dismissing his preoccupation. "Just thinking things through. We go in, observe, see who's talking to whom. Make a point of discussing what's been happening. Make it clear you're not going to be scared off, but that maybe holding off on the grand opening is a good idea."

"Do you really think we're going to learn anything?"

"Someone here knows something. Hell, maybe the whole town is in on it." He paused. "Do you know James Benson?"

Tim shook his head. "It doesn't ring a bell."

"He worked for Fire and Rescue. He is missing and presumed dead."

"What does that have to do with the lodge?"

"He's the brother-in-law of Paul Swain. His nephew is the one who set fire to the lodge."

Tim straightened his spine and glared at Sean. "Nephew?"

"Swain's son."

"Did you tell the police?"

"Not yet."

"Why the hell not?"

Sean should have approached this differently. "I don't trust that deputy," he said cautiously. "His reactions were atypical, and I find it suspicious that there aren't more cops in and out of that mine."

"You don't trust many people, do you?"

"I suppose not."

"I'll grant you Weddle—I don't know what to make of him—but he's not the only cop in St. Lawrence County."

"I've already put in a request to meet with the detective-sergeant assigned to the case. His secretary called to set up an appointment first thing tomorrow morning. Let's go inside. I'll buy you a beer. Anybody asks, you're postponing the resort."

"But I thought—"

"That was yesterday. Today, let's play their game. Callahan wanted us to postpone. We give them what they want and see where it leads."

They walked in and like last night, conversation halted momentarily as Sean and Tim ambled over to the bar. Even the band in the back hit a sour note. Sean sat down on the bar's far side, where he could clearly see both the front door and the door leading into the kitchen. The bartender was different from the one the night before—as different as you could get. Instead of old Reggie, this bartender was an attractive female—and one who knew she was hot. With long, curly dark red hair and big green eyes, she wore tight jeans tucked into well-worn boots.

She smiled as she approached them. "What can I get for you fellas?"

"Two drafts," Sean said.

Conversation resumed as soon as they were seated, though everyone's attention seemed to be focused on them. Sean observed there were twice as many people tonight as yesterday. It was Friday, after the dinner hour, in a small town and the Lock & Barrel was the only nightlife for miles. Sean never would have survived growing up in a town like Spruce Lake.

The redhead placed the beers in front of them. Sean noticed two scars on her left forearm. Too high to be a suicide attempt, but definitely a knife attack.

"I haven't seen you two before," the bartender said. "Let me guess—Adam and Tim Hendrickson?"

"Half right," Sean said.

"I'm Tim," Tim acknowledged. "This is my friend Sean."

She smiled brightly, but Sean sensed that she was observing them like specimens. She flirted, but not like Trina, the waitress. This woman was calculating; Sean saw it in her eyes, in the way she seemed attuned to everyone in the room, even though she looked right at him.

"I didn't think this town was big enough for two bartenders," Sean said.

"Reggie was feeling under the weather; I'm just helping out tonight."

"And do you have a name?"

She extended her hand and smiled seductively. "Bobbie," she said. She wore rings on nearly every finger; several diamonds and one large emerald stood out. If they were real—and they looked as though they were—she wore thousands of dollars on her hands. If fake, they were expensive fakes.

"Pleased to meet you."

"I heard about your troubles, Tim. The whole town is talking. I'm so sorry."

Tim shrugged. "Well, I really have no choice."

"What do you mean?"

"I have to postpone the opening."

She frowned dramatically, but Sean didn't think she was a bit sorry. She looked as if she was playing a part and enjoying every minute of it. "That's awful."

"I thought most of the people here were opposed to the Spruce Lake Resort," Sean said.

She shrugged. "I don't really have an opinion."

"Someone shot at me today," Sean said, watching Bobbie closely.

"Really? Who?"

"Don't know. But I'm going to find out."

Bobbie's neck muscles tightened—just briefly, but it was an interesting sign that she was irritated. "How?"

"I'm a private investigator. I'm pretty good at my job."

"Oh! A private eye. Wow. Like Sam Spade?"

Sean noticed that Bobbie ignored everyone except him and Tim. He found it odd that Trina, not Bobbie, was filling orders. Bobbie was trying hard to sound like a ditz, but her eyes were too sharp and observant. A man in his midtwenties sat at the end of the bar observing the three of them, trying to be discreet, but

Sean pegged him as security. Why did Bobbie need security?

He responded to her query. "Mostly computer work. Boring, really. Nothing like Thomas Magnum."

She stared at him blankly. "Who?"

"From the television show, *Magnum, P.I.* You're probably too young to remember—*I'm* too young to remember—but I caught the reruns."

She frowned, a flash of anger in her eyes. Why? Because she didn't know a television character?

"I don't have time for TV," she snapped and turned away, grabbing a rag from under the bar. "I gotta get back to work, boys," she said as if they were the ones keeping her.

"Of course," Sean said. She halfheartedly wiped down the bar, refilling a couple of drafts on the way without talking to anyone, until she got to the watchful guy at the end. She fixed him a Scotch and soda—light on the Scotch, Sean noted.

Bobbie was a nickname for Roberta. Was that sly woman Roberta Swain? Did she actually live in Spruce Lake, and if so, when had she moved back from Florida? Patrick hadn't been able to get a picture of her, but she looked about the right age, early thirties.

"That conversation was strange," Tim said quietly.

"Yep," Sean concurred. He watched the patrons. Everyone was trying *not* to look at Bobbie. They seemed deferential. Scared? Maybe. Angry. It was as though the whole town was in on a conspiracy to shut down the resort, and now the big guns were out.

With Patrick coming into town, Sean could cover a

lot more territory and keep an eye on Bobbie the relief bartender. After talking to him last night, Sean suspected that Henry Callahan knew all the town secrets. Maybe Sean could convince him to be forthcoming, even if he had to find a way to protect him.

"Are you ready to go?" Tim asked. "I don't think we're going to learn anything here."

"I've already learned a lot." He wasn't going to discuss what he suspected while they were still here. "It's only been twenty minutes. I want to see who shows up in the next hour. Since we've sat here, four people have stepped out, and now the band."

"Probably for a smoke."

"Probably," Sean said, not believing it for a minute. Smoking was the excuse. Someone had called in their sighting, and Sean wanted to know who.

Sean had swung by Ricky's house on the way to the bar and his car wasn't there, nor was there any sign that he'd been home since bolting this afternoon. If Sean could get him to talk, he'd protect the kid himself—or send him far from Spruce Lake. The U.S. Marshals had nothing on the Rogan family when it came to hiding people. But Ricky would have to be willing to share information and go all the way.

Could Paul Swain be running a drug operation from prison? Certainly a possibility if he was powerful enough. The police might not think the drug lab was still around, but that didn't mean he hadn't moved it nearby, or wasn't involved in another way.

Sean knew a bit about the international drug trade—his brother Kane had been fighting drug and human trafficking in South and Central America for twenty years. It was war down there—murder, bribery, corruption. It was the same here, but on a smaller scale. Cleaner. Cops were harder to bribe, though not impossible. Corruption existed, but not as blatant or as widespread.

But a town like Spruce Lake would be perfect for drug running. Near the Canadian border, remote, with people desperate to survive and no way to get out. The big cities in Canada had the same drug and gang problems as big cities in America.

What was it about the resort that scared them? Drug labs were everywhere, littering both urban and rural areas. A resort in the middle of nowhere shouldn't slow them down. Unless there was something about the location . . .

Sean had left the property maps in the cabin. Spruce Lake, the actual lake itself, was split between Hendrickson, Callahan, and federal land. But he didn't see how that would be crucial to the dealers. There had to be something else going on that the few people the resort would bring in would jeopardize.

Maybe it wasn't drugs. Maybe it was something else entirely. Which brought Sean back to: who would be hurt the most if the resort opened?

What bothered him at this point was the extent of the conspiracy. There had to be at least two people, other than Ricky and his uncle, who were involved. And a large number of people knew about it, and were either intimidated into keeping silent or part of the problem.

The swinging door leading from the kitchen burst open and Jon Callahan entered. He stopped abruptly at the sight of Bobbie.

She turned around and smiled. "Hello, Jon!" she said and waved from the opposite end of the bar.

Callahan didn't speak. He looked around at the patrons, most of whom had cut their conversation down to a whisper. Something in his face shifted, and he smiled. "Would you be so kind, sugar, and pour me a Scotch?" He sat down next to Tim.

Bobbie slammed a glass on the counter in front of him.

"Don't call me 'sugar,' *Boss,*" she snapped. The two stared at each other a beat too long.

"The Jameson will be fine," Callahan said.

She splashed a shot into the glass, then strode back across the bar to her security.

Callahan nodded at Tim. "Things okay out at your place today?"

"Other than some prick taking potshots at my friend," Tim said. Now that he was into the game, Tim was doing well, Sean thought. He let Tim run with the conversation.

"I didn't know," Callahan said. "I was in Montreal all day. Just got back."

"No one was hurt," Tim continued, "but I was thinking about what you told Adam last night. Maybe it would be best if we postponed the opening. I don't know who's screwing with me, but I can't take the responsibility of protecting my guests from some gun-toting lunatic. Adam is really torn up about it."

"He has his heart set," Callahan agreed, "but it's not forever. I'm sure things will get all smoothed over. And I'm happy to help with that over the next year."

"Thanks, Jon. I appreciate it."

Sean was missing a big piece of the puzzle. He

watched the crowd. Everyone was focused on Jon and Bobbie, as if they were waiting for something to happen.

Sean decided to add fuel to the fire. "I didn't think this town was big enough for two bartenders. Reggie was cute and all, but the redhead is cuter," he said with a wink.

"Reggie deserves some time off," Jon said. "I didn't know when I'd be back from Montreal."

Sean hadn't expected that answer. Obviously, Jon hadn't known Bobbie was going to be here. He observed the way his eyes watched her in the mirror behind the bar. Was this a turf war? Over a town of fewer than four hundred people?

Sean glanced around the bar again. No one was ordering anything, food or drink. Trina stood at a table in the far corner with two older men and an even older woman. Conversation was virtually nonexistent. The band was still out on break.

"Any news about the body in the mine?" Jon asked suddenly.

"Not that I know," Sean said.

"Did you check the missing persons in the area?"

"Yes, we looked through them. No one matched."

"I didn't know you saw the body," Jon said. "Didn't you say it was your girlfriend who found her? What an awful experience for such a sweet girl."

Sean didn't deny having seen the body, though Deputy Weddle and the Fire and Rescue guys knew that only Lucy had seen it. Sean's protective instincts kicked in. Was Lucy in danger because she was the only person to have seen Agent Sheffield?

He discreetly sent Lucy a text message to check in

and make sure she was all right while telling Jon, "Yeah, but Lucy's tough. She works at a morgue."

"Still, that must have been a shock."

"I think it was more of a shock that the body disappeared," Sean said. He watched Bobbie in his peripheral vision. Her head was turned away from them, toward the bodyguard, but her body language—the way her feet were pointed, her hair tucked behind her ear and her body turned just a bit *too* much in his direction—told Sean she was listening intently.

"How long are you staying on?" Jon asked casually. *Too* casually. Bobbie was definitely listening for the answer.

Sean shrugged. Bobbie looked over her shoulder, ostensibly to inspect her patrons' beers, but she made no attempt to refill their empty mugs.

Sean glanced at Tim. "It hasn't been much of a vacation, wouldn't you say?"

"Sorry about that."

Sean shook his head. "No worries. Lucy and I were talking about sticking around for a few days. Try to relax, give my leg a couple more days to get back full mobility. And I promised Deputy Weddle we'd be available for questions whenever the detective assigned to the arson comes around. I've never seen such disinterested police before."

"Odd," Jon said. "They are usually so responsive."

Bobbie sauntered over. "Can I get you boys refills?"

She wanted to talk. Sean didn't want another beer, but he nodded. "Thanks—Bobbie, right?"

She grinned. "That's right, sugar." She poured two more drafts for him and Tim. She glanced at Jon, and he held up his glass. She grabbed a bottle off the shelf and poured two fingers while glaring at Jon.

Sean had a sudden idea. He and Tim should hit Henry Callahan now, while his nephew was here. He didn't know how much time he'd have, but if they left and sped over there, he might have ten, fifteen minutes.

He drained half his beer. Tim gave him an odd look. Sean made a motion that he wanted to leave. He glanced at his phone. Lucy had responded to his message.

I'm fine. All quiet. You?

Good, she was safe for now, but he sent her a message to be diligent and to say he'd be late. He then inconspicuously snapped a no-flash picture of Bobbie. It was not quite three-quarters of a profile shot, but Sean couldn't risk getting closer or waiting until she was looking at him.

The band returned from their break and started tuning up their instruments. Sean used the disruption to stand, stretch, and put twenty dollars on the bar. "Jon, good to see you again. My leg's acting up; I think we're going to call it an early night."

"Stop by before you leave town," Jon said. "I'll buy you lunch for the road."

"Thank you, I'll do that." Sean tipped an imaginary hat to Bobbie. He sent the picture to Duke and Patrick when he walked outside and began to text. The air had turned much colder now that the sun was down.

Says her name is Bobbie. Possibly Roberta Swain. Five feet six inches, 125 lbs, dark red hair, might be dyed darker than natural, but is natural redhead (eyebrows). Has bodyguard or boyfriend who is in security. Approx. 180, five ten to six feet, blond, blue, possibly Russian or Scandinavian descent. Need to confirm Bobbie's identity, run through all databases.

"What was that about?" Tim asked.

"One sec," Sean said as he finished typing his message and sent it. "More work for my brother," he said with a grin.

He unlocked his truck. On the driver's seat was a torn slip of paper. Unlike the first warning this morning, this was scrawled in small, hurried block letters, but Sean knew it was from the same person.

Sean looked around, his hand on his gun. He didn't see anyone. He carefully picked up the paper, using the tips of his fingers to hold it by the corners.

I TOLD YOU TO GO HOME. NOW YOU CAN'T. THEY HAVE YOUR GIRL'S FLIGHT SCHEDULE.

TWENTY-TWO

Ricky parked at the abandoned farm behind Skyline Bible Church, then trudged through the fallow fields until he reached church property. He'd driven the back roads for hours, thinking about running away. But how could he? He had nothing. Finally, at sundown, he returned to town. He'd waited in the pine trees on the edge of the church parking lot for an hour until Reverend Browne finally left. He sat completely still, not thinking or feeling anything because he didn't want to cry. It was dark when Ricky slipped from his hiding place and ran across the street to the dimly-lit cemetery where he visited his mother at least once a week. Where soon he would visit his uncle Jimmy.

His grandfather, Lawson Swain, was buried here, but Ricky hadn't known him. He'd been convicted of murder when Ricky was three, and all he remembered was that Lawson had smelled of tobacco, rarely spoke, and when he did his voice was deep and scary and Ricky didn't know why his mother would squeeze him tight whenever they were in the same room as his grandfather. Ricky didn't remember anything about the trial and had never seen his grandfather again, until he was buried in this cemetery when Ricky was nine. That was two years before his father went to prison. Three years before he returned to bury his mother.

Ricky knelt in the damp grass of the small cemetery and stared at his mother's simple headstone. The soft lights outside the church enabled Ricky to see the angel carved above her name.

SWAIN
Abigail Anne
Beloved wife and mother
"The Lord is my Shepherd."
February 12, 1965–March 1, 2006

His mother had chosen the epitaph. His father wanted it to be "Vengeance is Mine, sayeth the Lord," but he had no say because he was in prison and Abigail had a written will.

Vengeance is mine.

Ricky was beginning to understand what vengeance meant.

Jimmy had been angry when Ricky told him about the fire and what happened at the mine, but his uncle was more scared than mad. He'd warned Ricky not to get involved with Reverend Browne, but Ricky hadn't thought about any of that. All he remembered was the pain and loneliness of losing his mother, then Joe Hendrickson. Reverend Browne had said he'd help get Ricky what he wanted most of all: a way out of Spruce Lake.

Anyway, Jimmy was a hypocrite. Telling Ricky to stay out of the business, but getting in deep himself. So deep that Ricky didn't believe him when Jimmy said it was to protect Ricky. Protect him from what? The monster? Ricky didn't believe she'd set foot in Spruce Lake again. If she did, Ricky would kill her himself.

He cringed as he thought of the last words he'd said to his uncle.

"You're a fucking hypocrite, Uncle Jimmy."

Ricky knew exactly what was going on in Spruce Lake. The drug trade was alive and well. And Ricky couldn't care less about it, other than it was his ticket out of here. What people did to themselves was their business; Ricky had no need to give up control of his mind and body to drugs. Maybe it was even his father who'd convinced him of that with all the lectures and warnings, ironic considering how his father made his money.

You're better than that, Rick.

His father had considered drug users weak and helpless, but he had no problem manufacturing the product that kept them dependent.

Ricky desperately wanted someone to tell him what to do, but he had no one to trust. He wanted to trust Sean Rogan, but why would that guy help him? He had to have an ulterior motive.

"Mom, I don't know what to do."

His voice was scratchy and thick. He swallowed and coughed, his head low.

Jimmy was gone. Reverend Browne wasn't acting himself. Something was happening, and it was the first time since his mother had died that Ricky didn't know everything that was going on in Spruce Lake.

He was scared and angry and there was only one person who might be able to help him, but Jimmy had told Ricky to go to him only in an emergency. Well, this was a fucking emergency! Jimmy was dead, and something big was going down on Sunday.

Headlights cut down the road as three cars turned toward the church. Ricky lay flat on the ground, partly shielded by his mother's grave marker. He didn't think they saw him. They were going into the church, eight or nine of them. Ricky knew all of them. The reverend. Andy Knolls, the weird guy at the Gas-n-Go who used to give only the girls free candy, until he touched Lisa Thompson's twelve-year-old breasts and her father beat him nearly to death. The creepy guy Andy hung around with, Gary Clarke. He wasn't from Spruce Lake; he hadn't shown up until Ricky's father went to prison. Some of the other regulars.

A fourth car drove up. It was a luxury rental, sleek and black. A blond guy got out. Ricky could read City Boy in his crisp jeans and black button-down shirt. And who wore trench coats in Spruce Lake? He looked mean, and Ricky might have been scared, but then he saw who got out of the passenger's seat and he was terrified.

The monster is back.

Even through his fear, Ricky had one thought.

Vengeance is mine.

The monster had killed his mother. She'd stolen the money that his dad had hidden before he went to prison. The money to pay for his mother's chemotherapy and surgery.

His mother had had a good chance of surviving if she'd had the necessary treatment.

And Bobbie had even known that when she took the money.

TWENTY-THREE

Sean drove Tim to his house and, after getting directions to the Callahans' place, he asked Tim to check in on Lucy. Sean had already warned her about the note he'd found in the truck. He didn't want to leave her longer than he had to, but he had questions he was certain Henry Callahan could answer.

As soon as he drove away from the Hendricksons', his cell phone rang. It was his brother, Duke, calling from California.

"Confirmed," Duke said. "Roberta Swain Molina, a.k.a. Bobbie Swain."

"That was fast." Sean had sent the picture less than thirty minutes ago. "She's married?"

"Widowed. Her husband, a known drug smuggler, was murdered in his bed and Bobbie left for dead in what the police believe was a retaliation killing. A killer for a rival cartel came in through a window, slit Herve Molina's throat, and attacked Bobbie. She fought back, but nearly died from blood loss. Their safe was emptied."

"It's not like those guys to leave a witness."

"She fingered him, but also told her husband's security chief who did it, and Molina's people got to him first. Tortured and killed him. His knife was found in the bushes outside the window with both Molina's and Swain's blood on it."

"That must have been hell to live through. Could have changed anyone."

"Don't lose sleep over what happened to Bobbie Swain," Duke said. "According to both Molina's cartel and others, she was just as ruthless as her husband. Kane heard the same thing, plus a nasty rumor."

"You called Kane?"

Their brother Kane Rogan knew near everything about the international drug trade.

"You said you needed the information fast. Molina's murder started a drug war. And Bobbie Swain walked away."

"Drug lords don't usually let people leave the business," Sean commented.

"Kane's theory was that she and Julio Gomez worked together to kill her husband, then Gomez turned on her, not wanting a witness. It's all about access—logistically, Gomez needed an inside accomplice to access her husband's safe."

"But Bobbie managed to survive and fingered Gomez."

"Molina's people never thought she was involved, and she walked away. It was a bloody fight between Molina's people and Gomez's. In the end, a third player rose to the top of the food chain. Someone named Theo Corbin, an American who is affiliated with some nasty people in Colombia."

Sean nearly missed the narrow, rutted driveway that marked the Callahan property. He made a sharp left turn and his truck barely cleared the old posts. A single light on the right illuminated a weatherworn metal sign:

H & E RANCH
MR. & MRS. HENRY CALLAHAN
SPRUCE LAKE, NEW YORK

Sean wondered how Jon Callahan felt living out here with his uncle. Unmarried, commuting three hours to Montreal several times a month. Unless he had something else going on—something illegal and lucrative. Agent Victoria Sheffield had been investigating white-collar crimes that crossed the border. Sean could see all the pieces of the puzzle, but he didn't know how they fit together—yet.

"Did you hear me?" Duke asked.

"Sorry, almost missed my turn."

"Kane speculated that Bobbie Swain had planned for Corbin to take over."

Sean's truck bounced over the potholes and he had to slow even more. "You mean she started the war between Molina and Gomez in order for a dark horse to come in and take over?"

"Bingo."

"Do you have any evidence? That's pretty damn cold-blooded."

"It is. There's no proof and little talk. But Corbin knows certain information that only Molina had—Molina and his wife."

"When did this happen?"

"Six years ago."

"Around the same time Paul Swain was sent to prison. Could that be a coincidence?"

"You tell me."

The driveway turned sharply to the left, then a well-lit house came into view. He turned off his headlights, drove past the house, and parked on the far side of the garage. The sudden silence was broken only by the tick of his cooling engine.

"I'm talking to Paul Swain tomorrow."

"Watch out for him."

"Kane have intel on him, too?"

"No, he doesn't track the domestic drug trade. Never heard of Spruce Lake or Paul Swain, and Bobbie Swain dropped off his radar when she left Miami. He's going to ask around, but doubts he'll find out anything in the next day or two."

"Meaning he's not going to try." Sean knew his brother well, better than Duke thought he did. Kane's priorities were always at the top of the list. He had quiet disdain for small-time drug action. The low-level players were easy to take out, but another asshole always popped up.

"I'll see what I can find out. Be careful, Sean. This woman sounds like a dangerous piece of work."

"I know exactly what she is," Sean said. "She's a monster."

"Excuse me?"

"I'll talk to you later." He hung up. Abigail Swain's letter to her son made complete sense now.

Paul Swain had something on his sister, some piece of information that was so big that it would get him killed in prison. It might put her in jail for life, or possibly even get her killed. If it was so big that it had kept Bobbie out of Spruce Lake and away from Ricky

Swain, it was likely connected to Herve Molina's murder.

Bobbie Swain sounded ruthless, at least the way Kane portrayed her. But his oldest brother didn't sugarcoat anything. A spade was a spade. A killer, a killer. No excuses, no explanations.

More than once Sean had threatened Duke that he'd head south and join Kane's team of mercenaries. It was the surest way to get easygoing Duke riled up. Duke had spent three months in Central America with Kane's team and returned a changed man. But Sean had never done it, and he'd always felt when he was younger that Duke thought he was too weak or too spoiled or too comfortable.

Sean saw the allure of fighting for something bigger than himself, fighting to save people from a fate worse than death. Rescuing young boys from the battlefield and giving them back to their mothers. Burning coca fields before harvest. Storming brothels where girls and women were held as sex slaves and bringing them to safety. Killing their captors because in some countries, there was no other justice.

But Sean feared that in such violent scenarios he might well lose his humanity. He could be trained to do what Kane did, but wouldn't emerge unscathed. He sometimes wondered if his brother was superhuman, because no one could do what he did with his soul intact.

Sitting in the truck, Sean considered another theory about the sniper. Someone in town knew precisely what was going on and wanted Sean and Lucy out of the way before one or both of them was killed. The sniper hadn't tried to kill him, true to his note. He thought he was doing them a favor.

Sean didn't like the game, and he wasn't leaving until he found out what had happened to Victoria Sheffield and Jimmy Benson. And he certainly wasn't leaving until he had Ricky Swain in his custody. The kid was a wild card, potentially dangerous and also in danger. He could get himself killed if he confronted the wrong people. Someone who would kill a federal agent could just as easily kill a teenager seeking vengeance for his uncle's death.

Sean quietly got out of the truck and pulled on a jacket. He walked up to the front door, acutely aware of the surrounding silence, marred only by occasional sounds of wildlife.

He knocked on the door, but it took a full minute before Henry Callahan answered. He stepped back, surprised by the visit. "Mr. Rogan."

"Is your nephew Jon here?"

"No, he's at the bar. Do you want to speak to him?"

"I actually came to talk to you. Do you have a minute?"

A flash of fear crossed the older man's face. He glanced over his shoulder, as if someone were there. Sean whispered, "Are you alone?"

Henry motioned for Sean to enter, then closed the door. "My wife, Emily."

She sat in a chair, white-haired and beautiful, but with eyes that were too bright, a handmade afghan on her lap, gently rocking her chair back and forth. A small, well-read Bible sat open on the blanket, the print so small Sean didn't think she'd easily be able to read it. Comfort, possibly.

"She had a stroke last year. She's in pain."

She looked stoned to Sean, but if she was in pain he wasn't going to criticize a septuagenarian for smoking a little pot, though he didn't smell the telltale signs.

"Henry?" Emily questioned. She looked toward them, but didn't seem to see them.

"Right here, dear." He walked over and moved the thick glasses that were on a string around her neck to her face.

She focused on Henry and smiled. "Dear. We had a lovely drive today, didn't we?"

"Yes, we did."

"Who is your friend?"

"He's a friend of Joe Hendrickson's. You remember Joe?"

"Yes, of course I remember Joe. Why doesn't he visit more often?"

"He died last year, honey. We went to his funeral."

Her smile faltered. "I remember." It was clear by her expression that she didn't.

"I'm going to take Joe's friend to the kitchen for a beer. Is that all right with you?"

"I'd like a beer, too."

"You don't like beer."

"I think I might."

"How about a martini? Extra vermouth and three olives?"

"That sounds lovely."

Sean followed Henry through a large formal dining room that didn't look as though it had been used for some time. One of the most famous reproductions of *The Last Supper* had a prominent position on one wall. Henry glanced at the picture, sadness in his eyes. He didn't stop until they were in the back of the house, where a country-style kitchen looked far more lived in.

He cleared his throat. "Excuse me."

His eyes were bright, not from pain or drugs, but emotion. "Usually, I'm okay with her forgetfulness, but it's been a hard week." He looked pointedly at Sean. "I think you know why."

"I need answers, Henry. What's going on in Spruce Lake?"

Henry sighed and pulled two bottles of beer from the refrigerator. He handed one to Sean and opened the other for himself. "I didn't tell Emily your name so she won't repeat that you were here. I don't want to put you in more danger than you're already in."

"Explain."

Henry shook his head and sat on a barstool, resting his elbows on the table.

Sean slammed his unopened beer bottle down on the kitchen counter. "I can bring in the cavalry—just say the word."

"And tell them what? You bring in the police, they'll find nothing, because your people need warrants. The bastards in charge will know before the ink is dry and destroy the evidence, then punish whoever they think turned them in. The devil you know . . ."

"I need your help," Sean said.

"Paul Swain was a ruthless bastard, but he took care of this town. As long as you were on his side, he took care of you. Someone turned on him."

"Who?"

"I don't know. When he went to prison and the cops left, some of the players changed."

Sean was getting frustrated. He didn't have time for a history lesson, and he wished Henry would just spit it out.

"I know a lot more than you think I do." The pieces were beginning to take form and Sean could see part of the bigger picture. "Before Paul Swain went to prison, someone undermined him. I don't know how—by threat, bribery, sex—but when she got enough people over to *her* side, she turned her own brother in to the cops. Though Swain was in prison, he had something on her—something that would get her killed or imprisoned—so she stayed away." As he spoke, Sean saw Henry's expression grow darker. He knew Sean was talking about Bobbie Swain.

"Bobbie Swain couldn't gloat or run the business the way she wanted, relying on people like your nephew Jon to keep it in line," Sean continued. "But something changed, and Bobbie's come back."

"Dear God, you saw her?" A look of terror crossed Henry's face.

"She was bartending tonight."

Henry's whole body sagged. Sean didn't actually *know* everything that he'd just told Henry, but he'd been working on the theory after hearing what Duke told him about Miami. *If* Bobbie Swain was cold-blooded enough to kill her husband and frame another drug dealer, she was certainly cold-blooded enough to turn in her brother Paul.

"Jon heard she was coming back," said Henry. "She called him, told him to convince Tim and Adam to postpone the resort. But you don't understand—Jon's not what you think he is. All he wants is to help people keep food on their table and a roof over their head. Protect them from Bobbie and her people."

"So that's why he bought up all the land? Put everyone into indentured servitude as a form of protection?"

"You should leave."

"I'm not leaving without answers."

"You won't find them here."

Sean turned away from Henry, frustrated but knowing that being a hard-ass with the old man wasn't going to get him the answers he needed. Henry was more than a little scared—for himself and his ailing wife.

He glanced around the spacious kitchen, circa late fifties. The brown appliances, though old, fit with the colorful tiles and collection of spoons on the wall above the gas stove. It was homey and comfortable. The dishes had been hand-washed and were drying in a rack on the counter. On the refrigerator were a variety of magnets from local businesses holding up faded pictures of Henry and Emily, some showing a younger, happier couple. Jon Callahan was in many of them. There were also snapshots from important events—his college graduation stood out.

Sean walked over to look at the pictures, but didn't really focus. He finally opened his beer and drank a long swallow. He'd taken the wrong tack with Henry. Maybe if he came back with Lucy, they could convince him to trust them.

Sean stared at one half-hidden photograph of Jon Callahan with a familiar blond woman. It was taken outside during spring or summer, the trees lush and green. He pulled it off the refrigerator. The blonde was turned partly away from the camera, so he only saw her profile, and her face was partly obscured by her long hair. But it was clear from her smile and their pose that she and Jon were more than friends.

He showed the picture to Henry. "Who is this?" He didn't need to ask, his gut told him he knew who the woman was, but he wanted to hear it from Henry.

Henry looked up with a long, sad face. "Jon's fiancée."

Sean hadn't been expecting that answer. "*Fiancée?*"

"She died."

"How?"

"You need to leave."

"My girlfriend found Jon's fiancée dead in the mine. Now her body is missing. Pack a bag for your wife, I'll get you out of town tonight."

"You saw my wife! She can't travel; she can barely remember what she likes to drink and eat. She's dying. She needs to die in her own home."

"Henry, you're not thinking straight." Sean ran a hand through his hair, wishing again Lucy was here. "Did Jon kill her? Is that why you're scared?"

Henry shook his head. "He loved her more than anything."

Frustrated and desperate, Sean said, "Did you know she was an FBI agent? Did she find out what Jon was doing—"

Henry cut him off. "You have to leave. If they're watching me you may have just signed my death warrant, Mr. Rogan. Leave now. I'm not asking again."

"Dammit, Henry!"

"Don't swear at me, young man!" Henry rose from

the stool. He still looked old, but he had fire in him. "You came to town three days ago and think you can solve generations's worth of problems? Spruce Lake has been on the wrong side of the law for more than a century, starting with Paul's great-grandfather, one of the original moonshiners in the county. Smuggling into Canada is as old as sin for our town. Alcohol, cigarettes, meth, marijuana—what's next? I don't know, but we'll be in the middle of it, and nothing you or I can do will stop it. These folks have killed for far less. And now that Bobbie Swain is in town—so help us God, she'll slash and burn on a whim if it strikes her fancy. I'm telling you to get out now, before you're not able to."

"Please, I need—"

Henry put up his hand. "Go, before Jon comes home. Last year, he would have agreed to help you. Now, I don't think he has a soul. Bobbie destroyed it. I can't do anything. I'm sorry."

Sean wanted to argue, but Henry was right—he couldn't be here when Jon Callahan returned. If only to protect Henry and Emily. Yet, Henry didn't seem to fear his nephew.

He handed Henry his card. "Call me. I'll drop everything to help."

Henry stared at Sean, tears in his eyes. "Leave Spruce Lake tonight, Sean. Take your pretty lady with you. And never come back."

Sean shook his head. "I'm not going anywhere until I stop that woman."

"You don't know Bobbie. She's a monster."

Sean had heard it before. "I've slain dragons before. I'm not going to be scared away by Bobbie

Swain." He walked out the way he came. Mrs. Callahan smiled at him. "Nice to see you again."

Sean understood Henry's fear. He was protecting his wife from a monster. Sean looked around the comfortable, simply furnished home. The handmade blankets. The clean, worn furniture. The older-model television. Stitchery on the walls, a framed hand-stitched ornate cross embroidered with the words *I am the vine, you are the branches.*

Simple home, simple people. If Jon Callahan was making a fortune in the drug business, he wasn't sharing it with his family.

He looked at Henry one last time before leaving. "Remember what I said."

On his way back to the lodge, Sean called Patrick. "I need to change the plans for tomorrow." He told his partner about the possible threat to Lucy. "Lucy's the only one who saw the body in the mine, and right now no one knows we've already identified the victim." He doubted Henry would say anything.

"So what are we doing to keep her safe?" Patrick asked.

"I need Noah to come with you on the commuter flight tomorrow morning." As much as he disliked Noah, the Fed was a former Air Force Raven and a good cop. Sean didn't particularly like the plan he'd come up with, but it was the best way to make sure nothing happened to Lucy on her way to Albany.

TWENTY-FOUR

Coming home is always bittersweet.

Ian and I finished inspecting the barns, the pleasing, sweet smell of drying cannabis making me proud of what I'd accomplished. This was the end of an era; I was ushering in the future. On Sunday, I would lead my men down a richer path.

"Are you ready to go?" Ian asked.

"A minute," I said. I told Ian to run through the plan again with the others. Though he was irritated, he agreed, leaving me alone.

I enjoyed Ian, but he was becoming clingy. On our return trip from Potsdam, we had to pull over for a fast screw. It was fun, but not as exciting as in the past. I appreciated Ian's attention, but he was too subservient when I wanted him to take charge.

I sighed and walked around the side of the barn farthest from the house, looking out into the dark valley spread all around. A coyote called, followed by another. I heard the flapping of wings—bats, I figured, this time of night. A perfect, crisp quarter moon sliced the sky, surrounded by a field of stars.

My empire.

As a child, Spruce Lake was truly my kingdom. I was the princess, my father the king, my brothers the two princes, the townsfolk our servants. Daddy taught us the power of fear. He'd never expected that it would be his daughter who learned the lesson best.

Paul was Daddy's pride and joy. Paul could do no wrong. I hated him because Daddy loved him best. As if being born with a penis gave him the right to the keys of the kingdom.

Paul became the king when Daddy died, even though Daddy promised to hand the reins to me. *Paul banished me when he saw I was a threat. That I was smarter than him, more ruthless, more focused.*

My brother lost his focus when he fell for a woman.

He was in l-o-v-e. I was eager to see how long that would last when I told the little lady just how our family made our money.

Sweet dumb little Abigail deserved to know who she had married. That Paul killed for Daddy. That he ran drugs up to Canada with the oh-so-proper Jon Callahan. That he'd screwed half the women in Spruce Lake. He especially liked to screw them from behind like dogs, and I had a few tapes to prove it.

When Paul was sixteen, he'd been pulled over for speeding by a cop Daddy didn't have in his pocket. A payload of pseudoephedrine was in his truck, and he could have been hauled in if the cop had an ounce more brainpower. I watched Daddy beat the shit out of Paul. It had been quite thrilling. I hated Paul, the Golden Child.

The day I turned eighteen, Paul stared at me for a long time. He said, "I want to kill you, but you're fam-

ily." I stared back. He turned around and walked to Daddy's desk.

"Ten thousand and I never want to see you again."

"Fifty thousand," I countered.

"Fuck you."

"Sick pervert. Like I'd really screw my own brother?"

He wanted to hit me, and I wanted him to try.

Unfortunately, he didn't. And though he gave me the fifty thousand, I regretted not killing him that day.

It took years to build my own empire. Though banished, I cultivated my own people in Spruce Lake. I learned about the drug business from the best and brightest. It took time, and what I had to suffer . . .

The night I killed my husband was the culmination of all that I had learned. I risked everything because I trusted no one. I had set it up all on my own. It was the only way I could ensure I would never be a suspect, by the police or Herve's people. All because of one small misstep, and Herve's suspicions, I knew my days were numbered. He'd started pulling away from me, and if I didn't act first, I knew that one night there'd be a bullet in my head.

I crushed a couple Viagra tablets into his preferred drink. I wanted him horny. I came to his bed wearing his favorite of my nighties, a white satin sheath. I apologized for talking to the wrong person, for damaging his reputation. No tears, because he'd know I was faking. Just a simple apology. Told him I didn't want to leave, that I loved him, but if he wanted me to go I'd go quietly. I was contrite the entire speech, even though inside my heart raced with anticipation and danger.

He said he didn't know if he could trust me anymore. That's when I showed a little emotion, just a hint of deep remorse. He patted the bed beside him.

When I sat on the silk sheets and Herve squeezed my breast, when I felt his erection against my thigh and saw the sweat bead on his forehead from his drug-induced excitement, there was no turning back. I didn't want to die, but nothing worth having means anything if there isn't a risk. Daddy always told me I had to take risks, be bold, be smart. And that night, I was all that.

Herve had always liked my sexual energy. My red hair and translucent skin. My voice when I moaned and gasped his name. I loved the theatrics of sex and the way I turned men into desperate, lustful creatures. I let Herve fuck me hard and made sure he enjoyed it. Never had I peaked so high, so long, so intensely as the night I last made love to Herve, knowing he would soon be dead.

After his first orgasm he was still hard, thanks to the drugs. I rolled him over so I was on top and grabbed the headboard to steady myself. Then I rode him hard, playing into his fantasy of a wild woman who couldn't get enough of her man.

Earlier, I'd taped a knife to the backside of the headboard—after Herve's security goon swept the room with a metal detector. I'd stolen the blade from an associate of Herve's he had been suspicious about, and set it up so the schmuck had no alibi.

I gripped the handle as I arched my back so Herve could get a face full of my breasts. He licked greedily, slobbering. It would have been a turn-off if I wasn't so jazzed about my plans.

Herve wasn't stupid, so I didn't hesitate. As soon as I had the knife in hand, I pressed my thighs down and tightened my body around him, knowing it was the best way to get him off. He closed his eyes, his mouth open and drooling, his face flushed. He called my name.

I slit his throat.

I had killed before, but never in such a raw, primal way. I cut him deep, without hesitation, because I knew I'd have only one chance.

He grabbed my hand, but had little control. I jumped off his body and watched as he died. There was so much blood—more than I expected.

But I could work with that.

I used the sheet that had fallen to the floor during sex and wiped the handle of the knife. I then cut my arms as if I were holding them up to my face to protect me. They might scar, but I didn't care—they would remind me of victory.

I cut one breast, my stomach, the back of my legs. My heart was racing, and I felt light-headed and wondered if I was losing too much blood. I tossed the knife out of the window, made sure there was blood on the windowsill, and screamed so loud my head ached. Then I hit myself with one of Herve's blue-and-white Chinese vases he said he bought for a hundred thousand dollars. Ridiculous to pay so much for something so impractical.

Blood flowed down my face into my eyes. I fell to my knees and crawled toward the bed. I was dizzy, and I looked down and saw that the cut in my stom-

ach was still bleeding. I hadn't realized I had cut so deep. I found the sheet again and pressed it to my stomach as my vision faded. I grabbed the phone and dialed for help, but didn't know if the call went through. Everything was a blur.

I heard people rush in. Shouts. And then nothing.

I woke hours later in the hospital, and the police detective told me Herve had been murdered and I was lucky to be alive. The two uniformed officers at my door asked me if I saw who attacked us.

I cried when I said yes, and begged them to protect me.

Herve's right-hand man heard me, and by the time the police found Julio Gomez, he was dead.

The war had begun, and I walked away scot free.

That was six years ago. I followed that victory with another. I knocked Paul off his high horse and put his ass in prison.

And now I was the Royal Queen.

I heard someone say my name, and remembered where I was.

"It's fucking cold out here, Bobbie," Ian said. He actually sounded irritated with me.

I turned to face him. He was huddled in a thick coat, the collar turned up past his ears, his hands stuffed deep in the pockets. I hadn't realized, until we'd arrived in Spruce Lake, that Ian was somewhat of a wimp.

"I was just admiring my kingdom," I said. "And remembering how hard I worked for it."

TWENTY-FIVE

Ricky Swain waited in the Callahans' garage for two hours before Jon Callahan returned from the bar. He'd parked by the lake so no one would see his car, then trekked through the back of Joe Hendrickson's property until he reached the Callahans'. At midnight, all but the porch light went off in the house. He huddled in his coat, pacing to keep warm, and hoped he wasn't making a fatal mistake.

But he had no other ideas. Asking Jon Callahan for help was his last hope to get out of this mess.

At nearly two in the morning, Ricky saw headlights turn onto the drive, pass the house, and stop in front of the detached garage. Jon didn't open the door, but started toward the house.

Ricky ran out of the garage. "Mr. Callahan!"

Jon jumped and reached into his pocket. Ricky put up his hands. "It's me, Rick Swain."

At first Jon looked confused, then angry. "What are you doing here?" he demanded.

"I have no place to go." Ricky's teeth were chattering and he bounced on his feet.

"You can't be here." Jon glanced around, as if worried someone was watching.

"I walked around. There's no one here. The lights went off at midnight." Ricky bit his lip. "Can I come in?"

Jon hesitated, then nodded and walked briskly toward the house. Ricky followed him through the back door into a toasty warm kitchen. Ricky's skin tingled in the heat.

"Thank—"

"Shh. Wait here."

Jon left the room and Ricky heard him close doors, then walk around upstairs. Ricky walked closer to the fireplace where wood still smoldered in the stove inset. By the time Jon returned, Ricky almost felt normal.

"Why are you here?" Jon asked.

"Before my mother died, she told me you were the only person I could trust in an emergency."

"Things have changed."

"I wouldn't have come if I had any other choice. I'm scared." There, he'd said it. Before he'd seen his Aunt Bobbie, he was worried—but now he was downright terrified. With Jimmy dead, there was nothing stopping her from going after *him*. Ricky had never known why his aunt stayed away, but his mother said as long as Jimmy was around, Bobbie didn't dare return to Spruce Lake.

Jon walked over to the counter and poured whiskey into a glass. He drained it in one gulp, then put his hands on the counter and stared intently at the tiles.

"There's nowhere else I can go." Ricky's voice cracked. "My Aunt Bobbie is here. I—I think she killed

Jimmy. And—and you know what she did to my mom."

Jon's voice was so soft Ricky almost didn't hear him say, "I know."

When he didn't say anything else, Ricky continued, speaking quickly. "I really screwed up, Mr. Callahan. I set the fire. I'm so sorry, I didn't want to, but everything just got out of control and—" Ricky stopped himself. He took a deep breath and collected his thoughts. "I know you and my father didn't always get along, but my mom trusted you, and so I have to trust you. Tonight, there was a meeting at the church. Bobbie was there, with Reverend Browne and everyone else my uncle Butch hangs out with. Even Reggie was there."

Jon's head snapped up. "Reggie? Are you sure?"

"Yes."

Jon rubbed his face with both hands. "Does anyone know you're here?"

"No, I swear. I parked behind the sludge pile near the lake and walked."

Jon went through drawers until he found paper and a pen. He wrote a line of numbers that at first looked like a phone number, but when he handed the paper to Ricky, he realized it was too long. "The bank is in Montreal. The first five digits are my safe deposit box number. The last seven are the pass code to access it. It's everything I have on Bobbie. It's what was keeping you alive. But with Jimmy gone—I don't know why she'd kill him when she's so close to finishing this deal."

"What deal?"

Jon didn't answer the question. "Do you know where the Fosters' summer cabin is?"

"Of course."

"The key is hidden in a box nailed to the underside of the second porch step. Do not turn on any lights, make a fire, *nothing*. Nothing that might attract attention."

"What about you?"

"I've made my bed—" his voice trailed off. "Don't worry about me," Jon said firmly. "I only need until Sunday, then this will all be over. But if something happens to me before then, you have to go to my bank. Understand?"

"Yes, but—"

"Do not leave the Fosters' house. If you follow my instructions, you'll be safe. But if Bobbie finds you, I won't be able to help you."

Ricky bit his lip and nodded. "What's really going on?"

"Go on, everything's changed and I need to get to work." Jon walked Ricky to the back door, distracted. "Wait."

Ricky was hoping for an invitation to stay, but Jon ran upstairs. When he returned, he handed Ricky a pistol. "Be careful, it's loaded."

Ricky took it, made sure the safety was on, and put it in his pocket. Without another word, he stepped into the frigid night and headed for the other side of Spruce Lake.

TWENTY-SIX

Lucy sat in the co-pilot seat of Sean's private Cessna while he performed a fuel and systems check. They'd left Spruce Lake at dawn, but now the sun was warming the air and the sky was clear and blue. A perfect day for flying. She sipped her coffee and watched Sean. He looked tired, and she knew he was still in pain from the stitches.

"Are you sure these extreme measures are necessary?" Lucy asked.

Because of the latest threatening note, Sean had altered their plans. Last night, he had asked Noah to fly with Patrick to Ogdenburg, and then fly Lucy to Albany in Sean's plane.

"Yes, I am," he said.

"It's not easy to sabotage a plane, especially with the security—"

"But it's not impossible," Sean said. "I can take you to nearly any airport in the country and in ten minutes show you how I could breach security."

"That's your job, Sean—you get paid to breach security."

He gave her a half-smile. "I am good, aren't I? But

I'm not so arrogant as to think I'm the only person in the country who knows how to exploit security weaknesses. There are at least three or four of us."

At least his sense humor was back. Last night had taken a lot out of Sean. He was worried about the teenager Ricky Swain, and alternately angry with and worried about Henry and Emily Callahan.

He took her hand. "Seriously, Lucy, they know you're flying out today. I don't know how, but they do. I have to mix things up. They could be waiting at this airport, in Albany, or be on the same plane. We don't know all the players, nor do we know what the stakes are. But if they were willing to kill a federal agent to protect their secrets, they will kill you."

"And you," she reminded him. "I'm worried about *you*. Like you said, they'll kill to keep their secrets."

He kissed her lightly. Unlike the peck last night, this kiss, though light, was filled with restrained emotion. His hands squeezed hers and he looked her in the eyes, holding her gaze with his. "I'm sorry about yesterday."

A weight lifted off her heart. Even though she still didn't understand everything that had happened yesterday between them when he clammed up and told her it was best she get out of town, she now understood it wasn't because he thought she was incapable.

She kissed him again. "Me, too. We're going to work this out." Lucy vowed to try to understand Sean's experience with authority, and not take his animosity personally.

"This is just hard for me."

"Me being a Fed?"

He shook his head. "Calling Noah for help," he said, his gaze focused on the horizon.

Now Lucy was even more confused. "Because he's FBI?"

"No." He looked perplexed. "For a Fed, he's not the worst out there."

"From you, that's a compliment."

"Don't you see it?"

"See what?"

He shook his head. "Nothing."

"Don't do that to me, Sean. You always tell me to spit it out. Or you just tell me what I'm thinking. Well, I'm not as good at reading your mind as apparently you are at reading mine, so I *don't* understand."

He tilted his head in disbelief. Well, if he wasn't clear, how could she understand what he meant? She wasn't psychic!

"Patrick would much rather have you dating someone like Noah than someone like me."

She laughed; she just couldn't help herself. That was the last thing she'd expected Sean to say. *Date Noah?*

He wasn't laughing with her, and though she was still smiling, she suddenly realized there was more to this than Sean was letting on.

"First, I doubt you're right about Patrick," she said. "My brother would probably prefer I date no one. But that doesn't matter, because what Patrick might or might not want is irrelevant."

"No, it's not."

"You think I make my decisions based on what other people tell me I should do? I'm perfectly capable of making my own choices in life."

"Patrick is different. Maybe you don't see it—"

"There's nothing to see!"

What was Sean keeping bottled up inside? She didn't understand, and she hated feeling that she was missing something. It made her apprehensive. "Let's not be mad at each other before I go to Albany."

He reached behind her neck and pulled her across the small space separating the pilot and co-pilot's seats. His heat-filled embrace sent her pulse racing. His hand went to her waist, under her sweater, pushing at the small of her back, holding her as close as he possibly could without bringing her into his lap. His mouth became aggressive, as if wanting to imprint the kiss on her, to kiss her so thoroughly that she wouldn't be able to forget. Lucy held him tight, shivers of desire running through her, a need to keep Sean close.

He turned her head and kissed her jawline, all the way to her ear. A faint moan escaped her chest and he put his hands on her face, his forehead pressed against hers. "I'm not mad at you, Lucy. I was never mad. I love you."

"I—" Her chest tightened. *Tell him! Tell him you love him.* "I'm not mad, either." Her voice cracked.

His phone rang. Before he answered, she saw disappointment in his eyes.

He let her go. "It's Patrick."

Sean walked Noah through the mechanics of his Cessna, shared some of its quirks, and closed with, "Any questions?"

"I was an Air Force pilot for ten years; I think I can fly a little Cessna."

"She's not a fighter plane," Sean said.

"I'll take good care of her."

Sean didn't miss that Noah glanced at Lucy, who'd watched the flight "lesson" with a bemused expression on her face.

"When are you returning?"

"Tonight," Noah said. "Considering what's been happening, you need all the help you can get." He handed Sean a file folder. "Here's everything you need to get in to see Paul Swain."

Though Swain was in a state penitentiary, Noah had contacted the FBI liaison and smoothed the way for Sean.

"I appreciate it," he said. It wasn't the first time Noah had pulled strings for him, and he didn't particularly like feeling indebted to him.

Sean took Lucy's hand. "Be careful, Luce." He pulled her into a hug. She stiffened, just a bit, but he didn't let her go. She'd never been comfortable with public displays of affection, and usually he respected her feelings, but this time he wasn't pulling back. He kissed her long enough to make sure Noah Armstrong understood that Lucy was off-limits.

When he stepped back, she touched his cheek softly and said, "*You* be careful, Sean Rogan. I'll be surrounded by FBI agents in a military-controlled building. You're marching back to the lion's den."

"I'll watch his back," Patrick called from where he stood leaning against the hood of the rental truck.

"Take care of each other," Lucy said. "I expect you both to be in one piece when we get back tonight."

Sean watched as Noah and Lucy climbed into his plane and Noah started the preflight check. He gave Sean a thumbs-up when he got clearance from air traffic control, and drove the plane toward the small-craft runway.

Sean leaned against the truck next to Patrick, watching until the Cessna disappeared in the sky. Patrick said, "You're jealous."

"I don't know what the fuck you're talking about."

Patrick laughed. Sean didn't. He strode to the driver's door and pulled it open, slamming it behind him. Patrick followed. "I'll admit, I like it."

"I thought you were my friend." Sean turned the ignition and drove too quickly from the field.

"I am. But in the three years I've known you, and all the women you dated before Lucy, not once did I see you jealous."

"I'm not jealous of Noah Armstrong."

But dammit, Patrick was right. He *was* jealous.

"It's a *good* thing."

"You're sick. Besides, I thought you wanted Lucy to dump me for someone like that Fed."

"I did."

"Asshole."

Patrick laughed. "You don't listen. When you called me last night and asked me to bring Noah here this morning to fly *your plane* to Albany with *Lucy*, I realized that maybe you have changed. It's been obvious for months that you don't like Noah, and I think it has less to do with the fact that he's a Fed and more to do with the fact that he's Lucy's friend. To call him for help shows a rare humility, but more important, tells me that you would do anything to protect my sister, even ask for help from the man you're afraid is your rival."

"Well," Sean said. "I don't think I've heard you

talk so much bullshit at one time. Rival? Hardly. That would mean Lucy is undecided, and she's not."

"I know. She loves you."

Just because Patrick said it so matter-of-factly didn't make Sean feel better. Because she'd never told him, and in fact he *did* consider Noah a rival. Because whether Patrick, or Lucy, or even Noah knew it, Noah was attracted to her. That Lucy liked and respected Noah contributed to it. And that was bad for all of them, no matter how Sean looked at it.

But if there was any silver lining to this epiphany of Patrick's, it was that he had finally dropped his opposition to Sean dating his sister.

TWENTY-SEVEN

Sean and Patrick entered the sheriff's office just after nine a.m. Saturday morning. Sean was supposed to be at the prison for his visit with Paul Swain at one that afternoon. He hadn't wanted to wait, but the cogs of the prison bureaucracy ran on their own time. Especially since Noah had moved heaven and earth to get Sean, who wasn't a cop, a private Saturday visit with Swain.

Detective Sergeant Kyle Dillard came out of his office to greet them. After introductions, he escorted them to his office and said, "I left a message for Deputy Weddle to come by, but I haven't heard from him."

"Probably skipped town," Sean mumbled.

He and Patrick sat in the chairs across from Dillard's tidy desk. On the wall behind the detective were several commendations from both the St. Lawrence County Sheriff and the Philadelphia Police Department. "You're from Philly?" Sean asked.

"Born and bred. Came here to get away from big city crime. Found out that small town violence can be just as bad." Dillard poured coffee into a mug from a thermos on his desk. "Did you get the copy of Weddle's report I emailed last night?"

"He's either a liar or an idiot," Sean said. "And I noticed he didn't report the sniper who shot at us yesterday."

"Sniper?"

Sean nodded and leaned forward.

"There *was* a body in the mine. Lucy didn't make it up; she wasn't scared and seeing things. She's identified the body as Special Agent Victoria Sheffield out of the Albany FBI office."

Dillard leaned back in his chair, but his expression was both grim and suspicious. "Why didn't you call me?"

"I wanted to talk to you face-to-face. After dealing with Weddle for two days, I don't trust him. And from what I've heard from people in Spruce Lake, he's been on the take for years."

"You'll have to put some names to those accusations," Dillard said.

Sean shook his head. "Not yet." He assessed Dillard as a straightshooter. "Are you familiar with the Swain family?"

Dillard nodded. "I was part of the joint task force that took down Paul Swain. Nine people went to prison. If I thought Swain was still running things in Spruce Lake, I would have called in the Feds. One thing I can say about that place—they take care of their own. Someone like me—I wouldn't get anywhere."

"You don't think Swain is managing his trade from the prison?" Patrick asked. "It wouldn't be the first time."

"I'd never say never, but he's closely watched. Two cops died during the operation—a meth lab exploded. Long story, screwups all around, but in the end we learned one of Swain's people set it up. A booby trap."

"How did you get the warrant in the first place?" Patrick asked.

"Someone turned state's evidence."

"Who?" Sean wondered if his theory about Bobbie Swain turning in her brother had merit.

"That information is above my pay grade. It's not in any of the official reports."

"An insider," Sean said.

Dillard shrugged. "That would be my educated guess. Someone very close to Swain."

"What if," Sean said, "this C.I. who helped the task force take down Swain and his cronies turned around and set up his—or her—own criminal enterprise?"

"Anything's possible," Dillard said. "Or, someone saw the opportunity to fill a hole in the distribution chain. I'll tap my contact with the DEA and see what he knows."

"Discreetly," Sean said.

Dillard frowned, and Patrick interjected, "My partner is concerned that there may be problems with some of the law enforcement. Especially after what's happened with Deputy Weddle."

"Weddle is a bad cop," Sean said bluntly.

"Not all cops are like Weddle." Dillard rubbed the back of his neck. "I pulled the GPS on Weddle's assigned vehicle. Though he officially clocked out at four p.m. on Wednesday, the day you found the body, his vehicle was at the Kelley Mine from eight-fifteen until nine-forty-nine p.m." He handed Sean a short stack of papers. "I shouldn't be sharing this with you, but you might see something I'm missing. It goes back seventy-two hours. Weddle has been spending a lot of time at the mine this week."

Sean scanned the GPS printout. It showed Weddle's exact route by time and location. He'd spent a lot of time in Spruce Lake. He lived nearly thirty minutes away in Potsdam, where his car was now.

Dillard added, "This week has shown a definite change in pattern."

Not only was Weddle at the mine Wednesday night—to remove Agent Sheffield's body?—but he'd gone back Friday late in the afternoon. That was after Lucy had told him there was evidence in the mine.

Sean looked carefully at the stops Weddle made after Thursday morning, when he first met Sean and Lucy at the mine. He first went to the Lock & Barrel, then back to Potsdam. On Friday he was at the Hendricksons' before noon—after Tim called about the sniper—then went to Reverend Browne's church for more than an hour. At 3:30, the deputy was in Colton for nearly thirty minutes, then went back to the mine for over an hour before returning to his residence.

"Who lives at 1020 West Mountain Road?"

Dillard typed the address into his computer. "The house is owned by Butch and Katherine Swain."

"He was there for nearly thirty minutes, then went back to the mine. That was after Lucy told him there was evidence down there. Which is probably gone now."

Dillard looked as though he wanted to argue. After all, Sean was making a grave accusation about one of his cops, but he closed his mouth.

Patrick said, "When did Weddle arrive home on Friday?"

"Six-ten."

"Where is he right now?" Patrick asked Dillard.

Dillard typed into his computer. "At his residence in Potsdam. At least his police unit is there. He has the day off. He could be using his personal vehicle."

"Are you planning on paying him a visit?"

"I suppose I am."

"How about a partner?" Sean said. Dillard hesitated. "Patrick here was a cop in San Diego for ten years. Does that help?"

Dillard gave him a half-smile. "A bit. You're both welcome to join me. Let me take the lead."

"We'll follow you," Sean said as they left the station.

There was no response to Dillard's repeated knockings at the small, post–World War II house of Tyler Weddle.

Sean had a bad feeling. Weddle's personal car was in the garage and his police unit in the driveway.

"I'm calling it in," Dillard said. He informed dispatch that he was entering the locked house of Deputy Tyler Weddle on a well-being check. He went to his truck to retrieve a small, one-man metal battering ram.

"If you don't mind," Sean said and pulled out his lock pick set. He liked the ease and finesse of picking a lock, and didn't understand why most cops went for the big guns, so to speak. In less than five seconds, he had the door unlocked.

"You two, go around back," Dillard said, notably impressed. "At a count of ten I'll announce myself and then enter. Do not enter until I give you the clear, though if he bolts—"

"Got it." He and Patrick jogged around to the back, keeping low beneath the line of the windows. "If he bolts, you'll have to chase him down." Sean was usually faster than Patrick in a sprint, but with his bum leg he didn't think he'd be any help.

At exactly ten seconds, they heard Dillard shout, "Weddle! It's Detective Sergeant Kyle Dillard! I'm coming in!"

Sean positioned himself just outside the door to watch the knob. Patrick was five feet behind him, against the house, gun drawn, ready to give chase if necessary.

"Boys!" Dillard called. "It's me."

Sean lowered his gun. As soon as Dillard opened the door, Sean smelled it. Vomit, alcohol, blood. Dillard's face was grim.

The back door opened into a small mudroom, then the kitchen. Dried vomit coated the sickly yellow counter and dripping sink. A bottle of JD had spilled on the table, soaking into a stack of junk mail and bills.

"I didn't do a complete search yet," Dillard said, "but I don't think anyone's alive in here."

The living room was clear. There were two bedrooms and one bathroom. The bedrooms were clear.

The carpet in the narrow hall outside the bathroom was soaked in water. A light trickle of water sounded from behind the closed door.

Dillard motioned for Sean and Patrick to stand back, then opened the door.

Sean wasn't sure what he thought he'd see, but he wasn't expecting a bloodbath.

"Dear God," Dillard said and glanced away.

"Glad I missed breakfast," Patrick mumbled.

Blood had spattered across the entire white-tiled room. Darker red arcs covered the ceiling in what looked like a classic cast-off pattern. Because the room was damp from the running shower, the blood hadn't completely dried. Some had dripped to the floor, drying in trickles of pink down the slick walls.

Weddle's butchered naked body was slumped in the shower, blocking the drain, as the water dripped steadily over it. Almost all blood had been washed from his flesh. His face was turned away from the door, but Sean could tell that Weddle's throat had been slit. He couldn't tell if it was deep enough to kill him quickly, or if the cause of death was the multiple slash marks covering his skin. They weren't simple in-and-out stab wounds, either. Whoever had killed Weddle used slicing motions—each cut shallow and methodical.

"Out," Dillard ordered. "This is now a crime scene."

TWENTY-EIGHT

As soon as Noah landed the Cessna, Lucy turned on her phone. She had a text message from Sean that gave her chills.

She said to Noah, "Deputy Weddle is dead. Murdered in his home."

By the time Lucy managed to get Sean on the phone, she and Noah were in a taxi heading to FBI Headquarters in Albany. "We just landed," Lucy told Sean. "I got your message about Weddle. I'm putting you on speaker so Noah can listen. What happened?"

"At first glance, it looked like he was attacked in the shower. But Patrick convinced Dillard to let him observe the on-scene investigation, and he's been keeping me updated. There were no defensive cuts on his forearms. At one point, he was bound with duct tape to a chair in his bedroom. They have a potential witness. Weddle's next-door neighbor saw a man and a woman walking away from Weddle's house Friday evening. The only reason she noticed them was that they couldn't keep their hands off each other. She thought it was tacky."

"No description?"

"No—it was almost dark. They walked two doors down from Weddle's and got into a dark truck."

Noah asked, "Do they have an estimated time of death?"

"The deputy coroner is the same idiot Lucy and I dealt with at the mine. He's not making any speculations. Patrick said the water messes with the timeline, but Weddle arrived home at six last night; he could have been killed anytime after."

"What water?" Lucy asked.

"After being tortured, the killers moved Weddle to the shower, where they slit his throat."

"To destroy evidence," Lucy said. "If the killers suspect their hair or blood or saliva might have gotten on the victim, the best way to contaminate it would be to drench it in bleach or water."

"The body looked like it was exsanguinated. There was blood all over the bathroom—ceiling and walls. Some had been washed away by the water. The floor and hall were drenched."

Sean continued, "Dillard is tied up at Weddle's house, and Patrick and I are about to head to the prison to talk to Swain."

Noah said, "Can you send me Dillard's contact information? I'm going to want to talk to him."

"Sending it to your phone."

"Anything on Jimmy Benson?" Lucy asked. "Did they find his body?"

"No word yet," Sean said. "Weddle's murder is the big news, but I'll remind Dillard to call when he hears back from the divers."

Noah said, "Ask if he pulled Benson's cell phone records yet."

"Damn, I should have thought of it."

"That's why they pay me the big bucks," Noah said, making Sean laugh.

Lucy relaxed. She had hoped that Noah and Sean could become, if not best buddies, at least friendly. Sometimes she felt as though she was walking on eggshells between her boyfriend and her trainer.

"How's my plane?" Sean asked.

"Still working. Keep me in the loop."

"You do the same." Sean hung up.

Noah drove into FBI Headquarters, showed the security guard his credentials, then parked. When they entered the building, they were greeted by ASAC Brian Candela himself.

Candela was in his midforties, with a conservative haircut and impeccable dark gray suit, even though it was Saturday. Lucy felt underdressed in her jeans and thin white sweater, even though she wore a blazer with it. Noah wasn't in a suit and tie, though he still looked sharp in khakis and a button-down shirt.

"Noah Armstrong?" Candela extended his hand. "Good to finally meet you."

"Finally?" Noah shook Candela's hand.

"You're Noah Armstrong, lieutenant, one of the original Ravens."

"You did your homework."

Candela shook his head. "My son is a Raven. Just finished training at Fort Dix. You're a legend among the recruits."

Noah laughed. Lucy glanced at him, startled. Had she heard Noah laugh before? She grinned.

"I doubt that, but I did write one of the manuals they're forced to study." He introduced Lucy. "Lucy

Kincaid, agent-in-training. She's working with me until she heads to Quantico in August."

Candela sobered immediately. "Ms. Kincaid, thank you for coming. As I'm sure you know, learning Agent Sheffield is dead has been tough on all of us, even though we didn't expect to find her alive." He gestured for them to follow. "Everyone is in the conference room."

Lucy hesitated. "Mr. Candela, I need to show you something first." She handed him the photograph of Jon Callahan and the blonde who may in fact be Agent Sheffield.

"Where did you get this?"

"The uncle of Jon Callahan," she gestured to the man in the picture, "gave it to Sean Rogan, the private investigator. We think the woman he's with is Agent Sheffield, but since it's only her in profile, we weren't certain."

"Who is this Callahan?"

Noah said, "He's an attorney in Montreal who lives in Spruce Lake and owns a lot property in and around town. He may have been involved with Paul Swain's criminal activity, though when I ran him, he came up clean."

"Have you spoken to him about Victoria?"

"No," Lucy said. "The situation in Spruce Lake is a bit difficult right now."

Candela nodded. "I'll let you tell the entire group. Wait here a second, I'm going to run this to the computer lab and get them started on facial recognition. I'm fairly certain it's her, but I need to confirm it. Then I can get a warrant to interview Callahan."

He walked down the hall. Noah said to Lucy, "Why are you nervous?"

She hadn't realized her nerves were showing. "I haven't briefed a room of FBI agents before. And the situation is tragic."

"You've held your own many times in far tenser situations. You're going to do fine."

"Thanks for the vote of confidence." She hoped he was right.

Candela returned. "We should have a confirmation shortly," he said. "Follow me, please." He led them down a long, gray corridor livened up by large posters of the scenic areas in the region.

Lucy had prepared herself for being questioned, but she wasn't quite prepared for the dozen people sitting around the high-gloss wood table. Some had Starbucks coffee cups, others small Styrofoam cups or water bottles. A young agent sat in the back with an elaborate computer system that would make Sean salivate, and a man and woman stood in the back talking quietly. When Candela stepped in, the woman approached.

Candela said, "This is Elizabeth Hart, our SAC. Ms. Hart, Noah Armstrong and Lucy Kincaid from D.C."

"Thank you both for coming. This is a highly sensitive situation, as you're aware, and I'm hoping that you have information that will help us find out what happened to Agent Sheffield." Hart motioned for Lucy and Noah to sit near the front of the conference room, where a projection screen had been pulled down in front of half a white board.

Lucy couldn't help but look at the wall of fifty-seven

fallen agents on the far side of the room. Every FBI office in the country had the same wall—it didn't matter where the agent served, anyone who died in the line of duty had his or her picture put on the Wall of Heroes in all fifty-six regional FBI offices, Quantico, and FBI national headquarters.

Would Victoria Sheffield be the next agent to grace the wall? It was a sobering thought.

Hart stood in the back while Candela took charge of the meeting. He introduced everyone to Lucy and Noah, including Supervisory Special Agent Marty Strong, who'd been Sheffield's boss, and Supervisory Special Agent Dale Martinelli, who'd been the liaison with the joint task force that had taken down Paul Swain six years ago.

Candela said, "Based on what Ms. Kincaid told me yesterday, we believe the body she found in the Kelley Mine was Agent Sheffield. I've brought you all up to speed with what I know. Ms. Kincaid, have there been new developments since yesterday afternoon?"

Lucy didn't expect to be put on the spot so quickly. She said, "We learned only a few minutes before we arrived that the deputy we suspected of being on the take was tortured and murdered in his home."

Her announcement was met with silence, then three people asked questions simultaneously. Candela cut them off.

"Chris, what's the situation with local law enforcement in St. Lawrence County?" Candela asked one of the other agents.

"Good relations with the Sheriff's Department," the agent said. "I spoke with the assistant sheriff this morning because the sheriff is out of town, and he assured me that they would be available to us. This was before they found out about their deputy being killed," he added with a glance at Lucy.

"How certain are you that he was a bad cop?" Candela asked her.

"Very certain." Lucy relayed the information they had, including the GPS tracking of his vehicle. She added, "He most likely went back to destroy evidence, but I collected some that I hope helps."

Lucy took the sealed brown paper bag from her backpack. "Because blow flies have a very specific life cycle that's impacted severely by the environment, I collected three maggots I found near where the body had been."

"I think Ms. Kincaid should go back to the beginning," Marty Strong said. "How certain are you that the body you found was actually dead?"

"I was an assistant forensic pathologist for the D.C. Medical Examiner; I know a dead body when I see one." She sounded defensive, but she wasn't expecting to walk into a quasi-hostile environment. She tried to remember that these people were grieving for their colleague. "The next day, when I realized the local cops weren't taking me seriously, we went down to the mine to photograph the scene."

"Yet you collected evidence."

"As I explained, the life cycle—"

"You're not an agent yet," Strong said. "What qualifies you in evidence collection?"

Noah rose from his seat, hands on the table. "If you feel the need to inspect Ms. Kincaid's credentials, talk to me after this meeting. For now, let her get through the facts of the case before you jump down her throat." He looked around the table before sitting down.

Lucy appreciated the support, but it intimidated her as well. She'd been questioning her decisions the entire flight here.

She told them everything she'd told Candela yesterday. She explained how the body was positioned, why she believed that the body had been naturally frozen in the mine, and how she determined, because of the clothes she wore, that the victim had been killed elsewhere. It took her more than twenty minutes, with only a few questions for clarification.

Everyone was staring at her. She glanced at Noah. He gave her a barely perceptible nod.

"It was the flower that suggested that the killer showed remorse. Someone placed a flower on her chest. I found it on the floor."

"Now she's a profiler," Marty Strong mumbled.

"Actually," Lucy said clearly before Noah could admonish the agent, "I have a master's in criminal psychology, and my brother is Dr. Dillon Kincaid, a renowned forensic psychiatrist who consults for the FBI and other agencies. I do appreciate the fact that everyone in this room has far more experience in the field than I do. But one thing I know better than most people is how killers think."

She walked to the white board and picked up a marker. She was hardly an artist, but she drew the body as best she could. "She was flat on her back. Her arms were crossed like this." She marked the drawing. "Crossed at the wrists. No one dies naturally that way." She drew the flower between the victim's hands.

As Lucy looked at her crude drawing, she had an

epiphany. She didn't know why she hadn't seen it before, but it was clear now.

"Whoever put her body here felt a deep remorse. Not only did he have a religious upbringing, but he probably considers himself religious. He laid her out as if in a coffin because he couldn't give her a proper burial. He went to the mine to visit her corpse, to pray and ask forgiveness for his crimes. She was his Snow White, but unlike the fairy tale, true love wouldn't bring her back."

Lucy's skin tingled painfully, as if a million ants were trailing up her body. She could barely stop herself from shaking the imaginary bugs from her skin. She was being watched, and worse, she had lost herself in her analysis, forgetting where she was, forgetting that she was standing in front of her future colleagues. She was the freak show. There was no doubt in her mind that they would find out exactly who she was, if they didn't already know what happened to her seven years ago.

Normal was so foreign to her she didn't even know what it meant anymore. All she knew was that it wasn't her.

She put down the marker and faced the room, even though she wanted to bolt. It was one of the hardest things she'd ever done—to stand there and be stared at.

Noah spoke, and Lucy quietly returned to her seat. He took her hand under the table and squeezed it, then let go. The gesture stunned her, and she didn't know how to respond.

He's just giving you a nonverbal pep talk.

She must have looked terrified for Noah to be so bold.

"Remember," he said, "besides Agent Sheffield, there was another victim to get out of the mine—the private investigator working the vandalism case was seriously injured when he fell down the mine shaft while pursuing an arsonist. As you all know, the rules of triage demand that we help the living before we deal with the dead."

Candela nodded. "I'm satisfied at this point, and we have a lot to get through so we can find out who killed Agent Sheffield." He motioned to the female agent sitting at the computer. "Tara has prepared a detailed list of all Agent Sheffield's electronic contacts up until her silence on January second." Papers were passed around. "And Agent Strong is handing out a list of key dates in the investigation."

Strong avoided looking at Lucy and said, "We now believe that she called her parents under extreme duress. There was no reason for her to cancel her vacation. When I last saw her, she was heading home to pack and catch an early morning flight. However, she never boarded the plane and we haven't found her car. Her personal car didn't have GPS installed—it was a 1995 dark blue Nissan Pathfinder."

Lucy was thankful that the focus had shifted from her and to the papers in front of them. Her stomach was so twisted she was in physical pain. She whispered to Noah, "I'm going to find the ladies' room."

He nodded, catching her eye. "You did good," he mouthed.

She didn't know why his praise didn't make her feel better, though she knew he was sincere. She excused herself and stepped out of the room. She leaned against the wall and took a deep breath.

The door opened behind her. She straightened, feeling sheepish to be caught in a state of near panic.

It was the SAC, Elizabeth Hart. She was tall and stately. Not pretty in the traditional sense, but what Lucy thought of as a handsome woman.

"I knew Victoria must have been dead," Hart said. "But I think they all were holding out hope. You understand this is a shock. Not simply because of where she was found, but because none of us knew what she was doing there. We've gone through all her records, emails, notes—she had no contact in Spruce Lake."

"Maybe it was personal," Lucy said.

"I saw the photo you brought. She looked happy."

"I gather she didn't mention if she was involved with Jon Callahan."

Hart shook her head. "Why hide it?"

That was a good question, and Lucy didn't have an answer.

TWENTY-NINE

Sean and Patrick sat in a small, windowless meeting room off the assistant warden's office at the state prison in Ogdensburg, twenty minutes west of Canton, right on the St. Lawrence River. They'd been reviewing Paul Swain's prison records for nearly an hour: Sean reading Swain's file and Patrick scouring the visitor logs.

Swain had been a model prisoner at the beginning; then, after a year, he started getting into fights and spending more time in solitary than not. Authorities had confiscated more than a dozen cell phones over the six years he'd been in the prison, plus four handmade knives. He'd killed a fellow inmate in a prison riot, earning him another twenty years on his twenty-five-to-life sentence. It was only recently, in the last year or so, that he had stopped getting into trouble.

"Look," Sean said to Patrick, "The first time he got into serious trouble was a week after his wife died."

"Makes sense. Wanted to be a model prisoner and not lose visitation rights with his family. Abigail visited him twice a week, once alone and once with their son."

"Did Ricky visit after she died?"

"No, but James Benson did."

"That could be another reason for Paul acting up—Benson not bringing his son to visit." Sean thought back to Ricky's letters from his mom. Sean had only skimmed most of them, but he had the impression Abigail was constantly apologizing for her husband to her son. Had she been trying to fix a bad relationship before she died?

"Benson visited the first Saturday of every month like clockwork," Patrick said.

"Any other regular visitors?"

"After Abigail Swain died—Reverend Carl Browne visited twice a year, until a year ago last March. That was his last visit."

"March? That's when Swain's behavior took a dramatic turn for the better."

"He had another visitor in March. A week before Browne." Patrick paused. "Joe Hendrickson."

"Hendrickson?"

"Stayed for ten minutes."

Neither Tim nor Adam knew about a connection between their father and Swain. His sudden visitation was of definite interest.

"Who else that month?"

"Other than Benson, no one." Patrick looked at the months before and after. "Except Jon Callahan. The last week of February, ten days before Hendrickson. Wait—" Patrick flipped through his notes, "Callahan also visited twice during the first year of Swain's incarceration."

If Callahan was as involved with Bobbie Swain as Sean thought, what was he doing meeting with Paul Swain? Were the brother and sister back on good terms? Perhaps Callahan was a messenger.

Sean's phone vibrated. It was a text message from Dillard.

The divers found a body. We just made a positive ID of James Benson.

"They found Benson's body," he told Patrick. He hadn't known the guy, but he was saddened by the news.

He responded to Dillard.

Don't forget his cell phone records. I'm particularly interested in the twenty-four hours after the arson fire.

Dillard sent back:

Got the preliminary report. No effort made to stop, signs that he sped up then turned sharply off the bridge. Possible DWI, accident, or suicide. More later.

Suicide? Sean hadn't expected that. "Why would Benson protect Ricky Swain for years, then kill himself when things in town started heating up?"

Patrick didn't have an answer.

"Anything else on Callahan?" Sean asked.

"He's visited Swain two more times," Patrick said. "February, two months later at the end of April, and again just after New Year's."

Sean frowned. Those dates seemed important. He pulled out the calendar on his cell phone. He'd already plugged in the important dates in the case. When Joe Hendrickson died, his funeral, when Tim and Adam moved back to Spruce Lake, their town hall meeting about the resort, each vandalism attack. And when Sheffield went missing.

"Let me see that," Sean said, grabbing the visitor logs. He input Callahan's recent visits and Hendrickson's lone visit. "Look. Don't tell me this is a coincidence."

Patrick stared at the calendar. "Well, fuck."

Last year, Callahan spent the full visitor's hour on a Saturday with Swain ten days before Hendrickson came for his one and only ten-minute visit. Three days later, Browne came for his last visit. The next morning, Joe Hendrickson was found dead of a heart attack.

"Did Swain put a hit on Hendrickson?" Sean wondered out loud.

"Didn't he die of a heart attack? He was in his sixties, right?"

"Sixty-four. And there was no autopsy. Tim said something about how he'd been under a doctor's care. If it was the quack who stitched up my leg, I wouldn't trust him with a Band-Aid."

Patrick said, "Look here—Callahan came the day after Tim Hendrickson had that town hall meeting, end of last April."

"When was his last visit? January of this year?"

"January third." Ten days after Agent Sheffield disappeared. "Sean, you're going to have to be extra wily with Swain. We've got nothing but theories, so the choice is between taking this information and running with it, and attempting to get something more out of him."

Sean looked closely at the log. "What's this?" he slid the file back over to Patrick. There was a five-digit number, not a name, on the printout. 19881. "No matter how I slice it, I can't make a date out of it," Sean said.

"I have no idea," Patrick said.

Sean noted the date on the log. December 23. "Do we have phone records, Patrick?"

"They're still printing those out for us."

"When you get them, see if there's anything on these dates." He circled the meetings. "And maybe you can ask the warden what this number means. Text me when you find out."

"Do you know who's *not* on this list?"

Sean stared at his partner blankly. Then it hit him. "Swain's brother."

"Bingo."

"That *is* interesting." Sean remembered that one of Weddle's stops before he died was at Butch Swain's house.

"Ready for Swain?" Patrick asked.

"Absolutely." He sounded more confident than he actually was as they left the assistant warden's office and walked through additional security.

"I'm confident you'll get inside his head," Patrick said. "Ten minutes and I'll bet he'll lose his temper."

"Am I that annoying?"

"You can be."

Paul Swain was not what Sean expected.

Sean faced the prisoner in a private interview room usually reserved for lawyers and their clients. Patrick and a senior guard were on the other side of the window, unseen, but Sean felt their presence. He had to play this right.

If Swain knew what he needed, he wouldn't just hand it over. Sean's only ace was to make Swain think he was looking for something completely different.

Forty-four, Swain had a handsome face and neatly trimmed dark hair. His palms and fingers were rough from labor, and there were scars on the back of his hands from fighting. A faded scar starting behind his ear and ending at his chin looked like it might have been serious at the time. There was a more recent scar at his temple, still red and raised.

Except for the physical scars, there was nothing about Paul Swain's demeanor that said *master criminal.* Even his quiet voice was well modulated.

"They told me you're not a cop."

"That's correct."

"Who are you?"

"Sean Rogan. Private investigator."

"Cop lite."

Sean shrugged and acted disinterested in Swain's approval. "I don't like cops as a rule. Good cops have their hands tied because of a system that favors pricks like you, and bad cops are worse because they abuse their power under the color of authority."

"And you're the noble knight in shining armor?"

He shook his head. "Not noble, and I'm certainly not a knight. But I hate bullies, whether they're cops or criminals."

"Applause," Swain said with a half-smile and leaned back in his chair. "Did you rehearse that just for me?"

"I didn't know you existed until this week."

"I have no reason to help you."

"I haven't asked for your help."

He rolled his eyes. "Then you're wasting my time."

"I've read over the files from your case," Sean lied smoothly. All he had was the names of the cops on the task force. "Agent Martinelli—what a prick."

"You don't know the half of it."

"I can imagine. They always make themselves look good on paper, but you and I know they fuck with the Constitution when they can get away with it." Sean leaned forward. "I've had my own run-ins with the Feds."

"Now you're just playing me, Rogan. Trying to be my friend. Acting all good cop with no corresponding bad cop."

"I'm not playing cop, good or bad. The last thing I want to be is subjected to arbitrary rules and regulations." That was certainly the truth. "You knew Joe Hendrickson, right?"

Swain didn't answer, just shook his head in disgust.

"I know you did. Spruce Lake had seven hundred ninety people at the last census, and we know that has dropped since. Cut in half, in fact. I was hired by his sons—Tim and Adam. Tim is the older one, Adam—"

"I know who they are," Swain said, impatient. "I don't need no goddamn family tree drawn for me."

First chink in the armor.

"They want to open a resort. Small scale, a few cabins, a lodge with ten rooms, nature walks, that kind of shit."

Swain leaned back again. "No one wants to vacation in Spruce Lake."

"Tourism is far from my area of expertise. Thing is, there's a group of people trying to shut it down, and guess who they're using to do it? Your son."

A bare hint of rage—the tightening of his fists. So small Sean almost missed it.

"To continue with the happenings in your hometown, Tim and Adam came up with a plan for a resort, and they've had repeated problems. Equipment destroyed. A cabin trashed. The kitchen set on fire. That's felony arson. Ricky is seventeen. He could be tried as an adult if some ladder-climbing prosecutor wants to set an example."

Swain's anger was growing, his eyes alert, his ears focused on Sean's every word though he didn't move a muscle.

"I'm going to lay it all out for you, Swain, because if you're behind it, you already know. If you're not behind it, I don't care if you know." Sean leaned back in the uncomfortable metal chair and pretended he was having a casual conversation, but in fact he was focused completely on Swain's "tell"—the physical giveaway that told Sean he'd hit a nerve. He was banking that Swain had one redeeming quality—the love of his wife and child. It was an educated guess based on Abigail's letters, his behavior after she died and Ricky stopped visiting, and the bits and pieces of information Sean had been putting together.

"Here's what I know. You're a smart criminal. I saw that right off in your file. No, I'm not stroking your ego, because I also think you're an asshole for manufacturing drugs. My sister died of a drug overdose. If I thought for a minute that you were part of her supply chain, I'd shoot you now. So we'll call you a smart prick."

No man likes being called a prick. Swain's tell manifested itself. Very subtle—he was good—but Sean was better. He'd played poker with his brothers for years and always won. Even his brother Kane the badass mercenary had a tell, though it took Sean years to figure it out.

Swain's tell was in his hands. They were cuffed in

front of him. When Sean called him a prick, his right index finger tapped once on the table.

"If I weren't in prison, I'd kill you."

"You might try," Sean said smoothly. "So back to the vandalism. It wasn't smart. In fact, it was amateur hour."

"You're boring me, Rogan."

"Your son led me on a pretty good chase. Over the hills and through the woods to the ventilation shaft on Travers Hill."

No reaction.

"He busted the oil tank of the ATV he'd stolen and it stalled out. He was scared and defiant with a mouth on him. I liked him, I'll admit. And he was smart—tricked me, and I fell down the mine shaft."

Swain smiled, but his finger was steady. He didn't know about the body in the mine.

"So I was pissed off. Tracked him down. Told him I would help, that I could protect him if he turned in whoever he was working for."

"You sure you're not a cop?" Swain grunted.

"I wouldn't trust just anyone to protect the kid, not with what I think is going on. Unfortunately, he got some bad news yesterday and disappeared."

Swain stared at him. "You claim to not like to play games, that you're going to lay it out for me. Then you play a fucking game. Spit it out or I swear I'll take you down. Where is my son?"

Sean leaned forward. "Jimmy Benson is dead. His truck went off the bridge in Colton, right in the lake. The evidence points to suicide or drunk driving. He sped up and intentionally went over the edge."

"Get out." Swain's voice was barely a whisper.

Sean leaned forward. "If you loved your wife and don't want her son dead you'll tell me what the fuck is going on in Spruce Lake. Or I'll assume you're behind it and beating up your kid is simply a life lesson you're trying to teach him. Why would Jimmy kill himself?"

Swain lunged forward. Sean didn't flinch. He knew if Swain got his hands on him, the guard would be in the door in two seconds. He prayed Patrick was able to hold him back now.

"I'll kill you!"

"Better men have tried."

Swain was red-faced. "Anyone touches my son, I'll slit their throat."

"From prison? That would be a neat trick."

"Let me rephrase," he said with forced calm, working to control his rage, "I'll have their throat slit."

"I think I have the answers," Sean said, pulling together the information he did have and bluffing about the rest.

"You know shit."

"I know that someone turned state's evidence on you, and I think you know who it is."

Swain was shaking his head.

"And you had damning information on this person, so damning that even though they fucked you and you ended up in prison, they couldn't take over your operation."

The finger tapped once.

"I don't know what information you have to keep this person in line," Sean said. "I suspect it's physical evidence, something that can't degrade. Tapes, disks, a computer hard drive, maybe photos, something that experts could prove weren't doctored. And you used that info to protect your son." He paused. "I read the letters your wife wrote to Ricky."

Swain's eyes darkened and narrowed. "You bastard."

"Something big is going down in Spruce Lake, and your son could easily get caught in the crossfire. Jimmy's dead, and Ricky is on the run."

"I don't know where you're from, Rogan, but here, we take care of our business ourselves."

"Your people aren't your people anymore."

Swain's right index finger tapped multiple times. He was thinking.

Sean leaned forward. "You haven't had a visitor or a call in the last week. Did you know that Bobbie is back in town?"

Swain stared at him, rigid. "Vengeance is mine, sayeth the Lord."

He'd been right. "You're setting her up."

Swain's voice was low. "Do you know what she did to my wife?"

"Your wife called her a monster. She stole your money."

"You don't understand. Abby was the one bright spot in my life. She had breast cancer, but she would have gotten better." He paused, uncertain.

Sean pushed. "Here's what I think happened. Bobbie had someone on the inside of your operation. She turned you in. Made sure the government had enough to lock you up for a long time. You hid some money for your family, but Bobbie found it. Your wife couldn't get the treatment she needed, and died nearly a year later. You've been plotting revenge, but so has Bobbie. She's been cultivating your son. I don't know who he trusted, but he was responsible for the vandalism at Joe Hendrickson's place. Now, Ricky is missing and Bobbie is in town, and she has your entire team in the palm of her hand."

Swain sighed and leaned back. "You were doing so good for a while."

Sean's phone vibrated, and he glanced at the message. When he saw the five numbers on the visitor log, he'd suspected it was a federal ID number, but wasn't sure. Patrick had come through: Victoria Sheffield had come to visit Paul Swain.

"You've been planning since the day you were incarcerated. Maybe things were going well, I don't know, but in December you had a visit from a very pretty blonde, an FBI agent. I don't know if she told you she was a Fed, or if she had some false identity, but she was here for forty minutes. I think she connected her undercover investigation into intellectual property theft with your former operation. This is where it gets a bit sketchy for me, because the Fed was in the white-collar unit. But she made the connection with Bobbie's operation here, probably with the help of Jon Callahan. She was a novice. Looking to prove her worth. She came in here tossing out her credentials and playing big, tough bitch cop, when in fact she was a twenty-something newbie desperately wanting to land a big fish." Sean was making it all up as he went along, adjusting based on Swain's reactions. "You told her to get the fuck out—because hell, *I'd* do the same thing. Unless she offered me something in exchange."

Tap.

"She's dead."

Swain laughed. That wasn't the reaction Sean was expecting. Had he got the entire scenario wrong?

Maybe some of the details, but he was certain Agent Victoria Sheffield came here to get Paul Swain to turn on his former associates.

"Who do you really work for, Mr. Rogan?"

"I am exactly who I said I was." He took out Sheffield's missing persons picture.

Swain definitely recognized her, but didn't say anything.

"She went missing officially on January second. Then you have a visitor on January third. Jon Callahan. He only visited you three times. A week before Joe Hendrickson died, right after he learned about Tim and Adam Hendrickson's resort plans, and the day after Sheffield went missing.

"So does Callahan work for you or your sister? Or both?"

"Where's Ricky?" Swain asked.

"I don't know."

Tap. Tap.

"Your brother has never visited you. Was he working for Bobbie all along?"

"Butch is an idiot."

Tap. Tap. Tap.

"What's going down in Spruce Lake?"

Tap.

Sean stood. "If Ricky dies, it's on you."

Swain jumped up and lunged for Sean. The guard burst in and Sean waved him off.

"Tell me, Paul. If you care one iota for that boy, tell me what I need to know to protect him."

"Do you know who you're up against? Do you know what Bobbie is?"

"I have an idea."

"You have no idea. When she was eight, she pushed her best friend down an exploration shaft in the Kelley Mine just to see what would happen. Those shafts are at least fifty feet. My father called it the Hell Hole and used to dump his problems down there. Our father was an evil bastard."

Sean barely refrained from commenting about pots and kettles.

"When Bobbie was ten, she shot my dog because I ratted her out when she broke Butch's fingers. Before I banished her, she nearly poisoned Abby and Ricky, to get back at me for chastising her in front of a guy she was horny about. Do you know what she did to her husband?"

"I do."

He seemed surprised, then shook his head with a half-smile. "You *are* a masochist. Why do you care? Most people would be running away screaming by now."

"Bobbie is a fucking psychopathic bully, and I hate bullies."

Swain stared at him, assessing Sean. Sean let him.

"Can you protect my son?"

"Yes."

"I'm dead serious, Rogan. Protect him or his fate is your fate. I still have friends on the outside. Friends no one even knows about."

For the first time, Sean felt a twinge of concern. How could he protect Ricky if he didn't know where he was hiding? *Could* he protect Ricky? How deep was the kid involved with Bobbie's people? Would he even trust Sean?

"You tell me what you know, and I will protect your son or die trying."

That satisfied Swain. He sat back down. Sean also sat.

"Talk to Jon Callahan."

Sean shook his head. "He's playing with her."

Swain laughed. "Hardly. He wants to kill her."

"Why? Because she's a whack job?"

"Whack job. I like that. No. She killed Joe Hendrickson."

Sean couldn't prevent the surprise from registering on his face. "Why?"

"Because Joe was talking to the wrong people."

"Be more specific."

"I can't. I still got to live in this prison, Rogan."

"And was Joe close to Jon and Henry?"

"Yes. And Joe looked out for Ricky, too, especially after Abby died. Joe and I didn't like each other, but I respected him. There are no honest men in the world, but if there were, it'd be Hendrickson. He left me alone, I left him alone. Bobbie had to make it look like an accident—a heart attack—because a lot of people would have been angry with her for taking him out. Jon was in over his head and Jimmy was panicking. Then Joe's sons show up in town with this foolish idea for a resort."

"Why does anyone care about the resort? It's not a big place."

"But it's *people.* Outsiders. Hikers." Swain realized that Sean didn't get that. "Let's say this. The product has changed. They need more space, warehouses, warmth. If you looked at the town's gas and heating bill, you'd be surprised."

They were growing pot. "There has to be more to this than a little weed," Sean said.

"Little? Hardly. And there is. And that's where the

problem is. Talk to Jon, if you can. He's changed. It got personal."

"And it's not personal for you?"

"It's business for me. I've protected my son as best I can from in here." He tapped his finger again. Maybe it was more personal than even Swain admitted to himself. "Bobbie wants to teach Ricky the family business, knowing I promised Abby he'd have a real life. She thinks it would be funny. And if he doesn't join her, she'll kill him. Not so much to get back at me, though that's part of it. But because she does not let anyone tell her *no*."

"Sweet little sister."

"Do not underestimate her."

"She must have a weakness."

"It depends what you consider a weakness. She's incapable of caring about anything except her goal. She likes to hurt people, and she won't hesitate. You can't reason with her. She's manipulative and a liar. She has a wicked, hair-trigger temper—though I've heard she's worked to control it. Our dad always said her temper would get her killed."

"Thank you." Sean rose, then turned back and said, "How is it personal with Jon?"

"Bobbie killed the woman Jon loved."

"And she killed the woman you loved."

Swain leaned forward. "That's why I'm helping Jon, even though he turned his back on me years ago." He called, "Guard! I'm ready." He said to Sean, "Remember. You promised to protect my son. I'm holding you to that."

THIRTY

Lucy took a few moments to compose herself before returning to the conference room. The group was adding her information to the timeline for Victoria Sheffield.

Lucy skimmed through documents related to Sheffield's original case, completely bored by the White Collar unit's methodical report, until she got to the bottom line and saw that the studio that had brought the case to the Feds estimated they lost over six million dollars on one movie alone.

Studio One was familiar to Lucy. Where had she seen that name before?

She had started going through her papers when her cell phone vibrated with an email message. Noah read his phone at the same time. It was from Sean.

Sheffield met with Paul Swain on December 23. I need to talk to both of you ASAP—without other Feds eavesdropping.

Lucy glanced at Noah. His jaw was clenched so tight she saw a small vein throb at the top of his throat.

He stood, and said, "You'll have to excuse me for a moment." He didn't ask Lucy to join him, so she remained where she was.

Sheffield's communications were rather generic, and listed from most recent to oldest. Lucy turned to the back of the packet and scanned the messages that came in prior to December 23. A full year before she disappeared, Sheffield wrote to her supervisor, Marty Strong.

I finally got a meeting with Studio One lawyers, along with G.T. from mounted police. We worked out the proprietary confidentiality agreement, I'm attaching it for approval.

Lawyers! That's where she saw Studio One. They were a client of the law firm Jon Callahan worked for. That was Sheffield's connection to Spruce Lake and her connection to Jon Callahan.

It didn't explain why she switched investigations midstream from intellectual property theft to drug running, but it was a place to start.

She wanted to say something, but the computer expert was continuing his presentation about the data analysis. He felt that none of the messages supposedly sent by Sheffield after the twenty-third were actually from her. Marty Strong disagreed.

Noah stepped into the room. "Brian, Ms. Hart, may I speak with you?"

Candela and Hart followed Noah out. What was that about? There were murmurings until the trio returned less than two minutes later.

Hart said, "Tara, Marty, Dale—you stay. Everyone else, you'll have to be excused for a few minutes."

Lucy rose and gathered her notes. This had to do with Sean, she knew it, and he was in trouble.

Don't panic.

If anything happened to him . . . her life would be empty.

"Lucy," Noah snapped, "where are you going? Sit down."

Lucy sat, startled by Noah's tone, and a bit irritated. Hart said, "I was referring to my unit."

When all but the seven of them had left, Noah said, "Sean Rogan is a principal at Rogan-Caruso-Kincaid, which is a security firm with high-level government clearance. They do quite a bit of work for different agencies, primarily Homeland Security, the DEA, and the FBI, and have several former law enforcement officers working for them, including Lucy's brother Patrick, who was a cybercrimes cop in San Diego." Noah turned on the speaker phone. "Sean?"

"I'm here."

"The room is clear. There are seven of us—Lucy, myself, the SAC Elizabeth Hart, ASAC Brian Candela, and Agents Marty Strong, Tara Fields, and Dale Martinelli."

"Your need-to-know team is quite large," Sean said over the speaker.

Hart spoke up. "With all due respect, Mr. Rogan, I didn't want to agree to this conversation at all, but Agent Armstrong convinced me to trust you. Please get to the point."

"Certainly, Ms. Hart. Agent Sheffield visited Paul

Swain in prison on December twenty-third. I read the report, and it said that Agent Martinelli was part of the task force, so you're probably familiar with the Swain sting."

"Correct," Hart said.

Strong interjected, "Why would she meet with a known drug dealer? Victoria worked white-collar crime."

"She went to Swain because in the course of her investigation of pirated DVDs she uncovered something bigger. Swain wasn't as forthcoming about what it was. I was hoping you'd all know why she was meeting with Swain, what she was doing in Spruce Lake, and how long she'd been involved with Jon Callahan."

Silence, this time of the stunned variety.

"You're pulling this out of thin air!" Strong finally said.

Martinelli said, "She wasn't even an FBI agent six years ago during the sting. How would she know Swain or any of the people in Spruce Lake?"

"I know how," Lucy said.

Everyone looked at her. She hesitated, not liking the attention.

Sean said over the speaker, "Shoot, Lucy. What do you think?"

"Agent Sheffield was undercover investigating the theft of intellectual property from Studio One. When I read her messages about meeting with the lawyers, it clicked. Studio One is a client of Jon Callahan's law firm in Montreal. They specialize in intellectual property, copyright, and other business matters. If she met with the lawyers, one of them could have been Callahan."

"That's a long, convoluted stretch," Strong said.

"It's the only connection she has with Spruce Lake," Lucy said. "And it would explain the photo of her and Callahan."

"Why would she get involved with a drug case without running it through the office?" Strong said.

Candela said, "Victoria was a good agent, but she had a history of acting without thinking."

Strong slapped his hand on the table. "That's not fair, Brian! We gave her a lot of leeway with this op because it was fucking movies!"

Martinelli said, "The Sacramento FBI office recently had several large stings taking down three separate pirating operations totaling more than one hundred million dollars. All the same signs were here. She might have thought she could bring us something bigger."

"Not on her own," Strong insisted. "Not like this."

"Are you too close to this?" Candela asked quietly.

Strong took a deep breath but said nothing more.

Hart said, "Our emotions are running high. Victoria was extremely bright, but she also was a maverick. None of that matters right now—we will find her killer. As far as I'm concerned, we're investigating the disappearance and murder of one of our own people. No judgments until we solve this thing. Is everyone clear?"

Everyone nodded their assent. Lucy felt ill, the mantra, *There but for the grace of God go thee,* running through her head. She could see herself following a trail that she believed in, especially if no one agreed with her. Especially if she knew justice and human lives were at stake.

"I might have an answer for you," Sean said, "but you're not going to like it."

"Theory?"

"Educated guess. Swain said one thing that is now perfectly clear. I asked him why Callahan wants revenge on Bobbie Swain. His answer? She killed the woman he loved."

"That's bullshit, Rogan," Strong said.

Noah disagreed. "It explains everything. Sheffield's connection to Spruce Lake, and why she was killed."

"How does it do that?" Strong demanded. "A lover's spat?"

There was more to Marty Strong's feelings for Victoria Sheffield than being a colleague, or even a friend. Lucy said, "Let's assume that Sheffield met Callahan through Studio One."

Strong cut her off. "That's a damn big assumption."

"Let her finish," Noah said with authority. Lucy glanced around at the others at the table and realized that though everyone else had both seniority and jurisdiction over Noah, he commanded the meeting.

Lucy continued. "They're working on the pirated DVDs and over time, Callahan tells her his concerns about Spruce Lake. It could be that she didn't take him seriously, or thought he was exaggerating, or wanted proof before coming to her boss. Whatever her reasons, she went to Spruce Lake one or more times to gather information."

Sean interjected. "That holds with what I got out of Paul Swain. He wants to destroy his sister for sending him to prison; Callahan wants to destroy her for killing Agent Sheffield."

"Hold it," Martinelli said. "Why not come to us? Even if we accept the theory that Victoria was investigating drug running on her own, when she was murdered, why wouldn't this Callahan come to us? Unless, of course, he's in on it."

"But," Lucy said, "there's no other way she could have found out about Spruce Lake except through Jon Callahan."

"We don't know that," Martinelli said.

Lucy did. Nothing else made sense. The theory she and Sean developed—most of it separately, she realized—worked.

Hart spoke up. "I'm inclined to agree with Lucy and Mr. Rogan." All eyes turned to the boss. "What I'm about to tell you is classified, but in light of this situation, you need to know. Roberta Swain Molina was in protective custody in Florida six years ago after her husband was murdered and she was left for dead by a rival drug cartel. She provided our office with key information and physical evidence that led to the takedown of her brother's drug business in Spruce Lake. Paul Swain had been one of the largest methamphetamine manufacturers distributing into Canada."

Sean said, "There's an alternate theory that Bobbie Swain orchestrated the hit on her husband."

"She nearly died that night," Hart said. "I know her background. Her mother died when she was a baby. She'd been grossly abused as a child, and finally escaped one violent family for another, marrying into the Molina cartel."

"I take it," Sean said, "you haven't been keeping tabs on her over the last few years?"

"There was no reason to. She just wanted to have a normal life."

"You might need to go back and fact-check," Sean said.

"Excuse me," Hart said, "I know more about this case than you do. You believe a convicted felon over an abused woman? Do you know what he did to her?"

Sean said, "After she got her brother Paul out of the picture, she walked in and took over."

"That's a serious accusation."

"I don't make it lightly."

Noah spoke up. "The situation is certainly volatile right now, and I think we should assess the intelligence we have and run Bobbie Swain through our contacts at DEA. We all know that they don't volunteer information, but if we have a name, we can get answers."

"Brian," Hart ordered, "take care of it."

Lucy noticed that the SAC had lost some of her polish. Was it because Sean challenged her, or because she was having second thoughts about her assessment of Bobbie Swain?

Lucy asked, "Do you have her interview on tape? A file with her transcript?"

"Yes. Why?"

"I'd like to read the file on Bobbie Swain, as well as

the sting six years ago. It might help us figure out additional connections."

Hart told Martinelli to pull the files, and said, "Whether Bobbie Swain had ulterior motives in turning in her brother—over and above her tragic upbringing—is irrelevant since everything she told us we were able to prove."

Noah said, "And what better way to get revenge and advance her own agenda. Right now, you have a dead federal agent who may have knowingly or unknowingly stumbled into a major drug operation. Paul Swain, believe him or not, has power outside the prison. He knows his sister turned him in. If she's innocent, she's in danger. If she's guilty, she's in danger. But more important, something big is going down in Spruce Lake, and a whole lot of innocent people are in danger."

Lucy's phone vibrated, and while Noah and Hart discussed facts and conjecture, she read the message from Sean.

It scared her. Not because Sean put her in an impossible situation of keeping information from the FBI, but because of the very real threat to his life.

Do not tell the Feds Bobbie Swain is in Spruce Lake. If they come in with their suits and attitude and cut her even an inch of slack, it will be a bloodbath. I don't trust Paul Swain, but I have other evidence to back up what he said. I fully believe that Jon Callahan has a dangerous plan of revenge, and it has to do with whatever is going down tomorrow. Paul is counting on it—he's using Callahan. I'm on my way to find him, because I think he's the only one who knows where Ricky might be. I promised Swain I would protect his son.

If anything happens, know that I love you.

Martinelli came in. "We have a problem."

A chill ran through her body. Lucy joined everyone in looking at the agent. He said, "The disk and computer files are gone."

"Gone? Misplaced? Checked out?"

"Gone. But the last person logged in to look at the Paul Swain sting operation was Victoria Sheffield."

THIRTY-ONE

Patrick was behind the wheel driving to Spruce Lake while Sean got to work on his laptop. "I really hope the Feds don't screw this up," Sean said.

"You were being difficult," Patrick said. "Maybe you need a lesson in diplomacy."

Sean glanced at him. "What was I wrong about?"

"Nothing, but you could have pulled out your charm."

"Maybe," he said without conviction. "So Victoria Sheffield took the disk of Bobbie Swain's accusations two days before she met Swain. Who else knew she had the information? And what was on the disk that could get Bobbie thrown in jail?"

"You're missing something," Patrick said. "That letter from Ricky's mother was written over five years ago. Sheffield took the disk five months ago."

"The question is, did she take it for Jon Callahan or for Paul Swain? What might be on it?"

Patrick considered. "FBI interview, supposedly friendly. They'd ask her tough questions, as well as the same question in different ways to see if her story changes, but if they considered Bobbie Swain a victim, they wouldn't have pushed too hard."

"Would they verify the information?"

"They did—they got a warrant based on her testimony and arrested nine people involved in drug trafficking."

Sean snapped his fingers. "If there's an appeal and the warrant is deemed illegal, what happens to the convictions?"

"Well, any evidence obtained because of the warrant could be thrown out. *Could* be, Sean. It's fruit from the poisonous tree. But in a situation like this—with a widespread drug network and multiple meth labs—they most likely had other evidence to back them up."

"Unless Paul Swain wasn't on the radar until Bobbie put him there."

"I'm not a lawyer, Sean. But I'd imagine that if she told the truth about her brother's operation, it didn't matter what her motivation was. Bad guys cut deals all the time. They do it to get reduced sentences, to get off, to save their life."

"She didn't cut a deal." Sean didn't know why it bothered him so much. Bobbie Swain was, as Abigail wrote, a monster. "Looking at the timeline—she kills her husband, injures herself, goes to the police a changed woman. They feel sorry for her, she gives them the sob story about how she was raised by a brutish father and abusive brothers and she wants it all to stop. They take down Paul Swain and in walks Bobbie, free and clear."

"Except she didn't. She wasn't in town."

"She was running things, nonetheless."

"That's going to be hard to prove."

"She's here now."

"Tread carefully, Sean. We don't have any proof that Bobbie Swain has committed a crime. There's a lot of circumstantial evidence, but nothing solid."

"The witness who saw two figures near Weddle's house."

"Who couldn't identify them in a lineup if she tried. She admitted she saw them from behind."

"If we can place Swain in Potsdam."

"Circumstantial. You'd need to have physical evidence that she was in Weddle's house."

"And you wonder why I'm not a cop. You *know* she's guilty."

Sean saw a new message on his email. "Dillard came through. Here are Jimmy Benson's phone records."

He scanned the numbers and compared them to a list he had compiled. "On Wednesday, Ricky called him at ten-thirty-one a.m. One minute, probably left a message. Benson returned the call two hours later. They spoke for three minutes." That made sense—Benson was on duty, he'd probably been at the lodge putting out the fire when Ricky first called. "According to Dillard, he left early Wednesday afternoon, taking sick time. We don't know where he was from then until he showed up at the Lock & Barrel. The bartender didn't remember when he came in, but he left shortly before seven. He made one call after he left the bar. Jon Callahan. Two minutes." One more thing to ask him about.

Sean glanced at the time. "It's nearly four. Let's regroup at the lodge, and I'm going to try to convince Callahan to come to us. If that doesn't work, we're going to the bar. Funny how both times I showed up there, he arrived within fifteen minutes."

His cell phone rang. "Hey, Duke," he answered.

"I set off a big alarm, so expect the weight of the federal government to come crashing down pretty quick."

"What happened?"

"I ran the bullet casings as soon as I got them this morning. I cut some corners that I probably shouldn't have, but nothing I haven't done before. I got a call from ATF."

"ATF?" The Rogan-Caruso-Kincaid agency rarely worked with Alcohol, Tobacco and Firearms. While they had high-ranking contacts at the FBI, in the military, and in Homeland Security, they had no go-to person in ATF.

"They didn't tell me anything, but they had a lot of questions. How I obtained them, who gave them to me, where had they been recovered, when—I told them shit, because to be honest, the guy who called was a prick and refused to answer my questions. However, I sent him to your pal Noah Armstrong. I hope he can get the answers."

"They were common casings."

"That's what I thought too, so I called in a favor with a friend of mine at the FBI lab. Emailed him pictures of the markings, and he told me the bullets were manufactured exclusively for law enforcement."

Sean considered that revelation. "That doesn't surprise me," Sean said, almost relieved. "I told you about the corrupt deputy."

"Maybe you're right, but that doesn't really explain why the ATF jumped down my throat less than three hours after I uploaded the technical data."

"Thanks."

"I don't need to tell you to be careful, Sean."

"Believe me, I'm watching my back on this one."

SAC Hart didn't want a copy of the remaining Swain file removed from the office, especially considering the missing documents, but she allowed Lucy to read it in the conference room. Lucy took extensive notes. She would much rather have watched or listened to Bobbie Swain, but the written statement was almost as good. On the surface, Bobbie said all the right things, tears timed just right to elicit sympathy.

Lucy had a difficult time reading the file and thinking that a woman had faked abuse. And maybe she *had* been abused. But it wasn't sexual, and Bobbie Swain stated as such.

Noah stormed into the room, Candela in his wake.

"Lucy, are you ready?" Noah's tone was severe.

"What happened?" she asked.

"The ATF called me. Bastards."

Noah kept his emotions close to the vest, like she did, and had always acted supremely professional. But right now, he looked as if he wanted to hit something.

He said to her and Candela, "The bullet casings from the sniper yesterday morning? Issued to ATF. They refused to give me any information, but demanded plenty. I had a few choice words with the jerk when he ordered me not to return to Spruce Lake." Noah shook his head. "He has no authority. After ten years in the Air Force I'm not easily intimidated."

Candela said, "They must know who shot at Lucy and Sean Rogan."

"Damn straight they do. But I also played them.

Sean's brother Duke gave me the heads-up about the ATF—he ran the casings against the database, then was locked out. Duke didn't tell them anything, not even where the casings came from. The ATF agent slipped by letting me know *he* knew where they were found. So I called Rick Stockton and told him I needed a favor."

Rick Stockton was a high-ranking assistant director stationed at FBI National Headquarters.

Lucy said, "I'm not following."

"Based on the tone of the call, I suspect they have an undercover operative in place."

Candela now looked as angry as Noah sounded. "They're not supposed to run an undercover op without informing our office. Excuse me, I need to talk to Elizabeth." He left Noah and Lucy alone in the conference room.

"If the sniper is an ATF agent, why would they shoot at *us*?" Lucy recalled that the bullets all hit the ground—it was something Sean thought odd at the time, but now it made sense. "That's a dangerous plan to chase us off. Sean returned fire; he could have killed the guy."

"Agreed. Stockton is going to call the head of ATF and get answers, but we need to leave for Spruce Lake now. Sean and Patrick need backup."

"Did you tell Sean?"

"He knows everything I know."

Lucy had already gathered up her notes. "I'm ready," she said. She glanced at her phone and realized she should have told Noah about Sean's earlier message. She glanced at the closed door.

Noah picked up on her quandary. "What is it?" he asked.

"You need to see this message from Sean."

Noah took her phone. He stared at it for far longer than it would take to read it.

Lucy finally said, "You're mad."

"This came in over an hour ago. He specifically told you not to share critical information with the FBI."

"A life is at stake."

"Sean follows his own rules." Noah stared at her. "Do you want to be an FBI agent?"

"I know what you're saying, Noah, but Sean has proven himself. He thinks—"

"Sean has proven himself in *his* business. His business doesn't always mesh with government business."

"You can't tell me you wouldn't do the same thing in his shoes—"

"You didn't give me the chance." Noah picked up his files and started toward the door. "Trust is a two-way street, Lucy. For all intents and purposes, you are my partner until you check in to Quantico. But I won't work with a partner who doesn't trust me." He looked over his shoulder at her as he opened the door. "Or whom I can't trust."

Lucy felt sick to her stomach when Noah walked out of the conference room. He was right. If she kept information from her partner, she put them both at risk.

Years ago, when her sister-in law Kate was a new agent, she had a partner who lied to her about something that seemed minor at the time, but spiraled into a deadly confrontation that got Kate's boyfriend and her partner killed and sent Kate on the run. The tragedy had changed Kate's life forever, and while she was now teaching at Quantico, it had taken her years to reclaim her life.

Lucy had enough tragedy and dark clouds hanging over her FBI career and it hadn't even started yet.

Lucy followed Noah out. He was talking to Candela and Hart in the foyer. "As far as this office knows," Hart was telling Noah, "there's no ATF operation in St. Lawrence County at all. I put in a call to the Brooklyn office, which would have to approve any undercover op in the state. I'll let you know what I find out."

"I appreciate it. Let's keep in touch," Noah said.

Candela said, "We're putting together a team to search the mine for Agent Sheffield's body and to gather further evidence, and Martinelli and Strong are packing to investigate her appearance and disappearance in Spruce Lake. But we need to confirm this new intel first. If we blow an ATF op, we'll have major problems."

"They should have told us," Hart said, frustrated, "but we have to go in quietly. Agents Martinelli and Strong will be flying into Ogdensburg first thing in the morning, but I instructed them to contact Detective Dillard first. If you need them, here are their numbers." She handed both Lucy and Noah business cards.

They shook hands and left. As soon as they got into the car, Lucy blurted out, "I'm so sorry, Noah. You're right. I should have told you immediately."

Noah let out a sigh and turned to face her. She couldn't read his face—Noah was only three years out of the Air

Force and still acted like the officer he'd been. "Sean is annoying, impulsive, and arrogant. He's also intelligent, knowledgeable, and courageous. There's no one else I would rather have on my team, but the fact remains, he's *not* on my team. He's on *your* team because he has one more redeeming quality—he loves you. I'm not his favorite person—" Noah put his hand up when Lucy opened her mouth to protest. "As far as the FBI goes, he has shown complete disdain for our mission, responsibilities, and rules. That he asked you to keep something from the FBI tells me he has no respect for your job or mine. That you chose to delay sharing the information tells me you're torn. Sean breaks the law whenever he wants—he always has a compelling reason, but where does it end? Someday he's going to land himself in hot water. He has an unusual knack for getting himself out of trouble, but he's going to make your life extremely difficult if you don't give him strict boundaries. And I fear he won't adhere to them anyway, so where does that leave you?"

Lucy rarely cried, which made the tears that burned behind her eyes that much more frustrating. Noah had clearly articulated each fear in her relationship with Sean and what it could potentially mean to her career.

"I understand. I *am* sorry, Noah. There's no one I'd rather work with in the FBI than you. I don't want to give you any reason not to trust me. I'll get through to him."

"If anyone can, it's you." Noah tried to smile, but it didn't quite work. He shifted in his seat and turned the ignition. "Love doesn't always work the way we want."

He wasn't looking at her, and Lucy had the distinct impression that he was thinking about a lost love of his own. She realized that Noah knew everything about her—her life was, unfortunately, an open book—but she knew next to nothing about Noah. There was much more to him than she had thought.

THIRTY-TWO

On the way back to the Hendricksons', Sean and Patrick stopped at the Callahan ranch. There was no answer at the door, which made Sean both worried and suspicious. Emily Callahan hadn't looked fit for travel, and after his argument with Henry, Sean hoped he hadn't pushed the old man into doing something rash.

Or maybe he did the smart thing and got out of town with his ailing wife.

At the lodge, Sean was torn over whether to tell Tim and Adam about Paul Swain's accusation that their father had been murdered. It came down to what Sean would want if he were in their shoes: the truth.

The four of them sat around the kitchen table and Sean filled them in on Weddle's murder and the highlights of his conversation with Swain. Then he said, "Swain believes that Bobbie had your father killed because he either went to the authorities or planned to go to the authorities about whatever operation Bobbie and her people have going on here."

"Dad was killed?" Adam stared in disbelief.

"There's no proof, but we think Jon Callahan knows who killed your father. I know this is difficult, but we don't have a lot of time. Patrick and I are going to find Callahan and stick to him like glue. He's up to his neck in this mess, but has his own agenda. I need you to help find Ricky Benson. He was manipulated somehow into setting that fire, and now I fear for his life."

"I can't believe Ricky's involved," Adam said. "He used to come fishing with Dad and me. Why would he do this to us?"

"I don't think there's anyone innocent in this town," Tim said.

"We need to get Ricky into protective custody," Sean said. "Detective Dillard is going to take him to his brother-in-law in Philadelphia—a cop he trusts—as soon as we find him. On our way into town, I checked at his house—he hasn't been back since he left me there yesterday. It's going to be dark in less than two hours. I'd like to get him out of the area before nightfall. Do you have any idea where he might be hiding?"

Adam paced. "None. I haven't seen him since I was seventeen and he was like eleven or twelve."

"I'm not going to lie. This is an extremely dangerous situation. Bobbie Swain has manipulated a lot of people. She's ruthless and vindictive. If she really ordered the murder of your father and the FBI agent we found in the mine, then she has been controlling this town for years."

"You're trusting the word of a convicted killer?" Tim said.

"I read between the lines."

"It sounds like you admire him," Tim said with disgust.

Sean forced himself to rein in his temper. "When lives are at stake, I'm not picky about who I deal with. The one thing I'm confident about is that Swain doesn't want his son dead or in the drug business. I promised I'd find and protect him. Ricky made some bad choices, but I'm not giving up on the kid, and neither should you. And, by the way, your father met with Swain in prison as well."

Sean hadn't wanted to get angry, but they were running out of time.

"Look," he said, "I had to understand how Paul Swain operated and how Bobbie Swain thinks so that I can stop that bitch. Trust me on this—she is far deadlier than either of her brothers."

"Adam," Patrick said, "put aside what Ricky did for now. Think hard. Where do you think he might possibly go to hide out?"

Adam asked, "Does he have a car?"

"Yes. It's not at his house and I didn't see it in town."

"There are two places he might go, if he stays in the area. The main entrance of the mine—there are two abandoned buildings, and lots of places to explore. The mine itself is dangerous, but we all knew how far we could push it. It was where we went to play as kids, or to make out as teenagers."

"Good. I need directions."

"The other place is across the lake—there's a rock grouping that looks like a family of bears. And when you get to the top, it's an amazing view of the valleys and mountains to the west. But the mine is easier to access."

Sean knew where he'd go if he were Ricky.

"I'll head up to the mine," Tim said.

"I'll take Bear Rock," Adam said. "I can get there on an ATV."

"Where's Annie?" Sean asked. "I don't think she should be alone."

"I sent her to stay with her sister in Massena," Tim said. "Until this is over."

"Be extremely cautious," Sean said, glad he didn't have to worry about another person. "Don't trust anyone. When you find Ricky, text me. We'll figure out if it would be safer to have Dillard come for him or you to take him out of town. Don't bring him back here—they could be watching. In fact, take a roundabout way to the mine, Tim. Look for tails. We don't want to alert anyone to our plans."

The four split up, and Sean and Patrick headed back to town. "I hope Noah hasn't taken off yet," Sean said, punching in his number.

"Why? We need the backup."

"I agree, but I have an idea to verify Swain's statement and maybe give us a leg up on what the fuck Bobbie Swain is planning. Other than me, Noah's probably the only one with the skill to pull it off."

Ricky had to get out of the empty house.

He'd done exactly what Jon Callahan had told him—stayed in the house, no lights, no fire. If there hadn't been plenty of blankets he'd have frozen his ass off. With his cell phone nearly dead, he decided to go to the car to charge it. He'd parked a quarter mile down an unmarked road from the Foster's vacation house. There was another cabin down here, abandoned. While his phone charged, he wandered up to Bear Rock. Before his death, Joe had taken Ricky here fishing numerous mornings. They'd usually cook up what they caught for lunch at the base of the rock. They'd rarely talk, but Ricky hadn't wanted to. It was great just hanging out with Joe, who never raised his voice, never lied to him, never brought up Ricky's father, the good or the bad.

Ricky sometimes talked about his mom. He missed her a lot the year after she died. He had resented Uncle Jimmy and the restrictions placed on him and the low-lying sense of fear that permeated the house. With Joe, Ricky had never been afraid. He could push everything out of his mind and just *be*.

He realized last night as he lay awake until dawn that the reason he'd decided to help Reverend Browne with the vandalism was because he was angry at Joe for dying, angry at Adam for wanting to change the place, and he desperately wanted someone to talk to. Reverend Browne was a man of God! He had buried Ricky's mother, and he'd been kind. And when Joe had died, he'd listened to Ricky.

But after what he'd seen at the church last night, Ricky knew that Reverend Browne wasn't his friend. The so-called holy man had used Ricky, and worse, he was working with the monster.

Ricky hated Aunt Bobbie so deeply that it scared him. He didn't like the rage and hatred buried deep inside. He'd had these disturbing feelings after his dad went to prison, after his mom died, after he found out Bobbie stole the money his dad had hidden away for his mom's cancer treatments. Joe taught him to let it go. To use it productively. To study hard and get good grades. To run off the negative energy. Ricky skied in the winter and ran in the summer, because sometimes the only way he could sleep and not remember the pain was if he was exhausted.

When Joe died, Ricky got angry again. In the isolation at the cabin, he realized that the reverend had used his anger, turning it against Adam and Tim.

Ricky sat at the top of Bear Rock and stared at the sinking sun. It had been a warm day, but now the air turned chilly. He stuffed his hands into his pockets, his fingers brushing against the small gun that Jon Callahan had given him last night for protection, but Ricky had never shot anyone. Could he kill a human being? He didn't know. Except, Aunt Bobbie wasn't human. She was a monster, through and through.

The sky was so clear, he already saw a few of the brightest stars shining from the heavens. Guilt and grief overwhelmed him, and he prayed that Adam could forgive him. He hoped Joe was up there and understood that Ricky didn't mean to hurt anyone.

A doe and her fawn walked by only twenty yards away, heading away from the clearing and toward the safety of the woods. Suddenly they froze, their ears at attention. Then Ricky heard what they did, a motor, far in the distance, but coming closer. The deer bolted into the trees, and Ricky almost followed, until he recognized the motor as belonging to an ATV.

He turned and saw the quad emerge from the woods and stop at the base of Bear Rock. Ricky remained alert, staying low on the rock, his hand wrapped around Jon's pistol. The engine cut out and the rider took off his helmet. It was Adam Hendrickson. He waved. Ricky didn't wave back.

He watched as Adam climbed Bear Rock. He slipped a few times, and Ricky scowled. They'd come here many times and Adam used to be so sure-footed. Now he was a soft city boy.

Ricky didn't budge when Adam sat down next to him.

"Leave me alone," Ricky said. He averted his face so Adam couldn't see that he'd been crying.

"Sean Rogan seems to think you and I need to talk."

"I don't want to talk."

"Talking to you isn't my idea of fun, either. Why did you do it? My dad *liked* you. He took you fishing and horseback riding, even when I wasn't around."

Saying nothing. Ricky stared at the horizon and wished he could disappear as easily as the sun.

"Listen, Ricky, there's a lot of stuff happening right now, and I'm willing to put this crap aside."

"Why? Go ahead, call the cops, have them arrest me."

"We're not turning you in."

"I wish you would." He meant it.

"You want your life to be over? For me to just send you off to juvie and be done with you? Do you think that's what my dad would have wanted me to do?"

"I don't know. I didn't—" He stopped. There was no excuse for what he'd done. He could have said no. He whispered, "I'm sorry."

"I know you are. Dad liked fishing with you, even when I wasn't here. I'm glad he had you around. I'm a little jealous that you knew him so well, and I only got him two months out of the year. But life isn't fair. Frankly, it sucks sometimes."

Ricky grinned, then masked it. Adam smiled. "It really does. But from now on, you're part of my family. That's what my dad would have wanted. And it's what I want." He paused. "I'm sorry about your uncle."

Ricky coughed to hide his sudden emotion. "Thanks."

"I need to call Sean and tell him I found you. Trust us, okay? Sean's going to keep you safe, but you have to listen to him."

"I didn't know Aunt Bobbie was in town. My father always hated her, but I never knew why. When he went to jail she came to see my mother. She—" He stopped. He couldn't do this. He didn't want to think about it anymore.

"Sean went to visit your father today. And we found out that Bobbie Swain had my dad killed."

Ricky shook his head. "It was a heart attack."

"He was poisoned. There was no autopsy because Doc Griffin signed off that he had heart trouble. I didn't know he *hadn't*. I should have been here. I could have saved him. Or at least known about his medical condition so that I'd known enough to demand an autopsy."

"Bobbie would have killed you, too, Adam," Ricky said. He stared at the glowing horizon. "She knew my mom had cancer and was going through chemotherapy. But with dad in jail and everything we owned seized by the government, we had nothing. Dad never had insurance because he had plenty of money selling drugs to pay for Mom's treatment. And she was getting better.

"Bobbie said she would pay for everything, Mom's treatment, our house, anything we needed. I thought she was an angel. And Mom told her no, said she was a monster."

Now the tears came and he couldn't stop them.

"Bobbie was furious. I thought she was going to hit Mom, so I stood between them. I would have killed her if she'd touched my mom, and I wouldn't have felt guilty."

"I would have done the same thing."

Emboldened, Ricky finished. "Bobbie said Mom would be dead within the year and I would be living with her in New York. Her exact words: 'I'll teach Rick the Swain family business like his father never had the balls to do.' I didn't realize until after she left that she'd stolen two hundred thousand dollars that my dad had hidden to take care of my mom."

He turned his head, hating the tears of rage that ate him up inside. Against his father for sheltering him so much that he didn't know what to do when threatened.

"How old were you?"

"Eleven. Mom died nearly a year later. We couldn't afford anything. Even my mom's inheritance from her parents—it wasn't big, but it would have paid for another round of chemo—the fucking FBI took it. After my mom . . . died . . . and my uncle Jimmy was my guardian. And for a while, it was okay.

"But after Joe died," he glanced at Adam, "Reverend Browne said I could hang out with him. I didn't know what he had planned. He's the one who wanted me to sabotage your place."

"Why did you run from Sean yesterday?"

"I didn't know why he would help me. Usually when someone offers to help you, they want to use you. But after I saw the reverend with Bobbie at the church, I was scared."

"So you went into hiding."

"I went to see Jon Callahan. My mom told me in an emergency I could go to Jon and he would help. But even Jon has changed."

"What did he say?"

"He told me to hide out at the Fosters' place and not leave until he came for me on Sunday. But I had to get out for a while."

"That's a good place to hide out. I'm going to let Sean and Tim know that I found you and we'll hang together until all this shit goes down. I don't want to be in the middle of it."

Neither did Ricky.

The Kelley Mine's field office was built up against the hillside, and though boarded up and abandoned for decades, it had been shielded from the worst of the weather and remained standing. It would be a good place to hide out—in fact, it looked like a good place for teenagers to party. Tim noted that some of the boards had been replaced within the last year or two, being far less weathered than others. But he didn't find any sign of Ricky here.

He approached the building cautiously, though he heard nothing except bird calls and the scurrying of rodents. He tried the boards. Most were firmly in place, but a few were loose, and he noticed one that appeared nailed in was actually on a hook.

His phone vibrated. He glanced down, and read a message sent simultaneously to him and Sean from Adam that he'd found Ricky and they were going to lay low at the Fosters'.

Tim responded that he'd meet them there, then pocketed the phone and assessed the building.

He carefully removed the large board, revealing a brand-new door with a padlock. Who would go to this trouble? There were plenty of abandoned buildings and houses in Spruce Lake. Why use this relatively insecure location?

He couldn't break the lock, so he tried the other boards. The plywood blocking the windows of the locked room had been nailed from the inside, so he couldn't get to those.

On the far side, where the building abutted the hillside, a two-by-four over one of the windows looked different than the others. Tim got out his Swiss Army knife and pried out the nails. He wouldn't be able to fit in through the opening, but he could see what was inside.

Tim shined his flashlight inside and his stomach turned sour.

An open box of C-4 explosives sat on the floor in front of him. It looked as though four bricks were missing. Enough to take out a building or three.

He surveyed the small room. There was a recent calendar on the far wall, a small metal desk and chair, and some boxes of wires and other electrical supplies.

The sound of a vehicle on the gravel road startled Tim. He propped the wood back up and skirted around the edge of the building to see who was coming. He heard but didn't see the car. He glanced at his truck, visible from the long drive. No sense in hiding. He bolted to his truck and reached the driver's side just as a big black F-350 came into view.

Two men with guns aimed at Tim jumped out of the slowing truck. He recognized them but didn't remember their names. The driver stopped and opened his door. Tim knew Gary Clarke from the Lock & Barrel.

"Tim Hendrickson, right?" Gary said.

"Hello, Gary."

"Funny thing is, we were looking for you."

"Funny thing that you found me here."

"Not really. We followed you from your place. I need Sean Rogan, but he wasn't there."

"I'll give you his number."

"Naw, you're going to tell him to meet you at your house. He's stirred up a bunch of shit, and I need to sit on him for a while, make sure he doesn't get himself hurt."

Gary motioned to one of the guys to grab Tim. Tim bolted, but hadn't gotten far when Gary shot him in the leg. He went down fast, vision blurred, hot bolts of pain shooting up his left leg. He grabbed his thigh. The bullet had gone in right above his knee.

One of the guys searched him, taking his knife, flashlight, and cell phone. He tossed the phone to Gary. "I'll just send Mr. Sean Rogan a little message that you'll meet him at the house in an hour." He looked at the phone, then started to laugh. "Shit, this is even better! I'm going to get a fucking gold star. We've been looking for that brat everywhere."

He grinned and said as he typed, "What time should

we meet?" A minute later he hollered and jumped in the air. "We've just redeemed ourselves, boys. I know where Rogan will be in an hour. We're going to get there first."

He pocketed Tim's phone and took his car keys. He tossed the keys to one of his partners. "Follow me." Gary glanced at Tim. Tim flipped him off.

"With that bum leg, I figure it'll take you a day or two to get back to your place, if you survive the night. Good luck."

They left.

The sun was nearly gone and the temperature would plummet. He glanced at the mine entrance, then at the outbuilding. The latter was closer, so he dragged himself over there.

He'd have to pry off another board or two to get inside, but he liked his chances of survival better in the building full of explosives than in the cold, deadly mine.

THIRTY-THREE

The sun was a thin line on the horizon by the time Noah flew Sean's Cessna over the greater Spruce Lake area.

Lucy had the Argus thermal imaging camera in her hands. "Is this going to work?" she asked. She was familiar with the imaging technology, but didn't think a handheld device had the range that surveillance aircraft did.

"It's top of the line," Noah said.

Lucy smiled. "Sean likes his toys."

"The weather is perfect and the plane is in good shape," Noah said, "but this is still a risky maneuver."

"I don't understand. Because of the trees? Or that it's getting dark? Do we have to fly too low?"

Noah glanced at her. "You didn't seem like a nervous flyer this morning."

"I'm not, usually." She wouldn't admit to it, at any rate. She didn't consider herself phobic about flying. She was just having a touch of nerves when they flew low over rolling mountains with trees suddenly popping up here and there while she looked for a barn full of cannabis through a thermal imaging camera.

"The terrain is not my primary concern. I've flown under far worse conditions. I'm more concerned about ground security. We may draw unwanted attention." He checked his gauges and slowly descended as they approached the town boundaries. "I don't think Sean realizes this is like finding a needle in a haystack."

They'd discussed strategy during the flight. Noah mapped the coordinates surrounding the greater Spruce Lake area and planned to fly in a circular pattern while Lucy monitored the thermal imaging camera. Barns or warehouses that might be growing marijuana would be easily spotted because of the extensive light needed to grow the crops indoors, which generated plenty of heat.

"Why didn't ATF inform the local FBI? That's protocol," Lucy said.

"Because they do whatever they damn well please." Noah shot her a glance. "A lot like your boyfriend."

"Is this going to be pick-on-Sean day?"

Noah grinned. "That might be fun."

Noah's phone rang. He glanced down at the center console. "It's Stockton. Answer it. I'm going to stay at this altitude so we don't lose him."

"Sean has a built-in cellular thingy," Lucy said, feeling stupid that she didn't remember the technical name.

Noah laughed, for the second time that day. "Why am I not surprised?"

Lucy answered the phone. "Lucy Kincaid."

"Hello, Lucy. Rick Stockton."

"Noah is flying. I'm putting you on speaker."

"Where are you now?" Stockton asked.

Noah said, "We're fifteen miles from the town proper. I'm beginning a circular rotation, starting wide. Lucy has the Argus. We're at the upper range of this unit's capabilities, but I still have visibility for the next forty minutes and can lower altitude if we see a potential hot spot."

"Good. I spoke to the ATF operations director in Brooklyn. Took me nearly two hours to reach him—I could have flown to New York and met him in person faster. He bullshitted me for the requisite ten minutes while trying to figure out what we knew, so I pulled my ace out of the hole and informed him that his operative shot at a federal agent who was on vacation and if he didn't give me everything he had, I'd make his life a nightmare."

"It worked?"

"As planned. But it's not good news. They have one deep undercover agent in Spruce Lake. Omar Lewis, going by the alias Omar Jackson. He's been in deep cover for thirteen months."

"That long?"

"A civilian contacted the DEA in January of last year regarding what he believed was an extensive marijuana farm. DEA was going to go in but ATF caught wind of the report and asked for leadership on it because one of the names in the file, Gary Clarke, was a known gunrunner with ties to the notorious Sampson Lowell. DEA stepped aside and ATF went in."

"Thirteen months is a long time."

"Yes, and there is no backup. Lewis reports weekly, and last asked that a team be ready within one hour on his call. Brooklyn has a team in Syracuse, which is two hours away. They informed Lewis, but he hasn't responded that he got the message. They're moving the team to Canton, but Lewis has yet to call them in."

"Anything else?"

"He's sending the files via courier, refuses to fax them. I swear, he's the most paranoid agent I've spoken with."

"Sir," Lucy said, "do you have a description of Agent Lewis?"

"Of course." The sound of flipping papers. "Thirty-nine, fourteen-year veteran of ATF. African-American—wait, I should say Jamaican-American. He was born there, came to the U.S. when he was three. Wears his hair very short or shaved, five foot ten, one hundred seventy pounds."

"The cook."

"You know him?" Stockton said.

"Omar is the cook at the Lock & Barrel. Sean and I saw him Thursday night. He stood out because he was the only black man we'd seen in town. No one paid him any attention, though. Reverse psychology—stand out so they don't think you're a cop."

"It worked. According to his boss, he's in with the number-two bad guy. But these past couple weeks, information has dried up. Lewis thinks there's a new player, but everyone's tight-lipped, so he didn't call in the cavalry yet."

"Did he report shooting at two civilians?" Noah asked.

"He didn't know, but isn't going to let his man get hung out to dry so refused to comment."

"Understood," Noah said. "Can he get word to Lewis about our presence?"

"He'll try."

"Sir, I don't think that's good enough."

Lucy said, "Who was the civilian who made the original report?"

"Joseph Hendrickson."

She glanced at Noah. "I think we—" She stopped as something flashed in the thermal camera. "Noah! Look!"

Noah glanced at the screen. "Bingo. Mr. Stockton, sir, we found our warehouse full of weed."

"I'll wait for your report."

Lucy shut off the cell phone and adjusted the camera. The red, orange, and yellow glowing colors over the external structure of the warehouse told them that it was well heated with high-wattage lights. "Wow. I didn't realize it would be so noticeable!"

Noah made a note on a pad attached to the console. "I got the location. We'll swing around and take another pass, then—"

"No—go north. Look at this." She pointed at the ground where there were clearings ahead.

As Noah headed north, one warehouse gave way to another about one hundred yards apart.

"Two warehouses?" Lucy asked.

"I think you're right." Noah looked at his map and the terrain below. "We're approximately four miles northeast of the town center. The population center is in town, and most of the larger-acreage properties are south and west."

"Could there be more?"

"Anything's possible, but look at the size of those buildings."

Trees dotted the area, which was relatively flat, but didn't provide a complete canopy. The warehouses may have once been barns—they were the same relative size and shape—but they'd been completely renovated. Likely insulated to keep down the cost of the electricity and heat. It would still cost a small fortune to run the facilities.

"I'm going east to follow that road down there," Noah said. "It appears that both those warehouses are accessible from it."

The road dipped into a valley and ended before the mountain began to rise again on the far edge of the Spruce Lake area, opposite from the Hendricksons' and Callahans' properties. Four new buildings were nestled in the valley, each half the size of the large barns they'd passed a mile away. A rambling ranch house spread out on the far side of the property, at the base of the mountain.

"Two of the buildings are possibles," Lucy said, showing Noah the screen. "The other two are dark. The house—very small thermal signatures."

Noah glanced. "People. We need to get out of here." He started his ascent and turned away from the property at the same time that three men ran from the house, and a fourth came from one of the buildings.

"They have semiautomatic rifles," Lucy said, sliding the camera back into its case.

She heard the rapid fire of the guns even over the plane's engine, sounding more like comic pops than weapons fire.

Noah increased speed and continued to climb. The window behind Lucy cracked. "Those are fully automatic," he said grimly.

A sharp metallic bang was followed by alarms in the cockpit and the sma'l Cessna dipped dangerously to the left. Noah's hands gripped the yoke, fighting to control their descent.

"It's the rudder," he said. "We have to land. Look for a road, an open field. No trees."

They were heading northwest and a small lake was directly beneath them. The sun was gone, they were flying in the twilight, and Lucy had a hard time distinguishing the terrain without any outside lights to point her to a road.

"Lucy, anything! I need to get her down while I still have some control." The propeller sputtered and Noah flipped a switch rapidly until it came back on.

Lucy saw a dirt road just the other side of the lake heading back toward the town. "On the left."

Noah glanced. "Twenty degrees left. I don't know if I can turn the plane."

As he moved the stick to go left the plane dipped precariously.

"Bad idea," he said.

"I don't see another road."

"I'm aiming for the field."

He couldn't regain the control he'd had before he attempted the turn, and they were dropping fast.

Lucy sat in the co-pilot seat, buckled in, gripping the strap hanging from the ceiling. Though Noah was tense, he had an aura of calm command even as the plane continued to fall. He worked the panel of switches and buttons like a master musician. There was a waxing crescent moon, hardly reflecting any light, but because the sky was cloudless and there was still a hint of light on the western horizon, she could make out the edges of the trees. The field was shorter than a football field with trees lined on the far end.

If Sean were landing under these conditions, he'd be talking to make both himself and her less nervous. Even when he was fully alert and in crisis, Sean always appeared relaxed and casual. Yet he had the same confidence that Noah had.

She missed Sean's manner. She could almost hear him saying, *"It'll get a little bumpy, Princess, but it's no problem for a Rogan."*

Noah said, "Get ready."

He had to turn the plane slightly to make it to the field and not hit the lake. The plane protested, sputtered, and fell three stories. Lucy's stomach rose and she tightened her grip. Noah leveled off for a few seconds, the tops of trees scraping the bottom of the plane, a thick branch hitting the front window. Lucy bit back a scream.

They touched the ground faster and sooner than she expected, and she bit her tongue. Blood filled her mouth and her eyes watered. She swallowed, her stomach queasy.

The plane bumped up, then came down hard. Noah held the controls firmly, trying to give no yield to the plane's natural momentum to turn or spin, but it was a battle between machine and nature and man, and they were losing, two against one.

The field was rocky and rutted, and they didn't roll, they bounced, coming down hard again. Lucy's head hit the side window. The window behind her that had been shot earlier shattered, the sound startling her, and this time she did scream. She couldn't hear herself over the noise of the plane.

Lucy had faced death before. While fear had been there, so had resolve and the will to live. Each time she'd had choices to make, and while her decision *could* have had a tragic ending, she was still in control. Having control kept her from panicking.

She had no illusion of control tonight. She could die, and it wouldn't be because she'd made the wrong decision, but fate. She could die, and Sean would never know she loved him.

He knows. He tells you often enough that you love him.

But he needed to hear it from her. Deep down, she knew he was waiting for it, insecure because she couldn't admit the depth of her feelings. Her nightmares now weren't just about her past. They were about losing Sean. Her fears held more power because they weren't just about her anymore, they were about *them.*

The plane lurched up again and Lucy saw her real fears, the ones she kept buried, in their full light: loss, loneliness, helplessness.

She had been so alone, even with her family surrounding her, until Sean walked into her life and taught her how to live and laugh. She was no longer lonely, in the deep, weary existence she'd had for years.

Love was a risk. Sean made it look so easy when he told her *I love you.* Yet when she looked at him, he was waiting. He was scared she didn't love him back, no matter how confident he was that she did. He needed her to admit it, because he knew she wouldn't lie.

She had to tell him.

She had to first survive.

The plane hit a boulder and forced them to an immediate stop, but the momentum kept the tail end going and she was looking at the ground through the front window. Then the plane continued to turn, and it hit the ground hard, upside down, and stopped.

She waited a minute, unsure if the plane was still moving, her heart racing, blood dripping from her mouth and head, her body bruised.

But she was alive.

"Lucy!"

"I'm okay."

"We need to get out." Noah undid his harness and turned himself around so he was squatting, his feet on the ceiling. "Shield your eyes."

He kicked at the door and it released.

Lucy fumbled with her harness, but her fingers weren't working right. She couldn't see what she was doing. Noah reached over and with one hand released the lock. She would have fallen on her head, but Noah took her under her arms and pulled her out.

"I'm okay," she repeated.

"You're bleeding and disoriented and shaking."

"Sorry," she said automatically.

He leaned her against the plane and said, "Sit for a minute. I'm going to grab what I can."

Her heart was racing and her hands were shaking as she brushed her hair away from her face and came away with blood.

Noah was at her side a minute later and took her hand. She tried to focus on him. "Lucy?"

"Fine," she said, her voice sounding as though she were speaking in a tunnel. "I'm fine."

He squeezed her hand.

"We can take a minute." He sat in front of her. "Let me look at that cut."

He shined a light in her face. "Good reaction, but you might have a mild concussion. I know I do." He opened a familiar black duffel bag. "Sean always comes prepared," he said. "Emergency supplies, extra guns, ammo. Black clothing—he even has a jacket in your size. And of course a first aid kit."

He took gauze and wiped the blood from her face, folded it, poured water on it, and wiped more. He then found a clean piece of gauze and said, "Hold this against the cut. I'm going to try to find a phone, then we have to go. They'll be able to find us real quick."

He stood and looked at the upside-down plane. "I don't think Sean will *ever* let me drive his car now."

Noah stepped away and Lucy smiled at his joke. She searched her pockets for her phone, but didn't find it.

In the distance, she thought she heard dogs.

"Noah?" she called.

He was already rounding the plane. "I heard them. We have to get out of here."

He handed her a gun from the duffel. "I can't find our phones, but there's a radio in the bag and when we find cover, I'll call this in."

He strapped the duffel to his back and pulled Lucy up. Her legs buckled and Noah caught her. "Okay?" he said.

She nodded. Noah wrapped his arm around her waist and helped support her as she started walking. "You just need to get your landlegs back," he said.

The dogs were getting closer, and now Lucy saw lights as well, but they were still on the other side of the lake. Once they reached the downed plane the dogs would pick up their scent.

They walked unsteadily across the field to the dirt road Lucy had seen from the air. It was easier to traverse than the rock-strewn field.

"I'm okay now," she said. "Thanks."

"Let's pick up the pace; I want to get off this road ASAP."

Over the barking dogs, they heard the roar of an ATV engine and they ran.

THIRTY-FOUR

The Lock & Barrel was nearly empty.

Sean and Patrick sat at the bar; each had a bottled beer in front of them that they hadn't drunk. Sean put down his phone. "That was Dillard. He knows where the Foster place is and is headed there now. ETA ninety minutes. Once Ricky is out of town, that's one less person we have to worry about."

"The bartender is very interested in us," Patrick said.

"It's pretty safe to say that he's probably in on it, too." Sean motioned for Trina to come over. She did so reluctantly. "Where is everyone?"

"Don't know." She shrugged, refusing to look at him. The bartender was still watching.

Sean smiled casually. "Odd for a Saturday night. We came in to say hi to Jon."

"I don't know where he is," Trina said.

Sean leaned forward. Keeping the smile on his face, he whispered, "I know there's trouble. I'm here to help."

She bit her lip.

"Smile," Sean told her.

She did. She looked ill. "Two more?" she asked brightly.

"We're good."

Sean waved to the bartender. "Reggie, do you know where Jon is tonight?"

"Nope."

"What about your boss?"

At first, Reggie didn't know what he meant. Then his eyes narrowed.

"Exactly. Your real boss. Where is she?"

"I'd tell you to get out of town," Reggie said, "but it's too late for that."

Reggie reached under the bar and Patrick had his gun out so fast Sean almost hadn't seen him move. "Keep your hands where I can see them," Patrick ordered. The bartender complied.

"Where is Bobbie Swain?" Sean said. "You can get her a message for me, right?"

Reggie glared. "I'm sure you don't want to do that."

"Tell her I know what's going on here, and there's a price for my silence. Have her call me and we'll talk. Got it?"

Reggie scowled.

"I'll take that as a yes." He put his business card on the bar and he and Patrick walked out.

"You bluffed?" Patrick said.

"I have to force her hand. If she thinks whatever they've got planned for tomorrow is at risk, she'll expose herself. If we can neutralize her, I can get Henry Callahan and his wife and Ricky Swain to safety."

"You know, it has yet to be proven that Bobbie Swain has committed any crimes," Patrick said.

"So she's wanted for questioning," Sean said. "Does that work?"

They got into the truck and Sean headed toward the Foster property on the far side of the Hendrickson land.

"You must know the woman is up to her neck in illegal activity," Sean said. "Drugs, perjury, conspiracy, murder."

"Without any evidence—" Patrick quickly added.

"Yet," Sean said. "That woman has been controlling this town for a long time. I just need one person to talk—and find whatever it was that Victoria Sheffield found that got her killed."

Patrick shook his head. "Yeah, wish it were that easy. When are Lucy and Noah getting back?"

"They should be done with the reconnaissance and landing at a small airstrip outside Potsdam."

His call to Lucy's cell went straight to voice mail. He tried Noah's. It rang six times, then went to voice mail.

He hung up. Cell reception in the air or the mountains was spotty. They'd left Albany nearly three hours ago, but they were making the loop around Spruce Lake searching for the drug warehouses Sean suspected were storing marijuana. Noah hadn't sent him a location yet to check out; maybe they hadn't found anything. Maybe Paul Swain had lied, hooking Sean in and diverting his attention.

Sirens cut through the air and Sean slowed down until he realized they were coming from the substation up the highway outside Spruce Lake and heading toward town. An engine and the chief's truck passed him.

"Scanner," Sean told Patrick.

Patrick opened Sean's laptop and logged into the law enforcement frequency for the area. Sean's program took the radio waves and converted them so he could listen over his computer.

Sean pulled over before he reached the turnoff that led to both the Callahans' and Hendricksons' places, and impatiently grabbed the laptop. It was his program; he'd find what he needed faster.

Small plane reportedly landed in distress three-point-two miles north-northeast of Highway 56 at marker A332. Survivors unknown.

Sean whipped the truck around and floored it, following the fire truck.

"We don't know—" Patrick began.

"We damn well know it's them. It's no fucking coincidence."

"Adam," Ricky whispered. "I hear cars."

He motioned for Adam to follow him to the back door, where they could see two trucks winding down to the valley where the Fosters' cabin sat. As they watched, the trucks rounded the last curve and turned their headlights to parking lights.

"We need to go," Adam said. "That's not Sean."

Ricky grabbed his backpack and Adam pocketed his gun and put on his jacket. They slipped out the back and were on the porch when the trucks stopped out front.

Vehicle doors opened and closed. "It's dark," a man's voice said.

Butch.

Butch was working hand in hand with Bobbie, but

Ricky knew no family loyalty from his uncle would save him.

Adam motioned to the edge of the porch. The house was on a slope, so they had to crawl under the railing and lower themselves down, falling the last four feet.

They crawled up the slope so they could observe the driveway. There were three men. "That's Tim's truck!" Adam said.

"Shh," Ricky admonished.

They both looked for Tim, but the guy leaning against the driver's door was Andy Knolls from the Gas-n-Go.

"Butch, search the house," ordered Gary Clarke. "Andy and I will walk the perimeter. Bobbie wants the kid alive, but he's a little prick. If I find him first, I'm going to teach him a thing or two about loyalty."

Ricky hated Gary. He wasn't from Spruce Lake; he was loyal only to Bobbie.

As they watched, the men disbanded. Fortunately, Andy went in the opposite direction of the slope they were lying against.

On the deck above them, Gary said, "We wait until the kid gets here—or Rogan. Whoever comes first. Bobbie wants Rogan for leverage, but either way, we can't go back empty-handed."

Adam and Ricky crawled along the slope at an angle so that when they emerged on the driveway, they weren't in the direct line of sight from the house.

Adam squinted at the driver's side of Tim's truck. "That looks like blood."

"Was your brother at the lodge?"

"He was looking for you at the mine."

Ricky didn't know how Bobbie's crew knew he was

here, but he couldn't think of any logical reason for Adam to turn him over to his aunt. And if it was Jon Callahan, why send him here in the first place or give him a gun?

"It'll take us twenty minutes to circle around to the ATV, but it won't take long to get to the mine entrance," Adam said.

Ricky hesitated. Adam said, "We can't stay here. He's my brother. I'm not going to bail on him. He needs help."

Ricky followed, still unsure what to do, but he didn't want to wait around here. "You need to warn Sean about Gary and Butch. Where's your cell?"

"In the house. Yours?"

"In my car."

"We'll get it when we pick up the ATV, tell Sean what happened, and find Tim."

Ricky hoped he wasn't making a mistake to trust Adam but he didn't see that he had a whole lot of options. They bolted across the driveway and disappeared into the dark.

THIRTY-FIVE

In the lights of the emergency vehicles, Sean saw his Cessna upside down in the middle of a small field. His heart tightened so fast he thought a heart attack couldn't be more painful. He jumped out of the truck and trudged across the field, barely registering that Patrick was behind him. Patrick was Lucy's brother and loved her as much as Sean did.

But he couldn't. No one loved Lucy like Sean. She was not dead. There had been no explosion, no fire, just the downed plane. She was unconscious maybe. Injured. But alive. She had to be alive.

"Hold it!" the fire chief called. Sean ignored him.

The pilot's door was open, the cabin empty. A temporary feeling of relief washed over him, immediately replaced by fear that they'd been thrown out on impact.

"Stop!" the chief called.

Sean told Patrick, "There's no one inside."

Patrick smoothed things over with the chief. "I'm Patrick Kincaid; that's Sean Rogan. It's his plane. My sister was inside."

"I'm sorry, you still can't be here."

"The pilot is a federal agent."

The chief frowned. "This is still a crash site."

While Patrick diplomatically argued with the fire chief to buy time, Sean walked around to the back of the plane. The plane had cut a deep path in the field. He saw the boulder it hit that caused it to flip over. But he didn't see a body. The rudder was completely broken off the tail from the crash, and he distinctly saw two bullet holes in the rear body of the plane.

Patrick approached. "I bought you two minutes. Noah and Lucy aren't here. They're okay." Patrick was trying to convince both of them.

"The plane was shot down." Sean pointed to the holes.

Then he noticed that the small external storage compartment was open. His duffel bag was missing.

"They're in trouble," Sean said, "otherwise they wouldn't have left."

He bent over to inspect the cockpit and spotted the thermal imaging camera. He didn't know if it had survived the crash, but he grabbed it.

"Let's go find them," Sean said to Patrick.

The chief called after them and Patrick turned around to hand him their business cards. "That's how to reach us. I'm sorry, we have to go."

Patrick drove while Sean checked the camera for damage. The case had protected it, in addition to the fact that this was one of the best-made, sturdiest devices Sean had ever worked with. He turned it on. The camera stored thirty images on its chip, and Lucy had taken six pictures that clearly showed evidence of marijuana greenhouses. The camera also marked their exact longitude and latitude.

"Paul Swain didn't lie to me. There are four warehouses."

"*Four*? Do you know how much pot you can grow in just one?"

"Oh, yeah, this is major. And this is just first pass. I wouldn't be surprised if there were more. There has to be a lot at stake for Bobbie Swain to return to town. Or she's just a psycho bitch."

Sean's cell vibrated. He looked down, hoping it was Noah or Lucy, but instead it was a code that told him someone was pinging his radio frequency. He switched his phone to radio and said, "Rogan here."

"It's Noah. Your plane was shot down but we're both okay. Can you track this signal?"

"Yes." He started typing on his laptop to run GPS, which he had in almost all his equipment. He directed Patrick to follow the signal to Noah's location. "Right at the main road."

"We're holed up in someone's house. They're not home, but the bad guys who shot our plane sent dogs after us and we can still hear them. I don't know how long I can hold them back."

Patrick turned on the highway and floored the gas.

"I have you. Five minutes. Keep the line open. How's Lucy?"

"Bumps and bruises, nothing broken but a little skin." He paused. "I'm sorry about your plane."

"I can replace the damn plane." He paused. "But if you even think about borrowing my Mustang, think again."

Sean heard Lucy laugh in the background and a weight lifted off his chest. She was alive, she was *fine*.

Patrick turned right on an unpaved road, following the GPS guide. Sean wished he knew the area better, because he could find a shortcut. But he couldn't risk it in the dark.

Over the radio, he heard dogs.

"Noah?"

There were shouts, and Sean heard Noah order Lucy to cover the rear. Someone was pounding on the door.

The two of them couldn't secure the house alone.

Noah shouted to make sure Sean could hear, "Four dogs and four or five suspects."

Sean checked his .45, then reached under the seat and grabbed his bag. Extra clips and a knife. He put the knife in his sock and pocketed the clips. "You ready?" he asked Patrick.

Patrick nodded.

They saw the lights from an ATV and a raised four-wheel-drive truck illuminating the house. Patrick turned off his lights and they rolled in silently, stopping to the side of the long driveway.

They both jumped out and ran along the edge of the property, behind a fenced chicken yard. Two of the suspects were behind the door of the truck, guns drawn, only a few yards from the house. One man stood behind the truck and controlled the dogs. Two more went around back. Sean held up his hand showing five fingers. Patrick confirmed the count.

"Dogs," Sean motioned to Patrick.

Patrick assessed the animals. "They're search dogs, not attack dogs."

"They look vicious to me."

"I'm pretty certain."

"You'd better be."

The dog handler had his work cut out for him, so he wasn't an immediate threat. Sean quickly assessed the area. There were no fences surrounding the property. "I have an idea." He motioned toward his truck. "Drive dark behind this chicken coop to the back of the house. I'll go on foot. On my signal, turn on the brights and that should buy us a minute. We'll disarm those in the rear and get Noah and Lucy out that way."

Patrick agreed, and Sean watched him move the truck into position before he ran low to the ground.

One of the suspects was about to kick in the door. Gunfire erupted at the front of the house, which startled him. Sean gave Patrick the signal and instantly, the back of the house was flooded with bright lights. Sean fired at each suspects' gun hand, disabling both men. He motioned for Patrick to disarm the two while he called, "Lucy! It's Sean!"

The door opened and Sean was relieved to see Lucy emerge. But he didn't have time for a reunion. "Patrick's grabbing their weapons. Get in the truck."

The gunfire stopped. Sean ran into the house and saw Noah behind a table he'd turned on its side. Noah took aim, but instantly saw it was Sean and tilted his gun down. "Out back," Sean said. "I'll cover."

Staying low to the ground, Noah ran past Sean while Sean fired four rounds out the front window that had already been broken by the earlier gunfire. As soon as Noah was clear, Sean followed him out the back.

He was punched from behind as soon as he was

about to exit. A gun was pressed into his head and his .45 was taken from his hand.

"Sean Rogan. My boss wants to see you. Come quietly, and she won't kill Henry and Emily. You remember them, right? You visited them yesterday. He said he didn't talk to you, but who do we believe?"

From the corner of his eye, he recognized the blond guy Bobbie had been talking to at the bar on Friday night. Ian.

"I should tell you, if I don't return with you or your girlfriend, Bobbie will kill the old farts slowly. She enjoys it. Come with me, and she'll shoot them in the head so they won't feel a thing."

Sean gauged the seriousness of the threat. He didn't know where Bobbie was staying, and they didn't have time to track her down. And after seeing what they did to Deputy Weddle, he knew they'd do the same to the Callahans.

"Sean! Come now!" It was Noah.

"I can shoot that guy, too. He's kind of bossy."

"I'll go," Sean said.

"Out the front. We don't need your friends getting trigger happy."

Ian snapped handcuffs around his wrists and Sean felt a surge of rage. He hated being cuffed, but went willingly. Ian pushed him to one of the trucks and into the backseat.

Sean recognized the guy sitting in the passenger seat. It wasn't hard; he was the only black man he'd seen in Spruce Lake.

"Go get the others," Ian told him. "Dead or alive. I'll wait here."

Sean fought against his cuffs. He may have just made the biggest mistake of his life.

Lucy helped Patrick secure the two men who Sean had shot in the hand. Both were bleeding, but neither injury was life-threatening.

"Noah, Sean hasn't come back out."

Noah went back inside the house. Something didn't feel right. Someone was watching her.

She reached for her gun at the same time she whirled around and faced a tall man with a gun pointed at her head.

"Frank!" a voice shouted from the corner of the house.

The man turned, taking his eyes off Lucy, and she dove toward the truck. A gun fired and Lucy almost thought she'd been hit, but she felt no pain.

Noah ran out of the house. His gun was aimed at a black man with a rifle. "Omar Lewis."

"Well shit, just go blow my cover after I saved the girl's life."

"Where's Sean?" Noah demanded.

"Bobbie wants him. She doesn't want you."

Omar fired his gun twice, into the side of the house next to the heads of two men who were tied up. "Don't say a word," he told them, "or I will kill you."

"What the hell did you do that for?" Noah said, not taking his gun off Omar.

"Keep it down," Omar said, his voice a low growl. "I have to leave the impression with the others that you and the girl are dead. If I bring you to Bobbie, she's going to only keep one of you alive. Trust me."

Lucy fumed. "Trust you? After you shot at us at the mine?"

"We'll chat later, sugar," Omar said.

Patrick also had his gun on Omar with one hand, and with his other helped Lucy up from where she'd dove away from Frank. She said, "There's four of us, we'll find a way to end this now. Noah—"

Omar interrupted. "I finally have Bobbie Swain Molina in the palm of my hand with Sherwood Lowell almost within reach and y'all come in and fuck it up. Do you know how long I've been setting up this sting? Tomorrow the biggest gunrunner in the U.S. would have been here, but I'm sure even Bobbie can't keep a lid on all this shit. Now I'm going to lose him, and have that bitch to deal with. Stay here until I'm clear. Meet me at the Lock & Barrel at midnight and I'll tell you where your man is."

"You have to tell him we're alive!" Lucy said.

Omar shrugged and slipped back around to the front.

Lucy almost ran after him, but Noah grabbed her and held her tightly around the waist. "Lucy. We'll find him." He turned her around to face him and gripped her firmly by the shoulders. "If anyone can get out from between a rock and a hard place, it's Sean."

She said, "But if he thinks we're all dead, he'll be reckless." She prayed Omar did the right thing.

Sean listened to the two men—Ian and Omar—but all he could think about was Lucy, dead.

"Where's Frank?" Ian asked as they drove away.

"The girl got the drop on him."

"I didn't like him anyway."

"Any word from the other team?"

"They're waiting for the kid to show."

Sean pulled at his handcuffs, rage fueling him. A primal cry escaped from deep in his chest and Ian glanced in the back with a smirk. "Don't hurt yourself, now."

"I'm. Going. To. Kill. You." Sean's breath came hard and fast and his vision clouded.

I'm sorry, Lucy. Oh, God, no.

His chest tightened to the point of physical pain, but he didn't care. Lucy was dead. He couldn't see her, hold her, kiss her good-bye. Just one last kiss.

Unshed tears burned his eyes and something deep inside twisted so tight that he felt broken. Paul Swain's words came back to him, in a haunting tone.

Vengeance is mine.

How could Sean live without her? It would be no life. If he got out of this alive, he would kill Ian and Omar and Bobbie Swain. He'd shoot them or choke them, but either way they'd be dead.

"Everything's working just fine now," Omar said from the passenger seat.

Ian disagreed. "Everything is fucked up, she's not going to be happy. Word is Lowell is backing down."

"That sucks, but maybe we can resolve it."

Ian laughed humorlessly. "He'll never work with her again. She's going to take out her anger on someone. Better him than me." Ian glanced in the rearview mirror.

Sean kicked the bench seat in front of him, over and over, the pain and anger still building inside until he thought he would explode, and still it grew.

Omar laughed. "Look, Ian, he's all choked up. Sorry, Romeo, it's not personal. But man, was your Juliet one fine lady."

Sean threw his body against the seat in front of him, not coming up with a plan, just reacting out of raw rage. Omar smacked him hard and Sean fell on the backseat, biting his lip to keep from screaming.

But his mind worked separate from his emotions. He repeated Omar's words over and over until he realized exactly what they meant.

Romeo thought Juliet was dead, but she wasn't.

Pushing the grief and anger aside, Sean focused on coming up with a plan. His emotions were still on overload, but he mentally repeated that Lucy was alive. He had to focus on his current situation, listen carefully, and take advantage of any opportunity.

He knew he didn't have a lot of time.

THIRTY-SIX

With Adam following in the ATV, Ricky drove his car to the Kelley Mine's main entrance. He was worried about being seen, but it seemed Gary Clarke and Uncle Butch were still at the Foster house waiting to surprise Sean.

He was preparing to send Sean a message about the trap and tell him what he was doing, but as he was about to press send, he feared that Sean was already in trouble—or dead. Instead, he called. A man answered who sounded nothing like Sean. Ricky almost hung up, then the man said, "Who's this?"

"Who's this?" Ricky responded.

"FBI Special Agent Noah Armstrong. You're calling the cellular phone of Sean Rogan."

Ricky sighed in relief. "I'm Ricky Swain."

"Are you all right?"

"Adam Hendrickson and I are looking for Tim. Three men came to the Foster house where we were hiding. They were driving Tim's truck, and are now waiting at the Fosters' for Sean to show up. My Aunt Bobbie wants him."

"And you are looking for Tim Hendrickson where?" asked the FBI agent.

Ricky hesitated. How could he be certain the man he was talking to was a real agent? And even if he was, he could be a bad cop—Ricky knew Deputy Weddle worked for his aunt.

"You still there, Ricky?"

"Yes."

"Sean's partner Patrick is with me. He says Tim was heading to the mine."

Ricky sighed audibly. He had to be legit, right? "I'm almost there."

"I need to advise you that it could be dangerous. It would be safer if you came into town. We're on our way to secure the Lock & Barrel and use it as a staging area."

"Adam is worried about his brother. We're headed to the mine first."

He heard voices, but couldn't understand what they were saying.

Then the cop said, "I'm not going to lie to you, Ricky. Your aunt has Sean."

"It's my fault. I should have found a way to warn him." Ricky frowned, wishing he knew what to do.

"It wasn't your fault, Ricky."

In the dark, he almost missed the road that led to the main entrance to the Kelley Mine. He turned quickly, and his car bounced down the long gravel and dirt road leading to the entrance. Adam was still right behind him. "I'll call you back," he said. "I'm at the mine."

"Ricky, promise me you'll find a place to hole up or get to the Lock & Barrel," the FBI agent said.

"All right."

"Keep your phone on you."

"I will." He hung up and stopped his car in front of the boarded-up building.

Adam was off the ATV before Ricky got out of the car.

"Tim!" Adam called, heading toward the mine entrance.

The door to the boarded-up building opened, startling both of them. Ricky reached for his gun, then recognized Jon Callahan.

"Jon!"

Adam turned around. "Where's my brother?"

"Gary Clarke shot him in the leg, but he's okay. Ricky, give Adam your car keys. Adam, take Tim to your house. Stay there; it might be the only place you're safe. Ricky, I need your help."

Ricky walked toward Jon. He didn't know what Jon had planned, but his mother had trusted him. Ricky needed to as well.

"No!" Tim shouted from inside.

"What's going on?" Adam said running toward the building. When he passed Jon, Jon grabbed him and pushed him to the ground. A gun appeared in his hand and Jon ordered Ricky, "Take his gun."

"What are you doing?" Adam asked. Ricky wasn't sure if the question was addressed to him or Jon. "Dammit, Jon! Are you part of this?"

He shook his head. "I'm part of the solution."

Ricky searched Adam and pulled his gun from his waistband. "I'm sorry."

"Did you plan this?"

"No, but he won't hurt anyone."

Jon grunted out a bitter laugh. "Not anyone who doesn't deserve it," he said. "Adam, Bobbie had your father killed. I have no choice anymore. She has to be stopped."

Adam slowly rose from the ground. "Sean told us he suspected my dad was killed because he'd contacted the authorities about some pot farms."

"It wasn't the marijuana; it's so much bigger," Jon said. "I turned my back on the pot because the town was surviving. What harm could growing a little weed do? It was better than the meth labs. But Joe figured out something else was going on. I agreed to help him find out what, but by then it was too late. Bobbie learned that Joe planned on turning over photographs he'd taken of her meeting with a gunrunner, a really nasty guy who's on the Most Wanted list. It's all coming to a head at dawn."

"Bobbie has Sean," Ricky said.

"I'm sorry." Jon turned toward the building.

Adam grabbed him by the arm and spun him around. Jon pulled back, held up his gun. "Don't do that again. I don't want to shoot you, but a bullet in the leg will slow you down."

"Didn't you hear Ricky? Bobbie Swain took Sean. He's in danger. You can't let her hurt him."

"I'm not letting her do anything," Jon said. "Until this week, she thought I was still in her pocket, that I was another one of her loyal lap dogs. I haven't been there for a long time. Just waiting for the right opportunity." He shook his head and stepped into the building. "I waited too long. She killed Joe, she killed Victoria, and I'm not letting her live through the night. But first, I have to make her suffer."

"Listen to yourself, Jon!" Tim spoke up from his spot on the lone metal chair in the building, which was really nothing more than a large, crumbling shack. His leg was bandaged, but he was pale and his eyes were bright with pain. Adam knelt by his side and checked the dressing.

"I know what I'm doing," Jon said.

"Who's Victoria?" Ricky asked.

"The woman I was going to marry." Jon motioned to the last three boxes in the room. "Ricky, that's the end of it. Grab them, one at a time, and take them to my truck."

"Don't help him," Tim said.

Jon ignored the comment. "Ricky, I need you to help set the trap. It's the only way I can make it work under the circumstances. It's my leverage to get my aunt and uncle to safety, and Sean if I can. I'll do everything I can to make sure you are safe. I owe it to your mother. I owe it to Jimmy."

"Jimmy?"

"I couldn't protect him, but I never wanted him to die."

Ricky asked, "Why did Bobbie kill him?"

"She didn't want him dead," Jon said. "She was furious that Victoria's body had been found. Jimmy didn't dump Victoria into the pit like she ordered. He'd laid her out properly. I promised him I was going to bury her this summer . . ." His voice trailed off.

"I don't understand," Ricky said.

"Victoria was my fiancée. I loved her. She was helping me plan a way to take down Bobbie, but Bobbie found out she was a Fed. And it's my fault she's dead because I told her it had to be off the books, I just needed some information. I didn't want her to get involved, but she overstepped and Bobbie found out. I don't know how, but she did.

"I couldn't have her dumped at the bottom of the mine! She wasn't garbage, she deserved a proper burial. Jimmy was just helping me. Tyler Weddle was freaking out that Bobbie had poisoned a federal agent, so Jimmy told him he'd take care of the body and Bobbie wouldn't need to know he flaked.

"Reverend Browne ordered Gary Clarke to bring Jimmy in alive. Bobbie would have killed him after the deal was signed, sealed, and delivered tomorrow, because then she can disappear again. She's real good at that. After she gets the money, she can hide. Certain people are definitely going to want her dead when we turn over the evidence that she killed her husband to start a drug war in Miami, all so she could prove something to God knows who."

All this was overwhelming, but it came down to the fact that Ricky's aunt was a monster. He picked up the box that Jon wanted him to carry. "Let's go."

"Thank you, Ricky."

Adam said, "Don't do it, Ricky. Don't be part of this."

"She killed your dad, Adam. She stole money. She is going to kill Sean Rogan, who you said was your friend. You don't know Bobbie like I do."

Jon said, "Adam, if you really want to help, get Henry and Emily out of the house." He glanced at his watch and began to grow more impatient. "They're tied up in the back bedroom, downstairs, where Uncle Henry moved my aunt after her stroke. I'm afraid

Henry is going to do something rash, and I won't be able to get to them for a while."

"You should put aside whatever foolish plan you've made and help your family!" Tim shouted.

Adam concurred. "We'll do it together."

For a split second, Ricky thought Jon waffled. He had no idea what Jon wanted his help with, but right now he could go either way. Whatever Jon thought was best. Because he was right about Bobbie—she was pure evil. She had to be stopped before anyone else got hurt.

Jon shook his head. "Uncle Henry understands. I have to do this. Victoria deserved better." To Ricky he said, "Take that box. We need to go."

They loaded the last of the boxes into Jon's truck while Adam helped Tim into the passenger seat of Ricky's Camaro. "I hope you both know what you're doing," Tim said solemnly as they drove off.

Jon followed them up the mine road to the highway. Ricky said, "I want to help Sean. I barely know him, but he was trying to help me and I feel like I owe him. And what about your uncle?"

"I'm hoping that when we start this series of events that Bobbie will be distracted enough for Adam to get Henry and Emily out of the house. I'd planned to get back there, but this works out much better."

"Is that where she took Sean?"

"I don't know. It's the best I can do for now." He glanced at Ricky. "I am really sorry about Jimmy."

Jon continued. "Jimmy called me for help. I couldn't. There was nothing I could do at that point, and I knew Bobbie didn't want him dead because of what your father and I have on her."

Ricky didn't respond at first, torn over what Jon was telling him about Uncle Jimmy. Then he asked, "Why didn't you and my dad just turn over the evidence you had on Bobbie when you got it? Why keep it?"

"Paul isn't a saint. Before he went to prison, Bobbie was playing a dangerous game with big-time drug dealers. Paul was having her watched. She killed a high-ranking lieutenant, and framed a rival cartel, then walked away with money and information.

"Before Paul could use the information he'd amassed, she set him up. He got sent away. But he kept the evidence—and she knew it. The only thing she didn't know was that he gave it to me. That's protected you for all these years. Bobbie would kill you just to spite your father."

"But that doesn't explain why you didn't turn it in when my dad went to prison."

In front of them, Adam turned the Camaro off the highway toward the lodge. Jon watched them a long moment, until he passed the private road and sped up.

"The same information that would put Bobbie in prison, or get her killed, would also be the end of Paul's life. The big drug cartels are ruthless and they always seek revenge. That Paul knew what happened and didn't give the information to the cops would get him more prison time, maybe—but because he knew and didn't give the information to one or both cartels? That will get him killed. Turning it over six years ago would have been suicide."

Ricky was beginning to understand the balance. He wanted nothing of the life his father had led. He didn't know if Jon had the solution, but anything was better than letting Bobbie go free.

"Okay, I understand. I'm in."

"Thank you." Jon turned off the highway toward the town proper, then passed through it.

"What is your plan?" Ricky finally asked.

"Destroy everything Bobbie Swain has built, not only here in Spruce Lake but everywhere she has her tentacles. Then set the final trap. When she steps in it, she's toast."

THIRTY-SEVEN

Noah slammed his phone on the table of the Lock & Barrel. "That was Tim Hendrickson. One of Bobbie's men shot him in the leg and left him at the mine. Jon Callahan showed up, then Adam and Ricky Swain. Callahan took off with several cases of C-4, and Ricky went with him. Voluntarily," he added.

They'd cleared the Lock & Barrel twenty minutes ago, which wasn't difficult since only Trina and two patrons were still there. Lucy suspected that everyone in town knew the FBI had taken over the bar, but there was nothing they could do about it now.

"Does Tim know what Jon has planned?" Patrick asked.

"Apparently, Callahan is out for revenge. He's planning on killing Bobbie Swain, but Tim doesn't know the details. Sean was right. Callahan was in love with Agent Sheffield and Bobbie Swain had her killed because she was an agent."

"Explosives?" Lucy said. "If he wants revenge, why blow something up?"

Omar Lewis stepped into the bar. "Because Jon Callahan has fucking gone off the deep end."

Noah had his gun on Omar as soon as he appeared at the door. He lowered his weapon. "That's a good way to get yourself shot."

"Then you're not a very good agent," Omar snapped. "I have a key. And so do half the bad guys in this town. I'd suggest you block off the service entrance, and that one," he jerked his finger toward the back room, "to protect your asses."

Noah said nothing, but walked past Omar and headed to secure the other exits.

Lucy demanded. "Where's Sean?"

"At the Callahans' spread. For the time being, he's leverage. She's not going to kill him yet."

"That doesn't make me feel better," Lucy said. She turned to Patrick. "We need to go get him out."

Patrick nodded grimly, looking first at Lucy, then at Omar. "First we need a plan."

"How can we trust this guy?" Lucy said. "He shot at us at the mine—he could have killed us."

Omar looked at her with disdain. "I was a sniper in the military. I intentionally missed. You're still here."

A jolt of sharp anger hit her. Lucy raised her hand to slap him, but Patrick grabbed her wrist. "Lucy, you have every right to be angry, but let's put this aside for now. Slap this jerk after we rescue Sean—that's our number one priority."

Omar said, "Like hell it is. He's a big boy and trained to take care of himself. We have a lunatic running around who's going to blow up something, maybe this whole fucking town, if we don't stop him."

"And then what? You won't be able to make your big bust?" Lucy countered. "Lives are at stake!"

"And lives are at stake if we don't stop a very dangerous man called Sampson Lowell. It's not just about the guns Bobbie Swain is going to store and ship for Lowell—it's *him*. He's my number one target. The guns that take down cops in street fights? They pass through Lowell's operation. The guns making their way to gangs, killing twelve- and thirteen-year-old kids? Lowell. The guns going to Mexico for the drug smugglers to import their shit? Again, Lowell. He is *the* pivotal cog of the illegal domestic gun trade and if he gets wind of the shit going down tonight, he'll be three thousand miles away." As Omar spoke, his eyes brightened and a vein in his temple throbbed. Sampson Lowell was his passion, his religion, his one focus. Lucy realized that nothing she could say would convince Omar that Sean's life—that anyone's life—was more important than taking down this illegal arms dealer.

Lucy looked over to see Noah standing in the doorway, listening. Omar saw him too.

"Agent Kincaid, may I speak with you for a moment?"

Lucy looked at him quizzically, then followed him into the storage room. "Isn't 'agent' a little premature?"

"Omar needs to think that you have as much authority as he does, because you're going to find Callahan and the Swain kid."

"I'm getting Sean."

"Let me do that. I'm taking Agent Lewis with me. I don't trust him."

"But if Sean is injured—"

"An FBI agent needs to take orders. You're the psychologist here. You figure out where Jon Callahan is going, and you're the one who can talk him down. You saw what I saw—Omar has tunnel vision. So does Callahan. Our priority is to save our team, Sean, and the innocent people in town. But I think we can do that and defuse the situation enough to set a trap for Sampson Lowell. If Omar is right and he's coming here personally, we can't miss this opportunity to capture him. But not at the expense of people's lives."

Noah was right. Her mind ran through scenarios, thinking like Jon Callahan, trying to understand his grief and guilt over losing his love, Victoria. His narrow-minded need for revenge against Bobbie Swain. "I understand."

She knew what was expected of her as a professional; she needed to put her personal feelings aside. Extremely difficult when the life of the person she loved was in grave danger. But she trusted Noah as much as she trusted Sean. For her, such faith was rare, and it had taken her years to develop the ability to have faith in anyone.

He hesitated, as if not quite sure how to reassure her. He reached out and put his hands on her shoulders. "I *will* rescue Sean. It's becoming kind of a habit."

"Don't tell him that." But Lucy cracked a half-smile.

"He saved my ass today which made us even, and I kind of prefer being one up on Rogan."

They walked back into the bar. Noah told Omar the plan hadn't changed and Lucy filled in Patrick.

"Sean will be okay," Patrick said to Lucy as much as himself. "He has nine lives."

"How many has he already used?"

Behind her, she heard Omar Lewis raise his voice. "I don't work with partners. You have no authority!"

Noah was firm. "My boss and your boss came to the conclusion that shooting at civilians, even without the intent to kill, is gross and negligent behavior. You've crossed the line, and I know all the reports you haven't filed, the check-ins you've missed, the orders you've disobeyed. I will take your badge and disarm you now, or you can do what I say."

"Fuck it all, I guess I have no choice."

"Good. You understand." Noah nodded to Patrick and Lucy. "I'm getting Sean."

The distant rumble of a powerful explosion shook the foundation of the bar and rattled the glasses. Lucy grabbed the counter and watched as three glasses fell off a shelf and hit the floor behind the bar.

"Holy shit!" Patrick exclaimed.

Omar kicked over a table. "I'll kill him!"

"Stand down, Agent Lewis!" Noah demanded.

"That came from the marijuana warehouses. Callahan must have blown them up! Do you understand what this means? Thirteen months of the perfect setup, gone." He threw a chair across the room.

Noah rushed Omar and pushed him against the wall. Several pictures fell to the floor, the glass breaking. Omar pushed back, but Noah had his forearm against his chest and the strength of both training and anger. "Listen to me, Lewis," Noah said. "I will not repeat myself. I am in charge from this moment forward. You will control your temper. You will do exactly what I say. Do you understand?"

Omar bared his teeth, breathing hard, his eyes narrowed. "Yes. *Sir.*"

Noah stepped back and Omar put his hands on the bar and looked down. "If you only knew how many deaths Sampson Lowell is responsible for."

Noah offered his understanding. "We'll get him. It might not be tonight, but we'll get him."

"Before how many more people die?"

"Are you with me? Or do I have to lock you in the storage room?"

"I'm with you."

"Good, because we're short on numbers and I need everyone working together."

Lucy had some sympathy for Omar and his fury at Sampson Lowell. There were some people in the world who didn't deserve to live, who were individually responsible for destroying the lives of countless others. There was no doubt in her mind that Lowell was one of the few so evil and ruthless, he needed to be destroyed. And she wished she could be part of taking him down, because she had known others, like him, who were so deadly that the justice system wouldn't be able to stop them.

But love had to win over hate, and saving Sean took precedence over stopping a bad guy.

"There will be another chance to take down Sampson Lowell," Lucy told Omar. "But if Sean dies, he won't have a second chance."

After Adam left Tim at the lodge, he drove his old beat-up four-wheel-drive truck as close to the Callahan property as he dared. He didn't know what kind of security Bobbie and her people had surrounding the place, but if Gary Clarke and the others were still at the Fosters' house, at least her team was divided. He knew these woods as well as anyone who had grown up in Spruce Lake.

The only way to get to the house and rescue Henry and Emily was to run through a clearing. He'd been in the house several times in the past, and from this angle, he could see the kitchen and living area brightly lit on the right, and a dim light on the opposite side of the house. All blinds were closed, and he hoped Jon was right that Henry and Emily were in the downstairs bedroom.

He sprinted across the clearing toward the faint light on the left, praying he wasn't shot in the back.

THIRTY-EIGHT

Tied to a chair in the Callahans' dining room under the reproduction of *The Last Supper,* Sean had been watching Bobbie Swain for two hours. She was a walking contradiction—strategic about her business, but with no common sense. Her voice had a melodic lilt, but her words were crude. She was volatile, but maintained a tight control over herself, so tight that Sean could see the battle raging behind her green eyes.

In fact, her temper was simmering, ready to boil over. She was having a harder time controlling herself, which could be problematic. When she was in control, she was shrewd and smart; when she was out of control, she was more of a loose cannon.

He needed to use Bobbie's temper against her, but *how*? An explosion brought his strategizing to an abrupt halt. Bobbie completely lost it. Any chance of calming her down or reasoning with her was gone.

She knew exactly what had happened and who to blame, which made Sean think the explosion wasn't wholly a surprise.

"I want Jon Callahan here!" she screamed at the guy named Ian. "He's the only one who has access to my explosives. I never thought he had the balls to fuck with me."

"Omar is out looking for him."

"Callahan walks in here, he's dead. The deal is *OFF*! You think Sampson is going to show up now? Do you know what Callahan has done? I had it all planned so perfectly. I would have slid into Sampson Lowell's operation so smoothly I would have ruled a bigger kingdom. I will slit Callahan's throat!"

"Bobbie." Ian's voice was calm, but Sean saw the concern in his eyes. "We should disappear. There will be cops and Feds swarming this place in under an hour."

"No, no, *no*!"

Ian was right, but Bobbie wouldn't listen to him.

"I know this area better than anyone," Bobbie said. "I'll get out just fine even if there are a thousand cops! I want the rest of the explosives, I want my money, and I want Jon Callahan on his knees begging me to kill him."

Sean had a choice comment, but kept it to himself. The last time he'd spoken, she'd hit him with a lamp, and his head still ached. With her extreme volatility, she'd likely shoot him next.

Ian's phone rang. As he looked at it, Bobbie snatched it from him. Her face reddened and her hand shook as she answered. "I will kill you, you fucking traitor!"

Obviously, it was Jon on the other end.

"Your family is as good as dead! Get them, Ian, so Jon can hear them beg for their lives!"

Sean strained against the handcuffs. His wrists were

chafed and sore, and he couldn't slip off the restraints. He had to find a way to help Henry and Emily.

Bobbie sneered into the phone. "Don't play me, Jon. I know you. You might think you've won, but I will kill you. You'll suffer more than you can imagine. If you think I don't know how—"

Ian returned to the living room without the older couple.

"Where are they?" Bobbie spat. Her face was red, her tone livid.

"They're gone. They must have left by the sliding door—"

"How did they get out? They were tied up! Are you against me, too? Are you working for Paul? Are you screwing him, too?"

"Bobbie, I've always been on your side. Only your side." Ian had his hands up. He knew she was volatile, but he thought he was safe. Protected.

After only two hours with this lunatic harridon, Sean knew differently. *No one* was safe from Bobbie.

"How did they escape? Tell me!"

Ian hesitated. That was his mistake, Sean realized.

"Did you do it?" Bobbie screamed. "Did you let them go?"

"Absolutely not!" Ian said. "I tied them together with duct tape on the bed, just like you told me to."

"And you're telling me that the old prick and his dying bitch just slipped out of the tape and walked away? Is that it?"

"No—I mean, someone cut the tape. It's there, on the bed. I swear."

"*Someone* cut the tape? *Someone* let them out? Do you understand what this screwup means? I lost my collateral with Jon Callahan! Do you think he cares about the fucking private investigator?"

She turned her gun on Sean, who sat just on the other side of the opening into the dining room. Sean sat stone-faced. He wasn't going to say a word, not when Bobbie wasn't thinking straight. She had to know that all her plans were already destroyed. If she were thinking, she'd get out of town now before the authorities arrived. With the explosion, they'd be sending in the troops and blockading the roads. But her rage interfered with her judgment.

"Bobbie," Ian said in a calm voice. "I'm sorry. I'll find them, bring them back here."

"No, no, NO!" Screaming like a child throwing a temper tantrum, Bobbie turned the gun on Ian and shot him three times in the chest.

Eyes wide, Ian hadn't seen the attack coming. He staggered for an agonizing five seconds before falling heavily to the floor, dead.

Tears streamed down Bobbie's face. "You made me do that! Why did you make me do it?"

Jon must have said something on the phone—Sean had almost forgotten he was still on the line. Bobbie turned her attention back to the conversation. "You're dead, too, you fucking bastard." She hung up.

Reverend Carl Browne—who was no man of God as far as Sean was concerned—ran into the room from down the hall. Sean had seen him when Ian and Omar first brought him in, but then he'd disappeared and Sean had assumed he'd left.

Carl stared wide-eyed at Ian's bloody corpse. "Why?"

"Henry and Emily Callahan are gone!" She threw a

lamp to the floor. "Jon Callahan just blew up my warehouse. That was *mine*!"

Carl evidently knew how to handle Bobbie. He changed the subject. "I found some of the disks, Bobbie."

She caught her breath, and smiled. "Thank you. For once, someone listens to me and does what I ask! And my money?"

"I searched the entire house. It's not here."

Bobbie whirled around, knocking a row of dainty figurines off a shelf. They flew halfway across the room and shattered on the hardwood floor.

"Where's Jon?"

"He set off the explosions," Carl said. "You know where he is."

"He wouldn't dare. I'll push him down that hole myself if he touches my stuff."

Carl glanced at Sean. "Should we kill Rogan now? I don't see any advantages to keeping him alive."

Bobbie glared at Sean, as though debating the value of his life.

Sean tried to avoid showing any reaction. A raw anger had him wanting to lunge for her throat. "He's probably still worked up about what happened to his girlfriend," Bobbie said. "But right now, he's the only hostage we have. With that explosion, the fucking cops will be all over the place, we may need a shield." She sneered at Sean. "And if you make this difficult, I'll spend my entire life hunting down every person you've ever cared about."

Carl's voice was calm. "Let's go to the mine and collect what's ours, then leave. The Feds will have enough to sort through. By the time they realize we're not here, we'll be far away." He glanced at Sean. "I'm still not sure what we do with him after we get out of the mine."

Bobbie stared at Sean for a long minute.

Then she smiled, and a shiver of fear ran up Sean's spine.

Adam carried the frail Emily Callahan from his truck into the lodge, followed by Henry.

"How is she?" Tim asked, leaning forward on the chair.

"She's scared and disoriented," Adam said. He carried her into the downstairs guest room. He told Henry to help himself to anything he needed, then he left Henry at her side, talking to her in soothing tones.

Adam returned to the living room and sat across from where Tim lay on the couch, his bandaged leg stretched out in front of him. He kept his voice down when he told Tim what had happened. "Bobbie Swain had them tied with duct tape. I cut them out, but Emily's wrists are raw and bleeding. You saw Henry—he looks like a ghost. How could anyone treat them like that?"

Tim said, "I called Agent Armstrong and told him about Jon Callahan and the explosives—then not fifteen minutes later, there was a huge explosion. You heard it. I think it was on the northeast side of town, up near the valley."

Henry stepped into the living room and shuffled over to a chair, where he sat heavily. "I gave Emily some cough syrup to help her sleep." He rubbed his eyes. "I need to get her to a doctor, but for tonight she's safest here."

"You both can stay as long as you want."

"I'm so sorry for everything. I should have told you at the beginning. I didn't know everything, just bits and pieces. Right now I have to stop Jon. It's my fault—I didn't realize that he was waiting for my call to start blowing things up. But right after I called and told him Emily and I had gotten away, I heard the first explosion."

"It's not your fault, Henry," Adam said. "I think Jon would have blown up the warehouses either way. You didn't do any of this."

"But I remained silent. For far too long. Jon's going to die. I'm the only one who can talk him out of this madness."

Tim rubbed his face. "I would go, but with my leg—and someone needs to stay with Emily. I'll make sure she's cared for."

"Thank you, Tim. You're a good man." Henry looked from Tim to Adam. "Your father would be proud of both of you."

Adam nodded. "For him, we need to end this peacefully. No one else has to die. Do you know where Jon is?"

"I don't know for certain. But I overheard Carl Browne talking to one of his people that the meeting was still on at dawn in the church. If Jon knows about that, and he has more explosives, then I think he'll go there."

Adam caught Tim's eye. Jon definitely had plenty of explosives to blow up anything he wanted.

Noah and Omar were hidden by bushes on the edge of the Callahan property, their breath visible. There was just one vehicle in sight, identified by Omar as the rental that Ian Galbraith, Bobbie Swain's right-hand man, had been driving. There was no sign of movement in the house, and the only noise was from emergency vehicles headed to the fire on the far northeast side of Spruce Lake.

Noah assessed the house. The brush and grass had been cleared for a hundred feet surrounding the house, but they had the advantage of darkness.

"You're sure the alarm is only on the house?" Noah asked.

"I'm sure."

On Noah's signal they moved in, circling the perimeter until they were in the rear of the house. Still no movement visible inside. Lights shined in a rear bedroom.

Gun drawn, Noah peered around the corner, looking for shadows or movement. All he saw was scraps of duct tape and ropes on the floor next to the bed.

The sliding glass door was cracked open, just a fraction. Noah motioned to Omar who silently pushed open the door.

Silence. No alarm, no voices.

A whiff of gunpowder hung in the air.

And the scent of blood.

The primary reason Noah hadn't wanted Lucy with him was because of the very real possibility that Sean was dead.

Omar looked as grim as Noah felt. He motioned to the ATF agent to open the door on the far side of the room. Noah put his back against the wall while Omar opened it and went out low. Noah aimed high.

Still no sounds.

They went down the wide hall side by side, Omar checking the doors to the right, Noah to the left, until they reached the end, which branched off—the left to the living room, the right to the backside of the kitchen. A quick look in the kitchen showed no one was there.

In the living room, they found the body. Noah breathed a sigh of relief.

"She killed Ian?" Omar was shocked. "They were bed buddies. Screwed like rabbits. Rumor was they got off killing together. He worshipped her."

"Seems she felt differently," Noah said. He looked around the room while Omar continued searching the house.

"All clear," Omar said when he returned.

Noah stared at an overturned dining chair and two broken lamps. "Sean, where the hell are you?"

Ricky huddled in his jacket outside the mine. The night was frigid, but still.

"How do you know Bobbie's going to show up here?" Ricky asked Jon.

"She wants her stuff."

Ricky almost didn't ask, but he was curious. "What stuff?"

"Do you know what C-4 goes for on the black market?"

"That was hers?"

"It was the down payment from the gunrunner she was supposed to meet with in the morning. That and a hundred thousand, which she'd already spent. The C-4 is worth more than that, but harder to move. She sold some and hid the cash until she could find a way to launder it properly." Jon laughed.

"She thinks she can play God and get away with it because she has for so many years," he said, sobering. "It ends tonight. Are you with me, Ricky?"

"Yes." He didn't know what else to say.

"There's one more warehouse. You do the honors." He held the remote detonator out for Ricky.

Ricky hesitated, but only for a moment. Drugs had driven his father, even if he hadn't done them himself. Drugs had destroyed his family, putting his father in prison and leaving his mother at the mercy of a monster. Drugs had fueled Bobbie's greed and revenge, and he didn't care if it was meth or pot—as long as there was a drug business in Spruce Lake, the town would never be free.

He flipped the switch and pressed the button. Nothing happened for two seconds.

Then the last explosion was twice as powerful as the first.

THIRTY-NINE

The blast from the latest explosion knocked Lucy and Patrick to the ground, and it was just good luck that they weren't any closer to the warehouse. Inside the structure the marijuana burned. They ran back to the truck, and Patrick sped away.

Lucy had barely caught her breath. "Jon's not here. No one is here."

"He's remotely detonating the warehouses."

"How far can he be?"

"Bombs aren't my specialty, but depending on the device he could be miles away."

"What will he target next?"

"He's already taken out the four warehouses. That's it."

"He has a bigger plan," Lucy said. She looked out the window, the horizon now ablaze. She was thankful it was spring and the ground was still moist from winter; the explosions could have started a severe forest fire. Even now, the firefighters had their work cut out for them. They had to wear special equipment or risk being drugged from the burning marijuana. Toxins in the air put everyone at risk. She hadn't heard of anyone dying just by being stoned, but she knew many cases of impaired drug-users doing stupid things and getting themselves killed.

Patrick's phone rang. "Get it—it's Adam."

Lucy answered. "This is Lucy. Adam?"

"I'm with Henry Callahan. We're at the church—Jon's not here. No one is."

"Does Henry have any idea about where else Jon might go?"

Lucy wanted to call Noah, but knew he'd contact her as soon as he had word about Sean. Not knowing was eating her up.

"None. He could still show up here. This is where they're supposed to meet the gun guy tomorrow."

"He's not going to show, not with all this police and fire activity. Which is," Lucy said, "probably exactly what Jon wants. To ruin Bobbie."

"Not kill her?"

Lucy considered whether Jon's revenge was more fatal-minded. She put herself in Jon's shoes. If Sean died—her heart skipped a beat, and she forced herself to think like a professional. If Sean died, how would she feel? What would be her raw reaction?

She'd want revenge. Tonight. And she would probably take it. But after four months? On a specific day, to also thwart the gun deal? She wouldn't. It was cold and methodical. Her revenge would be out of pain and anguish, not a calculated plot of murder.

"Why don't you stay there," she said to Adam. "In case Jon shows up. Let me know."

She hung up.

"That look on your face," Patrick said. "You're concentrating."

"There's no look on my face."

"There is. Think. Where would Callahan go? If he's dead set on getting revenge?"

"Wherever Bobbie is."

"The Callahan house."

"Noah would have told us. Unless something happened."

"I'll head that way." He sped up.

She sent Noah a text message. When they were only five minutes from the Callahan turnoff, Noah called her.

"Is Sean okay?" She didn't want to sound desperate, but she felt desperate.

"He's not here. Swain's bodyguard is dead. We think Bobbie took Sean with her. Any idea where?"

Her stomach twisted painfully. "Why would she take Sean with her?"

Noah didn't answer. Of course Lucy knew why: a hostage. She said, "If she encounters roadblocks she needs a ticket out."

"I have Ricky's number," Patrick said. "Call him."

"Noah, I'm going to try and reach Ricky. I'll let you know what I learn."

She hung up and dialed Ricky. He didn't answer. She sent him a text message.

Bobbie kidnapped Sean. We think she's going to either leave town or find Jon. Where are you? Are you still with Jon Callahan?

"Jon is the one with the control right now," Lucy said. "He's the one who wants revenge. As soon as I found Victoria Sheffield's body, Bobbie would have to know she'd be ID'd and the FBI would sweep in. Yet she stayed. Why?"

"Because she was playing the odds that Sheffield wouldn't be ID'd until later?"

"Perhaps. A narcissist, maybe? No one is as smart as she is? Not even the cops. That's why she had the body moved. If they don't have a body, they can't ID her."

"She didn't realize you're smarter."

"And Jon was in love with her." Lucy tried to put herself in Jon's shoes. For him, the real crime was Bobbie's killing Victoria.

She texted Ricky again.

Are you at the mine? Please tell me if Bobbie is there with Sean. He's in grave danger.

"Tim and Adam said the C-4 was stored at the mine, right?" she asked.

"Yes."

"And that's where Bobbie dumped Victoria's body. Vengeance. Jon wants her in the mine. For him, it's closure. Doing what he should have done months ago."

Ricky responded.

She's coming.

"We have to get to the mine. Ricky just confirmed Bobbie's on her way!"

As she sent Noah the information, she prayed they weren't too late.

* * *

Sean kept quiet during the drive from the Callahan house to the mine. Carl drove and Bobbie sat in the passenger seat, playing with her gun in her lap. Handcuffed in the backseat, he listened to their conversation as he considered his options.

Sean gathered that the explosives came from Sampson Lowell. He'd used Bobbie's operation to transport three cases to a domestic terrorism group. Sean tried to figure out who and where the group was, but Bobbie wasn't specific, nor did she seem to care. The group didn't have the funds for the entire shipment, so Bobbie had kept the remainder, which Lowell agreed to let her have as a sign of good faith in their gun distribution agreement.

As best he could figure, Lowell wanted to use Bobbie's pot warehouses to store the extensive collection of guns he sold—to anyone from foreign governments to revolutionaries to street gangs. Lowell didn't have a secure storage facility in the Northeast and while Spruce Lake was remote, it had the advantage of a nearby private airstrip, privacy, and an established and protected distribution network.

When the Hendricksons announced they were opening their resort, Bobbie feared tourists would come across her pot farms, and Lowell was nervous about the added influx of people. Bobbie wanted to delay the resort opening, at least until her operation with Lowell was up and running. Carl came up with the sabotage plan, thinking the Hendricksons wouldn't be able to open on time. When it became clear they still planned to open over Memorial Day weekend, Carl instructed Ricky to burn down the main lodge.

Bobbie had sold the remaining C-4 she'd gotten from Lowell and was supposed to deliver it to the buyer next week. That Jon used some of it to blow up her warehouses meant she couldn't fulfill her obligation. That put her name and trustworthiness at risk—not good for business. Worse, though, was that she'd just lost her entire inventory of weed, meaning she wouldn't be able to fill orders for months. Nor were her secure warehouses even standing. They would not be stowing Lowell's guns anytime soon.

Jon Callahan had effectively destroyed her entire operations in one explosive night.

Carl said, "Shoot him on sight."

"Don't tell me what to do," Bobbie retorted.

Sean couldn't see anything through the dark windows of the moving car. He calculated it would take only ten minutes to reach the mine. *Think, Rogan.*

"Arguing with Jon will only delay our departure."

"I want my money and the rest of the C-4."

If Sean were in her shoes, so would he. She needed the money to stay free, and alive.

"There are only a few places he could have put it. It's either with him or at the bar," Carl said. "He didn't have more than a few hours to hide it."

"Then we won't just drive up where he expects us. Pull over here."

Carl turned off the highway and onto an unpaved road. Sean had no idea where they were.

"We'll go in on foot," she said.

"It's thirty degrees out there!" the reverend objected.

"Come on, old man, you have a coat."

Carl didn't look happy, and Sean had no idea how far they had to walk.

"What about him?" Carl glanced back to where Sean was handcuffed in the backseat.

"We might still need a hostage when we leave. We'll kill him once we get into Canada. Make sure he's secure," Bobbie ordered.

Carl reached over the seat to check Sean's cuffs. He then wrapped duct tape around his ankles and a strip across his mouth. "Not that anyone's around to hear you. You just irritate me."

With the car heater off, the temperature plummeted. They hadn't given him back his jacket at the house, and Sean had on only jeans and a T-shirt.

As they sat in the car, Sean heard a truck on the highway pass them, then slow down.

"Who the hell was that?" Bobbie said. "It just turned down the road to the mine. White truck. Who has a white truck? It's not Jon's."

"Let's just leave," Carl said. "I don't like the feeling of this."

"We're not leaving without my money, or we might as well just turn ourselves in to the fucking police."

Carl sighed, resigned, and opened the car door.

Bobbie turned in her seat to look at Sean. She double checked the handcuffs and duct tape. "Stay put, sugar." Then she followed Carl into the woods.

Sean had rented a white truck. The last person driving it was Patrick.

FORTY

Omar stopped the truck on the edge of the road just before it opened into the Kelley Mine clearing. "We don't have the element of surprise. Callahan's waiting."

Noah glanced around the perimeter. "I don't see Lucy and Patrick."

"We were closer when they called."

Jon Callahan's vehicle was parked to the side of a small, boarded-up building that, at second glance, looked like several of the boards had been removed. Noah didn't see Callahan anywhere, but at this point, his job was to secure the rest of the explosives, find the teen Ricky Swain, and bring Callahan into custody, in that order.

He called Candela, who was now the liaison between the FBI, ATF, and local police.

"ETA?" asked Noah.

"Fifteen minutes to first explosion site by team Bravo, twenty-two minutes by team Charlie."

Noah and Omar were apparently team Alpha. "We need all available agents at the site of the abandoned Kelley Mining Company."

"Negative. I can send Team Delta your way. Twenty to thirty minutes."

"Sir," Noah said, "we have the alleged bomber's vehicle in sight. We believe he has a hostage who is a minor: Paul Richard Swain, Junior."

"A hostage or an accomplice?"

Noah wanted to give the Swain kid the benefit of the doubt, but he had to respond truthfully. "I can't say for certain, but we believe he's a hostage who has sympathy for his kidnapper."

"Understood," Candela said. "I'll see if I can reroute anyone your way, but the lives and safety of the local citizenry are our priority. There are four separate structure fires, and a small forest fire they're hoping to contain quickly. The main road into town has been roadblocked—no one is getting in or out."

Omar could hear the conversation and said, "There are a dozen ways to get off this mountain without even setting a wheel on the main road."

"Sir," Noah began.

Candela said, "Give me a few minutes to set it up. But you'll still be dark for fifteen minutes, minimum."

"Understood."

Noah hung up.

Omar said, "You know we can't just sit here on our butts for fifteen minutes."

He knew, but he didn't like strategically planning with only a hotshot ATF agent as his backup.

"And we don't have time to talk about it," Omar continued. "Callahan knows we're here. It's pretty damn obvious, don't you think?"

Noah put aside his dislike of Omar Lewis and made swift decisions. "We exit the vehicle. You go left along the perimeter, I'll go right and engage. You said he was the only person who knew you were undercover, correct?"

"Yes."

"Good. Stick to the shadows and focus your sharpshooter skills on the bad guys. I'm trusting you on this, Agent Lewis."

"You can."

Omar squelched the indoor lights before they opened the doors. He disappeared quickly, blending into the dark of night. Noah took the direct approach.

"Jon Callahan," he shouted, "this is Special Agent Noah Armstrong with the Federal Bureau of Investigation. I just want to talk."

He put his hands up to show he came in friendship.

"Jon, I'm here to help you."

He surveyed the surroundings. He didn't see anyone, but could feel eyes upon him.

He walked toward the building at the base of the hillside, near the mine entrance. The moon gave only a little light, but the fires to the northeast made the sky glow a deep orange.

The door was open; the place had been emptied. Whatever C-4 and equipment was inside was now either set to detonate or hidden elsewhere by Callahan.

Noah cautiously skirted the outside of the building. In his left periphery, he saw movement. It could have been Omar, but it didn't feel right. The ATF agent was too skilled to be spotted.

"Jon, I'm a friend of Sean Rogan. You know Bobbie has him, right? We don't know where she is or what she's planning to do to Sean. She sent someone to kill both me and my partner, Lucy Kincaid. You met her already. Sean's girlfriend."

Noah passed the building and glanced into the truck. The C-4 wasn't inside.

"Jon, you don't want to hurt anyone."

"Hold it." The voice was to his right, just on the other side of the truck. "Keep your hands up," said Jon. "I don't want to shoot you, Agent Armstrong, but if I have to I will. Bobbie is on her way, and this ends tonight."

"Correction," a female voice came from the hillside above them, "Bobbie *is* here, and you're going to give me my money and my C-4 or die."

Patrick had studied the area earlier in the day and decided they'd approach the mine from the back, which would take longer but give them better cover. Lucy deferred to her brother, but was nervous that they were taking too long to get there. They couldn't drive the entire way, and jogged a half mile to the mine, almost all uphill.

They regrouped behind an entangled overgrowth of blackberry bushes.

"Voices," Patrick whispered, nodding his head toward the mine entrance.

The clearing in front of the mine was a semicircular hard-packed area roughly the size of a football field. The mine was cut into the hillside, and based on the elevation of the ventilation shaft Sean had fallen in earlier, the tunnels inside must be graded downward. The building where the C-4 had been stored was on the opposite side of the entrance from where Lucy and Patrick were hidden, built up against the hillside.

Above it, the hill sloped up gradually about five feet, then leveled off where the trees began.

The glowing sky behind the mine illuminated the area, but details were hard to identify. Everything was framed by shifting shadows. Distant helicopters and the trill of emergency vehicles broke the silence, but here, at the mine, they had no backup.

"We need to get closer," Lucy said. She looked around for a way. "We'll go around the boulder near the entrance."

"If they see us we're sitting ducks."

"We'll only be exposed for a minute or two. As soon as we step into the mine, we'll be covered and much closer."

Lucy didn't wait for Patrick to concur. She started out, her heart pounding. She skirted the rock face, neither fast nor slow, until she made it to the entrance.

Someone was already there.

Gun drawn, she aimed it at the figure standing flat against the inside of the rough cave.

"Identify yourself," she demanded, in a coarse whisper.

"Don't shoot me. I'm Ricky Swain."

Lucy let out a quiet sigh of relief. "Lucy Kincaid."

"You're Sean's girlfriend."

"Have you seen him?"

"No. But my aunt Bobbie is outside somewhere and I'm worried. Jon thought—" Ricky shook his head. "I don't know what he was thinking. No one knows Bobbie better than me, and I told him this wasn't going to work. But I want to help him. I know how he feels."

From Ricky's vantage point, Lucy could see the

small building and Jon Callahan's truck about thirty yards away. Bobbie Swain was on the roof of the building, a gun on Noah and Jon who had their hands up. As she watched, a white-haired man emerged from the shadows. It was Reverend Carl Browne, she thought, though she couldn't see his face. Browne disarmed Noah and Jon. She glanced around quickly. Where was Omar Lewis? Was he in a position to shoot? He was a sniper, he could take Bobbie and the reverend down immediately. Or had he abandoned them?

Patrick stepped in behind her. "Dammit," he said when he saw what was happening outside.

"Ricky, this is my brother, Patrick. What is Jon planning?"

"He's going to kill Bobbie."

"He already lost his advantage," Lucy said.

Ricky didn't say anything for a moment.

"My mom told me if I had an emergency, call Jon. And he would fix it. He's fixing it."

"This isn't protecting you, not now. Jon is no longer the man your mother trusted. Look at his grief—Bobbie killed the woman he loved."

Lucy glanced into the dark mine. Two tunnels blacker than a moonless night, branched off. One of those led to where she found Victoria's body.

"Lucy," Patrick said and pointed to the ceiling.

C-4 had been pressed into the crevices around the mine entrance. Blasting caps were inserted into the C-4 at regular intervals, the wires all coming out to merge into one small box with a blinking red light.

"Does Jon have the detonator switch?" she asked.

Ricky didn't answer right away. "Aunt Bobbie will come in here. Then it'll all come down."

"You don't want to kill someone in cold blood," Lucy said. "Not even Bobbie."

"Don't talk to me like I'm a child!" Ricky said. He pressed the palms of his hands against his forehead. "She stole everything from me. My whole family is gone. Joe." His voice cracked.

"She kidnapped Sean. She's not getting away. Help me stop her without anyone else dying."

Patrick's attention was diverted from the C-4 to movement outside the mine. Lucy followed his gaze. Bobbie was forcing Noah and Jon toward the mine at gunpoint. Lucy didn't see Sean anywhere. Where had Bobbie left him?

She'd killed him.

Lucy refused to believe that. But she couldn't get the thought out of her mind.

"What's in here that she wants so badly?" she asked.

"A half-million dollars."

Patrick said urgently, "Lucy, we have to get out of here now."

Lucy said to Ricky. "He's right. Let's go."

He was still uncertain, and Lucy grabbed his arm to encourage him. Patrick led the way, then Lucy heard a female voice shout, "Ricky, stop."

Ricky did, forcing Lucy to stop as well. Lucy didn't know how she hadn't spotted Patrick. Then, from the corner of her eye, she saw a glimpse of his face. He'd stepped into a small, natural alcove in the mountain. If he stood still, Bobbie might not see him. But if she did, he was an easy target.

Bobbie walked to Ricky and Lucy. "You're the girlfriend." Her face twisted as she looked back at Noah. "You—you're both supposed to be dead!"

"I think—" Lucy began stepping to the left to keep Bobbie's attention on her.

"Not a word from you. Carl, watch them. Jon, come with me. You, this bitch, and I are getting my money."

From the second Sean knew Bobbie and the reverend were out of earshot, he started working on the handcuffs. They were too tight to slip off, a trick he'd done a few times in his life. But deep in the pockets of his jeans was a bobby pin. He remembered when he was little his sister had once told him she always had bobby pins in her hair and a rubber band around her wrist because they could solve any number of fashion emergencies.

Sean took the advice, but applied it to personal security. He always had a bobby pin in his pocket, pushed into a seam, so that on a quick search, it couldn't be felt. He couldn't risk it while being watched because he had to go through contortions to remove the pin and then to pick the handcuffs.

He had to remain calm and steady, because if he dropped the pin it would delay his escape, putting Lucy and everyone else at greater risk. He closed his eyes and felt for the small hole in the cuffs. He bent the bobby pin and inserted the thinner end into the lock. He moved it slowly around, using his skills and sense of touch and a hint of a sixth sense that had helped him more times than he could count. Clearing his mind, he pictured the inside of the lock, focused on seeing the pin hit the right spot to spring the latch.

Click.

Sean removed the cuffs and pulled the duct tape from his mouth, then let out a long breath as he tore through the duct tape around his ankles, which took him longer than picking the lock.

Free, he searched the car for a gun or knife, anything he could use as a weapon. The only thing he could find was an old tire iron, which he grabbed, then ran through the woods toward the mine.

He reached the edge of a cliff and stopped, his momentum almost taking him over the edge. But it wasn't a long fall—below him was the roof of a small building. To one side was Callahan's truck, to the other was the white truck. Now that he was closer, he saw that it wasn't his rental and he breathed a bit easier. There was still trouble, but Lucy wasn't here.

There was a lot of movement at the mine entrance, and he saw Noah and Ricky emerge, followed by Reverend Browne, who had a gun on them.

Timing was everything. Browne glanced back at the mine, distracted. Someone else was in there. Sean slipped down to the roof, then dropped off the side, out of sight from the entrance. That's when he saw Patrick, flush against the rock wall of the mine, tightly wedged in a crevice only yards from Browne's position. If Browne looked to the right, he'd see Patrick and have a direct line of fire. There was no way Sean could get to the group without being seen.

Trusting both Patrick and Noah to take advantage of the opportunity, Sean exposed himself to distract

Browne. He ran from the building, directly toward the group, his eyes on Browne's gun.

Browne turned and aimed his gun toward Sean. Sean dove for the ground, rolled to the right, and jumped up again. Browne was thrown off guard just enough for Noah to push Ricky down and put himself between the kid and Browne. Simultaneously, Patrick charged from his hiding spot and tackled the older man, pinning his gun hand to the ground. Noah disarmed him, then retrieved two more guns from the back of Browne's pants.

"Good work," Sean said as he ran over. He pulled the handcuffs he'd escaped out of from his pocket and said, "Let me."

Sean cuffed Carl, smug and satisfied. "One down. Where's that insane woman? And Jon?"

Noah said, "In the mine."

"Great—they're trapped. We'll wait for backup and then—"

A dark expression crossed both Patrick and Noah's faces. "Where's Lucy?"

"She's with them."

"Why are we standing around here?" Sean ran into the mine.

Patrick followed. "Wait, Sean!"

"Don't tell me to wait for backup, not when that lunatic has Lucy."

Patrick pointed to the ceiling. Sean looked up. At first he didn't know what he was supposed to see, then Noah shined a flashlight and exposed multiple charges sticking out of what could only have been the C-4 Bobbie had been ranting about.

"We need to pull every blasting cap out of the C-4," Noah said, reaching up to the charge closest to him.

Omar Lewis came in. "There's no one around the perimeter. Good work, Armstrong." Then he looked up. "Oh shit."

"Who has the detonator?" Sean demanded as both he and Patrick followed Noah's lead.

Ricky replied. "Jon."

FORTY-ONE

Jon and Lucy had flashlights; Bobbie had a gun. Jon took the lead, which meant Bobbie had the gun at Lucy's back. Every few feet she poked Lucy with the barrel, and Lucy tried not to stumble. She didn't want to fall down an exploration shaft a hundred feet to her death.

Jon whispered, "Keep your hand on the wall. Test each spot of ground before you step. About seventy feet in there's an exploration shaft."

"Give her the money," Lucy told him. She didn't want to walk that far into the mine. They had already started a gradual descent.

"Where is it?" Bobbie demanded.

"Victoria's coffin," Jon sneered. He stopped walking and turned to face Bobbie. In the yellow glow of the flashlight, he looked gaunt and determined.

He opened up his right hand. Inside was a small box with a switch. His thumb rested on the switch. "You're not getting the money," Jon told her. "This ends now."

"This is about a *woman*? She was an *FBI agent*! She only seduced you to get close to *me*."

"No. I knew she was an agent. She was going to save this town."

Bobbie stared at Jon in shock and disgust. "You knew?" She held her gun in his face. "You fucking *knew* she was a Fed?"

"She wanted to bring in a team, but we both worried you'd smell the operation. So we worked together. And you never knew there was another undercover operative. You're not as smart as you think, Roberta."

"Jon, stop," Lucy said, not wanting to antagonize Bobbie further.

"I'm sorry, Lucy."

Bobbie fumed. "You disgust me, you fucking traitor. I don't need you anymore, I know these tunnels better than anyone."

Lucy shouted, "No! Bobbie, Jon rigged the mine to explode. We'll all die!"

But Bobbie pressed the gun's trigger and Jon's chest exploded. His thumb hit the switch. Lucy screamed.

Sean had the last blasting cap in his hand when it exploded, burning the tips of his fingers. He dropped it and shook out the pain.

The mine stood. An echo of a feminine scream haunted him. Lucy.

"Fuck, that was too close!" Omar exclaimed.

There had been twelve blasting caps embedded in the C-4. C-4 was very stable and needed a spark to detonate; not even a bullet could set it off on its own. As soon as Bobbie disappeared down the tunnel, Omar ran up and tried to disarm the detonation device, but simultaneously the others pulled the blasting caps.

That quick plan had saved their lives.

"I'm going in." Sean had retrieved his gun from Carl Browne, and now shoved it in his belt. "I heard a gunshot." They all had, seconds before the blasting caps popped.

"You need me to guide you," Ricky said.

"Hold it," Noah said. "No way in hell I'm letting you walk in there unprotected."

"You can't stop me," Sean said, his voice low and calm, but his eyes burned with pain and anger.

"I have equipment," Omar said. "Wait one minute." He bolted toward his truck.

Sean didn't want to wait. The longer they waited, the more danger Lucy was in—if she wasn't already dead.

Patrick said, "Sean, think. You need a flashlight, rope, a radio. And Ricky, you're not going in."

"I know this mine. So does Jon. Bobbie thinks she does, but she hasn't been down here for years. Jon told her the money was where Victoria's body had been, but he didn't really put it there. He stashed it in Joe's house."

"Which means when Bobbie gets there and sees the money is missing, she'll lash out at Lucy," Sean said. "We have to beat her there, go in through the ventilation shaft."

"It'll take you twenty minutes minimum to drive over there—there's no straight path," Ricky said. "We have to follow. And quickly."

"I'm not letting you risk yourself, Ricky."

"This is my fault. I helped Jon. I knew I shouldn't

have, but Bobbie killed everyone who ever mattered to me."

"She's a sick psycho," Sean agreed, "and I'm not letting her get Lucy. Or you."

Omar drove up, his headlights illuminating the entire entrance. He jumped out. "I have a plan."

Sean's frustration hit overload. He didn't know if Lucy was dead or alive, and he didn't want to wait another minute.

Noah grabbed him and stared him down. "If that bullet was for Lucy, she's dead. If it wasn't, then she needs you to think smart. Or so help me, I'll cuff you and get her myself."

Sean's jaw tightened, but he nodded. "Tell me the plan, Agent Lewis—fast."

Lucy fell to her knees when Jon hit the switch, her arms covering her head.

Nothing happened.

She heard voices from the entrance. Judging from their steps, they were about thirty feet in.

Jon was on the ground next to her. She took his hand. "Jon—"

"I-I'm sorry. I didn't w-w-want to hurt you." His voice was labored and raspy. It sounded like Bobbie's bullet had punctured a lung. He struggled for another breath.

"It was an accident. You didn't mean to press the button." She wanted to believe it, but wasn't certain she could. "I'll get help."

"S-Stay left."

Bobbie grabbed Jon's flashlight and kicked him in his stomach.

"Don't!" Lucy shouted.

Bobbie kicked him again. "You blew up my warehouses!" Kick. "Stole my money!" Double kick. "Ruined everything!" Jon fell to his side. Blood dripped from his mouth.

"I w-w-would do it again," Jon gasped out. "Lucy. Be. Careful. W-what . . ."

She could barely hear him and leaned down. "What did you say?"

He whispered, "Not. There."

"He's going into shock." Lucy glanced over her shoulder at Bobbie. "If we get him out, we can keep him warm and put in a tube to help him breathe—"

Bobbie shot Jon in the head without hesitation, so quickly Lucy almost didn't register what had happened, even though his blood hit her face and chest. Then Bobbie aimed the gun at Lucy. "You're lucky I don't shoot you, too. You're an idiot to think I'd lift a finger to help that traitor. And besides, I need a shield in case your buddies follow us in."

Lucy barely heard Bobbie, didn't have time to fear for her own life. She hadn't expected her to shoot Jon so coldly. Her hands were covered in Jon's blood and half his head was now gone.

"Get up, Lucy. It's Lucy, right?"

Lucy slowly rose to her feet. She had one flashlight and no gun.

"Don't be stupid, and you get to be my hostage. You might even be reunited with your lover, who's tied up in my truck. I'll let you die together. Move. Stay to the left. Follow the tracks. But mostly, just keep moving. There is no way out but through me, and I guarantee if you run, you'll die. Either my gun or the mine will kill you."

Lucy stepped over Jon's body, her hand on the wall. She needed to talk to Bobbie, establish a connection, an understanding, but she was at a complete loss. She couldn't reason with someone so impulsive and violent.

Something brushed by her face and she jumped, stifling a scream.

Bobbie laughed. "You're so funny! It's just a bat."

Bobbie's tone changed. She'd gone from serious to humorous in less than a minute. But as Lucy thought back to what she'd said, even her threat had a hint of humor. She enjoyed it. She was in charge and she enjoyed Lucy's fear. She'd shot Jon because she wanted him dead—but she also enjoyed how the violence scared Lucy. It relaxed Bobbie. Put her in control.

It was all about control. When Bobbie felt things were out of control, she was rash and dangerous. When she was in control, she was still dangerous, but not rash. Methodical and calculating. She could change plans on a dime, and as long as she controlled the situation, she was happy.

Lucy said, "Sorry." She moved slowly down the tunnel. They were going at a downward angle—just steep enough that Lucy had to be careful where she stepped so she didn't slip.

Bobbie laughed. "I wish we had time to get to know each other. We're smarter than men. I always have been, at any rate. Smarter and sharper and more willing to do what it takes to get what I want."

"It's because people don't expect women to be ruthless and in complete control of our lives."

Bobbie pondered that as she poked Lucy with the barrel of the gun. "You might be right. Being looked at as soft and weak just because I'm a woman does give me a certain advantage."

"I heard about your grand performance when you turned over your brother to the FBI." Lucy's foot slipped and she grabbed the wall. It was cold and damp. Her whole body felt frozen, and the only thing that kept her moving was the adrenaline of fear.

"Like you said, being a woman has certain advantages."

"When I found out your brother had something on you that kept you from going after his son, I thought it might be the tape of your FBI interview where you lied about your dead husband and what happened, but this is something that he had on you six years ago, and Agent Sheffield stole the disk in December."

"No more talking. Just walking. Hey, I made a rhyme."

"Paul had already spilled the beans. Are you afraid someone else knows?"

"Shut up. Paul wouldn't say a word because he'd be dead. It's mutually beneficial that we both keep our end of the bargain."

They came to a split in the tunnel. She remembered Jon's words. *Stay left* had two meanings. Stay to the left tunnel or stay to the left of the tunnel? She shined her light down on the ground. The tracks split and went both ways.

"That way," Bobbie said.

Lucy walked slowly, but Bobbie wasn't patient. "Come on, move it!"

"I'm just curious," Lucy said. If she could keep Bobbie talking, they would go slower, and Lucy was all about caution right now. Her heart pounded. She feared falling to her death far more than she feared Bobbie's gun—and she was scared plenty of Bobbie's gun.

"You know what they say, curiosity killed the cat." Bobbie giggled.

"Do you think that after six years, the Molina drug family would still care that not only did you kill Herve yourself, but you stole everything in his safe? And that you turned over that valuable information to their enemies?" Some of this was conjecture, but Lucy bet she was right.

Lucy had been thinking about this situation for the last twenty-four hours. She didn't think it was a coincidence that Bobbie had made a deal with Lowell on the guns. He trusted her because she'd already been working for him.

"You've been working for Sampson Lowell from the beginning," Lucy guessed.

She expected a reaction, but not a simple admission. "You *are* smarter than the men."

"If I figured it out, the FBI will figure it out, too. And they have more information than I do."

"Shut! Up!" Bobbie pushed Lucy down the tunnel to get her moving. Lucy stumbled and dropped her flashlight. It didn't make a sound. It fell down a deep hole, the light bouncing off the ceiling until it broke or went out or was too far down to shine this far.

Lucy screamed.

"I don't need you," Bobbie said. "Meet the Hell Hole. You can join your fellow FBI agent Victoria Sheffield, Bitch Number One, at the bottom of the pit. But she had it easy. She was already dead before she went down."

Bobbie lunged for Lucy. Lucy jumped to the left, her back flat against the wall. Bobbie lost her balance and stumbled. She reached for Lucy, but her foot slipped into the hole.

Her hand wrapped around Lucy's ankle. Lucy fell hard as Bobbie pulled her down, grunting as she tried to use Lucy's body to climb to safety. The side of the exploration shaft began to crumble and Lucy felt herself falling.

Sean heard Lucy's scream. She was closer than they'd thought. They had been following the light ahead of them, their flashlights turned off, because Sean didn't want Bobbie to know she was being followed. Then the light changed, faded, and there was only one beam.

"They're at the Hell Hole," Ricky told him.

"Stay back," Sean ordered. He checked the harness Omar had strapped on him. The end was secured to the bumper of his truck.

Suddenly, everything went dark and Lucy screamed again. Sean turned on his light and rounded the corner.

Lucy was on the ground, clawing at the rocky bottom of the tunnel. Bobbie had her leg and was trying to use Lucy's body as leverage to climb out of the exploration shaft.

"Lucy!" Sean reached out.

She grabbed his hand. Her hands were slick with dirt and blood and she began to slip. Bobbie's weight was pulling her down.

"Ricky! Light!" Sean called out.

Ricky came around the corner and shined his bright light into the tunnel.

There was nowhere to gain traction. Nowhere to gain a foothold. Only his raw strength and the cable that strapped him to the truck held him in place.

He shouted into his radio and prayed they could still hear him, "I need more rope!"

Omar came back with, "That's it."

"I need more!"

Sean dropped his own flashlight and grabbed both of Lucy's hands. The rappelling vest dug deep into his flesh, making breathing difficult, as he strained to hold on to Lucy's hands.

"I'm moving the truck into the mine entrance," Noah said over the radio. "I can get you ten more feet, max. Omar, move," Sean heard before the radio went off.

Suddenly, the slack on the rope caused Sean to slide precariously closer to the edge of the exploration shaft. Lucy screamed as her legs went over the side. Bobbie shouted, "I'll kill you!"

Lucy screamed again, this time in pain, not fear.

"What?" Sean grunted.

"Knife. She cut me."

Ricky stood over the shaft with a small .22. Sean didn't know he had it. "No, Ricky."

Ricky shined the light into the pit where Bobbie held on to Lucy's legs. "Good bye, Aunt Bobbie."

Ricky fired the gun, and suddenly Lucy was out of the pit and in Sean's arms on the floor of the tunnel. He scurried away from the edge of the pit, the Hell Hole, and held her close. "God, Lucy, thank God. I can't lose you."

Ricky picked up the line, using it to guide him back to the mine entrance, giving Sean and Lucy a moment of privacy.

Noah's voice barked over the radio, "Report!"

"I have her," Sean said. "Lucy is safe. Bobbie Swain is dead. Give me a minute." He needed to just hold her. It had been close, too close.

Lucy clutched Sean, didn't want to let him go.

"I don't want to die without you knowing how much I love you," Lucy said.

She had finally said it, and though her entire body was shaking from fear and adrenaline and shock, her heart was no longer gripped by the fear of loving Sean. Her uncertainty was gone.

"I love you, Sean Rogan. I've always known it, but was too scared to say it. Still, you stuck with me."

They had issues they needed to talk about. Their lives were not safe or simple; they were dangerous and complex, and either of them could die at any time. This week had proven that—trouble found them. But they loved each other, and that had to mean something. It had to be stronger than their differences, more important than their egos.

Sean stared at her, wiping dirt and blood off her face. His expression was almost as if he hadn't heard her. "Luce—"

"I never want a day to pass where I don't tell you how I feel," Lucy said, holding his face in her hands. "You know the truth, you always have." She kissed him lightly, looking him straight in the eye. "I love you, Sean Rogan," she repeated.

Sean pulled her to him and kissed her fiercely, passionately. She lost her breath again and almost forgot where they were.

He leaned back, pulling her with him, resting against the tunnel wall. She didn't know if she could walk—her leg throbbed from where Bobbie had stabbed it, but the cut wasn't deep, just painful. Sean's heart beat rapidly against her palm. Then he smiled his impish grin in the pale glow of the flashlight and said, "I knew you'd come to your senses soon enough and admit that you're deeply and madly in love with me." His thumb trailed from her chin down her throat.

His voice cracked when he said, "I love you, too, Princess. And neither of us died today. I'd say it's a win-win all around."

FORTY-TWO

Two days later

Sean and Lucy walked into Albany FBI headquarters Tuesday afternoon. Sean was glad to finally leave Spruce Lake, confident that Tim and Adam Hendrickson could move forward on their resort. In light of the continuing police presence as local and federal authorities shut down the drug business and raided multiple buildings, seized several tons of marijuana, and removed all related computers and files, the brothers decided to postpone the resort opening until next year. Tim believed his financial knowledge and collateral would help bring redevelopment money into the area, and Adam planned to simultaneously open separate Boy and Girl Scout camps, something their father had dreamed about. They vowed to work closely with the people in town to develop a viable tourist area. Tourism wouldn't bring in the big money of drugs or gunrunning, but it also wouldn't get the townsfolk killed or imprisoned. Already, residents were calling Tim to thank him for standing up to the Swain family and for the first time in their lives, they felt both safe and hopeful.

Sean suspected the coming changes weren't going to be easy and nothing would be quite the same. But with enough people committed to rebuilding the foundation of Spruce Lake on legal businesses, there was definite promise.

After the adventure in the mine, Sean had hidden Lucy away in the cabin while Noah coordinated four law enforcement agencies that descended on the Adirondacks by dawn—the sheriff, FBI, DEA, and ATF. Every agency sent a dozen or more people, and Sean wanted nothing to do with the initial interviews and justifications. Noah's ability to organize the disparate groups into a unified team highlighted his military officer training, and Sean grudgingly admired his skill. He was more than happy to pass on any credit—or criticism. Sean just wanted to spend as much time alone with Lucy as he could. He'd never get tired of hearing her say *I love you.*

Their idyllic two days were over. They were called to Albany for a debriefing, and then would head home.

Lucy introduced Sean to the well-groomed Brian Candela, a stereotypical "suit" in the FBI. But his eyes were sharp and his manner professional. "We spoke on the phone the other day," Candela said.

"Good to meet you, sir." Being in this building made him uncomfortable, but Sean was trying to be polite and diplomatic for Lucy's sake.

"There are just a few of us in the conference room. Marty and Dale went up to Spruce Lake Sunday, will probably be there for a few weeks as they *weed* through all the facts and fiction." Sean grinned at Candela's obvious play on words, feeling more comfortable than he had when he first walked in.

Noah was sitting at the table with an older agent introduced as SAC Hart, a young woman, Agent Tara Fields, on loan from the cybercrime squad, and a secretary who typed on a steno machine like a court reporter.

"I know you're eager to get home," Hart said, "so we'll make this as quick and painless as possible. Agent Armstrong has already written his report, so we have most of the information we need."

Sean caught Noah's eye, but couldn't read his expression. Sean stood by every decision he'd made. But there were some things he didn't want in any official record.

Fortunately, the questions were straightforward and related solely to the facts. It took them not much more than an hour to recount the events from when he and Lucy first arrived in Spruce Lake to Bobbie's death in the mine.

Hart dismissed the secretary. "The official part is over. Off the record, I wanted to tell you that ATF Agent Omar Lewis is on official leave. ATF wasn't happy about it, but I insisted. He acted with complete and total disregard for your lives, contrary to all training and protocols. I suspect, however, he'll be back after an internal audit."

While Sean was still furious about the sniper incident, he'd developed an understanding and even some respect. "When the bad guys win one time too many, sometimes we have to bend the rules to stop them."

"Bending the rules, yes. Breaking them?" Hart shook

her head. "Nevertheless, ATF is livid that they lost Sampson Lowell after more than a year of field work and twice that in research. However, we're sharing everything we learn from those we arrested and the files we seized. Hopefully they'll get him next time."

Lucy asked, "What was in Jon Callahan's safe deposit box? Was it incriminating against Bobbie Swain as we'd thought?"

Candela nodded. "That and much more. First, all the evidence and files Victoria took from the office were in the box, including the tape of Bobbie Swain's interview in Miami where she turned on her brother. We've sent it to the Behavioral Science Unit at Quantico for further analysis, hoping we can learn something from her performance to help us in the future."

Lucy said, "She was certainly a unique personality, but she was also a cold-blooded sociopath."

Noah said, "I'll get you clearance to review the tapes, Lucy. You'll probably see something no one else did."

Sean glanced at Noah, agreeing with the Fed but wondering why he chose to lavish the praise on Lucy now. Then he dismissed his flash of jealousy. It didn't matter what Noah's feelings were, if they were professional or personal. Lucy loved Sean, and that was all he needed.

Candela continued. "The box also included a journal Callahan had kept recounting his early drug smuggling days with Paul Swain when they were teenagers. There was a falling out between him and Swain because Callahan had originally gone to law school to become a criminal defense attorney to represent Swain; while in college, Callahan decided to put it all behind him. He lived in Spruce Lake part time in order to keep his eye on things, but he knowingly turned a blind eye to the drug operation. After Swain went to prison, Callahan moved back permanently. But when he realized Bobbie Swain was behind it—and had covertly taken over her brother's operation—he worked out a deal with Swain to get inside her operation. Swain wanted his sister dead, and Callahan wanted her influence gone."

"And then she brought in Sampson Lowell," Lucy said. "Raising the stakes and the danger."

"Joe Hendrickson learned of the gunrunning plan—Callahan was unclear how—and he went to Callahan to do something. They agreed to contact the ATF, but at the same time Bobbie Swain's people found out what Hendrickson knew and poisoned him, having the doctor rule it as a heart attack. Callahan went to the ATF to speed up the investigation, and that's when Omar Lewis was sent undercover to work as the cook at the Lock & Barrel. Only Callahan knew Lewis was law enforcement."

"I'm still unclear why Jon Callahan brought Agent Sheffield in, and why she didn't inform your office," Lucy said.

"The first part is easy—you were absolutely right that Victoria met Callahan while investigating the pirated DVDs in Canada. They started seeing each other romantically. After Joe Hendrickson was murdered, Callahan told her everything. By this time, Lewis was already in place. Victoria thought if she reported what she knew, she'd be called off because it was an undercover ATF operation at that point."

"And she would have been," Noah interjected.

Candela nodded. "She still should have filed a report. There was nothing else about her in Callahan's notes until last December when she brought Callahan the files and evidence on Bobbie Swain. She'd been looking into Swain on her own, and coupled with the information she knew through her boyfriend, she came up with a plan. Apparently, the first meeting Lowell had with Swain was on January second—and Victoria got it in her head that she needed to be around to protect Callahan, who was playing the dangerous informant game with the ATF."

Sean asked, "How did Bobbie know she was an agent?"

"She didn't—Sampson Lowell did. He had scouts in town once he decided to work with the Swain operation. Apparently, his intelligence is exemplary. When he uncovered Victoria's identity, he canceled the meeting and told Swain to take care of it. She sent him proof that Victoria was dead. Lowell waited four months to ensure there was no increased police presence or chatter, then rescheduled the meeting for this past Sunday. Swain was providing storage and distribution channels for his gunrunning operation into Canada. It was a megadeal. If all went well Sunday, the guns would have been in the warehouses by midnight."

"And now Lowell has disappeared," Sean said.

"He's not our concern," Hart said. "He's ATF's problem."

Sean disagreed. Sampson Lowell was *everybody's* problem. But he kept his mouth shut.

"What's going to happen to Ricky Swain?" he asked.

"We're recommending leniency, and Detective Dillard is helping smooth things over with the prosecutors to give the kid probation and wipe his record when he turns eighteen. The Hendricksons aren't filing charges and Tim Hendrickson offered to serve as the boy's guardian. Dillard thinks they'll get what they want."

Sean was relieved. That someone was willing to step up and help Ricky meant he had a real shot at a future.

"We may have some follow-up questions," Candela said, "but we'll run them through Agent Armstrong. Again, thank you. Because of you, we know what happened to our field agent, and we can move forward."

After final good-byes, Noah walked Sean and Lucy out of the building. "I'll be returning to D.C. late tonight," he said. "Take the rest of the week off, Lucy. You can start fresh next Monday."

"Thank you, but if you need me to come in tomorrow, I—"

Sean cut her off. "*Monday* morning, Luce."

Noah smiled. "Monday is soon enough. Good work all around." Noah looked directly at Sean as he spoke. "This was a dicey situation and a testament to your skills that we all came through without major injury."

Sean was surprised at the clear compliment. "I appreciate that, Noah."

Lucy let out a breath and Sean glanced at her. She wanted everyone to get along, especially the people she cared about. He might not like that Noah was important to Lucy, but he loved Lucy. Sean vowed to make a real effort with the Fed.

Sean broke the awkward silence. "Now, there's the matter of you getting my plane shot down."

Noah nodded soberly. "I thought you might be a little upset, so I've taken care of it."

Sean couldn't hide his surprise. "I don't get it."

"I called in a friend of mine, a former Air Force mechanic who now works at Lockheed. He's flying in this afternoon to take your plane to his shop."

"You don't have to do that," Sean said in all seriousness.

"I know." Noah extended his hand. Sean shook it. Then Noah grinned broadly and winked at Lucy. "You never know when I'll call in the favor."

Sean returned the good will. "Anytime."

Read on for

LOVE IS MURDER

An original novella

by

Allison Brennan

Published by Ballantine Books

Dear Reader:

Love Is Murder takes place a year before the events in *Love Me to Death,* the first Lucy Kincaid novel. I hope you enjoy reading this adventure about Lucy and her brother Patrick as much as I enjoyed writing it.

Special thanks to Dr. D. P. Lyle for help on medical questions, and my pal Toni McGee Causey for a quick, early read. My husband, Dan, was particularly helpful this time around with brainstorming. And as always, thank you to the Ballantine and Writers House team.

Happy Reading,

Allison Brennan

ONE

Twenty-four-year-old Lucy Kincaid had certainly needed a break, but skiing hadn't turned out to be quite as much fun as her brother Patrick had promised. In fact, Lucy had spent more time *in* the snow than *on* the snow. Snowsuit notwithstanding, she was cold, wet, and miserable.

"I told you I didn't know how to ski." Lucy shivered in the passenger seat of Patrick's truck. She put her hands directly in front of the heater vent.

"You just need more practice. We'll try again tomorrow."

"No."

"Wimp."

"Is it wimpy to not want to freeze my ass off?"

For just a second, Patrick took his eyes off the curving mountain road. "Since when have you been a quitter?"

"It happened the thousandth time I hit the snow."

Patrick laughed. "You weren't all that bad."

"It's no fun to fail."

"You're just cranky because everything usually comes so easy to you."

"Not true," Lucy protested, though she wondered if her brother was right.

Patrick grinned.

"You think this is funny?" she asked.

"I think you're scared."

"I'm *not* scared."

"Are too."

"God, you're a brat."

Lucy stared out the passenger window as they carefully made their way back down to the lodge where they were staying for the four-day weekend. The winding mountain road was treacherous in parts, and the increasing wind coupled with the falling snow didn't help. She found it strange that less than two hours ago, they were skiing under bright blue skies dotted with white clouds, but during the thirty minutes they'd sat at the coffee shop at the base of the ski lifts the sky had darkened, as if a gray, fluffy blanket had been laid over the mountains. The snow flurries had begun blowing almost as soon as Patrick started the ignition.

"I'm glad we didn't take the snowmobiles this morning," Lucy said. "We'd be coming back in this."

"We're almost there." Patrick's expression had grown from light to concerned as he slowed and kicked the SUV into four-wheel drive.

The drive to the Delarosa Mountain Retreat yesterday afternoon had been lovely, with striking scenery and crisp fresh air. Lucy loved the outdoors, though she preferred it at least forty degrees warmer. Now, unfamiliar with the treacherous road, she was as tense as Patrick, and wondering why the weather report had told them a "mild" storm system would be passing overnight, when it was four in the afternoon and this was no mild storm. With every passing minute the snow increased, and Lucy suspected a blizzard would be in full force before sundown.

She trusted Patrick to get them safely back to the lodge and hoped that though fierce right now, the storm would quickly pass.

She closed her eyes, considering Patrick's comments about how she didn't take failure well. While she was in great shape from running and swimming, being fit didn't seem to matter when she couldn't find her balance on those damn skis. She was more than a little irritated that she'd failed her first day skiing because anything athletic usually came easily to her. In fact, most things came easier to her than to others. She studied in school, but never as much as her peers. She'd been an honors student, received two bachelor's degrees and a master's from Georgetown, and spoke four languages fluently. And because her mother had nearly drowned when she escaped Cuba, Rosa Kincaid made sure every one of her seven children could swim. Lucy ended up being on the swim team in high school and college and had been scouted for the Olympics, but she couldn't commit the time and energy such an opportunity required. After she'd been attacked on the day of her high school graduation, her priorities had changed dramatically.

Lucy came from a military and law enforcement family. Her father was a retired army colonel; her oldest brother, Jack, was also retired army. She had a cop for a sister, a private investigator brother, and another brother who was a forensic psychiatrist. They'd all married into law enforcement in one way or another. Patrick was a former e-crimes cop, and now worked for a private security company with Jack. Joining the FBI seemed not only natural, but what Lucy was supposed to do. She had everything planned—she would submit her application this summer. It could take up to a year to go through the testing and review process. In the meantime, she had plenty of work with her new D.C. medical examiner's internship and volunteering at a victims' rights group.

She opened her eyes to see if the landscape had changed. The snow continued to stream down at a forty-five-degree angle, the wind rocking the sturdy truck.

It didn't look as though they'd get another opportunity to ski this weekend. Secretly she was pleased. She didn't like being so cold her teeth chattered, though at the same time she wanted a second chance. She didn't want to return home a failure at the one new thing she tried and didn't get immediately.

A bright green flash to her right, up the mountainside, caught Lucy's eye. She leaned forward and immediately recognized that a person was rolling rapidly down the steep, tree-dotted slope. As she said, "Patrick! Someone's in trouble!" she saw the tumbling figure smash into one of the trees. The person grabbed the trunk and tried to stand, but that only sent him falling again, trailing a streak of pink behind him.

"I see him." Patrick stopped the truck as quickly as he dared on the icy road. He turned on his emergency lights and they both got out of the car. The icy, damp air hit Lucy's lungs before it registered on her skin. She trudged to the back of the SUV and grabbed the first aid kit, then followed her brother, fighting the wind-driven snow.

Above them, the man grabbed at a sapling, caught it, and stopped. He was still twenty feet from the road.

"That's Steve," Lucy said, recognizing the lodge owner's twenty-year-old son now that they were closer. It seemed to be getting darker by the second, the blinking lights in the front and rear of the car turning the snow alternately red and yellow.

Patrick called out, "Lie on your back and slide!"

At first Lucy didn't think Steve had heard, but then he turned around and lay back. The snow was stained red where his head had rested. She couldn't see an injury, but as she watched, blood seeped from his scalp.

"Let go!" Patrick commanded.

Steve complied and slid down until he hit the slush on the roadside. He tried to stand, but stumbled and fell, unmoving.

Patrick reached him first. "Lucy, get the first aid kit—it's in the back."

"Got it." She knelt next to Steve and unlatched the red emergency kit.

"What happened?" Patrick asked Steve, brushing the snow from his face.

"I'm okay," he said.

"We saw you hit your head on that tree up there. Lie still a minute." Patrick began inspecting the young man's body for breaks. "Tell me if it hurts anywhere."

The cold could send him into shock, especially if he had internal damage. Lucy wanted to get Steve inside as quickly as possible, but they had to make sure moving him wouldn't make any injuries worse.

"I'm fine," Steve repeated.

"Can you move your legs and arms?"

"It's just my head."

Lucy handed a thick gauze bandage to Patrick, who pressed it on Steve's still-bleeding wound. "Head injuries can be serious," Patrick said. "You need to lie still for a moment. I'll tape this up, then we'll get you in the truck."

Lucy handed Patrick pieces of tape and he affixed the bandage. Steve didn't protest. Other than the gash on his head from hitting the tree, he had only a couple of minor scratches on his face. His body was well protected with a GORE-TEX jacket and pants over layers of clothing.

"I'm freezing my ass off," Steve said. "Let me up."

Patrick helped Steve sit up, watching his eyes carefully. "Just hold it right here for a minute. Are you dizzy?"

"I was just stupid."

"What were you doing going up that slope?" Lucy said. "It's too steep."

"I didn't walk up the slope," he said, as if she were an idiot for asking. "I slipped at the top."

"So you decided to take the fastest way down to the road?" Patrick joked, helping Steve to his feet.

"Ha-ha." Steve rolled his eyes, trying to pretend he wasn't in pain, but his hand clutched his stomach.

Lucy said, "What's wrong?"

"Nothing," he snapped. "Are you going to give me a ride or do I have to walk?"

Patrick helped Steve to the truck, and Lucy put the supplies back. She made sure the heater was at maximum, and handed Steve a blanket while Patrick started back down the mountain.

"I don't need it," he said.

"Humor me." Lucy smiled. Steve probably felt stupid and clumsy, which contributed to his foul attitude. He grumbled, but took the blanket and closed his eyes.

They'd met Steve briefly yesterday afternoon when they first arrived at the Delarosa Mountain Retreat. He was young, didn't talk much, and seemed conscientious in his considerable duties running the lodge. It didn't seem likely that he'd make a dumb mistake like getting too close to an unstable ledge.

"Steve," Lucy said, "what were you doing up there?"

"I was coming back from inspecting our outlying cabins—we close them in the winter—and checking for animal tracks. We have been having some problems with four-legged predators, and I wanted to make sure they hadn't returned. I knew the storm was going to get bad as soon as the sky turned, so I took a shortcut. Stupid."

"Why didn't you take a snowmobile?" Patrick asked.

"They were all out when I left, and I can't get to two of the cabins with my truck. I do this all the time," he said defensively. "I just lost my balance. And my favorite skis."

He didn't open his eyes, and Lucy couldn't tell if he was telling the truth.

She said, "I checked the weather report this morning. They said light snowfall overnight, clear tomorrow. I can't believe they were so wrong."

Steve laughed once. "Weather systems change often, especially in the winter. I've lived here my entire life and when I saw the report this morning, I knew the system was going to shift as soon as the wind shifted. Weather reports are more reliable now with satellites and historical data all computerized, but minor changes in one location can have a chain effect, especially in the mountains."

"How long do you think it'll last?" Patrick asked.

Steve looked out the window. "I think we're in for the weekend."

"What?" Lucy exclaimed.

"We can get you off the mountain if you want, but tonight is going to be a blizzard and I don't advise it."

"I'm not going anywhere tonight," Lucy said.

Patrick grinned. "What did you do, Luce? Send a prayer up for a blizzard to get you out of learning to ski?"

"On the contrary, I decided that I was going to learn how to ski if it was the last thing I did—just to prove to you that I'm not scared of failure."

"I shouldn't have said scared. You're not scared of failure, you're just pissed off. You don't like it when you can't do something your first time out. And you just said *learn how to ski,* meaning you have no intention of failing."

"Why would I try if I expected to fail?"

"Indeed. I rest my case."

Lucy was confused and sighed heavily. "Brothers."

Patrick drove across the pressed gravel road that was now covered with a thick layer of snow, but the lights lining the lodge's entrance helped guide him to the barn, which had been converted into a large garage. Steve jumped out of the truck and opened the barn doors. Patrick drove in and parked where he had earlier, next to the Delarosa truck. He got out and helped Steve close the doors against the fierce wind.

"I need to gather up supplies and check the generators," Steve said. "You should get inside before the storm gets worse."

"With that bump on your head, you shouldn't be out walking around," Lucy said.

"I don't have a choice. I'm not risking damage because I slacked off."

"I'll help you," Patrick said.

"I don't need any help."

"Then I'll tell your stepmother that you whacked your head. Based on her mother-hen attitude, I don't think she'll let you leave your room."

"What do you care?" he asked petulantly.

"I've been the recipient of a nasty head injury," Patrick said. "I know how unpredictable they are."

Lucy didn't say anything. Her brother had been in a coma, thanks to the man who had kidnapped her nearly six years ago. She still felt a pang of guilt that Patrick had been so severely injured while trying to rescue her. She thanked God every day that he was alive, breathing, and awake. Since his recovery, they'd grown much closer than they'd been growing up. Their ten-year age difference had been huge when she was ten and Patrick was twenty; now, at twenty-four and thirty-four, it didn't matter much.

"Fine," Steve said, "if you promise to not say anything to Grace. She's a worrywart."

"Promise."

Lucy didn't think that was a good idea, and she was surprised that Patrick agreed to it.

"It might be kind of hard to hide that bandage," Lucy said.

"I'll take care of it. We need to get this done before full dark."

"I'm dressed for it," Patrick said. He nodded to Lucy with a look that said he'd keep an eye on Steve, and she felt marginally better heading inside to the lodge.

"I have plenty of extra snowshoes," Steve said. "Lucy, stick to the path—there is ground lighting that shouldn't be buried by the snow yet. It'll land you right at the porch." He handed her a pair of snowshoes.

"I've never walked in these."

"It's not hard, and if you go out in those boots you'll sink into the snow and it'll take you longer to get to the house."

She strapped on the snowshoes and left the barn. Steve was right, it wasn't difficult; she just had to lift her feet up completely and take wide, deliberate steps. She could see the house only fifty yards away, though visibility was definitely worsening. The wind was at her side, wanting to knock her over, but she kept an even pace.

By the time she reached the porch several minutes later, she was winded from the exertion, but exhilarated.

The lodge was a larger replica of the Ponderosa, the home of the Cartwrights of *Bonanza* fame. But the main floor was eight stairs up from the walk, and Lucy had to take the snowshoes off to climb the stairs. She opened the door, the wonderful aroma of simmering stew reminding her that she was starving. Falling down a lot apparently worked up a huge appetite.

The interior, while bigger than the Cartwrights' fictional home, was decorated in the same Gold Rush–era style with simple wood furniture and old rugs. Clean and polished, there were no contemporary touches aside from electricity and indoor plumbing. The Delarosa Mountain Retreat was technology free: no television, no computers, no cell-phone reception.

Lucy wasn't so sure how she felt about that, but they'd be here for just three days. Maybe it was time to unplug, and really, what was a few days? They'd be out of here no later than noon on Monday. In fact, only twenty minutes down the mountain there was a ridge where they'd noted they had cell-phone reception, and fifteen minutes farther there was the small town of Kit Carson, with a restaurant, grocery, and gas station, plus a few dozen residents. Not that Lucy was planning on going to any of them and pleading like an addict, *"Please, can I log on to the Internet for just five minutes? I'll pay you."*

Lucy started up the stairs to her room when Grace Delarosa, Steve's stepmother, stepped into the foyer. Her face fell when she saw Lucy. "I thought you were Steve. He was supposed to be back by now."

"He and Patrick went to bring in supplies and check the generators."

"Was he okay?"

"What do you mean?"

"He hasn't been himself lately. I'm worried about his health. He's so much like his father, doesn't want to go to the doctor. But I finally convinced him because he was getting dizzy so often, and while they couldn't find anything wrong, when the doctor wanted to do more tests, he refused."

Lucy thought about Steve's tumble down the mountain. She bit back the truth, and said, "Patrick will keep an eye on him."

Grace smiled tightly. "Thank you. We're having dinner early. Appetizers are already in the dining room."

"Great, I'll change and be right down."

She started up the stairs and heard Grace say, "What do you want now?"

Lucy glanced over her shoulder, startled, thinking that Grace was speaking to her, but all she saw was Grace turning the corner toward the office.

Lucy's room was the first on the left at the top of the stairs. Patrick's was directly across from hers. There were six upstairs guest rooms in the lodge, two larger suites and four single rooms. Earlier, she'd learned that Grace and Steve lived in the small cottage behind the lodge, and Grace's sister, Beth, had taken the caretaker's room downstairs, adjacent to the office and kitchen.

Lucy had met the three couples staying at the lodge when she and Patrick first arrived. Alan and Heather Larson were thirty-five-year-old workaholics from the Silicon Valley who'd taken the snowmobiles to town in order to check their email. She'd almost laughed at the time, but now realized she'd been suffering the same technological withdrawal.

Kyle and Angie DeWitt were about Lucy's age, and according to Beth they spent more time in bed than anywhere else. From their lovey-dovey display at the breakfast table, Lucy wasn't surprised. She admitted to being a bit jealous of the newlyweds, as well as hopeful.

Jealous that she didn't have a close relationship like they did—she didn't know if she was capable of that, for she certainly had never shown such outward affection for her ex-boyfriend, Cody. And hopeful that maybe there was someone out there for her whom she could love as much as he loved her.

But that was in the future. She wasn't going to look for it. Sometimes she thought her life experiences had jaded her to unconditional love. Or worse, made her incapable of trusting someone enough to love.

She suspected someday she might be in a relationship more like the Larsons'. They obviously liked and respected each other and had a lot in common—work, intelligence, a dry sense of humor; they even looked alike, both tall brunets, nice-looking but plain, wearing almost identical wire-rimmed glasses. Lucy could imagine herself marrying her best friend out of comfort.

But Cody was your best friend, and you turned down his proposal.

Or maybe she'd fall in the camp of Trevor Marsh and his wife, Vanessa Russell-Marsh—complete opposites physically and in personality. Breakfast this morning had been interesting with Trevor's boisterous laugh and Vanessa's cool demeanor. While Vanessa was model-beautiful, Trevor was a bit overweight and looked a little like a cherub. She was at least two inches taller than he and they seemed mismatched, though they had an obvious silent communication going on that suggested they'd known each other for a long time. Lucy had liked Trevor's lack of pretension.

If she weren't so hungry, Lucy thought as she

stripped off her damp clothes in exchange for a warmer—and dry—outfit, she would go right to bed. She was physically exhausted. But dinner first.

A scream pierced the silence, a sound so anguished Lucy immediately knew that someone was in pain.

But she feared it was much worse.

TWO

As soon as Lucy stepped out of her room, she heard shouts coming from Trevor and Vanessa's room. She ran down the hall to the last room on the right just as Kyle swung open his door across from the Marshes' room. He was bare-chested, and Angie had on a short robe. Both looked stunned, but Kyle took action and ran into the Marshes' room ahead of Lucy.

"Vanessa," Trevor moaned his wife's name. Tears dampened his face as he shook the lifeless body on the bed. "Please wake up!"

Kyle froze inside the doorway. Lucy pushed him aside and went to Trevor's side. She didn't have to feel for a pulse; it was obvious that Vanessa had been dead for at least an hour. Her half-opened eyes were glassy and already had a thin, cloudy film over them, and her jaw and eyelids had noticeably stiffened.

"Trevor, put Vanessa down," Lucy said calmly.

"W-why?" he cried.

Lucy quickly assessed the large room. It was L-shaped, with a couch and desk in a small area directly in front of the entrance, and the bed in the larger area to the left. Clothes had been draped carefully over the sofa, as if someone was deciding what to wear: a simple black dress; jeans and a cashmere sweater; and a blue sweaterdress. Matching shoes were lined up beneath each outfit.

Vanessa was on the bed in a thick white terry bathrobe, similar to the one Lucy's sister-in-law had given her for Christmas last year. Vanessa's long, golden-blond hair was damp and a bit stringy, as if she had brushed it after getting out of the shower but it had nearly dried before she could style it.

A prescription bottle was on the nightstand, along with a glass of white wine. Lucy squatted to read the label without touching the bottle, remnants of her training with the Arlington County Sheriff's Office—not that this was anything but what it seemed.

The prescription was made out to Vanessa Russell for Seconal. Seconal was a common temporary sleep aid. The thirty-day prescription had been filled two months ago and appeared half-full—not uncommon, with the direction to use as needed for insomnia.

The DeWitts were still standing in the doorway when Grace came through saying, "Excuse me, please, excuse me."

Lucy looked up. "Grace—"

"Oh my God, what happened?"

"You need to call the police."

"Police? Why? Is she—"

"She's dead," Trevor moaned.

"But how?" asked Grace.

When Trevor didn't answer, Lucy did. "We don't know."

Trevor rocked Vanessa's body in his arms. "I don't understand. Why would she do this?"

"What happened?" Grace repeated.

"It could have been an accidental overdose," said Lucy. "We don't know how many pills were in the bottle. It's an older prescription."

Grace frowned. "But—she took pills, right?"

Lucy couldn't say. On the surface it looked like Vanessa had taken sleeping pills—but there was no suicide note, no indication that she'd intended to harm herself. But if she wanted to take an afternoon nap, why take Seconal, which came with the warning to take only if you could sleep for eight hours because of possible side effects? Not that people followed the rules of their medications, but if Vanessa had been taking the drug for a while, she'd know its potential dangers.

That there was a nearly empty glass of wine was also disturbing, because anyone who regularly took sleeping pills knew alcohol enhanced the effect of the drugs, even within normal dosage.

Alan Larson popped his head into the room and Lucy said to Grace, "Get everyone out of here. Please."

She wasn't a cop, but she'd been at enough crime scenes to know that contamination was a big problem. Not that this was a crime scene; it was technically an unattended death, but Lucy felt compelled to protect the body and the scene as much as possible before the police arrived.

Grace walked over to the guests and said, "Please go downstairs. Give us a moment." She closed the door over concerned protests.

"Trevor," Lucy said firmly, but with great deliberation and calm. "Trevor." She waited until he looked at her before she continued. "You need to put your wife down."

Trevor stared at her. "Who are you?"

"Lucy Kincaid. We met last night, remember? At dinner, with my brother Patrick. You talked to him about how you grew up in Laguna Niguel. We're from San Diego originally. Do you remember?"

Trevor nodded. "Can you help Vanessa?"

"Trevor, Vanessa is dead. You need to put her down."

He blinked rapidly, then he looked at his wife as if he hadn't realized he was still holding her in his arms. He stared at his dead wife for several moments. Grace tried to talk, but Lucy silenced her.

"Oh, dear Lord." Trevor layed Vanessa's body back on the bed. He stood and looked at her lifeless body, finally understanding there was no bringing her back.

"Grace, please take Trevor downstairs," Lucy said.

"You need to come, too," Grace said.

"I will. I want to cover the body." That wasn't the complete truth.

"We can wait."

"Trevor should go now." She looked at Grace pointedly, and she didn't know if the hostess understood, but she did walk Trevor out of the room.

"Let's get a cup of tea, all right?" Grace said as she led Trevor out to the hall. She shot Lucy a scowl, but didn't insist she join them.

Kyle DeWitt was still hanging out in the hall. Lucy said to him, "Please go to the barn and get my brother."

"Can he do anything?"

"He was a cop for nearly ten years; he'll know what we need to do since I don't think the police or an ambulance will be able to reach us tonight." Lucy also knew they had limited options—they had to get the body someplace cold to slow decomposition. Otherwise, as the gases and bacteria broke down, there would be a horrid stench, especially in the warm lodge. If the authorities couldn't reach them by morning, they would have no choice but to move the body.

After Kyle left, Lucy closed the door and locked it before going back to Vanessa's body. Six years ago she couldn't have imagined viewing a dead body much less touching one, but between the Sheriff's Department and the morgue, Lucy had lost any squeamishness she might have had.

She hesitated before touching anything else in the room. She saw a pair of leather gloves on the dresser, which she remembered Vanessa had been wearing that morning. Lucy put them on, then inspected Vanessa's body. Touching her skin, she realized that rigor wasn't well developed. Lucy would guess from the facial muscles and thin, cloudy film over her eyes that Vanessa had been dead at least an hour, but because rigor was still limited to the outer extremities, she didn't believe she'd been dead longer than three hours. If she had more training, she might be able to pinpoint time of death more closely. The sooner a body was discovered, the more accurately the time of death could be determined, but coroners had more tools at their disposal, as well as more experience.

Lucy glanced at her watch. 5:24 P.M. Vanessa had died roughly between 2:30 and 4:30 in the afternoon.

Lucy was confident that she'd been dead longer than an hour, but three hours was a guess, so she pushed her window to 1:30 P.M. Patrick had been an e-crimes cop and never liked forensics, but he might have more insight.

Lucy studied her surroundings, imagining the likely scenario that had led to Vanessa's death. Shower. Bathrobe. Pills. Lucy had a degree in criminal psychology, but had studied a variety of mental illnesses, including depression. Identifying a suicide was difficult, but there were reliable indicators. Lucy hadn't seen any of the standard signs of depression in Vanessa Russell-Marsh, though many clinically depressed people didn't show outward signs, especially if they were on meds. Vanessa had been the quietest at dinner, but introverts were uncomfortable in groups of strangers and, like Lucy and Patrick, the Marshes had arrived yesterday afternoon. Vanessa seemed to have had a quiet affection for her more extroverted husband, and had been polite if a bit standoffish.

Suicides sometimes made themselves attractive prior to killing themselves—showering, putting on makeup, dressing in their nicest clothes—so that their loved ones would see them at "their best." The shower itself didn't throw Lucy off—it was that Vanessa had showered but *not* dressed or made herself up.

Yet if it was an accident, why would she take sleeping pills in the middle of the day? Especially Seconal. It made no sense, and made it appear more like a suicide than an accident. Still, just because the bottle was there didn't mean Vanessa had ingested the pills. The bottle was half-filled and closed. But if she hadn't overdosed on sleeping pills, what had killed her?

Lucy continued her visual examination of the body. Vanessa's fingernails and toes were painted dark red, and the polish appeared fresh—no chips. Lucy couldn't remember if Vanessa had painted nails last night, or what color they were.

Her engagement ring was a huge marquise-cut diamond. Too ostentatious for Lucy, but it fit Vanessa and she could see Trevor giving it to her. Her wedding band, however, looked like an antique: a thin, unpolished gold band with seven tiny diamonds embedded in an intricate pattern. Though dwarfed by the engagement ring, Lucy thought it was the more interesting and attractive piece of jewelry.

What a waste, she thought. Vanessa was a beautiful woman, newly married to a man who appeared to adore her, and she was dead.

Always look from the inside out. Husbands, boyfriends, exes—nine times out of ten, when a woman is found murdered, it's someone she knows.

Lucy frowned. Murder was a far cry from an accident or suicide. But the idea stuck in Lucy's head that Vanessa hadn't died naturally or by her own hand. Lucy looked at the scene like a cop.

"It could be natural causes. She could have had an embolism or an aneurysm," she whispered to herself.

Lucy had some medical training and a few human biology classes that enabled her to land the internship at the morgue, but she was more interested in the process than in actual autopsies, despite her assistant pathologist certification. She had no idea how to inspect the body for signs of such natural causes of death, but it would be clear in an autopsy.

Maybe she was too suspicious. Did Lucy really expect the worst in every situation? She didn't want to think that she was such a negative person, but when she worked on a body in the morgue, she was most interested to learn the cause of death—natural, accident, or murder? At the Sheriff's Department, she'd worked closely with one longtime cop near retirement. Joe Marquez's philosophy was, "Everyone is guilty of something." Lucy hadn't believed it, but in Joe's life more often than not people lied, even if they weren't killers or rapists. Wives lied to protect their husbands; women lied about assaults out of fear; juveniles lied about minor crimes because they didn't want to get into trouble—and sometimes to see if they could get away with it. Fear of cops was a motivator for many, but Joe didn't have a lot of faith in people or the system. Had some of Joe's skepticism about the human condition rubbed off on her? Or was it her own past experiences that made her unusually suspicious?

She opened the bottom drawer of the dresser where in her room extra sheets and blankets were stored. They, too, were in here. She covered Vanessa's body with a sheet and said a quick prayer. As she was about to cover her face she noticed something on the side of her neck.

Lucy carefully moved Vanessa's hair and turned her head slightly to get a better view. A tiny red pinprick below Vanessa's ear looked suspiciously like a needle mark. She cursed herself for not having her cell phone with her to take a picture, but since there was no reception up here she'd left her phone in the car. She searched the room, looking for another camera. If the Marshes didn't have one, she'd ask the others, though she'd then have to explain why.

Vanessa's death now appeared much more like murder.

THREE

A loud knock on the door was followed by Patrick calling out, "Lucy! It's Patrick."

She again put the sheet over Vanessa's body in case anyone else was with him, and ran to the door, the digital camera she'd found in Vanessa's purse now strapped to her wrist. Kyle DeWitt was there, along with Steve. She didn't want anyone else in the room, and said, "Out of respect for the deceased, I think only Patrick should come in."

"What's going on?" Steve demanded. "Is Mrs. Marsh really dead?"

"Yes," she said. "Please—"

"Oh my God." Steve ran his hands through his mop of hair. He looked panicked. "This is terrible. What more could go wrong?"

The comment was cryptic, but Lucy didn't ask him to elaborate. She caught Patrick's eye and signaled to get rid of the other men. Patrick blocked the doorway. "Steve," he said, "I need you to contact the Sheriff's Department."

"They won't be able to get up here—"

"Call them. You have a landline, right?"

"Yes, but—"

"I know, it might be down, so try now before the storm gets worse. Tell them we have a deceased female, cause of death unknown, and to send a unit and coroner as soon as possible. Get a contact name and number, and tell them that there's a retired police detective on scene."

"You?" Kyle said. "You're young to be retired."

"Long story." Patrick handed Steve one of his Rogan-Caruso-Kincaid business cards. "That's my contact information and P.I. license number. I'll call in as soon as I have something to report."

"But what happened to her?" Kyle asked.

Lucy hesitated, then said, "I don't know."

Patrick glanced at her. Lucy was the world's worst liar, and Patrick realized the situation was serious. "Kyle, would you go downstairs and tell everyone to see what they can do to comfort Trevor? As soon as Lucy and I get a handle on this, we'll be down."

He closed the door before either Steve or Kyle could object, then turned to Lucy and said, "What's going on?"

"I found a needle mark on Vanessa's neck."

Patrick walked over to the body and was about to remove the sheet when he saw that Lucy was wearing gloves. "You do it."

"They're not latex, but it's better than nothing," she said.

"You must have been suspicious from the beginning to put them on."

"Well, a little. The lid is on the pill bottle."

"So?"

"Suicides aren't usually so tidy. She could have put it on, out of habit, but then there's the fact that she took a shower, but didn't dress. I just thought—be careful. All the training beats it into you."

"You can say that again."

She pulled down the sheet. "Do you see it?" She pointed to the mark.

"Yes, but you must have been looking to notice something so small. At first glance, it could be a pimple or minor skin blemish."

"I saw it and—" She stopped and turned Vanessa's head more to the right. "She's had a face-lift. It's good work, too—I didn't notice the marks at first, but I wasn't looking for them."

Patrick stared. "I can barely see anything."

"Like I said, excellent work. But right here under her ear—" She put her finger on the tiny scar. "And there's minimal tightness, so I think she already had good skin and complexion, no excessive sun exposure. She's someone who has been well taken care of most of her life."

"Someone killed her," Patrick said flatly.

"I think so, but I couldn't say definitively. We should secure her body and this room."

"How long has she been dead?"

"One to three hours."

"We need to question everyone. But Lucy—if the killer suspects that we're on to the fact that Vanessa Marsh was murdered, no one here is safe."

"I understand."

"I don't think you do. Lucy, you've never been able to lie. Let me ask the questions, okay? I'm going to tell everyone that we need to move the body to a cold environment for health reasons."

"That's true."

"Then you can say that." Patrick rubbed her arm. "Then I'll say we have no idea what happened, but it looks like an accidental overdose or possibly natural causes."

"Before I saw the needle mark, I thought embolism or aneurysm."

"Good—"

"But will anyone believe she took sleeping pills in the middle of the day and accidentally overdosed?"

"Not everyone thinks like a cop, Lucy. We need to search this room now, before we move the body. I'll need help—Steve and Kyle."

"Do you think Trevor killed her?"

"The husband is always the first suspect, and often guilty."

"He just doesn't seem—" She cut herself off. Killers didn't always look the part. "I like him," she said simply.

"So do I. But we're cops in this scenario. You didn't kill her and I didn't kill her. Therefore, right now we're the only people we can trust. Got it?"

"Got it."

"I'll start here. You take the bathroom and their luggage."

Lucy started in the bathroom. The shower floor was still damp; the hair dryer was plugged in. She put herself in Vanessa's shoes—take a shower before dinner, dry her hair before dressing. She'd set out her clothes—another indication that she planned to go downstairs to eat. Vanessa's makeup, jewelry box, and toiletries were organized neatly on the counter. She wouldn't leave the hair dryer plugged in all day. She would have put it away. The meticulous way the bathroom was set up indicated that.

How did the killer get the needle into Vanessa without a struggle? It had to be someone she trusted to get that close. And what drug could have such an immediate effect that she would have no time to scream or fight back? It would have to have a paralyzing effect. Had she been drugged while lying in bed? Then why had she lain down in the first place?

Maybe Trevor came in and suggested a midday lovemaking session. They got into the bed and during foreplay he injected her. Up close and personal. Intimate. Watched her die. Was she surprised? Did she beg for her life or demand to know why?

There were few convenient drugs that could kill instantly, but if Vanessa was incapacitated that would make it easier for her killer.

Lucy stepped out of the bathroom and said, "Patrick, the wine by her bed. We need it for evidence."

"What are you thinking?"

"She was drugged before she was injected. There's no food in here; the wine is the only thing." She took a picture of the wineglass and pill bottle. She'd already photographed the body and the puncture wound. She wished Trevor hadn't moved the body, because lividity hadn't set in. She could guess, based on the slight discoloration along the right curve of Vanessa's waist, that she'd been lying on that side for over an hour when she died. Because Trevor had now laid her on her back, the blood and fluids would be pooling on her underside.

Still, Lucy had taken the pictures and hoped someone with more experience than she had would be able to decipher them.

"If I ask Grace for plastic bags for evidence collection, she'll be tipped off that we think Vanessa was killed," said Patrick. "I think it's best we keep the likelihood of homicide to ourselves."

"I have some ziplock bags," Lucy said.

He raised an eyebrow. "You normally carry evidence bags around with you?"

"I keep them for travel. Makeup, toothpaste, shampoo. I have some that haven't been used."

She opened the door and was startled when she saw lodge owner Grace and her sister, Beth, in the hallway. Had they been listening at the door? Lucy didn't think so, but she made no assumptions.

"I don't understand what's going on," Grace said. "Why did you and Patrick lock the door? What happened to Vanessa? Trevor is distraught—"

"I thought you were going to stay with him."

"Angie and Heather are with him in the library," Grace replied. "He didn't want tea. I gave him Scotch. Steve told me you had him call the sheriff. What happened to Vanessa?"

"We don't know exactly," Lucy said, obfuscating.

Patrick walked up behind her. "Vanessa is dead, and the sheriff needs to be notified about any unattended death. I can't tell whether or not she died of natural causes. I don't know her medical history. I need to talk to her husband first, and then hopefully the sheriff can contact her immediate family and doctor and see if there was some other contributing factor to her death."

"Oh." Grace sighed and rubbed her face. "I'm sorry, it's just so distressing that someone died here at the lodge. Steve is really upset."

Lucy said, "Steve said something strange. He said, 'What more could go wrong?' Do you know what he meant?"

Grace shook her head, but Beth said, "Grace, we can't keep it secret." She put her arm around her sister's shoulders. "There have been several mishaps since Leo died. One of our main generators broke down. It was under warranty, but it still required us to close for two weeks before it could be repaired. The root cellar was left open one night and most of our food was eaten by a bear. That cost us thousands, to repair the door and replace the stock. And Steve had an accident last month, totaled his truck, and was lucky he wasn't injured. That boy has been working himself too hard, trying to make this place into everything his father wanted."

"Leo was special," Grace said. "He had a way about him."

Beth frowned. "He also left a lot of things undone, spent all his savings to keep the place up. We can't simply avoid the seriousness of the situation. And with Steve's illness—"

"Beth, please!" Grace rubbed her temples. "It's going to be fine."

"What about Steve's illness?" Patrick asked.

"He's been forgetting things," Beth said, ignoring Grace's plea. She lowered her voice. "We think he forgot to secure the root cellar. But he won't go back to the doctor, and we're both worried sick about him."

Patrick said, "We need to move the body."

"Why?" Grace asked.

Lucy said, "The warm house will accelerate the rate of decomposition, and the smell will spread. In addition, there are health issues to take into consideration, as all the bedrooms share ventilation."

"I didn't think about that," Grace said. "But where? How?"

"I'm going to ask Alan and Kyle to help me move Vanessa's body to the root cellar," Patrick said.

"But our food is down there!" Beth said.

Patrick said, "Can you bring up as much food as you can store inside? Anything that isn't canned or vacuum-sealed. Lucy and I will wrap the body securely, to minimize any contamination. And if you have any large plastic sheets, we could use them."

That would have dual purposes, Lucy thought. It would also preserve evidence on the body for the coroner and sheriff.

Beth paled, and Grace said, "I'll get it. The food we can't fit in the lodge, we'll bring to my house, Beth."

As they walked down the hall, Lucy overheard some of their conversation.

"You need to sell this place, Grace."

"It would destroy Steve. I can't."

Lucy hurried down to her room and retrieved her baggies—she had four that she hadn't used—and returned to Vanessa's room. "Let's use these judiciously."

"The wine. I want to save the glass as well—but we can put it in a paper bag."

"That I don't have, but there's stationery in every desk. We can wrap it in that."

They preserved the wine and the glass, then finished searching the room. Lucy went through Vanessa's purse. She hadn't changed her driver's license, it was still under her maiden name of Russell, but there was a copy of the marriage certificate. They'd been married in Phoenix, Arizona, last week. The best man was Nelson Russell—Vanessa's brother maybe?—and the maid of honor was Christina Morgan.

Lucy went through the camera one last time to make sure she had taken all the pictures she thought the police would need. The body, the wine, the pills, the general layout of the room, close-ups of the possible lividity and the needle mark. She'd also taken pictures of Vanessa's hands and arms, which didn't indicate that she'd fought back—no obvious bruising, scratches, broken nails, or fibers. She scrolled through earlier pictures and noticed that Vanessa or Trevor had taken many pictures of the grounds—the lodge, the barn, the surroundings. Some were dark and hadn't come out, but Lucy didn't delete any. She didn't want any photos to be missing—each was digitally numbered.

The earliest pictures were of Vanessa and Trevor on their wedding day. They seemed happy. Trevor beamed at Vanessa. The wedding was lavish, at least from what Lucy could tell from the few pictures saved on the camera.

She set aside the camera. She looked through Vanessa's address book, then went through her receipts.

"Anything?" Patrick asked.

"Nothing that stands out to me."

"I'm going to insist that no one come into the room,

and ask for all the keys, but that's no guarantee that there isn't an extra floating around."

"Grace probably has a master key."

"I wrapped her body in the sheet and top blanket," Patrick said. "When we get the plastic sheet, I'll move the body. Find Steve and ask what the sheriff said. Then we'll talk to Trevor. It's time for you to put that criminal psychology degree to work, sis."

FOUR

While Patrick and the others took Vanessa's body to the root cellar, Lucy found Steve in the lodge's office. He sat slumped at the desk with his head in his hands.

"Hey," Lucy said softly, sitting across from him. "You okay?"

He shook his head. Though he had a lot of responsibility, he was still a young man, not even twenty-one, and this situation seemed to be taking its toll. He picked up a quart carton of orange juice that was on the desk next to him and took a long gulp. Drinking from the carton reminded Lucy of her brothers growing up. Her sister Carina would have a shit fit if she caught them, and always found an innovative way to get back at them. Once, Carina poured hot sauce into the orange juice. Patrick had been the brunt of that spicy etiquette corrective.

"Did you call the sheriff?" Lucy asked.

Steve looked up. He tucked some papers under the desk calendar before saying, "Yes. There's no way they'll be here before noon tomorrow, and that's still contingent on the storm. They'll know more in the morning. They ran Patrick through their system, I guess, and said he should determine what's best to do with the body until they arrive."

"Patrick is taking care of it. We need to close off that room, however."

"Why?"

"Health reasons."

He didn't seem to find Lucy's answer odd. That she was becoming a better liar didn't please her.

"Who has keys?" she asked.

"The guests would have two. There's an extra here. I have a master key for every room."

"May I have it?"

"I won't go in."

"I know, but Patrick wants to control the keys."

Steve now looked at her suspiciously. "Why?"

"I'm just doing what my brother asked. I'm not a cop."

He pulled the key from his ring and handed it to her. He then reached over into one of the boxes and handed her an extra key. "I don't have the other two."

"We have Vanessa's, and Patrick will get Trevor's."

"Tell me what's going on."

"Anytime a healthy person dies, it's never a mistake to be extra cautious. But I'm certain the coroner will clear everything up as soon as the body is examined." She then asked, "What other things have been going on around here?"

"What do you mean?"

"Upstairs you said—"

"Oh." He waved his hand in dismissal. "I was just feeling sorry for myself."

"This has been a hard year for you. When did your father die?"

"Last March. Nearly a year ago, but I still miss him so much." His voice cracked and he looked away. He took another pull on his orange juice.

"I'm so sorry. Beth told me there had been some mechanical problems, with the generator, then the bear in the root cellar—"

"Grace thinks I left the door unlatched, but I didn't. I've secured that root cellar every night since I was eight."

"How long have you been feeling dizzy?"

"That has nothing to do with anything."

"Maybe, but I'm worried about you."

"Why should you care? You don't even know me."

True, and Lucy didn't have an answer. She was sticking her nose into other people's business. "I have some medical training, and the dizziness and fatigue and imbalance could be a sign of something serious."

"Look, I spent three days in the damn hospital in Jackson right before Christmas. They said my blood pressure was a little low, but not dangerously so, and they ran their battery of tests. Everything came back normal 'cept for borderline anemia. So I'm on an iron supplement. Grace shouldn't be talking to everybody about my problems. It's all under control."

"You fell off a cliff today, Steve."

"I just slipped."

"For a kid who grew up in these mountains, I think you'd know better."

"I can't spend any more time in a hospital. Grace can't run this place alone, and without at least some guests, we won't survive the year. I don't want us to sell the lodge. I can't disappoint my dad like that. I didn't think we'd ever be in this position. Dad always had an emergency fund, but—"

"But what?"

"It's gone. Grace said he didn't want to tell me that the lodge had been running in the red for the last few years, and he was using his savings to keep it afloat." Steve put his head back down. "I can't lose my home. It'll be like losing Dad all over again."

Looking for Patrick, instead Lucy found Heather Larson in the dining room. The vacationer from the Silicon Valley was loading food on a plate, but no one else was eating.

"I thought I'd bring Trevor something to eat, though I doubt he'll touch it," she said. "Still, he'll need something to soak up all the Scotch he's drinking."

Lucy winced. He'd be difficult to interview if he was falling-down drunk.

"Did she kill herself?" Heather asked, just like everyone else had.

"We don't know."

"It's so awful, either way, but I hope it was natural. For Trevor's sake. He's such a nice guy."

Lucy had thought so, too, until his wife ended up murdered. "They both seemed nice, though Vanessa was quiet."

"She was a bit weird. I never thought she'd kill herself though."

"Weird? How?"

Heather shrugged. "Maybe I should say she was interested in strange things. Like this morning. Alan and I were up early to take a walk. She was standing by the barn taking pictures through the window."

Lucy remembered the dark images on Vanessa's camera, but she had assumed the camera had just gone off in her purse or something. She'd have to look more carefully at the detail.

"And then when I told her Alan and I were going to town, she asked me to mail something for her."

"And why is that strange?"

"It was a postcard with a short message. 'You are right. We win.'"

That was odd. "Who did she mail it to?"

Heather shrugged. "It went to Phoenix, but I didn't pay attention to the name. I showed it to Alan, though. Maybe he remembers."

A gust of wind burst through the house, and a door slammed shut. Lucy ran to the foyer and saw Patrick and the other two men covered with snow, their faces red. "That was miserable," Alan said. Lucy didn't know if he was talking about the weather or moving Vanessa's corpse.

"Is it locked?" Lucy asked.

"No bears will get into that place," Patrick assured her and showed her the key to the padlock. He pocketed it, then took off his jacket and hung it on a rack near the door.

"Alan," Heather said, "do you remember that postcard Vanessa asked us to mail?"

"Of course."

"Who did she mail it to?"

"Nelson Russell."

"There you go," Heather said to Lucy. "Why do you want to know?"

Lucy shrugged. "Just curious." She glanced at Patrick, nonverbally telling him she'd clue him in later. "Patrick, Trevor is drinking heavily. You might want to talk to him now."

"I'm bringing him this food—" Heather began.

Lucy took the plate. "I'll take it for you."

"I am frozen solid," Alan said to his wife. "Let's go upstairs."

Lucy followed Patrick into the library. Kyle joined them. Angie sat with Trevor, holding his hand while he sobbed. The room reeked of Scotch. Angie looked to be at her wit's end.

Lucy said to Kyle, "We'll relieve Angie. She needs a break. You two should get some food and relax. It's going to be a long night."

"Good idea," Kyle said, escorting his wife from the room.

Patrick shut the door. He sat down across from Trevor. "I'm sorry for your loss."

"Two years. We waited two years to get married. Two wasted years."

"I know this is difficult. But—"

"We were both married before. But her ex-husband was an asshole and my ex-wife was just nuts. That we met up again after all those years—"

"Again?" Lucy asked.

"We dated back in high school, after my family moved to Phoenix from California. Vanessa and Nelson—her brother—became my closest friends. Then we went to different colleges, got married, all those things that people do. I always loved Vanessa, and when my divorce was final I moved back to Phoenix and we started seeing each other again. For two years.

Taking it slow, because we wanted to make sure—" He coughed to cover up his distress.

"You come from a wealthy family?"

"We both do. Vanessa's dad was in the construction business. He always did well, but in the eighties his business took off. He retired ten years ago, left it to Vanessa and her brother. They've done even better. She's so smart." He put his hand to his mouth. "She was. She was so smart. She wouldn't kill herself. She loved life. Everything about it."

"We don't know that she killed herself," Patrick said. Both he and Lucy were closely watching Trevor's reaction. His grief seemed genuine.

"She didn't," he said as if Patrick's statement needed additional emphasis.

"Was she on any medication?"

Lucy hadn't found any prescriptions in the Marshes' room other than the Seconal.

"No."

"But she took sleeping pills."

"Sometimes, but only when we travel because she doesn't like sleeping in strange beds. She took one last night because she couldn't sleep, but that's it."

"Was she acting depressed lately? Did she get any bad news?"

Trevor shook his head.

"And your relationship was good?"

"Yes! We just got married!" He wiped his nose with the back of his hand. "I love her so much."

He reached for his Scotch glass and saw it was empty. He stood and grabbed the arm of the couch for support.

"Maybe you should slow down," Patrick cautioned.

"Leave me alone. Just leave me alone!"

Patrick put an arm on Trevor to steady him, then eased him back onto the couch.

Lucy asked, "Was Vanessa close to her brother?"

"Very. Two peas in a pod. Nelson was one of my best friends. We're a year older than Vanessa. He's my brother-in-law now—" Trevor choked back a sob. "This will kill him. Why did this happen to Vanessa?"

"A coroner will make that determination," Lucy said.

"I need to know. I just need to know that she was happy. That she didn't—" He pressed his palm against his forehead.

"What did you do today after breakfast?" Patrick asked. That had been the last time he and Lucy had seen the Marshes.

"We went on a walk. A long walk to this vista with an amazing view. We talked. Thought about how nice it would be if we could have a vacation home up here. Phoenix is so damn hot—and I suggested we go to Kirkwood and check out some properties. Vanessa asked if I would do it alone; she wasn't up for snowmobiling. Beth went with me, and it only took thirty minutes to get there. We stayed a few hours, got back at three or so. I went to check on Vanessa, but she was sleeping and I left—What if she was in trouble and I could have helped her?" His voice rose in panic.

But Lucy caught what he'd said. "She was sleeping? You went into your room?"

"I opened the door and saw her lying on her side, curled up like she sleeps. I let her rest. But when she didn't come down by five, I went back to wake her up and she—" He broke off.

Trevor had put himself at the scene of the crime during the window when Vanessa was murdered.

"Are you sure she was asleep?" Lucy asked.

"I don't understand, of course she was asleep."

He could have been mistaken. She could have been dead, but looked asleep. The eyes often opened as the muscles in the lids contracted during early stages of rigor mortis. But she might have been sleeping. Or drugged, in order for the killer to inject her with whatever killed her.

But she was presupposing that Trevor wasn't the killer.

"Where did you live before you returned to your hometown?" Patrick asked.

"I went to college in Boston, and stayed there. Met my first wife. We moved to Dallas so I could be close to my team."

"I don't understand."

"I owned the Dallas Kings."

"The baseball team?"

He nodded. "I sold it during the divorce, to my ex-wife. I bought it for her, anyway, but at least I got my money back, and more. Treena was the sports nut. So nutty that after I caught her cheating on me the second time with a player, I filed for divorce."

"And what do you do where you can buy and sell baseball teams?"

"Do?" He almost smiled, though his blue eyes were still watery and rimmed red. "I'm an investor. Venture capital. I invest in companies I think have promise, in exchange for a small percentage. I'm good at what I do. Out of twenty-nine investments this last decade, twenty-two were successful."

"Define successful."

"Five years ago I invested five hundred thousand in two college students to develop tracking software that helps businesses target their most likely customers. I gave them a little advice on how to sell the software—instead of flat-fee licensing, they get royalties on the license. In two years, they were netting over one million a year. Last year, it was three million. I own twenty percent of the company. In five years, I've more than tripled my initial investment. That's my most successful venture to date. I love those boys like they're my own sons."

Patrick seemed impressed, but he was always into technology. Something felt wrong to Lucy, though. "Trevor," she said, "why would you and Vanessa spend your honeymoon at a lodge like the Delarosa? I'd imagine that you could buy your own cabin anywhere you wanted."

"Vanessa saw a brochure for the place and wanted to visit. We're going—" He stopped himself, leaned back and closed his eyes. "We were leaving for Hawaii on Wednesday. Now—I have to call her father and brother. Oh, God, how are we going to make it without Vanessa?"

Lucy and Patrick stood in the dining room, dishing up lukewarm dinner. "I don't think he killed her," Lucy said quietly.

"It could be an act."

"Could be."

"You don't think so?" he asked.

"No. You didn't see him with her body. I don't think that could be faked."

They sat at one of the round tables. "Maybe we're wrong," Lucy said. "Maybe that mark isn't an injection."

"It wasn't a bee sting."

"We won't know until an autopsy."

They ate for a moment in silence. Lucy added, "The lodge here is struggling. Steve said his father spent their savings keeping it afloat."

"Upstairs, Beth and Grace were talking about selling."

"Beth was," Lucy reminded him. "Grace was worried about Steve."

"What if Vanessa wanted to buy the Delarosa?" Patrick said. "With Trevor's money, she could easily afford it. Probably could with her own money."

"A place like this, with all the land, so close to Kirkwood? It's worth a lot."

"Then why is Steve so worried? He could get a loan on it."

"I don't know—maybe there already is a big mortgage."

"We can look into that easily enough. But what if Steve heard that Vanessa wanted to buy the lodge? Maybe she persuaded Grace or Beth. Steve wouldn't want to sell—"

"You're suggesting he killed her?"

"If Grace owns the place after his dad's death, then she could sell whenever she wanted."

Grace might have been worried about Steve's health. She could have thought selling the lodge was the right thing to do. "But," Lucy said, "we don't know if she owns the land, or if Steve does, or both."

"We can find out."

"We'll need to go to the recorder's office, or—"

"Or I can look around here."

Lucy frowned. "You need to be careful."

"I know what I'm doing."

She didn't want to believe Steve was a killer, but he seemed so distraught. Perhaps his mysterious illness made him act rashly.

There was something premeditated about Vanessa's death. Who keeps hypodermic needles lying around? Who has poison at their disposal—and knows how to use it?

"You need to be careful, too, sis." Patrick said.

A crash from the kitchen had Lucy and Patrick bolting up from their chairs. Patrick pushed open the swinging door into the kitchen and found Kyle DeWitt on the floor, struggling to stand.

Patrick squatted next to him and helped him sit up. "Whoa, Kyle, hold on a second. What happened?"

"I just felt dizzy."

"And fainted?"

"I guess." He touched his forehead. A bump was already forming.

Lucy walked over to the refrigerator for ice and stepped into a puddle of spilled juice amid broken glass.

"Sorry," Kyle said. "I dropped my glass."

Grace rushed in. "What happened?"

"I'm fine. Really." The guy looked embarrassed. "Just slipped."

Grace stared at the mess on the floor.

"I'll clean it up," Lucy offered.

"No," Grace snapped, "I'll do it." She strode over to a cabinet and grabbed some rags and a broom and dustpan.

Lucy and Patrick exchanged glances. She was wound tight. Maybe they all were tonight, with a dead body in the root cellar.

"You *fainted,*" Patrick said. "You didn't just slip."

Grace said, "We're at a seventy-five-hundred-foot elevation. The air is thinner up here." She knelt to pick up the biggest pieces of glass.

Lucy said, "Grace is right. The thin air could affect you, especially if you overexert yourself. Usually symptoms of high-altitude sickness don't occur until eight thousand feet—"

Grace cut her off. "That's arbitrary. People are affected differently."

"True," Lucy said, though she didn't completely agree. The human body processed oxygen at different ranges comfortably; it was when the atmosphere started to thin at eight thousand feet that the oxygen level sharply declined. Kyle was a grown man, physically fit, and he shouldn't have a problem here. But she wasn't going to quibble over five hundred feet. "Do you have a headache?" Lucy asked.

"No, I just felt light-headed and dizzy. I didn't really faint."

Patrick helped Kyle to his feet. "I think we're all tired and under stress. You should go to bed. We all should."

"Good idea," Grace said.

Angie walked in. "What's wrong?" She looked at

the bump on Kyle's head. "My God, Kyle! What happened?"

"I slipped. It's nothing."

"It's not nothing!"

Lucy handed Angie the makeshift ice compress she was holding. Angie put it on his head. "Ouch, that's cold!"

"Let's go to bed," Angie said. "I need to keep my eye on you."

He kissed her, then pulled her into a hug. "I'm fine, babe, really. You can have your way with me."

Angie hugged her husband back tightly, her voice filled with emotion. "You'd better be."

"Hon, I am. Really."

Kyle kept his arm around his wife, and they said good night to the others as they walked out together.

Lucy watched them leave the kitchen. She reflected that even after two years with Cody, she'd never felt that comfortable with him, where she could joke about their sex life or show public displays of affection. With Kyle and Angie it was entirely natural, not in any way forced. Their affection showed in their expression, how they looked at each other, how they touched each other. It was the subtle hints that showed Lucy that Kyle and Angie truly cared for each other, the little things that Lucy had worked hard to remember when she and Cody were still together, but usually forgot.

She wondered if she would ever find someone where she didn't forget those small touches that said *I love you*.

FIVE

Lucy couldn't sleep.

Her first night here, it had been the silence that kept her awake. Tonight, it was the howling wind as the snow continued to fall. That, coupled with the disturbing thought that someone in this lodge had murdered Vanessa Russell-Marsh.

She tried a hot shower, and while that eased her sore muscles, it did nothing to help her sleep. Finally, she put on her robe and left her room just after midnight. There was no light under Patrick's door, but she knocked anyway. "Patrick?" she said quietly.

She heard a moan and movement. Patrick opened his door, alert. "What's wrong?"

"Nothing. I—" She felt stupid. "I can't sleep."

He groaned. "Warm some milk in the microwave."

"Never mind. I'll go find a book to read."

She half-expected Patrick to go downstairs with her, but he closed his door and went back to bed. She wasn't surprised, she supposed. They'd had a busy and strenuous day, physically and emotionally.

The hall lights were left on low throughout the lodge. Lucy padded silently in her slippers down the staircase, across the foyer, and slowly opened the double doors to the library. They'd left Trevor there to sleep; Grace had made up the last available room for him, but he was too drunk to walk upstairs and had ended up back on the couch.

Angie DeWitt gasped. "Oh, you startled me!"

"I'm sorry," Lucy said. "I didn't know anyone was up."

Angie was curled in a chair wearing a fluffy robe, a stack of books next to her. Trevor was snoring on the couch, all blankets on the floor. "I couldn't sleep and thought reading would do it, but Kyle can't sleep with the light on. And I wanted to check on Trevor. He was so upset. Justifiable, but—I didn't want him to do anything stupid."

"You have a kind heart."

She shrugged. "Kyle says I have a bleeding heart, but I just laugh at him. He can act like a hard-ass sometimes, but he's the sweetest guy on the planet, especially when he doesn't think anyone is looking."

"That's when it's most important," Lucy said. "I won't stay long. I just wanted to grab a book since I couldn't sleep either."

Lucy perused the bookshelves, but nothing jumped out at her. She realized that she was worried about Steve Delarosa, and Grace, and Trevor Marsh. She couldn't get Vanessa out of her mind, or the cryptic postcard she'd had the Larsons send her brother. Lucy didn't want any of them to be guilty of murder.

She found it doubly odd that Kyle DeWitt had fainted—or nearly fainted—and complained of being dizzy. Very similar to Steve. Had the two of them been somewhere that no one else had? Could Vanessa have been exposed to the same thing and been killed by it?

There was no place for any of them to go now. And with Grace and Beth both living here, it didn't seem likely that whatever was causing the dizziness was airborne.

Lucy understood Steve's deep desire to keep his family lodge running. Businesses were hurting everywhere, and it couldn't be cheap to maintain this place, especially with only six guest rooms in the winter, and a few cabins open in warmer weather. The food, the heating, the generator for electricity, routine maintenance. And losing Leo to a heart attack had been doubly tragic, because being this isolated had delayed getting him quick help. And then for Steve to find out that his father's nest egg was gone . . .

Lucy liked the family and wished she could help. That was one of her greatest assets, Patrick had always told her, as well as one of her greatest weaknesses.

"You want to save the world, Lucy. But sometimes the world doesn't want to be saved."

How many times had she heard that! She wanted to scream, *"I don't care!"* But she did care. About the world, and the people in it. And she could never seem to sit idly by and watch good people suffer.

But what could she do? She wasn't a doctor; she couldn't examine Steve. She wasn't a businesswoman; she couldn't tell the Delarosas how to run their resort. She wasn't even a cop yet. She shouldn't even like any of these people personally, knowing that one of them killed Vanessa Marsh.

Logic reasoned that the person who had killed Vanessa knew her. The only person fitting the bill was Trevor Marsh, her childhood sweetheart and new husband.

Unless . . .

What if someone else at the lodge also knew Vanessa? Trevor said that Vanessa's ex-husband had been an asshole. What if he was lurking around?

She shivered. *Don't be such a conspiracy nut!* Where would he hide while it was a gazillion degrees below zero and a blizzard raged outside? And poisoning or faking a suicide attempt was hardly the standard method of a jealous or vengeful ex-husband.

A chill ran over her skin, raising the hairs on the back of her neck. At first she thought it was only her, but she noticed that Angie pulled her bathrobe tighter around her neck. Trevor's snores halted momentarily, before the annoying noise returned.

Lucy grabbed a book without looking at the title and said good night to Angie. She entered the foyer and saw a wet spot on the hardwood floor, right inside the main door.

She stared. She'd watched Grace Delarosa dry the floor after Patrick and the others came back from securing Vanessa's body. Grace and Steve had gone to their house via the door in the kitchen, which was closest to their cottage.

Someone had gone in and out. Or out, then back in.

Who? And why?

Lucy ran up the stairs, taking two at a time. She knocked on Patrick's door. There was no answer.

Her heart pounded in her chest. She had the extra key to Patrick's room and used it to unlock his door.

"Patrick?" she called into the dark.

He moaned from his bed.

She turned on the lights. He was lying in his bed, the covers kicked off, his bare chest bathed in sweat. His face was flushed. She rushed to his side and felt his head. He was warm.

"Patrick, what happened? What's wrong?"

"Hey, sis."

His words were slurred. He grinned.

"Patrick, what is wrong? Are you sick?"

"I'm fine. Really, I can drive. Nope, well, Carina is the designated driver again."

She frowned. Carina was their sister. She and Patrick were thirteen months apart in age and had been very close growing up. The last time either she or Patrick had seen Carina was at Christmas, two months ago.

Thirty minutes ago she'd woken him up and he'd sounded fine. Groggy, but normal. Now he was hallucinating.

She looked around the room. Thirty minutes . . . there were lots of drugs that had a thirty-minute or less reaction time. Maybe after Lucy had woken him up, Patrick had drunk something.

She saw nothing on his nightstand. In his bathroom there was a water bottle, half full.

She ran back to Patrick. "Did you drink the water in the bathroom?" She picked up his arm and let it go. It flopped back to the bed. He tried to raise it, but couldn't.

Patrick looked at her. "I'm so glad you're here. But why did you do it?"

"What?"

"If you'd just told me, I would have fixed everything."

Lucy didn't know if he thought she was someone else, or what he was thinking, but his comments and physical symptoms told her he'd been slipped a sedative that suppressed his central nervous system. A date rape drug, like Rohypnol or ketamine, or a Mickey Finn—but why on earth would Patrick be drugged? Had someone tried to incapacitate him to prevent his investigation of Vanessa's murder?

That meant Patrick had already learned something that the killer feared would expose him.

Lucy and he had been together the entire time. Except when Patrick had gone out to stow Vanessa's body, and when she'd gone up to bed he'd been talking to Steve in the office.

"Patrick, please."

"Don't worry about me. I'll be fine."

Then he moaned and Lucy knew what was next.

She turned him to his side and he vomited.

SIX

Lucy could not trust anyone.

She'd stayed awake most of the night watching over Patrick. After he vomited, she cleaned up and helped him stagger across the hall to her bedroom. She gave him water from the tap, not the bottle left in her bathroom. He was still hallucinating, but mostly he slept.

She was angry beyond measure—Patrick had been in a coma for nearly two years. Any drugs that depressed his central nervous system could potentially put him back into that coma. The doctors didn't know why he'd reacted in the first place—he'd been conscious prior to his brain surgery after an explosion had injured him, causing swelling in his brain. The surgery saved his life. One doctor believed that the coma was a direct result of the brain surgery—that after the damage had been fixed, he'd simply gone to sleep for two years. Another doctor believed that Patrick had an adverse reaction to the anesthesia, based on his medical history. When he was nine, his appendix had burst and he'd undergone emergency surgery. He'd been in a coma for two weeks then.

Whatever it was, any sedatives were incredibly dangerous for Patrick.

Lucy watched him sleep deeply as the digital clock turned from 5:59 to 6:00. She'd woken him up every hour just to make sure he could be awakened. He'd mumble something unintelligible, then quickly fall back to sleep.

Lucy wished she could ask someone to watch her brother, but she was going to have to leave him alone. It was time to talk to the sheriff herself.

She crept from her room back to Patrick's. Though she had cleaned up after him, his room smelled foul. She went through his notes and found the sheriff's name and number that Steve had given him. Would Steve have passed along the information if he were the killer?

The house was still silent. She walked downstairs and peered into the library. Trevor was still on the couch, no longer snoring, but bundled under a blanket. Angie must have put it back on last night.

Lucy closed the library door and padded silently to the lodge's office. She picked up the phone and was relieved to hear a dial tone. Outside, the wind still blew like an angry god, dawn barely visible in the white that rained down around them.

"Alpine County Sheriff's Department."

"Sheriff Mackey please."

"He's not in right now. This is the dispatcher. How may I assist you?"

"This is Lucy Kincaid at the Delarosa Mountain Retreat. Sheriff Mackey spoke with Steve Delarosa yesterday about an unattended death. We have a serious problem up here, and I need to talk to the sheriff immediately."

"One moment."

She was put on hold. Lucy didn't know what the dispatcher was doing. She waited impatiently.

A small stack of papers was tucked under the desk calendar, making it lopsided. She vaguely remembered that Steve had been reading something when she'd walked in last night.

She pulled out the papers and unfolded them. The top pages were a handwritten letter in bold, confident block letters dated over two years ago from Leo Delarosa to his son, Steve. The bottom pages were a formal last will and testament.

She read the letter first.

Son,

Today is your eighteenth birthday. I hope to be here to watch you drink your first beer (legally!) and get married (you'll find the right girl, just be patient) and have a child of your own.

But my heart attack last year was a wake-up call for both of us. I don't know how long I'll be here, whether I'll live to see my grandchild or not. Because God sometimes has ideas about things that we don't understand, and because I'm not too good in talking about my feelings and all that crap, I decided to write this letter.

My words don't always come out right. They sound like criticism, like when I told you that you were too smart to get a C in Algebra. What I should have said was, "Son, you're a smart boy. I'm proud of you and proud of your grades. I'm disappointed in the C because I know you can do better. But I'm not disappointed in you."

I've never been disappointed in you, Steve.

You were the best thing that happened to your mom and me. We didn't think we could have kids—hell, we tried often enough! And then you came. She loved you the minute she found out you were growing inside her belly.

Your mom would be proud of you today. God took her home way too soon, and I cursed Him for it. You needed your mom. I wanted you to have her in your life more than the ten years you had her. I needed her.

Damn, I'm going to cry now. I just want you to know that I'm proud of you, and I'm proud that you want to keep the Delarosa growing in the spirit that your mom and me always wanted. I won't blame you if you decide you want something else, because I know a bit about wanderlust. I was in the navy for three years because I needed to get off the mountain. But the mountain called me home.

I have taken care of you and Grace. Grace means well, and she wants to please me, but she doesn't love the Delarosa like we do. That's why I changed my will to reflect that you and Grace need to agree to sell, and not until you're twenty-one.

Steven John, you are a smarter young man than I was. If you sell, you sell free and clear. There is no debt, thanks to your grandfather. You remind me a lot of my dad. I was proud of him, too, but more than that I admired him.

I admire you even more.

You'll do the right thing for you, for Grace, and for the mountain.

Until then, I've still been contributing to the nest

egg, as your mom liked to call it. Sometimes a little less than I wanted, but always at least a token, every month since the day I married your mom. We joked about how we'd travel to Hawaii and Tahiti and Bora-Bora. Always someplace warm. Hell, I never wanted to go to any of those places (except Hawaii, I'll admit), but that nest egg will keep the Delarosa running during the lean years.

I hope you never have to read this letter. I'm going to tear it up when you're twenty-one and write a new one. But in case I'm too stubborn or stupid to remember to say it, I want you to know, son, I love you.

Dad

Lucy read the letter twice, tears in her eyes. No wonder Steve was so heartbroken over the debt . . .

Would Leo have told his son in a letter that wouldn't be read until his death that the mountain was debt free and there was a nest egg to run the place "during the lean years" if it weren't true?

Did that sound like a man who had been running in the red for years?

Someone had lied.

Either Leo Delarosa lied about the nest egg, or the nest egg had been stolen.

Or it was hidden somewhere.

She scanned Leo Delarosa's will. It appeared standard, and showed the amendment where Steve and Grace would have to agree to sell.

There was also another clause. The right of survivorship.

If Grace dies, Steve gets the mountain. If Steve dies, Grace gets everything.

Yet right now, there didn't appear to be anything left to have.

"Ms. Kincaid?"

Lucy had forgotten she was on hold with the Sheriff's Department.

"Yes, Sheriff Mackey."

"Sorry to keep you waiting. I've been out in this godforsaken blizzard half the night. What can I do for you?"

"Did you speak to Steve Delarosa last night?"

"Yes, he told me one of the guests had died at the lodge. That you all thought she might have killed herself, or had an accident."

"My brother Patrick was a San Diego detective. Vanessa Russell-Marsh was murdered."

"That's a one-eighty from Steve's call."

"Patrick didn't want to alert the killer, but I work for the coroner's office in Washington, D.C., and I'm pretty certain that Mrs. Marsh was injected with something in her neck. And last night, my brother was drugged."

"Is he all right?"

"He will be. But he's out for the rest of the day, and I don't know who drugged him or who killed Vanessa. We're in trouble here and need you."

"I wish I could help, but there's no way I can get up to the lodge. The roads are all closed; we can't even reopen until the snow stops."

"What about cross-country skis? Snowmobiles? Something?"

"It's treacherous from here, but—I have two deputies who know this county better than even Leo Delarosa."

"You knew Steve's dad?"

"Hell yeah, we went to school together. He was older than me, but we played on the same football team. Good man."

"And Grace?"

"Well, I met her at their wedding. Pretty lady."

"You don't know anything else about her?"

"No, can't say that I do. After Leo's heart attack, he didn't come into town as much."

"Could you run her and her sister for me?"

"You know what you're asking for?"

"Yes, I do."

"What's her sister's name?"

"Beth Holbrook. Beth is probably short for Elizabeth."

"Right—Steve mentioned Grace's half-sister came to help at the lodge. Keeping the books, I think he said. She used to be a bank manager or something."

Beth kept the books? That made sense—she knew that the lodge had been running in the red, and she seemed to have specific knowledge when she mentioned the problems to Lucy.

The sheriff continued. "Why would either of them want to kill a guest? It doesn't make sense."

It might not make sense to them now, but it would when they solved the crime. She simply said, "Someone killed her."

SEVEN

Lucy checked on Patrick. He was still lethargic, but no longer hallucinating. "What happened?" he asked.

"Someone drugged you. I think it was in the water bottle. Don't eat or drink anything I don't hand you personally."

He tried to sit up, but groaned. "Why am I in your room?"

"Don't you remember? You puked all over yours. I cleaned it up. You can thank me later." She spoke lightly, but she was hugely relieved that Patrick was better.

She gave Patrick water from the tap. "Only tap water. I'm going to grab some food from the pantry."

"I can't eat."

"You need to eat something. I'm going to look for chicken broth. In a can."

"What have you learned?"

"First, I need to know who you spoke with when we weren't together yesterday. You tipped someone off. That's why they drugged your water."

"I used to be a damn good cop, Lucy. I didn't tip anyone off."

"You acted like a cop investigating a murder. Wouldn't that be tip-off enough for the killer?"

Patrick still looked ill, and Lucy wanted him to rest. "I spoke to the sheriff," she said. "The blizzard won't be letting up soon. He can't get the coroner here, but he's working on sending two deputies. There's no guarantee they'll be here today."

"So Steve did talk to the sheriff. Good." He sipped some of the water Lucy had given him. "I spoke to Kyle and Alan after we moved Vanessa's body to the root cellar. They were both a little unnerved. Neither seemed to be hiding anything. Kyle was very worried about his wife."

"She was sitting up with Trevor most of the night in the library. She said she couldn't sleep." Lucy remembered the water by the door. "There was a puddle of water on the floor after I woke you up. In fact—it was after I went to the library. I was in there about fifteen minutes."

"If it was my water that was drugged, they would have had to have done it before that. I took a leak and drank half the bottle after you woke me."

"Where did you get the bottle?"

"It was in the bathroom when I—" He hesitated. "I'm not sure. I don't remember it being there when we checked in Thursday night, but it was there last night when I went to bed. I didn't think about it."

"When were you out of your room yesterday?"

"All day. We left about nine-thirty to go skiing, came back at four, found Vanessa at five-thirty—I went to my room to change after we moved her body, between seven and seven-ten or so. Then back at eleven."

"Can you remember if the bottle was there when you changed?"

Patrick closed his eyes, thinking. "No, it wasn't there."

"You're certain."

"Yes. I brushed my teeth and used a glass for water. When I came back at night and brushed again before bed, the glass was gone."

"Mom would be so proud of you."

"What for?"

"You probably flossed, too."

Patrick threw a pillow at her, then groaned. "I feel like I've just been beaten up."

She sat on the edge of the bed. "You'll be fine." *Thank God.* "We were together most of the evening, except when you went to talk to Steve."

"Steve and I were talking about how his great-grandfather bought this land and built and lived in the cottage. The kid was really upset, but I felt it had less to do with Marsh's death and more to do with his physical health."

"Did you see either Grace or Beth?"

"I didn't see Grace after Kyle collapsed in the kitchen. Beth was talking to Trevor and Angie later in the evening, but I didn't talk to her alone."

Lucy straightened her back as something occurred to her. "Kyle said he was dizzy."

"Yes. Altitude sickness."

"I doubt it. He broke a glass, remember? It was juice. Steve was drinking orange juice from a carton yesterday."

"You think the juice went bad? Or—" Realization dawned on Patrick. "You think they were drugged."

"I read a letter Steve's father left him in his will. It was written two years ago, when Steve was eighteen, and Leo said there was plenty of money to support this property, even during the lean years. That was his exact quote. I think Steve believes his dad lied to him."

"In a will?"

"Yes, but I don't believe he lied. I think there was money. Beth was a bank manager before she came here, and she's the one who mentioned that Leo had spent all the emergency funds."

"You think she stole the money? Why?"

"This property is worth a small fortune, at least I'm guessing it is. It's close to the ski resort, it's in its own little valley, and has its own road. With no mortgage, it's owned free and clear. But if there's no money to keep it going or to expand—which according to Steve was his father's dream—then they would have to sell."

"And how does that benefit Beth?"

"I don't know that it does, but we don't know how much money was in the accounts in the first place."

"If she's guilty, we can't ask her."

"But we can find the books."

"Lucy—"

"I know what to look for. Beth has her room off the kitchen. I'll get Angie to keep her occupied."

"You trust Angie?"

"Yes, but I'm not going to tell her why."

"I'll do it." Patrick tried to stand, but fell right to his knees. His skin paled.

"Or not." Lucy helped him back into bed. "Patrick, you stay here. My plan is contingent on the killer thinking that you're too sick to investigate and we're just waiting for the sheriff to come for Vanessa's body."

"Lucy—you need to be careful."

"I promise."

"Why would Beth drug Steve?"

"I don't know. Maybe to distract him—or Grace—from her embezzlement." She frowned.

"Okay, spit it out."

"I don't know. It's Grace, too. She was really angry about the spilled juice."

"When Kyle fell?"

"Yes. It seemed . . . over the top."

"It's a stressful time," Patrick pointed out. "A dead guest, her sick stepson, then another guest fainting."

"You're probably right."

"But Luce—trust your instincts. Please. Don't trust anyone. My gun is in my truck. I didn't think I'd need it, but I want you to get it. If it's safe to go for it."

"Where? Under the seat?"

"Yes. I have a holster strapped to the underside. It's loaded. Extra bullets are in the glove compartment. It's a forty-five; are you comfortable with that?"

She smiled. "Jack taught me everything I know about guns." Jack was their oldest brother and retired Army.

Patrick rolled his eyes. "I thought I gave you some good lessons."

"You did. But you know Jack. Repetition."

"Yeah, don't I?"

Lucy wanted to check out Grace's and Steve's rooms as well. They were in the cottage, and that was on the way to Patrick's truck.

"What?" Patrick read her expression and snapped. "You're thinking about doing something you know I won't like."

"You're right."

He paused. "Well?"

"You won't like it." She stood. "Stay here and be sick. If anyone comes, moan. If anyone offers you food, don't eat it. I'll be back as soon as possible."

"Lucy, wait—" He sat up, but became immediately queasy and lay back down.

"Trust me," she said and left.

Beth had just put out a small breakfast buffet. She looked like she hadn't gotten any sleep. "How are you doing?" Lucy asked.

"I'm worried about Grace. This has been so hard on her. And Steve—the poor kid. I don't know how to make it better, and it's killing me."

"My brother woke up sick this morning."

"Sick? Like a cold?"

"Like puking-his-guts-out sick. I cleaned up after him, but I was hoping to get some ice and a little juice or something."

"Of course."

Lucy followed Beth into the kitchen. Angie was there, as Lucy had prearranged.

"Oh, good," Angie said to Beth. "I was hoping you could help me with Trevor. He went up to the extra room, but he's hungover and distraught and I don't know what to do. Kyle is no help, he doesn't know what to say, and you were so good with Trevor last night."

Beth said, "I have the perfect hangover remedy." She started gathering supplies, then turned to Lucy. "Oh, let's take care of Patrick first."

"I can do it. You talk to Trevor. I'll bring juice to my brother. Maybe some chicken broth?"

"In the pantry. I can prepare something for you."

"No, really, it's okay. I need something to do anyway; I'm going stir-crazy."

Less than two minutes later, Angie and Beth left with a tray for Trevor. As soon as Lucy heard them on the stairs, she slipped into Beth's bedroom.

It was a suite, with two rooms and its own bath. Beth was tidy—her bed was made, her dirty clothes in a hamper, her furniture arranged just so. Careful to leave everything exactly as she'd found it, Lucy quickly searched Beth's room for anything that would connect her to embezzlement or drugging Steve. Beth didn't have a computer in her bedroom, which meant that the books were kept either on the office computer or in the cottage.

She did find a box of letters to Beth from a man named Andrew Simon, Corporal, U.S. Army. They were all sent from an APO address in Afghanistan. Ten letters, written in the months she'd been living here. She had a P.O. box in Kit Carson, which Lucy recognized was the same address that the lodge used. Would she use the same address if she was hiding something? Or would she have opened her own post office box?

Lucy opened the most recent letter, dated three weeks ago.

Dearest Beth,

Our last letters must have crossed in the air, now I understand better why you need to help your sister. Of course family is the most important thing, and I'm so happy that you've become so close to your sister after everything that happened when you were kids. I love you more for your devotion. It was my selfishness to want you closer during my rare leaves, so we can be together.

The Delarosa sounds like exactly what I need when I get out in August. I had planned on reenlisting, but knowing you are waiting for me, three years for my country is enough. I can't tell you how I feel when I get a letter from you. I am counting the days, and will write when I have my final discharge papers. I wish we could email like we did before you moved to your sister's, but I reread your letters every night. Keep them coming, love.

I'm so sorry the lodge finances are in such dire straits. If anyone can turn it around, it's you. Steve sounds like a smart, determined young man. I look forward to meeting him.

I hope you can convince your sister not to sell, at least before I can spend a week or ten making love to you in paradise.

The picture is me and my squad before we went out on recon two weeks ago. Buddy didn't make it back. He's the one in the Jeep. He was a damn good man.

Love you, Beth, with everything I am.

Andy

Lucy looked at the picture, and her eyes immediately went to Buddy in the Jeep. Her dad was working on base by the time she was born, and her oldest brother, Jack, had enlisted when she was still a toddler. She knew what these men went through.

Was the fact that Beth was dating a soldier clouding her judgment? Lucy hoped not, but she hadn't found anything in Beth's room to indicate that she was embezzling money.

Lucy carefully put the letter back exactly as she'd found it and the box on its shelf, next to a framed photo of a man in uniform that had to be Andy. She went through the bottom drawer of Beth's desk and found bank statements. Up until last April, she'd had deposits of a little over five thousand dollars a month. Since April, she'd made small monthly deposits of fifteen hundred dollars. Unemployment? Rent checks? Did her sister pay her a salary?

Beth hadn't withdrawn much money, either—she had a balance of just over nine thousand in her checking account, about the same in her savings, and two CDs of ten thousand dollars each, maturing at different times, both purchased before she'd moved here.

Suddenly, Lucy felt guilty for poring over Beth's finances. There was nothing here to show that Beth had been stealing. She put everything back and would have left, but someone was in the kitchen.

Steve and Grace.

Heart thudding, she eavesdropped.

"Please, Steve, don't do this. Your health is more important to me than anything."

"I need to. On Monday I'm going to Jackson and getting a mortgage. I need you to sign with me."

"You'll be in debt for the rest of your life. You'll put yourself in an early grave. I can't go through that again. Not what I went through with your father. Him dying in my arms because we couldn't get him to the hospital fast enough."

"Please, don't—"

"We can sell. That will solve all our financial problems."

"I'm not selling!"

"Beth, tell Steve that a mortgage isn't the solution."

Beth must have stepped into the kitchen, or had been silent at first. "Actually, I've been thinking it might be a good option. Not a large mortgage, but ten percent would be more than enough to replenish the emergency funds. I'll stay here, at least another year, and work out a budget and growth plan. It's my forte."

"But it's not about the lodge, it's about Steve!" Grace said. "His health."

"You need to go to the doctor, Steve," said Beth. "I'll help you with the mortgage papers—we'll go to my old boss, he'll find us a good program. But then you have to promise to go in for the tests."

"All right," Steve agreed.

"I don't think this is a good idea," Grace said.

"It's a win-win," Beth said. "Steve gets what he wants, you get what you want. Steve, can you help me clean up the guest rooms?"

"Sure. Thanks, Beth."

"You've grown on me. I want you happy and I want you healthy. Okay?"

Lucy didn't know if Grace had left, and she couldn't open the door to check. Though she wasn't dressed for the weather, she went out the side door and walked around the porch to the front door. The snow was still falling, but didn't seem as severe as earlier this morning. Drifts had accumulated against the porch and she couldn't see the stairs. She shivered and tried the front door, but it was locked.

Dammit, this wasn't a smart idea. She knocked, getting colder by the second. She knocked again and the door swung open.

Grace said, "What are you doing outside dressed like that?"

"I stepped out to get fresh air and must have locked the door, or someone else did. I was only out here for a few minutes."

She shook off in the foyer, feeling like a wet dog, her long hair already damp against her cheeks. She tucked it behind her ears. "Thanks," she added when Grace didn't say anything.

"Beth said your brother was sick."

"Stomach flu, I guess. I don't know, but he's finally sleeping again. I think I'll go check on him."

She walked upstairs, feeling Grace's eyes on her back.

EIGHT

Fifteen minutes later, Lucy was bundled in ski clothes. She knocked on Angie and Kyle's door. Kyle opened it. He was disheveled. Angie leapt off the bed and headed for the bathroom; Lucy noted she was naked.

Lucy blushed. "I'm sorry—I didn't mean to, well—"

"It's okay. Is Patrick feeling better?"

"Yes, but still queasy. Can I come in?"

"Sure."

He closed the door behind her. Angie emerged from the bathroom in a robe.

"I need your help," Lucy said.

"Like when you asked me to talk to Beth about Trevor?" Angie asked.

"Right. I need to go to Patrick's truck, but I don't want anyone coming with me. At least, anyone but one of you."

"I don't get it," Kyle said.

"I have to trust someone, and I don't have anyone else. Alan and Heather are probably fine, but Patrick thinks you're on the up-and-up."

"What's going on?" Kyle asked.

"I don't know," she said, not willing to give up the fact that Vanessa was murdered. "But *something* is weird around here, and I think Patrick figured it out but then he was drugged. He's not sick—he was intentionally drugged. And he doesn't remember what he did last night." That wasn't a total lie.

"Was Vanessa drugged, too?" Angie asked, wide-eyed.

"I honestly don't know. But I talked to the sheriff, and he's working on getting deputies here by the end of today, but there's no guarantee."

"I'll go with you," Kyle said. "What do you need?"

"Well, I need a lookout because I'm going to search the barn. And Patrick's gun is in his truck. And then—I need to get into the cottage."

"You're going to break into Grace and Steve's house?"

"No, not exactly. I have a key." She'd taken it from the office where everything was neatly labeled, even the extra key to the cottage. Considering Beth's immaculate room, Lucy wondered if Beth had reorganized when she came over the summer.

"I'll be downstairs in five minutes," Kyle said.

Lucy turned to leave. Then she asked, "Yesterday, when you were dizzy, what had you been drinking?"

"Orange juice, why?" Then he shook his head. "You think there was something in the juice? Is that what Patrick drank?"

"No, but Steve has been dizzy and I saw him drinking orange juice last night." She asked Angie, "Did you have some?"

"No, and I told Kyle he should have asked."

"I just wanted some juice. Beth said to help myself between meals."

"That was your third glass."

"It was good."

What could have had that fast of an effect? Or was it simply the quantity? And what would have caused light-headedness or fainting?

"I'll see you downstairs."

Leaving was much easier than Lucy had thought. She and Kyle traversed the fifty or so yards to the barn. She'd already verified that Grace and Steve were both in the main lodge. Beth was cooking soup in the kitchen for lunch. Lucy couldn't count on the cottage remaining vacant, but she would have to take her chances.

The wind had died down, but the snow still fell. It was almost picturesque, except that she could barely see the barn. She had never seen such odd light before—almost everything appeared gray or white through the thickly falling snow. It was both eerie and beautiful.

And silent.

Because there was no wind, it took only a couple of minutes of plodding through the snow to reach the barn. Lucy went in through the regular door, which was unlocked; the large main doors were braced from the inside to keep them from breaking off in the heavy winds. The barn was dark, and she didn't want to turn on the lights and attract attention. Angie had been instructed to tell anyone who asked that Kyle had walked Lucy to the garage to get something for Patrick, but why encourage followers?

She went straight to Patrick's car and retrieved his gun.

"What are you doing?" Kyle asked.

"This is just a precaution."

He looked skeptical. "I don't like this. Someone's going to get hurt."

"Kyle, I trusted you; I need you to trust me."

He was torn. "I don't like guns. I don't like what's going on here. Tell me the truth."

"Vanessa was murdered."

He paled. "How can you be sure?"

"We can't until an autopsy, which is why Patrick secured the body in the root cellar. The only people who were in the house during the time of death were Trevor, Beth, Grace, and possibly Steve. Alan and Heather returned from town at four, which is on the tail end of the window, and you and Angie were on a walk. Unless you lied and conspired to kill a woman you'd never met before this weekend."

"We *were* on a walk! I didn't kill anyone." He was too stunned at her comment to be insulted or angry.

"I also suspect that she was drugged before she was killed. Again, I can't prove it. But we have a lot of circumstantial evidence to back it up."

"Why?"

"That's the million-dollar question." Why indeed? Lucy was still missing a few pieces to the puzzle. She hoped to find them in the cottage.

She threaded the holster through her belt and tucked the gun inside her thick ski pants. It wasn't visible with the bulky clothing, but there was no way she'd be able to hide the .45 on her person once inside, even if she wore an oversized sweater. She'd have to think of something.

She walked around the barn, looking for anything that didn't belong. There were a lot of tools, Steve's truck, a Jeep Cherokee, and a classic Mustang.

She looked in the glove compartment of the Jeep first. It belonged to Beth—Elizabeth Ann Holbrook. It was registered in San Rafael, California, and Lucy wrote down the address. Beth's car, like her room, was immaculate. Service records were folded neatly in the pocket of her car manual. The Jeep had been serviced at the same place she'd bought it four years ago. She found a business card holder. Beth had been a manager at a national bank in San Rafael.

She had the knowledge to embezzle, but what was her motive? Jealous of her sister? Needed the money? Nothing in her bank statements seemed to indicate a need for funds, but Lucy knew she could have hidden accounts, could be in debt, could be involved with something nefarious.

Nothing else in the car gave Lucy more information. She next went to the Mustang.

"What can I do?" Kyle asked.

"Look for anything that seems out of place—something that doesn't belong in a barn or garage."

In the Mustang's glove box was the registration. Grace Delarosa, at the lodge. Behind it was an older registration. Grace Anderson, Orlando, Florida. She was about to put it back when she saw there were three other papers.

Grace Ann Summers, Chantilly, Virginia. Grace Brooke Jackson, Monterey, California. The last,

Grace Marie Holbrook, with a Phoenix, Arizona, address. That registration had expired nine years ago.

Phoenix. Vanessa was from Phoenix.

Heart racing, Lucy wrote down all the names, addresses, and dates and put them back in the glove compartment. She couldn't get into the trunk, which needed a key because the classic model didn't have a trunk release.

"Kyle," she called.

"It's hard to look for something when you don't know what you're looking for," he said.

"I know. I found what I need."

"What?"

"Let's steer clear of Grace for a while."

"You don't think—"

"I'm thinking nothing right now except I need more information, and I'd rather not talk to her first." She also needed to call the sheriff again and give him Grace's aliases, and tell him that she'd once lived in the same town as the deceased. Phoenix was a big place, but it was too much of a coincidence.

Lucy thought back to Vanessa's message to her brother.

You were right. We win.

What did she mean?

Trevor hadn't called Vanessa's brother yet, and Lucy wanted to be there when he did. But if she let on to Trevor that Vanessa's death was a homicide, she didn't know what he would do, or if she could control his reaction. It was best to keep the information to themselves.

Leaving the barn, Lucy looked toward the lodge. Visibility was still poor, but she didn't see anyone walking around on the porch. The lights in the cottage were off. She turned back to Kyle. "I need you to go back to the house and hang around the porch. Delay anyone coming to the cottage." She looked at her watch. "I need ten minutes."

"You're going to search that place that fast?"

"I know what I'm looking for." Or she had a good idea.

Kyle reluctantly agreed, and he and Lucy parted ways at the short path—at least, she thought the path was where she turned, buried deep in the snow—that led to the cottage.

She opened the door with the key she had taken. More silence, though as she listened she heard a ticking grandfather clock. The hum of the refrigerator. The deep drone of the generator.

She quickly assessed the layout. There were only two bedrooms, no den, and one great room that had a kitchen and dining area attached to it. She went to the room that was obviously Grace's and immediately searched her drawers.

At first she found only clothing. She went to the closet, which was packed with thick winter clothes. The floor was a mess of clothes that had fallen off hangers and shoes and folded blankets.

If Lucy needed to hide something, where would she hide it? Not under the bed—though she checked there quickly. Grace wouldn't have wanted Steve to find it, even accidentally.

She thought back to her brothers and how they never liked to talk about "girl stuff"—namely menstruation. Carina had once told her that she used to hide her chocolate in a Tampax box so Patrick wouldn't steal it.

"He never looked there, didn't even consider it."

Lucy went to the bathroom. The bottom drawer was filled with feminine hygiene products. She opened every box and there it was.

Maybe she didn't know what she was looking for specifically, but she had certainly found it.

A box full of pill bottles. Prescriptions for Thyrolar, made out to Grace Marie Holbrook, and several prescriptions made out to Leonardo Delarosa. She lined them up by date—first a basic diuretic, common for high blood pressure. Then lisinopril, which was a stronger medication. That started after his heart attack three years ago. Then six months before his death, the doctor increased the dosage.

There were pills in some of the bottles. She opened one and it was coated in a fine powder—more powder than would naturally rub off the pills from friction. Lucy looked in the drawer and found a small mortar and pestle—a classic tool used for hand grinding. Such as to grind pills into a fine powder that would more easily dissolve in liquid. And the bitter taste would be masked by a strong-flavored drink. Like orange juice.

The front door opened and Lucy quickly put everything back and closed the drawer.

"Angie and I wanted to use the snowmobiles this afternoon if the snow lets up," Kyle was saying.

"I think tomorrow."

Lucy breathed in relief. It was Steve. But she didn't want him to know about Grace, not yet. Not until the police arrived.

"Are you sure?"

"Yes. Look, Kyle, I'm sorry, I'm just really tired. It's been a long couple days and I need to check the barn, the wood—"

"Let me help. Please, I'm going to go insane in that house without anything to do."

"Okay. Fine. I just need to get my parka."

Two minutes later, they were gone.

Lucy didn't want to tempt fate. She watched out the window until she saw Kyle and Steve go into the barn, then she left the cottage and retrieved her snowshoes from where she had stashed them out of sight, around the side. She crossed over to the lodge, retracing Steve's and Kyle's tracks.

She saw something odd to her right where the root cellar entrance came out of the ground on the side of the house. The doors were open.

Who had gone down there? Trevor? The killer? Patrick had the key—but he was in no condition to check on the body.

She needed someone to investigate with her—she wasn't going to go down in the cellar alone, especially when no one knew she was checking it out. She stepped toward the lodge, but movement on her left startled her. She turned and saw Grace Delarosa skiing rapidly toward her. Before she could move, Grace had rammed into her, sending Lucy sprawling into the snow.

She struggled to get up, the snowshoes making it difficult, and Grace grabbed her arm. Lucy opened her mouth to call for help, and Grace backhanded her with a gloved hand. Lucy tasted blood and spit into the snow.

She felt a pinprick in her neck and hit at it. Something warm trickled down into her shirt.

"You're too late," Grace said and she pushed Lucy back down. Lucy tried to talk, but her muscles weren't working right. She tried to stand, then crawl, but couldn't control her limbs.

Grace dragged her to the root cellar. Darkness ate at the edges of her vision.

"I'll be long gone before anyone knows you're missing." She reached into Lucy's pocket and pulled out Patrick's keys.

"W-why did you?" Lucy managed to whisper.

"You're so smart, you figure it out."

Grace pushed Lucy down the rough earth staircase that led down into the root cellar and closed the doors. Lucy heard the lock slip into place.

Everything was black.

She lost consciousness.

NINE

Lucy woke up not knowing how long she'd been unconscious, but certain she was freezing. Her face was flat on the frozen ground, her cheek numb. The musty smell of damp earth brought images of a graveyard to mind, and her heart quickened. She opened her eyes, but it was pitch-black in the root cellar.

She slowly got up on all fours. One snowshoe had broken off when Grace had tossed her down the stairs. She turned to sit and take off the other.

Her muscles felt weak and uncoordinated, but she didn't think Grace had gotten enough of the drug into her. There had been an instant effect, but she didn't seem to have any lingering side effects. She had to find a way out. What if Grace hurt Steve? Or someone else? Was Patrick okay?

Thinking about Grace drugging her brother pushed Lucy through the pain. She was sore everywhere, but nothing was broken. The padding of her winter clothes had protected her from the fall. She reached to her lower back and found Patrick's .45 still there.

There should be a light switch somewhere. She felt around the hard-packed dirt floor to make her way to the wall. Her finger touched plastic, and her stomach rolled as she realized she'd been sitting right next to Vanessa's body. She crawled away until she reached a metal shelving unit. She stood up, knees cracking and muscles still weak. She held the shelf as she shuffled along the edge until she found the wall. It, too, was hard dirt, and she felt for a switch. There was none.

"Of course not," she said out loud, her voice startling her in the dark silence. It would most likely be suspended from the ceiling; the root cellar was cut out of the earth to preserve food without refrigeration. The light would probably be tapped into the housing electricity.

She considered the layout of the house. What room was directly above the root cellar? She could find something to bang on the ceiling and maybe someone would hear her.

She realized she was directly beneath Beth's room.

Lucy hesitated. Beth could be part of the scam to steal money from the Delarosa estate. She had no way of knowing whether or not the sisters were in this together.

She'd heard Grace lock the root cellar, but Lucy had to try to escape. She found the stairs and crept up, crawling at the end as the ceiling got lower. She pushed the thick wood doors. They didn't budge.

But she heard something. Two men's voices. They were getting closer. Steve and Kyle?

"Steve!" she cried out. She banged on the door. "Help! Steve! Kyle! I'm trapped!"

Silence, then Steve called through the doors, "Lucy?"

"Yes!" She relaxed with relief. "Thank God. Get me out. And don't talk to Grace!"

"What did you say about Grace?"

"Get me out and I'll explain everything."

"Hold on, I know where the spare key is."

Spare key? That was what Grace must have used.

"Get the key from Patrick!" Lucy called.

Kyle said, "Steve went inside. What happened?"

"Grace locked me in here. She tried to drug me, too, but I didn't get the full dose. It's a muscle relaxant, and I think that's what she used on Vanessa before she killed her." If Vanessa had been incapacitated with a muscle relaxant, Grace could easily have suffocated her. Lucy hadn't thought to look in Vanessa's nose and throat for cotton fibers from a blanket or pillow—but often those fibers were visible only under a microscope. An autopsy would provide a definitive answer.

"Grace killed Vanessa?" Kyle asked. "Why?"

"I don't know," Lucy admitted, "but Grace has at least five identities, including one in Phoenix where Vanessa is from. She took Patrick's keys. Did you see or hear his truck leave?"

"No," Kyle said. "Steve and I just came from the garage—no one was there. Patrick's truck was still there."

What was Grace up to?

"Kyle, how long has it been since you and Steve went to his house?"

"Fifteen minutes? Twenty at the most."

That meant Lucy had been knocked unconscious for only a few minutes. And since Patrick's truck was still here, Grace was still here and was probably planning something. What? Was she in her cottage packing, thinking she had more time?

"Lucy? Are you down there?"

It was Patrick. "What are you doing out of bed?"

"I'm fine." He unlocked the padlock and opened the doors. The light from outside poured into the cellar and Lucy instinctively shut her eyes. She crawled out and Patrick stood her up. "What happened?"

"Grace ambushed me and locked me in the root cellar. She took your keys."

"Why would she take my keys and not use the lodge truck?"

"You have a better truck," Lucy said. "Or maybe so we don't follow too quickly. I don't know." She looked around. "Where's Steve?"

"He went to find Grace," Patrick said.

"No! She's been drugging him for God knows how long. I found prescription thyroid and blood pressure medicines in her bathroom—dozens of bottles. The pills had been ground into a fine powder. Thyroid medicine increases your heart rate, and blood pressure meds lower it—" She frowned. "What was she doing with Leo Delarosa's blood pressure meds? He should have been taking them, especially after his heart attack."

"Unless she withheld them or swapped them out," Patrick said.

"If she was giving Steve the blood pressure meds, that would explain his dizziness and fainting. And Kyle"—Lucy looked at him—"you drank the orange juice that Steve had been drinking earlier. That's how she did it."

"Why?"

"So she could control and sell the land. This place has no mortgage on it, it's worth a small fortune, and I'll bet she embezzled the money Leo left to run the lodge."

"You know what you're saying?" Patrick said.

Lucy nodded, shivering more from her deduction than from the cold. "She killed Leo."

"Let's get inside and contact the sheriff," Patrick said, "and get everyone in one room."

They started toward the stairs to the porch, and that's when Lucy saw Steve standing at the top. His face turned from shock to rage.

"What did you say?"

"Steve, we need to get everyone in the house. Everyone. We need to talk."

"Tell me what you meant—who killed my father?"

Lucy stepped forward, her boots sinking into the snow. Fast was not an option, but she moved as quickly as she could, worried that Steve would do something stupid. "We'll talk about this inside."

"Tell me!" he shouted.

"Steve, I don't have definitive proof, but I found your father's heart medication ground into powder in Grace's bathroom."

Steve looked perplexed.

Lucy realized why the thyroid meds were also ground up. "I think she was giving him her own thyroid medicine instead of his blood pressure meds."

"I don't understand. Why would she do that?"

"Thyroid medicine can increase the heart rate. Since your father already had high blood pressure, if he wasn't taking his meds and then was given something to make his heart work harder, the combination could bring on a heart attack or stroke. It's not predictable—Grace couldn't have known when it would happen, just that it would eventually. Then when she found out she couldn't sell the land, she took all the money she could from your accounts. Maybe she took the money before he died, I don't know."

"But *why?*" Steve wailed, his pain and anguish evident in his voice. "My father loved her!"

Lucy had some ideas about what had motivated Grace, but didn't want to share them now, not with Steve so volatile. She glanced at Patrick and nodded toward Steve. Patrick stepped next to him and said, "Let's go inside. The sheriff will take over."

As they stepped through the door, they all heard an engine start. A half minute later, the barn doors were nudged open by Patrick's truck. Grace was at the wheel.

Beth walked into the foyer. "Close the door! You're letting the heat out!"

Steve turned on her, pushed her back. Her eyes were wide in fear, and Steve shouted, "Did you know? Did you know your sister killed my father?"

The shock on Beth's face was palpable. Without waiting for an answer, Steve pushed Patrick and stomped out the door, grabbing cross-country skis from the rack.

"Steve, wait for the sheriff—"

"No! She killed my dad. It all makes sense. Everything makes sense now."

Lucy tried to stop him, but she couldn't move fast through the snow, and Steve was on the skis before she could reach him.

"Patrick!" she called out. "The snowmobiles."

Patrick said to Kyle, "Call the sheriff now. Give him my truck description, license plate 5K55567. Tell them Grace may be armed and dangerous. There's only one road out of this mountain—they need to meet up with her before she hits the highway."

"That doesn't give them much time—twenty, maybe thirty minutes."

"Then tell them to haul ass."

Beth looked shell-shocked. "I don't understand what's happening."

"We can't explain now," Lucy said, "but your sister is a killer. I'm sorry."

"I thought—" she hesitated. "I thought we'd finally become close. I guess I was wrong."

Patrick said to Lucy, "Get everyone in the library and stay there. I'll get Steve."

"You're not going out there alone," she countered.

"Dammit, you're not a cop!"

"Are you going to argue with me or cooperate? You were drugged last night, Patrick. Grace is a killer and Steve's emotions are running high. You need backup. Let's go."

She gave Patrick no opportunity to argue. She walked toward the garage where the snowmobiles were stored. Without snowshoes, it took longer. Patrick waved her over to the tracks his truck had made; walking on the pressed snow was definitely easier.

By the time they reached the garage, Grace and Steve had a six-minute lead and the steadily falling snow was covering up their tracks. Patrick uncovered the snowmobiles. "Why don't we take Steve's truck?" Lucy asked.

"We need to make up time, and we'll never catch up to her before Steve. Trust me, snowmobiles are faster."

He started one up, then motioned for Lucy to take it before he started the next. This was only the second time Lucy had ridden one of these vehicles—the first time being two days ago when they arrived at the lodge.

Patrick led the way. As they passed the lodge, Kyle came out and gave them a thumbs-up. She hoped that meant he had spoken to the sheriff. With that, Patrick rode off and Lucy followed.

They stayed on the path left by the truck. Lucy noticed that Steve's skis had diverged from the road, leaving a clear trail through the trees.

She sped up and motioned for Patrick to stop.

"What?" he shouted.

"Steve went that way," she pointed down the mountainside. "We should split up."

"Hell no."

"He's going to cut her off. He knows these woods better than anyone."

"I don't care, we're not splitting up."

"We may not catch up with her in time, and I'm worried for Steve. Please—I'll follow him."

"And what if you get lost?"

"I'll stick to his trail. I can catch up to him and stop him from doing anything stupid. You focus on Grace. We're wasting time."

It was clear Patrick didn't want to agree, but Lucy took his silence as assent. She rode back to where she'd seen Steve's ski trail, worried that the heavy snowfall would cover his tracks faster than she could follow them. But he'd been traveling fast, leaving deep gouges in the snow, and Lucy easily found the path he'd left.

Lucy started slowly because she was at a dangerous downhill angle. But it leveled off a bit and she picked up speed. The trees started far apart, but the more she went down, the denser they became. She paid close attention to the tracks, because if she lost them she would have to backtrack, and she might not be able to find his path again. Worse, the snow was making it difficult to see more than twenty or so feet ahead of her, and she had to slow when Steve's tracks started swerving between trees.

Several minutes later, she saw a green figure in the distance. It had to be Steve, in his bright green jacket, and he was moving at a rapid pace. She sped up a bit, but stayed tense and focused on his trail. She didn't know this area, and didn't know if there was a deep gulley or drop-off.

She made good time. But just as she was getting closer to Steve, he suddenly turned sharply to the right and disappeared from view.

Lucy sped up, and spotted him. Steve lay unmoving in the snow.

She stopped the snowmobile and jumped off. Steve was trying to get up. One ski had come off.

"What happened?" she called.

"A rock. I wasn't paying attention."

She didn't know if she believed him. She thought he might have gotten dizzy and collapsed, or lost his balance. "Steve, Grace has been drugging you, too. You can't do this—"

"Why are you trying to stop me?" he said as he got to his feet.

"The police are on their way to Kit Carson. They have a description of Patrick's truck and Grace. She's not going to get away."

"This is between me and that woman."

"Steve—please, I don't want you to get hurt."

"She killed my father!"

He pushed Lucy down and stomped toward the snowmobile.

"Steve!"

He jumped on. Lucy scrambled up. "Don't leave!" She suddenly grew terrified that he'd go and she'd never find her way out. She was in the middle of the forest with no visible paths, and the snow was masking her trail down the mountain.

Steve said, "Get on the back. You have ten seconds or I'm leaving without you."

Lucy had no choice—Steve was distraught and determined. She jumped on the seat behind him. He started off so fast she nearly fell off, so she grabbed him around the waist, holding tight. He drove the snowmobile much faster than she did, but he had more experience and knew where he was going.

He swerved, then sped up, driving far faster than could possibly be safe. Lucy closed her eyes and held on tight, fearing that this was it. Steve would crash into a tree and she'd be dead.

When he slowed about five minutes later, Lucy opened her eyes and saw they were approaching a road. To her left she saw Patrick's truck coming down the mountain. Patrick was right behind it on the snowmobile.

At their trajectory, they'd hit the truck when they reached the road.

"Jump!" Steve shouted.

Lucy feared she knew exactly what Steve was planning.

"No, Steve!"

"Jump, dammit, I'm going to stop her."

"Don't—"

"Do it!" He slowed a fraction, grabbed her wrist that was still tight around him, and twisted it until she cried out and let go. She fell off the back and hit the snow, stunned. But nothing felt broken.

She watched in stark terror as Steve sped up and made a beeline for the road. This was suicide! She couldn't stop him. She scrambled up, but the snow was so deep she sunk in past her knees.

Steve timed the collision perfectly, jumping off the snowmobile at the last minute. Grace swerved to avoid crashing but fishtailed and slid on the icy road, losing control. The truck slid past the snowmobile and into the embankment.

Lucy reached the road as Steve opened the passenger door, because the driver's side was pressed firmly against the mountainside. He grabbed Grace and pulled her from the seat. Patrick stopped behind the truck and shouted, "Let her go! Steve, the police are coming. Let her go."

"You killed my dad!" Steve screamed and slammed Grace against the hood of the truck. "Why?"

Grace didn't answer. Instead, she kicked Steve in the knee. He lost his footing on the icy ground and let go of her. She took two steps away and pulled a gun from her pocket. She pointed it at Steve and shouted at Patrick, "Step away from the snowmobile. I'm taking it."

Patrick slowly moved away. "The police are on their way. You're not getting off the mountain."

"Move faster!" she ordered.

"We know your aliases."

"I doubt you know all of them," Grace snapped back.

"Why did you stay so long?" Lucy asked. "Why didn't you just take the money and run? Why'd you have to kill Leo?"

She laughed. "Wouldn't you like to know?" She jumped onto the snowmobile.

Grace started down the road. Lucy couldn't let her get away.

As soon as Grace passed her, Lucy retrieved Patrick's gun from the holster and, just like Jack had trained her, took aim and fired. Three bullets right in the back of the snowmobile. She didn't know where it was most vulnerable, and she didn't want to shoot Grace, but she hit the engine. It began to smoke, and the snowmobile wobbled. Grace's pant leg caught fire and she swerved and jumped off, rolling in the snow.

Patrick was fast and jumped on Grace before she had a chance to retrieve her gun. Lucy held the gun on her while Patrick disarmed her and turned her facedown into the snow. Grace cried out in pain, but Patrick didn't take her bait.

Lucy told Steve, "Patrick has handcuffs in his glove box."

He didn't move. "Give me the gun, Lucy."

"No."

He moved toward her and Lucy turned the gun on him. "Steve, I don't want to shoot you."

"Just give me the gun. I need to do this."

He was wild-eyed with grief.

"No."

Steve stepped forward and Patrick shouted, "Stop!" He had Grace's gun aimed at Steve. "We have her, Steve. She's going to prison for the rest of her life."

Tears spilled from his red eyes. Steve sunk to his knees, releasing a cry of anguish.

Lucy retrieved the handcuffs and handed them to Patrick. He cuffed Grace and sat her up. "It's over for you, too, Grace."

"It's all conjecture. There's no proof of anything."

"Don't be so sure," Lucy said. "The orange juice you drugged. It's still in the refrigerator. Steve himself is evidence—the next stop is a hospital for a blood sample."

"But there's no proof I did anything. What you might have seen in my house? Well, I doubt anyone will ever find it again."

"I'll testify."

"There's no evidence."

"There's Vanessa Russell-Marsh's body."

"Nothing connects me to her."

"Phoenix."

"A lot of people live in Phoenix."

"Nelson Russell."

"Doesn't matter," Grace said, though her confidence faltered. "You can't prove I did anything to anyone."

Lucy suspected she was correct. She said, "You're a con artist. You conned Nelson Russell and he sent his sister to collect what you stole. She sent a postcard to her brother that said, 'You were right. We win.' Did Vanessa demand repayment or she'd tell Beth and

Steve what you did to her brother? Perhaps that would make them suspicious about Leo's missing money. Did she threaten to turn you over to the police?"

"Vanessa was a fucking bitch!" Grace exclaimed. "They hired a private investigator to find me, and she thought she was so smart coming up here and surprising me. But the joke's on her."

"You killed her and planned to leave, but you got greedy," Lucy said. "You wanted Steve to sell, so you pushed him harder. Told him his father had squandered all his money. Increased the blood pressure meds you were giving him so that he'd get sicker. Maybe get himself killed, because he was working double time to keep the lodge running. You had Beth on your side because you made her feel sorry for you. Poor Grace, you were barely holding on, you were suffering because you were trying to save Leo's dream for his son—while all along you had been sabotaging it."

A four-wheel-drive sheriff's truck came into sight. Grace squirmed.

"You're going to jail," Patrick said. "Once we talk to Beth and Vanessa's brother, you'll be begging for a plea agreement."

The sheriff put on the lights and over the speaker came, "Put down your weapons."

Lucy put her gun on the hood of Patrick's truck, and Patrick walked over and did the same thing. The deputy got out of the car. "Who's Kincaid?"

Patrick introduced himself and handed the deputy his private investigator's license and business card. "I had the lodge call you about Mrs. Marsh's murder, and we have reason to believe that Grace Delarosa killed her. We also have reason to believe that she killed her husband and attempted to kill her stepson."

"Frankly, you're going to have to get in line." The deputy walked over to where Grace knelt in the snow, head low. "Grace Marie Holbrook, you're under arrest. You have the right to remain silent."

As the deputy read Grace her rights, he walked her to the back of the truck and locked her inside. Then he returned to the three.

"What did you mean, deputy?" Patrick asked.

"Well, we ran the names you sent us, and one of the aliases, Grace Ann Summers from Virginia, popped up with an active warrant for murder."

"How long ago?" Patrick asked.

"Nearly six years."

Steve said, "She came here looking for a job six years ago this June. My dad hired her and they married a year later."

"She was probably hiding out," Patrick said. "Taking another name, living in another state, she could have stayed here forever."

"Probably," the deputy concurred. "I'm going to take her in, but two deputies are on their way to the lodge to take down statements. Do you need help with your truck?" he asked.

Patrick surveyed the damage. "It looks like we can dig it out."

"Don't wait too long. The storm will pass tomorrow, but it'll only get worse tonight."

He tipped his hat and left.

TEN

The sheriff's deputies arrived Saturday evening and took everyone's statement. They stayed the night because they couldn't get off the mountain, but by dawn the snow had stopped and pockets of blue could be seen above.

The drama of the weekend had taken its toll on the guests, and Alan and Heather left Sunday morning, followed by Kyle and Angie. Trevor, after making arrangements with the coroner to send Vanessa's body to Phoenix, also left. Patrick and Lucy decided to stay one more night to help Beth and Steve make plans.

"The good news is Grace isn't as clever as she thought," Patrick said. "I spoke to Vanessa's brother this morning, and he told me everything. Grace and Nelson Russell had been engaged. Vanessa suspected Grace had stolen an expensive painting, even though Grace had come up with an excuse as to why she had it in her car. Russell forgave her, but agreed to test her honesty. He set up a sting of sorts, but Grace figured it out and stole 150,000 dollars in cash and jewelry that had been in the Russells' safe. According to Russell, he didn't care about the money, but the jewelry had been in his family for generations. They've been looking for the jewelry and Grace ever since."

"How did they find her?" Steve asked.

"Through your website. When Trevor and Vanessa decided to find a mountain lodge to honeymoon at, they researched dozens, including the Delarosa. On the page was a picture of Grace and Leo. Though not a close-up, Vanessa thought she'd recognized her and hired a private investigator, who confirmed it. She told her brother she'd investigate, and if it was Grace, she'd demand the return of their jewelry. According to Russell, who hasn't received the postcard yet, the message meant that he was right, she still had the jewelry, and they won, because Grace promised to return it in exchange for them not turning her over to the police."

"So why did Grace kill her?" Lucy asked.

Beth said, "Because she doesn't have the jewelry." Everyone turned to look at her. "It's my fault! I sold it for her." She rubbed her temple.

"Why?"

"She told me Leo left it to her in the will, and I had no reason to doubt her. She said she needed the money so she wouldn't have to tell Steve that Leo had spent their savings. I believed her. Dammit, she was my sister!"

"You didn't know any of this?" Steve asked.

Beth shook her head. "Grace is ten years older than me. We weren't close growing up, Grace always resented our mother for divorcing her dad, and then remarrying. Grace left home when she was eighteen. I'd see her every couple of years, and she was always nice to me. Generous, talking about her travels."

"How did she make money? What did she tell you?"

"She was a nurse for years. Then she met her first husband, in Orlando. When he died, she came into some money. I didn't really ask her much about that."

"She was a nurse?" Lucy asked. Beth nodded. "That makes sense. She'd know how meds work and interact."

"I'm so sorry, Steve. I really didn't know."

Steve took Beth's hand. "I believe you. But we still have no money left."

"Don't be so sure about that," Patrick said. "The police will go through all her finances and bank accounts. You'll have dibs on it as soon as they get it straightened out."

Beth nodded. "I'll go through the books and find out how much she took. And I'll stay. It's the least I can do."

"You don't have to." Steve looked around the dining room. "Maybe I should close down."

"No," Beth said. "Please—I love this place. My boyfriend is in Afghanistan. I sent him pictures, and he wants to live here when his tour is up. Andy is going to need a place like this. You'd like him."

"You'd stay? Even though I can't pay you or anything?"

"I have a roof over my head and food to eat, and we'll find a way to make it work. I'm not giving up on you, or the lodge."

Lucy rose and faked a yawn. "I'm beat. Patrick?"

He picked up on her cue and followed her upstairs. "What's wrong?"

"Nothing. I just want to give them time alone. This is a lot to digest."

"Tell me about it. You want to ski tomorrow?"

Lucy looked at Patrick as if he'd grown a second head. "No. I've had enough snow for a lifetime. I'm still freezing from yesterday."

She opened her door. "You think they'll be okay?"

"I think they have a lot to deal with, but yeah, I think they'll make it. Steve works hard, and he loves this place. Getting over what happened to his dad will take time, but Beth is solid. I think she'll be good for him."

"And when her boyfriend gets back from Afghanistan, maybe the three of them can make a life together." She paused. "Do you think there's someone for everyone?"

"What brought this on?"

Lucy felt uncomfortable talking to her brother about relationships, but she pushed forward anyway. "I didn't love Cody."

"I know."

"Maybe I didn't give him a chance."

"You dated him for nearly two years."

"What if I won't know what love is when I see it?"

Patrick sighed. "You don't see love, you feel it. You'll know. I liked Cody, he was good to you, but if you don't feel the same way, getting married would have been a huge mistake." He gave her a hug. "You'll find the right guy, someone who will love you and protect you, someone who makes you happy and makes you laugh. Someone will walk into your life when you least expect it and sweep you off your feet. You won't be able to imagine your life without him."

Lucy smiled. "That's really sweet."

"And he'll know if he breaks your heart, he'll have to answer to your brothers."

She laughed. "What are you trying to do, scare this fictitious Mr. Perfect away?"

"If he really loves you, he won't be scared off so easy."

Lucy kissed her brother on the cheek and went into her room. She changed into her sweats and T-shirt and crawled under the thick down comforter.

She hoped Patrick was right. She hoped someday she would find someone to love.